Praise for

DISHONESTLY YOURS

"Krista and Becca have created a world that I not only love being a spectator to but wish I could be a part of. The characters, the twists, the cons. . . . I couldn't get enough!"

—Elle Kennedy, *New York Times* bestselling author of *The Score*

"Krista and Becca Ritchie have outdone themselves with *Dishonestly Yours*! It's fresh and innovative and artfully crafted from the very first page. The tension is delicious, and the twists kept me turning the pages late into the night. I was absolutely consumed by these characters and their stories. This is definitely one of those books I'm going to find myself thinking about for years to come."

—Elsie Silver, #1 *New York Times* bestselling author of the Rose Hill series

"Fresh, deliciously angsty, and sizzling with slow-burn tension that kept me glued to the pages. *Dishonestly Yours* is a must read!"

—Samantha Young, *New York Times* bestselling author of *The Love Plot*

"This story was addictive! Unique premise. Intriguing plot. It will leave you craving more."

—Devney Perry, #1 *New York Times* bestselling author of *Shield of Sparrows*

“A roller coaster of a read, with twists and turns galore. Krista and Becca Ritchie give us a cast of characters to root for as they fall in and out of their lives of crime. *Dishonestly Yours* shows us that love can be both messy and sweet—like the perfect strawberry.”

—Jen DeLuca, *USA Today* bestselling author of *Ghost Business*

“Dark and sexy, *Dishonestly Yours* deftly deals in captivating twists and deliciously angsty love. The Ritchies stole our hearts with every page.”

—Emily Wibberley and Austin Siegemund-Broka, authors of *Seeing Other People*

Berkley Titles by Krista and Becca Ritchie

WEBS WE WEAVE SERIES

DISHONESTLY YOURS

DESTRUCTIVELY MINE

DANGEROUSLY OURS

ADDICTED SERIES

RECOMMENDED READING ORDER

ADDICTED TO YOU

RICOCHET

ADDICTED FOR NOW

KISS THE SKY

HOTHOUSE FLOWER

THRIVE

ADDICTED AFTER ALL

FUEL THE FIRE

LONG WAY DOWN

SOME KIND OF PERFECT

DANGEROUSLY OURS

KRISTA RITCHIE AND
BECCA RITCHIE

BERKLEY ROMANCE
NEW YORK

BERKLEY ROMANCE
Published by Berkley
An imprint of Penguin Random House LLC
1745 Broadway, New York, NY 10019
penguinrandomhouse.com

Book design by George Towne
Interior art: spiderweb © Sveta Aho / Shutterstock

Library of Congress Cataloging-in-Publication Data

Names: Ritchie, Krista author | Ritchie, Becca author
Title: Dangerously ours / Krista Ritchie and Becca Ritchie.
Description: First edition. | New York : Berkley Romance, 2026. | Series: Webs we weave
Identifiers: LCCN 2025043488 (print) | LCCN 2025043489 (ebook) |
ISBN 9780593549599 trade paperback | ISBN 9780593549605 ebook
Subjects: LCGFT: Romance fiction | Novels | Fiction
Classification: LCC PS3618.I7675 D36 2026 (print) | LCC PS3618.I7675 (ebook)
LC record available at https://lccn.loc.gov/2025043488
LC ebook record available at https://lccn.loc.gov/2025043489

First Edition: May 2026

Printed in the United States of America
1st Printing

The authorized representative in the EU for product safety and compliance
is Penguin Random House Ireland, Morrison Chambers, 32 Nassau Street,
Dublin D02 YH68, Ireland, https://eu-contact.penguin.ie.

We loved with a love that was more than love.

—EDGAR ALLAN POE

ONE

Hailey

"You're saying it's already noon?" I ask while I slip out of black rumpled bedsheets. I pat my arms and limbs to ensure I'm real.

This is real.

I'm not lost in my head. I'm not asleep. *I don't think*.

I slip my fingers down my fair skin, brushing over my hip bones and a camo-green lacy thong, then up to a strappy neon-blue sports bra. My underwear choices are on-brand for my life right now.

Mismatched. Mixed-up. Disordered.

I bolt for the digital clock at my bedside and crouch down to inspect the numbers. It says 12:03 p.m.—and logically, I should believe my own eyes, but historically speaking, I'm having a *little* bit of a hard time with the concept. Two weeks ago, I experienced a hallucination so vivid, I ran barefoot through the grounds of the Koning estate and found myself locked in an old storm shelter. Where I believed I was being violently *murdered*.

Turns out, I locked myself in there. Alone.

Big, *big* whoops.

Reality washed away the delusion . . . eventually, and I found the answers about our births that I'd been searching sleeplessly for. But the aftereffects of being bamboozled, deceived, *conned* by the people we trusted most—the godmothers and godfather: the ones who raised me, my two brothers, and the Graves triplets—have seeped deeper into me than maybe they have for my best friend, Phoebe.

I question everything at every turn. I don't want to. I want to believe the wall is a real fucking wall and my feet are truly planted on the floorboards. That I'm really in this cute little loft above Baubles & Bookends, a bookstore in Victoria, Connecticut.

My reality.

One I created. *I* asked Phebs to live honestly with me on the coast of New England last summer. *I* asked Phebs to join my *Mystic Pizza* dream, where we were supposed to have normal romances and normal jobs (we are still country club servers, at least). I advertised this version of us living our best Julia Roberts lives. Perfect, lush hair days. Romantic small-town entanglements worthy of the big screen.

No deception.

No cons.

But it's been hard for me to stop what I was raised to do, and the only reason I wanted to retire this trade was for Phoebe. I would've done *anything* to get Phebs to quit the family business. Her role is damaging. I saw it *damaging* her . . . maybe before she even did, and I couldn't watch anymore.

We're grifters. We move. We run once our pockets are loaded and it's time to choose a new rich mark, but I want to stay in this reality I've created for my best friend. I want it to be mine, too. So the ground has to be stable. This has to be *real.*

But . . . "It-it can't be noon," I stammer. "It was just *nine* in the morning." I back up from the digital clock like it's a mini explosive.

"Hailstorm."

I freeze at the deep, comforting voice behind me. *Familiar.* Masculine. He's a strong, soothing rush of cold water against my mind. I wake up to the sound of Oliver Graves.

His fingertips touch the top of my head, and I rotate with the movement of his fingers, like he's twisting a tiny porcelain version of me in a music box.

I peer up at his twinkling caramel-flecked brown eyes. Ones I've stared into for so long that I can't reliably count the exact years. Facts: I'm twenty-four, and I've known Oliver since I was born, but memory recollection is said to begin around three and a half to four years old and is typically tied to an emotional or unusual event.

I remember him when I believe I was four.

I remember his arm curving over my shoulders as he tried to comfort me. We were left on a windowsill nook in a fancy Newport estate. I can't remember whose home it was. I can barely remember what we were doing there.

I do remember feeling lost. I remember wondering why I couldn't play with Phoebe. So I kept to myself. Said very little. Gazed out the window. Even in my quiet shell, Oliver found me and gave me a great sense of relief.

Fear has no home in my body when he's around. Strange how that is, but everything about my life could be classified as abnormal.

I skate my eyes over his mesmeric features. Olly is *beautiful.* Pieces of his hair curl around his ears—the strands not long enough to be a bother, but not short either. I've sunk my fingers into his glossy hair at its natural dark-chocolate-brown color, and I've slipped them into the dyed lighter walnut shade he has today. Grabbing and clutching as he pistoned into me.

Like he did late last night.

He's not naked now. His white tank shows off carved biceps. The elastic waistband of his black boxer briefs accentuates the toned V-line of his muscles that I've trailed my tongue down once or twice. Okay, closer to a hundred times.

The problem: I've hallucinated Oliver before. I followed him into the storm shelter—or rather, a *figment* of him. One that I could never physically catch and grab.

Yet, gazing at Olly here and now, I'm not scared.

I feel myself ease, even as I say, "There's a probability I never woke up this morning. That I'm still dreaming."

"Hands." Oliver holds out his, and I instinctually place my hands in his hands. His eyes never leave mine. His smile stretches as he rubs his thumbs along my palms. "She feels real to me."

I nearly smile back. "Really anxious?"

"No, you have steady hands, Hails." He lifts my palms to his cheeks, rests them tenderly against his jaw, and I breathe deeper, feeling—truly *feeling* Oliver. I glide my fingers over his slight stubble from not shaving yesterday. I thumb the soft skin beneath his glittering eyes.

The stress tensing my body begins to slip away. Because he's not staring at me as if losing my mind is synonymous with a face full of pus-laden boils. He's staring at me as if I'm perfectly Hailey.

As if I'm pretty.

Inside. Out.

Mad and all.

It's what he's good at—making people feel loved. He's a trained flirt. He could cause a married woman to fall head over heels for him at first casual greeting. Which he has done. Multiple times for various con jobs. One of which I even constructed.

He's the chameleon. An integral player on the board. I'm the mastermind. The one moving the pieces.

It's not our roles that made me think we'd be an ill-fated couple. I've just never believed we could be anything more than fuck buddies, given both our proclivities to sleep around and bang anyone with a pulse. But lately, he's only been sleeping with me, and I've only been sleeping with him and . . . Jake Koning Waterford.

Which he knows.

They both know about each other, but they've been avoiding each other to uncomplicate what should just be *casual* sex. I'm having casual sex with my best friend's charming brother *Oliver*. And with the town's treasured resident *Jake*.

Not to mention, Phoebe has spent a good majority of the year fake dating Jake while I was fucking him, so yeah . . . I am a great friend.

"Hails?" Oliver lifts my chin, and I realize my hands have slid off his face. "Where'd she go?"

"Down the rabbit hole."

"Not without me, I hope." He's more serious. It's hard to detect because he can expertly control his facial muscles, and the light never dims from his eyes. But I know Oliver well enough to see what he likes to hide. Before I ask for the real time, he's already telling me, "Twelve-oh-five."

"But I did wake up at nine this morning?"

"*We* did. Then I started reading to you." He grasps my shoulders, holding me still so I don't swivel in a dazed circle. "Which made you fall back asleep."

I blink hard, remembering. *"Little Red Riding Hood."*

He smiles. "Your obsession with wolves endures."

I have been researching all about them. "Thanks for indulging."

"Always and for never," Oliver teases after I peel out of his grasp and search the bed for my phone. I feel him staring at my bare ass. He can't see the smile trying to pinch my lips or the stinging heat against my face. I try not to advertise how much I enjoy our banter.

Because maybe he'd overdo it if he knew. I'd be just another girl he's reeled in emotionally and spit back out. And this isn't about emotions.

Not for me. Not for him. It is just sex.

Which . . . is precisely the cause of my current predicament. Sex. Intercourse. Sperm meet egg.

I'm pregnant.

The fact shoots to my brain every now and then, most especially when I'm clutching a toilet and spilling my guts up. But when I'm with Oliver, I'd like this knowledge to take a backseat.

Tell him. No, not today. He'll ask, *Who's the dad?* And the truth is, I don't know whose sperm defied the condom and rebelliously fertilized my egg. I'm luckily in a period of my life where there are only two possibilities.

Thank God.

It could have been worse, I've been telling myself. I've been sleeping around since I was a teenager. Sex is an energy release. It's the purge of adrenaline after a job. It's necessary in my life, like coffee in the morning or dessert after dinner.

I know the risks, but I've always used protection.

It could have been worse.

My two possibilities aren't even bad. I just hate that this will change the status quo. I'm not ready for it to. Which is why only Phoebe knows, and it will remain purely an *only Phoebe* situation until I gather the mental fortitude to include the others.

Anyway, I only learned that I'm incubating a human a week ago. It's sunk in about as well as a pool floatie. If not for the nausea and my nipples being so sore that shower water feels like a form of archaic torture, I would demand the doctor to run the test again.

Eight weeks.

I'm only eight weeks pregnant. I have time. As long as I stop losing sense of it, that is.

Hurrying around, I peek under pillows, detangling the fluffy comforter. No phone appears.

My mind whirls in too many directions. So . . . I fell back to sleep while Oliver read to me then. I didn't intend to sleep this late, but he must've wanted me to. Which is good. I need sleep. I've been trying to sleep more, in fact. Insomnia is a beast I've needed help to beat, and it still rears its horned head every single night.

The name of my new personal game: *Do Not Lose This Baby*. I can't think about whether I'll even be a good mom when I'm terrified I might cause this baby's demise before it's even born. Lately I've felt like a wrecking ball inside my own body. Like I cause more harm than good, and I want to prove to myself that I won't harm this baby.

I snatch my phone deep under the sheets, and my eyes widen at a missed message from Addison Tinrock. My mom. Just not in the biological sense. "Shit, *shit*."

"What shit?" Oliver asks while I shove my phone in his chest and beeline for the closet.

My pulse is going haywire as I fling aside grungy shirts and cargo pants. "Today is Saturday, April 21, 2012."

Oliver flips my phone in his hand like a pancake. "Is there something significant about the date? Other than the obvious."

"The obvious?" Why do I have so many cargo pants? I need a dress. Uh, not *that* dress. Too see-through. Very nightclub in Miami, which is the last place I wore it.

"The obvious: it being two weeks since your little brother decided that *poison* was a practical tool to pull like it's the fifteenth century and we're the Borgias." He catches my gaze, and his smile peeks out. "Down with the queen. Off with her head."

Claudia Koning Waterford is . . . deceased.

Jake's mom.

By Trevor Tinrock's doing. My nineteen-year-old brother—he went off-script. It was unplanned. A mistake . . . well, okay, it was premeditated by Trev, but for the rest of us, it was unintended. Claudia was our mark, but Phoebe should've pulled the rope via blackmail.

We never had the opportunity to cage Claudia in her own misdeeds.

Two weeks have passed, and everything is messier since Jake didn't inherit the entire Koning fortune and all assets, but rather, Claudia's will detailed a complicated split between her firstborn and thirdborn son.

Trent (asshole) and Jake (not an asshole . . . very sweet, actually).

All we wanted was for Jake to become *sole* heir. He needed to obtain everything. Then he'd pay us out.

But it's not impossible to salvage the scattered pieces of the Koning job. It's still alive.

I tear a simple black dress off the hanger. Prada—one of the last designer dresses I kept and didn't sell on the internet for cash, just to pay rent. "It's not the obvious," I say quickly to Oliver while I shimmy out of my strappy sports bra.

He comes over and helps tug the dress down over my head. "Then what?"

I fix my platinum-blonde hair out of my face while he zips the fabric at my hip. I try not to concentrate on the tingling sensation as his knuckles brush my bare flesh, the zipper ascending with his hand. "Um"—I breathe out—"Phebs and I made lunch plans with the godmothers."

Surprise coats his eyes. "That's big."

"I know." Heat bathes my face again. This time with nerves. The lunch is the first big olive branch we've extended to our moms since they confessed their lies in the storm shelter. Both Phoebe's brothers and mine knew we'd been toying with the idea of mending broken fences with the godmothers.

Rocky was the most irritable, but that's to be expected. He never loved the godmothers the way that we did. The way that we still somewhat do.

Oliver has a hand on my lower back. It's casual, reassuring. I've always liked his touch. His gaze falls to my phone, which he's clutching. He reads my mom's text aloud: "Where is Cogsworth?" He arches his brows at me. "I thought my sister told Addison to stop with the riddles?"

"Phoebe thinks they're distressing me, but uncovering a riddle isn't what's distressing. It's the fact that she's saying I'm late." I pull out of his reach and find heels at the bottom of my closet, explaining fast: "Cogsworth is the clock from *Beauty and the Beast*. She's reminding me to check the time."

"I know what the text meant," he says easily while skimming the length of me. "I'm not the rich boy who needs a

Tinrock-Graves history book." It would sound like a jab at Jake if it weren't for his lighthearted tone and inching smile.

"I didn't think you were Jake." Though, I do explain a lot to Jake Waterford. Because he wasn't raised as a con artist like us, but he's been an ally. I nuzzle my toes into dark velvet heels. Not appropriate for springtime, but it'll work. *"Oh."* I drop down and inspect my toes. *"No."*

Oliver strolls closer. "Did you grow a sixth toe? The magical marvel of Hailey Tinrock."

"I'm not a polydactyl. Just a girl with the ugliest chipped toenail polish." I pick at the black flakes on my big toe. "*Shit.* We're going to a five-star restaurant. I think the cheapest thing on the menu is fifty bucks. My mom is going to make a comment."

"Is the point to try to please her?"

"No, I just don't want to spend half the lunch hearing, 'This is why you should be a part of the elite and not the working class. So you can afford a basic pedicure.'"

"Fair enough." He dips his head close to mine, his lips ghosting against my ear as he whispers, "Let's venture to the bathroom." Every secret he shares with me sounds sexual, and likely it's because we have a sexual relationship.

We are sex partners.

And I'm carrying his baby. *Maybe.*

Maybe this baby is Jake's—but these facts are changing . . . things. *Things have changed, Hailey.* He doesn't know it yet, and guilt tries to pummel me.

Later.

Later.

I'll tell him later.

"Okay," I breathe. *Okay.* I wipe my sweaty palms on my thighs. I have horrible "tells" in comparison to Oliver, Phoebe, and Rocky—those three are masters of deception. I'm not great. They can all see when anxiety mounts like I'm ascending Everest without an oxygen tank.

Oliver hooks his finger with mine, and I pop into focus as he guides me out of the room and to the only bathroom.

No one else is in the loft this morning. Just us.

While I hurriedly comb a brush through my hair, Oliver leans against the sink, a little slouched as he cups my ankle and paints my toes with metallic black polish I picked out. I balance well, but every time I teeter, he lifts the brush off my nail and slides his other hand up my bare calf, clutching me tighter.

Feeling him stabilize me steals my breath once or twice.

The sensual look he slips me isn't helping. His *I know how to fuck you into oblivion* eyes are enticing. He entices me, and I can't . . . I'm late. Like, in every worst way a person *can* be late, I've been late.

"It's in Rhode Island," I mention, using my comb to create a center part in my hair. "The lunch."

"An hour away."

"Yeah, I'm meeting Phoebe."

"You want me to drive you?"

"No, *no*. I'm capable. I can drive." I've always been one of the better drivers among our families.

He dips the brush into the polish. "Of course you can, Hailstorm." The smile in his voice is fuel when I'm on empty. I'm eager to receive his faith in me, even if it's manufactured purely to make me feel good. I don't care.

I love how my lungs swell with his encouragement.

Our eyes fasten in a quiet, easygoing beat, and I want to ask where he'll be today. I'm afraid he'll say, *With Collin Falcone*.

Collin was Trent Waterford's former best friend. I hate that Olly's role has been to pry Collin away from the firstborn heir, which enabled Rocky to become Trent's number one BFF.

Unfortunately, Collin is a cokehead. Which means Oliver has had to partake in these hedonistic, drug-fueled nights reserved for bored trust-fund babies like Collin.

Every time I've surfaced the possibility of a role switch, Oliver says, "This is where I need to be, Hails. You even said it yourself. It's the best position."

Best position for the job. I didn't mean it was best for him. But for Oliver, they might as well be one and the same. He's a lot like his sister, Phoebe, in that way. Willing to take the harder tasks if the outcome means success for the team.

I think about Oliver a lot.

For too long, really. Even how he's unlike Phoebe. How he's so goal oriented that he'd race toward every checkered flag for the thrill. How he loves pushing his limits during jobs. How he'd choose the path with the most obstacles, the one that's farthest away. How he'd run until his legs broke and his heart gave out.

I think there is no stop in most of us, but for Oliver, he will run himself too hard, too fast, before anyone else has a chance to catch him.

I've always worried about putting him in a role that'd hurt him. I'm afraid I already have. *My fault*. When things go awry, it falls on me. I made the blueprint. So I made the error.

"Hailey, really, are you paying attention?"

Oh . . . fuck. That's not Oliver.

I blink into the clear, vividly bright present. I sit across from a formidable, stylish woman who could pose as a high-society New Yorker as much as she could a hardball attorney. But she's not posing as anyone other than herself today: Addison Tinrock—my mom.

What the fuck, what the fuck, what the fuck? I think over and over. Trying to calm my panic, but how the hell did I even get here?

"Hailey?" Her cold voice is tinged with concern. More than she usually grants me, but it's why I wanted to reach out. I could tell she's been genuinely worried about my welfare since she saw my breakdown in the storm shelter. It's been nice to see she cares on a deeper level about me and not just what I can do for her.

It's what I choose to believe, anyway. There is a small possibility she wants me close so I can continue working for her, but my brothers and I have already established those bridges will never be rebuilt with our parents. Any jobs we pull, we need to have our own autonomy.

They can't call the shots anymore.

"Um, yeah, I'm here," I say, doing my best not to stammer. A light coastal breeze blows through the sunny patio of an upscale seafood restaurant. The wicker chair creaks beneath my ass as I reach for my ice water. Condensation wets the glass, which means I've been here for minutes, at least.

I need to check my phone.

I need to check the parking lot.

Did I really drive?

Did Oliver end up bringing me?

"I actually need to make a quick call." I scooch back.

"Hailey, wait—" Her concern spikes in an odd way. She's afraid I'm ditching her, that I'm retracting the olive branch.

"I'll be back. Really, I will be. Stay, p-please."

She lowers back down at my insistence. Wind musses her new bangs, still a shade of auburn red. I assume she's still waiting for Elizabeth Graves to show up. Just like I am Phoebe. Because neither is here, and our table is set for four.

Leaving, I weave through the crowded patio. I don't make a scene. Too many people mind their own business. Every teak table is occupied. Chatter, the sounds of the sea, and speakers playing Tchaikovsky will drown our forthcoming conversation into incoherence from eavesdroppers. It's a perfect place to meet.

I should remember arriving.

I should.

"Think, Hailey, think," I mutter to myself. *Bad habit*, speaking my thoughts aloud. Bad, bad, bad.

And thinking—thinking is likely why I'm missing passages of time. I was in my head, wasn't I?

I try not to sprint through the restaurant. I almost crash into the ginormous fish tank, but once I swerve around the hostess stand, I push the double doors into the glaring sunshine-soaked afternoon.

Then I rock to a full stop.

My old faded green Honda is parked beside a sleek sapphire blue Porsche. The man leaning against the luxury sports car could belong in *Pretty in Pink*, *Mystic Pizza*, any Julia Roberts or John Hughes movie. Born to a fortune of blue-blooded New England aristocracy. He's a man in numbers (twenty-eight), but also a man in how he carries his body. Confident in who he is, confident in his ideals, confident in his actions.

He straightens up and spots me from across the parking lot.

I see the concern tighten his striking blue eyes. I wonder if he sees the confusion in my gray ones.

Jake Koning Waterford.

Why is he in Rhode Island?

TWO

Hailey

Did Phoebe invite you? Did the godmothers?" I whisper as soon as I reach Jake's side. He's impeccably dressed in navy slacks, a crisp white button-down, and shiny leather loafers. Like usual, his brown hair is artfully styled to peak high-class standards.

For a flash, I remember disheveling those strands as he kissed between my legs. I remember the hungered way he looked up at me as his tongue circled my clit.

I gulp hard.

Focus, Hailey.

Jake towers above me in the parking lot. Tall like Oliver, maybe even an inch taller than him, and his strong jawline clenches as more dark concern narrows his gaze. He casts an apprehensive glance at the restaurant, as if expecting Addison to rush out after me, but mostly, he's assessing me head to toe. "No, they didn't invite me."

"Did I?" It sounds like a silly question out of context.

His concern hikes. "No, Hailey. I drove here after I talked to Carter."

"Carter?" *What?* I almost sway backward, but Jake shields my eyes from the sun with his hand, and I stay fixed on him.

"Stuart Cartwright," he clarifies. "The only Carter I know. My oldest friend."

His old boarding school roommate, who happens to be my family's forger. And *also* my ex-fling. I used to fantasize that Carter would be *the one*. The long-lasting forever romance—back when I thought I'd eventually have a whirlwind con artist love story like my parents.

The fantasy blew up when A.) I learned my parents lied to me and they seemed less like people to emulate and more like a cautionary tale and B.) I realized Carter and I no longer want the same things.

He will always be on the move. I want to stay in Victoria for more than a few seasons.

The want feels more like a *need* now that I'm pregnant.

I shake my head slowly. "Why Carter?"

"You talked to Carter on your drive here," Jake says, pausing to let his words jog my memory, but all I remember is Oliver.

"No . . ."

"Look at your call history. He said he called you, and you picked up and told him you were driving to Newport for lunch at Briny Pearl."

I fumble my phone out of my studded crossbody purse. Sure enough, I have an answered call from Carter. "Thirty minutes ago," I mutter.

Jake opens the Porsche's passenger door. "Here, sit. You look pale."

"I'm always pale." I'm dazed staring at the phone.

"Paler than usual."

I feel dizzy, so I sink down on the black leather interior. Jake bends close, extending an arm over me to reach the cupholder. His bicep skims against my shoulder, and our gazes touch for a heady second.

His sandy-brown hair rustles with the wind, and I get lost in his cerulean-blue eyes, dreamy and idyllic like a perfect summer sky.

Jake Waterford has felt unreal.

Like another figment of my imagination. There was a time or two that I wondered if I'd made him up. If my mind had conjured him back when we moved to the quaint, delightfully romantic Connecticut town. The hot landlord to shepherd me and Phoebe into our new honest living.

Then we found skeletons under his bed—he faked his little sister's death; he'd been friends with Carter—and I knew he had to be real. My brain wouldn't construct someone this complex with sister baggage and parental issues and boarding school connections to my yearslong crush. He wasn't simple.

I thought maybe I needed simple, but I found myself liking that he was so complex.

I still find myself liking him.

Even now, as he grabs a three-fourths-filled water bottle for me. I love and hate being doted on and taken care of. I love feeling important enough to matter, but I hate how it's synonymous with being weak.

"Drink this." He unscrews the Evian and hands it to me.

"Thanks." I take small sips. "What did I even tell Carter?" I vaguely begin to recall climbing into the car and clutching the wheel.

"He said you were mostly talking about Oliver."

"Oh God," I mumble into a heartier swig of water.

Jake nods more strongly. "Yeah," he says flatly, then rises to a stand. He stays close.

It's no secret that Carter and I banged in the past, or that I'm now having casual sex with both Jake and Oliver. The *causal* situation (emphasis on casual) shouldn't be awkward, but the more Oliver and Jake avoid each other—it is.

"What did I say?" I ask.

"Mainly that you were concerned about him. You think he needs a new role. Then you were rambling. Carter couldn't follow your logic, so he called me after he hung up and said I should check on you. He's not in Victoria."

"I heard." Carter flew to Manchester for a long weekend. He's unsure if he'll return to town or not.

I pick at the label on the water bottle. Jake remains standing, holding the hood of the car as if he's touching my head, but he's not touching me. He's more careful with me than Oliver is. I love and hate that, too.

"Well, you found me. I'm okay."

"Are you?" He lifts his brows. "Do you even remember driving here?"

"A little . . . not enough, probably." I've told him that I lose time while I'm stuck inside my head. I have trouble being in the present moment. It's a persistent problem, but it's been heightened to these extremes since I learned my parents deceived me and my insomnia reared its ugly head. "It'll come to me. It usually does." We lock eyes again.

He's the town heartthrob. A quintessential Prince Charming who has women swooning the second he enters a room. Every lady at Victoria Country Club will be trying to pair their prim and proper daughters with him.

Even if I wasn't a server, even if I wasn't a grifter, there is *nothing* about me that screams *debutante*. I'm a goth weirdo with a brain that never sleeps and a heart that's never been up for grabs.

Yet, I've told him things I shouldn't. He knows more than he needs to. And that's how I first knew I liked Jake. It's also how I know I've been letting him reach my heart.

Maybe he's touched too much of it.

"You shouldn't drive, Hailey. Not while you're still recovering. It's only been two weeks since you hallucinated—"

"I haven't hallucinated since then," I say with a nod. "I'm getting better." I nod again.

He nods back. "It's okay if it takes a while."

No, it's not. I wrap my arms around my abdomen, hoping I'm not drawing attention to my uterus.

Jake's frown deepens. "What's the rush? Because if it's about me and my brother and this unfinished job—"

I pop out of the car, pushing the Evian into his hand. "There's always a job. It's not the job. It's . . . it's just me."

He shifts his weight uncertainly. "You put too much pressure on yourself. This isn't life-or-death here anymore. You can breathe."

"Almost. We're almost there." I tie my hair in a low pony out of my face.

"Hailey . . ." he starts, but I'm already walking toward the restaurant.

"Don't wait for me. Phebs is coming. I'll ask her to drive us home."

"How is she getting here?"

"The bus, I think."

Jake shakes his head in slow-growing confusion. "You girls . . . I don't get you two. She could've asked me for a ride."

"You both *just* broke up." It was a fake breakup to their fake romance, but it was recent nonetheless.

"What about Grey?" *Grey Thornhall*—Rocky's alias in Victoria. "Why couldn't he drop off Phoebe?"

"She didn't want to be seen out with her ex-husband right after ending things with you."

Jake doesn't like this answer. It means he's the reason she's taking public transit. He's also blamed himself for being the reason Rocky and Phoebe have been secretly dating for half the year and not a public couple. But he's not the reason.

It's just the job.

We all have our roles. We all play pretend. It's only fun when we can see all the pieces. When we know what's real and what's fake. I want it to be fun again.

I think it can be, but that involves staying out of my head. My phone buzzes as I hurry back toward the restaurant.

Carter: You should tell them. About the bun in the oven.

Did I tell Carter I'm pregnant?! My eyes bug, and it takes a lot of control not to stall out. Jake is waiting for me to reach the doors to Briny Pearl, likely afraid I might pass out midstride. I manage to go inside the restaurant, the cool AC hitting me all at once, and I sink down on the rattan bench near a life-sized mermaid sculpture.

I call Carter.

"Ailey!" He picks up on the first ring, his East London accent thick along with his joviality. Carter is rarely somber. I've always liked that about him. "Nice chat we were 'aving earlier."

"The one where I purged everything in my head?"

"Not everything. Trust, you were skirting around things, too."

I'm quiet.

"Oi, you better be breathing, or I'll do worse on you and call your big moody brother."

I smile a little. "Rocky would hang up on you."

"Not when I say it's about you."

That's true. "Did I tell you that . . . ?" I can't finish.

"That you've got a bun in the oven. You mumbled it. Said you've been keeping it to yourself. You and Phoebe. Now me, I reckon."

I intake a sharp breath. "Carter—"

"I didn't tell Jake. You barely meant to tell me, and you know me and you, Ailey. I'm not going around spilling all you share. This'll be the same."

I exhale.

"Ain't that the sound of beauty."

"Breath?"

"Life."

His words drive deeper through me, and I place a softer hand on my flat belly.

"They should know," Carter says in my silence.

"Who?"

"All of 'em. Best way to protect the future Tinrock progeny is if the whole team knows."

"Not yet."

"Thought you'd say that." I hear his laughter before it comes. "I'm finishing up a passport for Mum's friend, but I'll pop in and out of Victoria when I can. Hit that Uncle Ned?" He's telling me to go to bed. I understand some Cockney slang. Not as much as Oliver.

"Fly safe," I say, then call Phoebe after I hang up.

"Ew, this bus seat is *nasty*," she says upon answering. "I seriously could not find one that didn't have a random white or brown stain. Buses shouldn't have fabric seats. This needs to be illegal."

"They know." I stand up, heading toward the patio so as not to worry my mom. I've been gone long enough.

"Who knows what?" she whisper-hisses.

"The baby. Carter knows."

"What the *fuck*?" she curses harshly. "You've got to be fucking kidding me—"

"My fault—"

"Never your fault," she says. "He probably weaseled it out of you."

"That would still be my fault," I whisper, skirting around a server and her bowls of lobster bisque.

"I'll never believe it is, so you need to live with my delusion."

I smile a little, loving my best friend during a crisis. "I'll explain everything later. Ride safe."

"Pray I don't get a rash."

"I'll let Oliver know so he can pray in every language."

"Perfect. Love you."

"Love you, too." We hang up, and I take a readying breath as I push into the patio. My mom nearly springs out of her chair upon seeing me. Her overwhelmed relief slams into me like a monster truck, and it feels . . . good.

She really wanted me back.

THREE

Hailey

"You look a little clammy. Do you need more water?" My mom is about to flag another server.

"I'm okay." I catch her hand across the table, stopping her. She jolts at the sudden touch as much as I do. We're not a physically affectionate mother-daughter pair. Not like Elizabeth and Phoebe.

Even so, my mom turns her hand, letting my fingers slip into hers for the briefest of moments. She squeezes the tips of them in the subtlest expression of care. Here I was, expecting a lengthy lecture about not being put together enough.

After releasing her hand from mine, she clasps the stem of a wineglass filled with a pale-gold liquid. The Sauvignon Blanc tips me off that she'll be having oysters on the half shell. It's an Addison Tinrock staple, and despite everything we've been through, a part of me is honored she's let me see her likes, dislikes, and true personality when so much of her life is a careful fabrication.

I prefer seeing the truths. I never want to be fed lies again.

Water laps gently against sailboats and yachts in Bowen's Wharf. It's not a secret how much the godmothers love Newport, Rhode Island. How along the Cliff Walk they'd admire the rows of Gilded Age mansions. How they dreamed of one day being so rich and powerful they could buy the Vanderbilts' summer home themselves.

I love the scenic New England coast. *Pleasant*. The salty air and smell. It eases me as much as the escalating chatter around us. Ladies in flowing silk dresses scoop mussels out of shells and sip rosé. Lost in their own universe. Oblivious to ours.

I take a deeper breath and ask, "What were we talking about before?"

"Phoebe and Rocky."

Of course we were. Their names typically leave my mom's lips as easily as *hello* and *goodbye*.

Phoebe and Rocky.

Rocky and Phoebe.

My older brother and my best friend.

Two people who have been vital organs in my life as essential as lungs and kidneys and the black heart that pumps in my chest. Brain fog begins clearing. Little pieces of our lunch convo return to me. "You were asking for updates," I state. "Haven't you heard the gossip at the club?"

Addison and Elizabeth have been frequenting Victoria Country Club since Claudia's funeral. They've already established false identities as ritzy, boutique New York matchmakers—which is why we're meeting outside of Victoria. It'd raise too many questions if they were spotted out to lunch with me and Phebs in town. We could brush away the skepticism, but it's easier to avoid altogether.

She watches me tear a packet of Sugar in the Raw. "Yes, I've heard about the breakup. You really can't escape the news about Phoebe Smith, Jake Waterford, and Grey Thornhall." She takes a stiff sip of wine. "It's this town's version of *Dawson's Creek*."

She knows I love those soapy shows, even if they aren't her favorite. I scoot closer to the table and say, "Except part of the love triangle was fake, which makes it not really a love triangle at all."

"For the best. I can't imagine anything more needlessly complicated than a real-life pull between two men. Phoebe avoided a headache."

I try to think of anything but Oliver and Jake. "What's the public perception of the breakup?" I stick to the job. Stable ground.

"Claudia's friends at the club are unsurprised. No one honestly believed Jake would last with Phoebe long term, and those with daughters have already gone rabid. Julia Kelsey's mother is trying to set the poor girl up for polo lessons with Jake."

"As expected," I mutter, my stomach weirdly knotting picturing a flock of women hovering around Jake. I can't imagine Jake lifting Julia off a horse without feeling dizzy. I should drink water, but I dump my sugar into a cinnamon latte macchiato, a splurge when I've been mostly living off drip coffee these past months.

This will be my only burst of caffeine today, so I plan to savor every sip.

"What do you think?" my mom asks.

"About?" I lift my gaze to hers, seeing her assess me a little too intensely.

"About Jake."

I blink, not knowing what to say, considering she has *zero* clue that I'm Jake's fuck buddy. A secret I shall not be inviting her to share. And she's not asking if I'm sleeping with Jake—that'd be ludicrous. We've been very discreet, and the only reason a select few people know is because I told them.

"Jake . . . ?"

"And Phoebe." She gives me a puzzled look. "You're sure you're fine, Hailey?" She waves a server over, just to ask them to adjust the umbrella. Shade bathes me once more, and I thank them before they leave. "Better?" she wonders.

I nod. "I think it was a good, amicable breakup. There was no screaming match. No slap to the face. She didn't push him in the pool, and he didn't stomp angrily away. Phoebe should come out unscathed."

The two of them stopped attending social functions together. People asked questions, and they've told the same story. Jake is mourning over his mom's unexpected death two weeks ago, and now he's too busy dealing with the messiness of his inheritance to give time to a relationship.

They're officially *over.*

My mom sets her wineglass on the table, a whisper of a smile lifting her lips. "It was a clever breakup. Using Claudia Waterford's death as the impetus. It painted them both in a good light. Was that you?"

She's asking if it was *my* plan.

I nod again. "They asked for my help."

"As they should. You're brilliant." She says it as if it still exists within me. My smarts. As if they haven't been lost with my mind.

A familiar surge of pride pours through me. I used to bottle up her compliments like medicine, downing them during low times to give me boosts. These days it's harder to hoard them. So I let the compliment flow through me and away like a single shot of dopamine.

She stares off at the patio railing for a beat, then takes a longer sip of wine. "If the Koning job is still on . . ." She pauses, hesitating to continue or not.

"It is still in motion. We haven't called it quits." Once Jake has full control of his dynasty, he's agreed to give us each a million dollars for helping him. It's a long con that was severely flubbed when my little brother offed Claudia.

Jake doesn't deserve to be abandoned halfway through, especially after our mistake cost him his mother, and the payout will be a windfall we all desperately need.

"Then what's the point of Phoebe breaking up with Jake?" she questions.

"Because she loves Rocky."

"She can love Rocky and still fake date Jake." Her advice is to do by example—since she's been with my dad in the real sense while they've pretended to be with other people for cons—but we aren't trying to follow in their exact footsteps.

Clearly this hasn't sunk in for her yet.

"She'd rather be with Rocky publicly."

Mom shakes her head slowly, her fingernails tapping the teak table. "The better play is for Phoebe to remain with the thirdborn heir to a billion-dollar fortune, especially while he's fighting with his brother for the inheritance."

I can't disagree. It is the smarter move. But I'm still warring with how to protect the people I love versus protecting the job. "Phoebe and Jake's breakup won't impact the job that much," I defend.

I've weighed the cost, and I'd rather my best friend be blissfully happy with my older brother than be tortured with the idea that they can *never* be publicly together.

"You know what would be easiest." Her eyes bore into mine. There is no question. Because I'm conditioned to see the seamless path to secure a fortune. The one she taught me to locate.

"She's *not* marrying Jake," I say more strongly.

"Would he agree to it?"

I shove back from the table, feeling sick.

"Hailey, it's just a question," she says quickly. "I'm not pushing. I'm just . . . trying to gather data." Her breathing shortens. She's nervous? I've never had this much power over her, I don't think. She's never been this afraid to truly lose me.

"It doesn't matter if he would or wouldn't marry Phoebe." I'm not giving her all the information. She's not using me as a resource into the mind of Jake Waterford, and I hate the implication that Phoebe can be persuaded to do anything. That the only roadblock would be convincing Jake. "Phoebe wants to be romantically and truthfully with Rocky. What Phoebe—my *best friend* wants—is all that matters."

Phoebe has never been selfish. She's never wanted *anything* for herself at the cost of the team, and the fact that she wants my brother publicly is big.

"Okay. *Okay.*" She places her hands on the table to calm the strain between us. "You are aware, though, that marriage between Phoebe and Jake would guarantee more than a million—"

"I'm aware," I cut her off.

I can't lie to myself. I know a marriage is what I would suggest if feelings weren't in the way. And maybe not just Phoebe and Rocky's feelings . . . maybe mine, too.

She releases a soft sigh, uncertainty flashing in her tightened eyes. She wants me and her to be okay, but she can't help but dole out nuggets of advice. I prepare for another. Unsurprised when she says, "Your life here is dependent on the outcome of that job." She means my financial stability. "Unless you'd like to pull one in another city. You can always leave Victoria—"

"No, thank you." I sit a little straighter. "We'll be fine here as servers."

"And how have you managed in one of Connecticut's *richest* towns as a server?" *Not well.* "Have you been dependent on your landlord?"

Yes. I swallow a sip of macchiato. "Jake has covered our rent for more than a few months," I admit.

She leans back with a slight smile, liking this answer. "You should keep squeezing him."

Guilt flips my stomach. "It's not like that. He's just being kind."

"And you're using his kindness to your advantage." She slips designer sunglasses over her eyes. "I'll have to tell Bethy all isn't lost with you two. Somewhere, deep down, you and Phoebe know this is the right path."

I'm not so sure myself anymore. I despise the insinuation that I'm using Jake for his money. All my mom sees is what he can provide us, and I haven't envisioned him as a pot of gold I'm trying to reach. It'd make me no better than all the ladies scrambling to be the next Mrs. Jake Koning Waterford.

But he is supposed to pay us out at the end.

So am I really any better?

I want off this Jake Waterford merry-go-round, so I begin thinking about my childhood. About the jobs I never questioned because I'd receive little details when I did.

You weren't a part of those, she'd say. *I can't incriminate you. That time is long gone, Hailey.*

I want to know her past. Because it's mine, too. "I was in Newport when I was little, wasn't I? Around four?"

"Around then." She picks up her wine again, her voice incredibly stilted, but the warning look in her eye tells me to *drop it*.

I won't. Not anymore. "You said you adopted me so Phoebe would grow up with another girl. Like you and Elizabeth were childhood friends. Well, I remember being at a fancy estate with Oliver, but why was I separated from Phoebe? Why keep me from her when we were little?"

She peers around.

At first, I think it's to avoid my question, but I realize she's just calculating how many people could be listening over the music, chatter, and sea.

"We were in Newport for a short time back then." She speaks in a quieter tone. "A piggyback job."

I assume they befriended New England socialites, then influenced them to pay their tabs and hotel fees with promises of "I'll get you next time, of course" only to then disappear. "Did something go south?" I ask.

"Not at all. It went perfect." She takes a tiny sip, staring more at the liquid than at me. "But it was necessary to have Phoebe be with Brayden."

Brayden. Rocky's birth name. "You were trying to pair Phoebe and Rocky together *that* young?"

"*No*," she emphasizes like this is absurd. "Brayden was . . . he was a traumatized little boy. He had these screaming fits, and the only way he'd calm down was when he was around Phoebe. We didn't know why he felt safe with her, and we didn't question it. So when we were in Newport at a family's estate, we didn't want a meltdown from my six-year-old to cause attention. The *horrible* woman we were deceiving would make comments about ill-mannered children, and she'd cast us aside if she thought mine made a scene."

I process this slowly. "You could've let me be with Phoebe *and* Rocky then."

"You were a shy child. It was better if you were around Oliver. He made you less skittish—darling, stop . . ." She trails off, and I catch myself picking at my cuticles while she catches herself lecturing me.

Tension builds between us.

My face contorts as mistrust circles through me. "Or . . . you were attempting to match me with Oliver. To see which pairing would stick—"

"You were *four.* We cared more about whether you all were fed, bathed, clothed, and if you'd say anything inappropriate to the wrong people." To their marks, she means. "We were only twenty-seven back then. We weren't thinking decades ahead."

I want to believe you.

God, I do.

It hurts that there's *any* doubt. But I spent months in tormented, sleepless nights trying to track down the holes she left in her lies.

She can see the pain cross my face. I don't have to say words. Not when it comes to her. We speak through our eyes. Her carriage rises in a deep, aching breath.

"I'm telling you the truth," she professes. "I'm honest *now.* With *everything.*"

"I'm trying to believe that." The pieces of our relationship are large fragmented shards, and maybe with time, they'll be able to be glued back together one day.

But right now, I can't shake how she spent my entire life making me believe I was her biological daughter. Making me believe Trevor and Rocky were my biological brothers.

In reality, I was adopted from foster care. Trevor is the son of a rich, elitist couple like the ones we scam. My parents, Addison and Everett Tinrock, paid the couple's surrogate to give the newborn to them instead.

And Rocky . . .

He's the only one with murder all over his backstory. While I might never know my birth name, his is Brayden Wolfe.

The Wolfes.

They're one of only three founding families of Victoria, and Varrick Wolfe conned his way into the Wolfe family, married into their dynasty, and decimated it from the inside out.

It's hard to think about Rocky's origins without picturing my mom and dad in their early twenties—younger than I am now—caught up in a con gone horribly wrong with Varrick. They trusted him until his plans took a sinister turn, so they tailed him one dark night in Connecticut. They saw him run the Wolfes off a bridge, the car plunging into the watery depths of the river below. Instead of driving away and dusting off their hands and consciences of this cruel malice, my parents pulled their car over.

My dad jumped off the bridge and into the water, attempting to rescue anyone he could from drowning in that river.

Out of a family of five. He could only save the one-year-old in the backseat.

The one-year-old they would raise as theirs.

The one-year-old that would come to be a vital organ in my life.

My big brother.

I know I shouldn't offer my love to two people who were complicit in the demise of Rocky's birth family, but it's difficult to hate them. My mom didn't have to stop the car. My dad didn't have to jump into the river. And they chose to keep Rocky in fear that Varrick would finish off the Wolfe line.

It was to protect him.

In a way, I think most of their decisions—good and bad—have been to protect all of us.

As someone who constantly weighs pros and cons, who thinks about every variable in a job, I can understand when there are no perfect choices. Only ones that come with consequences we can live with, and they chose to live with these horrible lies.

My only wish is that they told us the truth sooner. Trusted us when we became adults and especially when we questioned their stories, but I think this was something they were willing to take to their graves until they realized it was going to cost their relationship with us completely.

Rocky will say they didn't want to lose their pawns in the game of grifting.

But I'm not so cynical.

I truly believe my parents love me, and I'm not going to torture myself anymore by doubting that. I've seen how it's chipped away at Rocky over the years. That won't be me. Especially not *now.* The last thing I need in my life is stress.

Do not lose this baby.

FOUR

Phoebe

Fuck the bus. Fuck Rhode Island (sorry if you live here). And fuck my creepy *fucking* birth father, who's making me check over my shoulder a hundred times a minute.

"He is *so* fucking weird," I say harshly into my phone. "Not the interesting kind of weird, but the I-will-butcher-you-in-your-sleep type of fucked-up freak."

"You want to drop another *fuck*?" Rocky snaps hotly.

"You plan to pick it up for me?"

"Fuck no."

My scowl pinches into a smile, but my power walking stride never loses blistering heat as I trek from the bus stop to Briny Pearl. I'm very late to the lunch with the godmothers and Hails on account of my lack of forethought about how painfully slow the bus would be.

"Let's return to the part where you said you saw him," Rocky says, his voice deep and coarse like harsh sandpaper against my ears.

Him. "That creep wishes he were as cool as Jason Voorhees."

"Your sick fascination with the ugly fuck from *Friday the 13th* isn't dispelling the father-daughter comparisons here."

I skid to a full-blown halt right outside of Briny Pearl. I glare at the pirate ship wheel on the restaurant's navy-blue siding. "I'm *not* like my dad. Take it back right now."

"Only if you stay on topic. For fuck's sake, Phebs. I'm going out of my mind picturing him tailing your bus."

"Like I said, he was waiting at the bus stop in Victoria. I thought he was going to follow me on, but he just waved me goodbye with a creepy smirk."

"Use another fucking adjective."

I hate that I love Rocky's aggravated, serrated edges. I might be a freak in the sense that I like being cut up by him, but I refuse to believe I share more than a genetic code with Varrick Wolfe. Personality, uh-uh—we are *not* the same. Not that we're on speaking terms. He's just done the stalkerish loitering thing.

I expel a molten breath. "Picture a fortysomething version of Christan Bale in *American Psycho*. That was his pompous, punchable smile."

"Great. Did he know you were going to Newport?" Rocky asks.

"Unsure." I fix the spaghetti strap to my slim pink dress, then bend at the knees to retie the loose ribbon on my white wedges. "He knew I was leaving Victoria to hop on the bus, at least. Maybe my mom told him. She's been keeping in contact with Varrick." It's been a point of contention among me and my brothers and her, and I feel ill even imagining her spending two seconds with a man who *murdered* Rocky's entire family.

What else is he capable of?

My skin crawls, and as I scan my surroundings, my body tightens in preparation to throw a fist, knee a groin, or run for my life. Luckily, I'm alone near the sunny entrance of the restaurant. Just me and some potted yellow daylilies.

"You didn't think to call me on the bus?" Rocky questions. It sounds like he's power walking as angrily as I just was.

"I did think about it, and I thought that you would've followed me." I hear the slam of a car door over the phone. It swells my lungs, knowing he's quick to be there for me, but at the same time, this isn't one of those cases where he should show up. "You can't come here." I hear the engine. *"Rocky."*

"Give me one decent reason."

"It'd look exceptionally shitty banging my ex-husband shortly after breaking up with the town sweetheart."

"I'm not going to fuck you in Rhode Island, Phoebe. I'm just making sure you weren't tailed."

My face flames. I open my mouth, but I replay the gritty mean tone he had with me. And now I do just want him to fuck me in Rhode Island.

He must hear the shift of my breath. Because he says, "Don't worry, I'll destroy your cunt later."

I glare. "*If* I let you."

"Funny you think I won't just take you anyway."

I'd flip him off if he were near me. I chew the corner of my smile. "Threatening me with a bad time."

"Always. I'm fuck out of good times."

"Same." I love how deranged this conversation is, and *shit*, I really need to go to lunch. I'm stalling now. "I need to go. I love you. Bye." I hang up, not giving him the opportunity to serve an *I love you* back. It feels like a victorious declaration of love. One that doesn't need reciprocation.

While gathering my dark blue hair into a messy high pony, I barrel into the fancy restaurant and offer a brisk smile to the hostess. "I'm meeting someone on the patio." Then I follow a server out into the glaring sunshine, squinting as I locate Hailey, Addison Tinrock, and two empty chairs.

Confusion knits my brows. How is my mom still not here? I plop down unladylike into a free wicker seat. "Hi, Hails," I greet my best friend, happy to see signs of good sleep since I spent the night at Rocky's boathouse and didn't wake up in our loft. No dark circles under her eyes. Her platinum-blonde hair is combed and tangle-free. I catch a glimpse of her toes, which have a new metallic polish.

Go, Hails.

Smoky shadow accentuates her gray irises. She appears reserved and standoffish, but her smile peeks at me over a sip of coffee. Her black lipstick leaves a stain against the rim, and I watch how her body relaxes like she's relieved I'm a part of the lunch.

I smile back, then notice Addison staring more at the door. Maybe she's expecting her own best friend to trail after me, but my mom is nowhere in sight.

"So, Addison, did you happen to tell your old creepy friend that I'd be here today?" I stretch forward like this is an interrogation. Because it *is*. My trust in her and my mom hasn't just been on thin ice. It's plummeted into hypothermic waters. They're lucky Hailey and I have retrieved it, but like hell am I holding it in my hand just to get frostbite.

I believe in actions more than words.

"My old creepy friend?" she repeats like I doled out a freezer-burnt dessert when she's only ever been fed Michelin-star soufflés.

"Six-foot-something. Dresses like he's old money. Clean-shaven. Very fit. Probably runs ten miles to the soundtrack of babies crying. Stupidly good-looking according to ladies at the club who need checked for cataracts, but he's grotesque to my own two eyes. *That* old creepy friend. You know, the one you lost touch with back in '86 in Victoria."

Addison sends me a sharp reprimanding look to lower my voice.

I'm not feeling *demure*. I've learned too much. Like how our parents ran jobs with Varrick Wolfe in the eighties. They have history with him that we don't. They *know* him, and I simultaneously want nothing to do with the man while also wanting to know everything about him. The latter, mostly to protect myself.

"I haven't said a word to Varrick," Addison says, pushing a plate of oysters toward me. Even as my stomach grumbles, I don't take the distraction.

"But my mom has," I state, knowing she's been popping in and out of Stonehaven since Claudia died. The historic mansion is located on a tiny island a short boat ride from the Victoria harbor, and it's belonged to the Wolfes since they founded the town in 1887. Unfortunately, Varrick married into the Wolfe dynasty before he killed them off, so he has sole claim to the residence.

Hailey frowns at me. "You think Elizabeth tipped him off that we'd be here?"

"I think someone did, seeing as how he was waiting for me to get on the bus."

"You took the bus?" Addison puts two fingers to her temple, sinking backward like a migraine is coming on.

"That's what you're getting out of this?" Irritation claws at my insides. Their priorities seem fucked-up. The godmothers are more worried about me and Hails ditching our grifter lifestyle than anything else. Rocky would say they don't want to lose their assets they've cultivated for twenty-four years, but I've always believed it's deeper.

They're worried Hailey and I won't live the lives they've

dreamed for us. All they've ever wanted was for us to have it *better* than them. From what they've said, they grew up poor as dirt, and they scraped their way to the upper echelons of society. So seeing their daughters choose the bottom-feeder lives they fought to escape—it must hurt a little.

At least enough to burst a blood vessel in Addison's temple.

"If Bethy tipped him off, she would've had a good reason." Addison reaches for her wineglass. "The *last* thing she'd do is put you in harm's way. The only reason she's entertaining that ghoul is to protect you, Nova, and Oliver."

I clench down on my teeth. My heart pangs as guilt begins to gnaw from the inside out. I have no idea if my mom even loved Varrick. She was only twenty-two when she ran from Connecticut. From him. Pregnant with triplets.

He couldn't have been much older than her. What was their relationship even like? Were me and my brothers conceived out of hate? Was it forced? Do I want that answer?

It'd paint a graphic picture of her present interactions with my dad at Stonehaven. I should have these facts rather than bury my head in the sand, but my throat swells with emotion. I can't ask Addison for those exact details when they need to come from my mom.

"Has there been signs of life?" I ask, my voice scratchy and edged. "What if he threw her into the bay?"

"He didn't throw her into the bay . . ." Addison says, but her forehead wrinkles again. She downs the last sip of white wine and only eases when she glances left. She immediately rises from her chair in relief. "There you are."

Elizabeth Graves is . . . a mess. My mom struts in with disheveled, bed-head hair. It's dyed a pretty honey blonde that seems a little too yellow in the sunlight. Her peach blouse is severely wrinkled—her leather Birkin halfway unzipped.

She's not always drenched in Hermès, Cartier, and Dior, as she'd say, "Real wealth doesn't need to be flashy." And Addison would add, "Wealth whispers." But my mom does usually appear like she's a walking celestial perfume ad. Ready to grace your life with heavenly charm.

She's not angelic right now. She's evoking hangover chic. Is her mascara smudged?

After Addison and Elizabeth hug, my mom sinks down in her seat while greeting too brightly, "Hi, spiders." Her smile is too caked on. *Phony.* "You're both looking cute today."

I open my mouth, but a server interrupts us. "Would you two like anything to drink?"

"Water's fine," I say.

"I'll have what she's having." My mom points to Addison's empty wineglass.

"We'll take a whole bottle," Addison chimes in. "Four glasses, please."

Hailey slumps in her chair, cupping her coffee in two tight palms. I slip her a subtle reassuring look before waving a casual hand at the server. "That won't be necessary. Just two glasses for them."

"You sure?" My mom smiles to draw mine out. "You have a reason to celebrate." She must detect my confusion because she adds, "Your breakup with Jake."

Right . . . "No, we're good," I tell the server. "Just two glasses." Once she disappears from earshot, I explain, "I'm sure it's a hundred-dollar bottle. At minimum. Hailey and I didn't come to this lunch flush." I pick up a menu. "I'll be lucky to afford the breadbasket."

It's not a lie, but it's not the real reason we're sober.

I'm protecting Hailey's baby secret. To my fucking *grave.* I won't tell a soul, not even my boyfriend. Her brother. Not until she's ready to share this news—which she's not. She literally just found out a week ago.

My mom zips up her Birkin. "Aren't you dating Rocky, bug? He can pay for you."

"For a lunch he's not even attending?" I set down the menu, my stomach tossing. "That's demoralizing."

"More demoralizing than taking the bus here?" Addison retorts.

Elizabeth lets out a shocked breath. "You didn't."

I growl out a sigh. "Okay, the real issue isn't my mode of transportation." I rotate toward my mom beside me. "Did you tell Varrick about this lunch?" My frown deepens into pits of concern. "And why do you look so . . . ?"

She flattens her hair quicky, almost embarrassed. Flustered. This woman could make a period stain appear like the latest fashion trend. I've never seen her wear embarrassment—not a single day of my life. Hell, she's never been this *ruffled*. Even on the drive away from an abusive mark who left a handprint on her cheek, she'd have perfect posture in the car.

She spends a great deal of time untwisting the knotted chain of her gold heart-shaped locket before reaching for her water. "I left our beach rental in a hurry," she explains with a barbaric slurp. Water drizzles down her chin. She curses under her breath, dabs the spill with the cloth napkin. "I did mention to him that I'd be meeting you for lunch. I didn't tell him where we'd be."

We go abruptly silent as the server returns with a wine bottle, another dozen oysters, and a creamy crab dip. Tension mounts as she slowly pours a taster for Addison. None of us put on a façade that everything is okey fucking dokey. Even my mom's smile—a tiny gesture to expel my worry—has vanished.

Once the two wineglasses are filled and the server leaves us, I angle back toward Elizabeth. "Why tell that creep anything at all?"

"I'm trying to reason with him, bug, and . . . and that means being open. He can tell when I evade."

"Can he be reasoned with?" Hailey asks, a lot less hostilely than I would.

"I don't know." My mom perches her sunglasses on the top of her head. I almost feel bad for the heat off my questions when I notice the deep bags under her eyes. "There are things he wants and things he clearly doesn't."

We all look unsettled.

Addison starts piling mignonette sauce onto her shellfish with a little spoon, her shoulders more constricted.

"What doesn't he want?" I ask.

"A payout. I offered him a portion of the Koning job, and in return, he would leave Victoria permanently."

My brows spring. "You did *what*?"

"It was necessary—"

"No, you don't get to include him in a fucking *job* without including *all* of us in this decision. We don't even know him, and that job was ours." We involved our parents because we needed their help, but they weren't supposed to ever take the helm.

I am hurt.

Rocky will always believe the godmothers want to control us, and so badly, I want my mom to prove him wrong. But if she continues yanking the strings from us, then how are we anything but her puppets?

Hailey looks ashen. "You told Varrick we're trying to screw over Jake's brother?"

"He already suspected since Phoebe was dating a Koning

heir." Her eyes flit worriedly between me and Hails. "I promise I wasn't trying to undermine any of you kids."

"We aren't kids," I mutter angrily under my breath. "You should've told us before posing *anything* to him."

"It was my idea," Addison pipes in quickly, attempting to redirect my anger to her. News flash, I'm pissed at both of them. "I told Bethy we could potentially use Varrick to finish the job you all started. If he promised to leave once Jake's inheritance is secured, it'd solve two issues at once."

My jaw unhinges. "So, now he knows we don't want him in this town?"

"He already *knew*," my mom professes deeply. "He's not an idiot, spider. He's known we've been avoiding him for years because I've kept you and your brothers a secret from him." She's already confessed how he's aware I'm his daughter now. It makes his whole Michael Myers knockoff routine a little more unnerving.

I teeter toward concern for her again. "Is he angry?"

"No . . . he's . . . impressed that we managed to deceive him." She downs her wine in minutes before pouring herself another glass, not even waiting for a refill from the server.

"But he doesn't want to help us with the job?" Hailey wonders, genuinely curious.

I really wish Rocky were here. My emotions burn too hot. At least he'd share in the overflowing rage. Maybe then I wouldn't feel like I'm overreacting.

"He's uninterested in the money," my mom says dazedly, just staring at the ice beneath the oyster shells.

"That's not a shock, right?" I chime in. "He has the Wolfe family fortune. What does he need the money for? He's been hibernating in that mansion for how many years?"

My mom chokes on a sharp noise. "You think he's spent

over two decades as a hermit? In a three-story mansion on an island? With no yard and the only way in or out is by boat?"

My lips pull downward. "That's what everyone in town believes . . ." I trail off, realizing how wrong I am almost instantly.

"A town myth he uses to his benefit, bug," Elizabeth says, almost sadly. "That man has been traveling the country under different aliases. He only just returned to Victoria when Emilia Wolfe became sick and died."

Hailey stares around the patio before looking between the godmothers. "So he'll leave again if he leaves often. It's logical."

Addison turns to Elizabeth.

Elizabeth frowns at the crab dip, then pours a third glass of wine, and downs the entire thing in one gulp.

"Bethy—"

"We can't pay him to leave, Addy," my mom declares. "It's not what he wants. It's not why he's staying in Victoria indefinitely."

Addison sets an uneaten oyster on her plate. "You can't live your life with a monster—"

"It's not me either," she whispers, as if this is a fragile secret. "He's not interested in me."

Cold drips down my spine when her brown eyes veer over to mine. "He wants all six of you."

My stomach drops out. "For what?"

"As we thought, he's been observing you to see how well we raised you, but he'd prefer to have you all in his back pocket. He wants you to trust him more than you trust us. He might even attempt to sway you against us."

Addison sends an apprehensive glance to my mom. My head spins, and Hailey digs her nose and mouth into her forearm before springing up.

Oh shit. She's going to be sick. She shoos me not to follow, then rushes toward the bathroom. I wonder if the fishy smell from the oysters is upsetting her already queasy stomach. This pregnancy hasn't been kind to her on the morning sickness front.

Addison swings her head toward the door. "Is Hailey ill?"

"We drank a lot of wine last night. I think the hangover mixed with oysters is getting to her," I lie casually.

"Should I go check on her?" Addison asks, more to Elizabeth than me. It's an odd question from someone so supremely confident in any role she takes. But I suppose the role of *mother* has been tarnished a bit. She doesn't know exactly where she stands with Hails.

"I'll text her," I offer, sending Hailey a quick message on my burner: **You okay?**

Her response is almost instant:

"Assumptions confirmed." I slip my phone away. "It's the hangover." I thread my arms over my chest and drop my voice so only they can hear. "So . . . if he'd prefer to use us in the art of confidence games, then why hasn't he said *boo* to me? Seems like he's done a pretty shitty job convincing us to be a part of his one-man team."

Slowly, Elizabeth reaches into her Birkin and pulls out six envelopes. She hands me the stack, Rocky's alias written in cursive on the top one.

Grey Thornhall

Elizabeth never blinks as she says, "That's about to change."

FIVE

Jake

I fold an envelope. My name is scrawled in black ink over the letterhead: JAKE KONING WATERFORD. No return address. I slip it in the back pocket of my navy-blue slacks after hanging up the phone.

I called Hailey the second I found the envelope underneath my Porsche's windshield wiper. It's definitely not good how often she circles my thoughts, not good that my first instinct was to reach out to her—not good that I'm headed to her now.

Most of my life, I've been revolting.

Pushing against expectations set before birth. Probably before I was even conceived, my mother had an idea of who she wanted her thirdborn son to be, and I'm pretty positive I was only half of what she desired.

Athletic, *perfect*. Studious, *even better*. Proper, *outstanding*.

Questioning . . . *unacceptable*. Challenging, *we can't have that*. Rebellious, *he must go*.

With no peep from my weak-willed father, I was sent to

boarding school for most of my youth. Because she hated that I called her out for being every fucking thing I didn't want my mother to be.

Vindictive. Petty. Cruel. Her high standards could never be reached by most staff. She went through valets, assistants, chefs, and housekeepers like seasonal decorations. Discarding them as if they were the wrong type of ribbon and garland for the year. She only ever remembered the names of the nanny and butler. They were the only ones she'd bother to keep around for decades, a way to tell herself she was so loyal, so *giving.*

It was bullshit.

I told her exactly what I felt each time she canned household staff, like Chef Lydia, who'd just returned from maternity leave after giving birth to twins.

"She looks so different . . ." Mom crinkled her nose in distaste, then waved her hand. "She's better off elsewhere. She'll have more time to take care of herself."

I let out a tight, irate laugh. "She just gave *birth.* Not that her appearance should even matter."

"Jacob, please. Not today."

She loved my oldest brother because he never held a mirror to her face. Trent was Claudia . . . *is* Claudia in so many terrible ways. It's been two weeks since she died, and I keep wishing he'd join her.

I keep thinking, *What the fuck is wrong with me?* That I want my own brother to die. I never considered that I could be someone who'd put a hit on their own family. Screw them over to protect others? Yeah, I tried to do that—I'm still trying. Kill them . . . no.

I don't want this dark desire to exist anywhere but in my head.

This year, everything has felt like love or death.

Fitting earbuds in my ears, I play music off Hailey's iPod Nano and leave my Porsche parallel parked on Main Street. She loaned me the Nano after I asked about what music she likes. The bands she listed off sounded fake.

"The Peanut Butter Bandits?" I'd said with raised brows.

"Death metal."

"You're joking with me."

"No, really." She handed me her iPod Nano. "Keep it." We were on my catamaran. In my bed. Lying under the silky ocean-blue sheets. I sat higher up against the headboard.

"For how long?"

"No time limit."

I watched her slide out from under the covers. My eyes were drawn to every beautiful inch of Hailey—not just her slender legs, the slight curve of her hips, her small breasts and pink pebbled nipples, but in how she glanced back at me, pieces of her platinum hair hanging in her gray eyes. Her brown roots were growing in like tar spilling into white sand.

She was seeing if I was watching her.

She was . . . studying me. I smiled a little, my brows creased in more intrigue. Because I was trying to make sense of her, too. I'd been thinking how she wasn't shy about being naked. Yet, she was strangely reserved. Cold. Not affectionate in any sense I knew. I'd never encountered a girl who asked me flat out, "Do you want to fuck?" while also in the same breath waited for me to make the first move.

That same night, I'd eaten her out so very slowly. Just to watch her reactions. Her thigh spasms. Her breath hitches. The soft, pitching moans as her lips parted. When she orgasmed, her eyes were so intensely fixed on mine—like she was trying to rip into my soul—that some would likely find it unsettling. I couldn't stop staring at her. I wanted inside her brain to know *exactly* what she was thinking.

I'd been a second from asking, but then she'd panted, "Can you do that again? With your tongue. I really liked that."

I smiled, bigger than I had in so long. Months? Years? Nothing about Hailey added up in my mind, and I liked it. I liked that she just didn't make sense to me right away. I liked that I had to keep contemplating her. "This?" I'd dipped back between her thighs, licking her swollen clit. She'd tasted so sweet. I could've been down there for too many hours. Less when she began to wince like it'd been painfully sensitive. I'd begun to pull away.

"Keep going."

"Hailey—"

"I like the feeling." Her next earnest, nearly begging "*please*" won me over, and I'd sucked her while she cried into a full-body twitching orgasm. Quickly, I'd slipped two fingers inside her soaked pussy, feeling her contract around them, and she'd moaned into a whimper, "Don't move."

Hailey knew exactly what she liked and what she wanted.

I was so fucking turned on by her, I could barely think at all.

When she caught her breath, I lay beside her, wiping away leaked tears from the corners of her eyes. Surprised when she let me, more surprised when she nuzzled her body against my side, her cheek on my chest. I was about to wrap my arms around her, but she'd grabbed my wrist, then said, "Will you stay down there?"

She'd meant between her legs.

"My hand?"

She'd nodded. "I like the pressure."

So I'd cupped her pussy, adding friction every now and then

with my fingers, which soothed her to sleep. I found her enthralling, bizarre, maybe even troubled. I knew she was searching for answers about her parents at the time, and I'd been helping her any way I could.

I kept telling myself that also meant sleeping with her, but I knew I wanted to be inside Hailey. I wanted to see if I could get her off I think as badly as she wanted to see what made me hard. The answer has been *her*.

No book in any library has gripped me as much as she has, and it's been fucking *maddening*.

On the catamaran, with the iPod Nano in my grip, I kept my eyes on Hailey as she gathered her cargo pants and mesh shirt off the floor. She wasn't in a hurry, but she wasn't making a point of delaying either.

"You can stay," I said.

"That's okay. That Valentine's event is happening soon at VCC." *Victoria Country Club*. "I need to be there for work."

"For the Hunt? It's not even five a.m." I checked the bedside clock, then glanced back as she buttoned her pants. "Katherine isn't expecting you to be there this early."

Katherine Rhodes is her boss and the maître d' of the club, overseeing guest relations and managing staff. She's also been more of a mother to me than my own mother. But she's *extremely* particular. Stringent. She takes pride in this town and the club, and anything she sees as a threat to the values she has upheld, she dislikes.

Hailey and Phoebe have been dislikes for her, but that's diminished a fraction of a fraction throughout the past year. Mostly because she thinks I've been in love with Phoebe.

I've hated that I lied to her, but there was no better path. Katherine revered my mother, saw her as generous and *kind*. She was the nanny. *My* nanny. Once my siblings and I were grown, my mother gave Kathrine the esteemed country club job as a token of her generosity.

It did keep Katherine loyal to her. And I needed my mother to truly believe I was going to potentially marry Phoebe.

"I have to go home and take a shower," Hailey said, sliding on her mesh shirt.

"You're welcome to shower here."

"My shower is fine." She was avoiding my gaze now.

"Can we talk?" I asked.

"About what?" She slipped on socks, then reached for her combat boots.

"About what just happened."

Her fair cheeks went rosy. "We fucked. You went down on me twice. I wanted to blow you, but I think I fell asleep. Then I woke up, and we talked about astrology and music. You're an Aquarius—said to be deeply intellectual, independent, and rebellious—but I don't believe in horoscopes, even though they do matter."

"Why do they matter?"

"Because other people believe in them, and that belief holds weight." She gave me an inching smile. "I didn't tell you that part last night."

"No, you didn't." I wanted to smile back, but uncertainty still hammered into me. Instead, I just shifted out of the bed, my bare feet hitting the floor. After I stood, I grabbed my watch off the dresser. Careful to give her space.

Now she was bashful seeing my cock. It confused me. "Hailey—"

"It was just sex," she said. "We don't need to complicate this."

I frowned. "You showering here complicates this . . . how?"

"It just does." She laced her boots.

I scraped a hand through my hair, knowing I shouldn't want more. Because I agreed, "It is just sex." I couldn't have a relationship with her. I couldn't do *serious*.

Not just because I was fake dating Phoebe at the time, but because it wasn't safe to be committed to anyone who could potentially be collateral damage in this war between me and my brother.

It's still dangerous.

Maybe even more now than before.

It's been two months since the Hunt, and we still call our relationship "just sex." The more I learn about her, the less I feel like it is.

As I leave my Porsche, loud rock beats blast in my ears, and I hustle toward Baubles & Bookends.

While most of my adolescence was spent in New York, all my summers were in this seaside Connecticut town. I love the sticky heat off the coast, the way the streets flood with bouncing kids as school lets out, the nostalgic smell of charcoal from Danny's Dockside Grill. Sunsets melt like orange freeze pops, and nighttime feels alive with fireflies and bullfrogs.

I might've been the son of an eleven-figure fortune, a kid with a distinguished lineage dating back to the 1700s, but I was always just the third. Able to run off and buy cookie dough ice cream, race through Main Street like a vagabond child, and I found myself kicking soccer balls with other teenagers on the grainy beach as foamy waves crashed to shore. Always knowing in the back of my head that my family owned half the town. That our money came from one of the most popular, well-recognized beer franchises in the world.

The guilt came later.

When I realized my summers were blissful and free while my little sister's were tormented and caged. She might've been the fourthborn, but she was the only girl, and our mother had planned Kate's life down to the hour. Sometimes the minute.

I don't know what brings more grief: knowing my sister never experienced these idyllic, joyful summers in Victoria or the fact that this might be my last.

My brother might take everything from me. He's already started to.

Hailey's fury-laced music bleeds into my veins. I can't hear the *woof* of Archer Fitzpatrick's Saint Bernard as he walks the giant dog along the cobblestone or the beep of cars being locked as vehicles park outside Symphonies on the Pier for dinner.

But I falter when I turn my head . . . and I spot Oliver Graves.

Fuck. He's across the street, nearly parallel with me on the other sidewalk, and it's clear we're headed in the same direction. The loft above the bookstore.

He has a casual but quick stride, his hands in pockets of tailored khaki slacks. His designer sunglasses match the jet-black shade of his short-sleeve linen shirt.

Oliver dresses like he frequents yachts in the summer and chalets in the winter. Like he was a silver-spoon kid who never lived without a trust fund. I never would've questioned his wealth had I not learned the truth.

I stay in time with his lengthy gait. Our builds are very similar and we're around the same height. *I bet I'm stronger.* Not a competition.

I breathe out a lengthy breath. Then glance over at him again. He's not peering over at me. At all. He's so unconcerned. Unbothered.

There's something about him that simultaneously stands out and blends in, and I can't put my finger on what it is.

Maybe it's the way he carries himself. Like he's unshackled by life. Or maybe it's just that he's bewilderingly attractive. I might have the jawline, but his features are striking as they balance between daring and safe. Treacherous and harmless.

If Phoebe Graves is considered stunningly beautiful, I don't even know what you call her brother Oliver.

What I do know: he's on the side of the street I need to be on.

Can't avoid him forever.

With a deep sigh, I cross the road at an intersection, waving politely to Mr. Eddington, who stops his Mercedes for me. Picking up my pace in a slight jog, then I slow right beside Oliver on the cobblestone sidewalk.

I pry out an earbud.

Without looking at me or breaking pace, Oliver says, "The king has returned." His smile inches upward.

I've stopped being surprised that the Graveses and Tinrocks have eyes in the back of their heads. They're not just con artists. They are *born and raised* con artists. I'm still wrapping my mind around what that actually entails because they're incredibly secretive about how they grew up. What they did. Where they did it.

"Quoting *The Lion King*?" I say, pulling out my second earbud, barely able to hear him over the heavy female vocals.

"You are the Disney prince."

"And that makes you . . . what?"

He tips his head toward me. "Everything all at once."

I find Oliver frustrating. At least I know that Grey (Rocky) is a raging, angst-driven asshole. I don't know who Oliver is other than Phoebe's brother and Hailey's . . . friend with benefits, I guess.

"Everything all at once, huh?" I side-eye him while we keep a steady pace.

His smile slants higher. He twirls a set of keys on his finger. Keys to *Hailey's* loft. Keys he shouldn't have since she's not supposed to make copies, and I know that because I'm her landlord.

She must've given them to him.

I take out the iPod Nano from my pocket to shut off the song.

He lifts his sunglasses to his head. Pushing back his thick hair, he sees the screen of the Nano. "Animal Alpha," he names the band. "You thieve that from Hails or did she give it to you?"

"I wouldn't steal anything of hers."

"You should try." He outpaces me, just to spin around and walk backward. He maintains complete eye contact. It's impressive he's not tripping or concerned he might bump into a chalkboard sign. "Hone your fledgling skills, Koning. Or would you prefer I pick up your slack?" He puts a hand to his heart. "I've been known to carry deadweight. Don't take it personally, I like lifting heavy things."

His biceps bulge in his short-cuffed black sleeves. I shouldn't stare at his muscles—because it's obvious he's being fucking *figurative*. From what I know of Oliver, he's all wit and charm, but I didn't notice his strength—not until the night my mother died. When he shed his jacket and attempted to open a metal storm shelter at my family's estate.

I try to hold his gaze and not outwardly size him up. "I didn't realize I've been deadweight."

"You didn't feel me carrying you?" He cracks a smile.

"Just the opposite, actually." My eyes flit down to his

hands. His knuckles are scabbed over, some bandaged with butterfly tape. I'd been at that storm shelter . . . as he tried to break Hailey out with his fists.

He gives the keys one last spin before pocketing his battered hands. He jerks his head, making his sunglasses purposefully fall over his eyes. He's a cool fucker, but I can't tell if it's just a front.

It shouldn't spike my interest in Oliver, but I feel myself wanting to know more about him. Likely because he spends plenty of time with Hailey. I just need to know she's being treated well.

He falls back to my side. "I'm guessing you heard about the letters."

"Only because I got one, too." I pull out the envelope from my back pocket and pass it to him.

He raises it to the sky, but the light isn't bleeding through the paper to reveal anything inside.

I look him over. "Hailey said to wait to open it. We're all doing it together?" I heard they each received one from Varrick. Oliver's birth father.

We don't bring up the relation or the sender.

"That's the plan," he confirms, reaching the apartment door beside Baubles & Bookends. He unlocks it, then gestures me forward into the stairwell with him. Once we're inside, he whispers, "If you have the chance, *always* walk in front of the mark. It's easier to eavesdrop when they're behind you. Tips and tricks of the trade." He pushes the envelope firmly into my chest, then pats it lightly.

I take the letter from his fingers, my muscles flexing. "Still trying to corrupt me?"

"Corruption or preparation?" He cocks his head in

thought. "Or are they one and the same?" He hooks his sunglasses to his collar. "If Rocky taught Trevor even half of what he knew a whole lot sooner, then maybe our little psycho wouldn't be straggling behind us, but like I said, I don't mind picking up the slack."

Rocky has offhandedly mentioned to me that he didn't want his little brother to turn out like him. Which is likely why he's been slow to teach Trevor the art of being a silvertongue. He's only just recently started taking him under his wing.

"Right." I breathe out, staring up at the staircase that leads to the loft. The expelled breath doesn't untense my body. My jaw even clenches.

Oliver glances between me and the loft while sliding a piece of gum into his mouth. "Secrets are no fun unless you tell—"

"Everyone?"

"No. Just me." His smile reappears as he rests against the stairwell's railing to face me. I nod a couple times, shove my letter in my back pocket, and study the length of him. I imagine if we found ourselves alone together, he'd warn me to stay away from Hailey.

I keep waiting for the *Back off, motherfucker*, the sneer between his teeth, the serrated glare . . . and I realize I've been around Rocky too long. That's his blunt, aggressive routine—growling at me to piss on someone else's territory and to get the fuck off his.

I'm on defense with Oliver, but how can I play offense when I can't even give Hailey more than what we are right now?

Silence clings to the air, especially as my eyes hit his.

"And now he's more interested in me," Oliver states, reading me too easily. It feels intrusive because I can't reach into his thoughts. Let alone analyze his feelings. He might as well be an Etch A Sketch, the image disappearing before I see a thing.

It's . . . exasperating. Every time I'm around this guy, my brain is a stampede of Thoroughbreds released from a starting gate.

He points up toward the stairs. "Loft? Or me? Where's your head at, Koning?"

"On Hailey." I sound protective. I don't really know him. I just know her.

He blows a bubble. Completely, totally . . . *unconcerned.* "Like minds." He winks.

It's hard to believe he doesn't care that I'm sleeping with Hailey when he and I have been actively ignoring each other for weeks. *Can't get into this right now.* Regardless of the thousand and one messages I'm dealing with from lawyers, staff at the estate, country club employees, renters from my other properties—I'm responsible for this job they've taken on. Because I enlisted their help to blackmail my mother.

I brought them into my mess, and I care about them coming out of it unscathed.

The letters—I don't know what they could be about. But I do know there's another issue. I release a tight breath and glance at the door to the loft again. "It's not a secret exactly."

"Then what is it? A problem?"

"Yeah." I unpocket my set of keys. "The girls don't know it yet, but they're going to need to move out."

His brows crinkle. "And why's that?"

"My mother owned the loft. She was going to sell it to Varrick Wolfe, but when she died, that transaction fell through. So now Trent and I have been fighting over it since this asset wasn't specified in the will. He knows I want it because my 'ex-girlfriend' lives here." I use air quotes to refer to Phoebe. "He's gunning too hard for it, and I need to let it go in order to retain other properties."

I still can't decipher Oliver. He chews casually on his gum. "Well, fuck. Looks like you've just made Hailey homeless." At this, he strides up the stairs, and I follow behind, exactly where he advised me not to be.

SIX

Rocky

"Don't," Nova warns me.

I'm leaning against the fridge in the coastal two-bed, one-bath loft above Baubles & Bookends, loosely gripping the neck of a Koning Lite and staring down the shut bathroom door several lengthy feet away from us.

Nova is seated on a rattan barstool. Did not ask him to be in eyesight of me. Did not ask him to tell me what to fucking do on this ugly Saturday night.

Letters are stacked beside the brewing coffeepot and a Seaside Griddle mug (Trevor swiped it). My name on the top envelope, and no, I haven't ripped that shit open because, for one, whatever Varrick Wolfe has to say *will* piss me off, and two, I'm already naturally pissed off, and three, I don't go rogue. We all agreed to wait until everyone is here. It's dumb as fuck to take matters into my own hands without consulting the others first.

Something I *sincerely* hope my little brother has learned the past two weeks.

"Don't what?" I snap at Nova. He's going to need to spell it out and not do his whole stern soldier routine with me. I'm not in the mood.

He grinds his jaw, a stubbled goatee and mustache grown in, but he recently buzzed his hair again. His beer bottle—and Glock—rest next to an opened Gambit comic book he's been reading.

Nova Graves, already prepared for the ending. Let's hope it doesn't conclude with a bullet to a head.

His expensive Piaget watch catches the light as he points to the bathroom. "Don't go in *there*."

"I'm not moving, dumbass."

"You're considering it."

He's not wrong.

I've been staring down the bathroom door ever since Hailey and Phoebe rushed inside. We were in mid-conversation about their lunch with the godmothers, and Phoebe suddenly carted Hailey away with an abrupt "We need a moment alone. BRB."

"BRB?" I arched my brows at her. "What are you—fifteen?"

She diverted her gaze from mine and sprinted to the bathroom, tugging my younger sister behind. "Be right fucking back," she said too urgently, too rushed. The heat of her words flamed out. "Don't follow us."

Concern bludgeoned me. *"Phoebe."*

"I'm serious, Rocky." She slammed the door, but I caught her brown eyes right before she disappeared from sight. No hostility in them. She seemed panicked. It's been bothering me, coupled with the fact that something has felt off with Phoebe this past week.

At times, she's been more withdrawn. While other times, she's hung on to me as if we're in shark-infested open water together, drowning in the raging deep blue sea. Desperate, needy, starved affection—to ensure I'll never let go.

I won't release my grip on Phoebe. *I can't*. If someone tried, they'd need to hacksaw both my fucking hands.

Her clinging tighter to me—not unusual, especially since we've been together for real.

Feeling her pull away afterward like she never meant to hold on in the first place—that's new. I get the sense she's scared about something, but Phoebe was taught to be emotionally brick walled and iron willed. Being vulnerable isn't as easy for her.

I know this.

I know *her*. (Too well.)

Ignoring Nova, I take a harsh swig of beer. Replaying the past thirty minutes, I wonder what the fuck I missed before my sister and my girlfriend evacuated like the floor was lava. I hadn't been dissecting them. I'd been glaring, *stewing*, over how Elizabeth Graves took it upon herself to share information about the Koning job with Varrick.

It even angered Phoebe, which honestly surprised me. I thought she would've made excuses, saying we need her mom's help. But Phoebe has been really struggling to reconcile the Elizabeth who cares for her and the Elizabeth who betrayed her. Our parents would have to reconstruct the *Titanic* and hope it doesn't sink to row their way back to me.

To reach the others, it'll be much easier now that the truth is out and our parents are acting like this is some fresh start while they assist us in finishing the Koning job. It's exactly why I'm more on guard. Protecting Trevor, Hailey, Oliver, Nova, and Phoebe is ingrained so deep in me, and the wider they open their arms to our parents, the more I want to step in front of them and take the blows.

But I can admit that Elizabeth, Addison, and Everett have been crucial for this con. Hell, Everett is still the staff manager at the Koning estate, and now that Claudia is gone, the godmothers have swooped into her social circle to take advantage of her grieving friends. Becoming closer, gaining more influence in the town.

I've accepted that the godmothers are assets to us as much as we are to them. Because if they weren't involved in the recent job to screw over Claudia Waterford, then she would've never added Jake, her thirdborn son, to her will before she died.

Jake's insufferable prick of an older brother only inherited half of the Koning estate, half the Koning properties, half the Koning fortune. There was a path where Trent could've owned *everything*, and if we walked that road, staying in this town would be a specific circle of hell I wouldn't want to reside in.

I just hate that we might be playing this game from behind now if Varrick knows as much as we do. I hate that the godmothers can't defer to us, even when we've been adamant they need to.

More than that, I hate that I might've let my aggravation for them cloud my awareness for the people I truly love. I hate that I'm standing here while something is clearly going on with Phoebe.

It's driving me insane.

"She's allowed to have some space from you." Nova turns a page of his comic. "So give my sister some fucking space." It's a protective brotherly threat.

And I'm not nice. "Your sister who prefers to be choked out and superglued to me until my skin tears off—that sister?"

His glare is violent. "She wants to talk to her best friend privately for a minute. Let her."

Jesus Christ. He's still so wound up around the idea that I could be bad for Phoebe. I eye the bathroom, then him. "And that doesn't worry you?"

"They're friends and women, Rocky. We don't need to always be a part of whatever they're discussing."

"I'm *dating* Phoebe."

"So?"

"So, if something were wrong with her, I'd expect her to fucking tell me." I grimace up at the ceiling light. "That's not true, because your sister would prefer I morph into one of your silly little comic book characters and read her mind." I flash him a tight smile.

His brows harden. Then he shuts the comic. "What do you think is going on? Is it Varrick?" Visceral heat blazes off his pinpointed gaze. And I thought the Big Bad Wolfe's name pissed off me and Phoebe. Nova has been irate since learning he's Varrick's son. I doubt he ever wanted a father who'd be capable of murder. Nova loved Everett. Obeyed Everett. My so-called dad, who I would've traded in for a cardboard cutout of Shrek or Donkey.

I shake my head slowly and place my beer on the counter beside the fridge. "It can't be about your father. He makes Phoebe angry more than scared."

"Then what?"

"She ran into Trent, maybe. He came on to her and she's not telling me." My phone buzzes in my black slacks, and I pry it out. "Speaking of the firstborn fuckbag." It's what Phebs calls him, which makes me eye the bathroom again before pounding out a message with my thumb at my waist.

Trent Koning Waterford has been texting me every five goddamn minutes.

To party with him.

I'm running out of creative ways to brush off my fake best friend. When really, I just want to tell him to go fuck himself with a chain saw.

"Have you considered you're just paranoid?" Nova asks.

"I'm listening," I say while I text.

"Jake's oldest brother is still a threat to Phebs, especially now that she's seemingly single. You have to pretend to be Trent's closest friend, so it's harder for you. You're imagining the worst before it's even happened."

Yeah.

I press send. "How do we know it hasn't already happened, Nov? She's a dog toy in a feud between two brothers. She knows it, man. I know it. *You* know it."

He crosses his buff arms. Rigid, more primed for a shit-storm. "We're all watching Trent. When would he get the chance?"

"The country club. Her place of work."

"He doesn't go to VCC anymore. He's frequenting the fucking Mariner's Club." It's an older, more exclusive establishment owned by the Wolfes and resides closer to private docks. Less beach but better anchorage for yachts, sailboats, catamarans. "Which is where you and I've been the past week, Rock."

We're now cardholding members of a rival country club. In the Konings' division of assets, Jake Waterford was granted Victoria Country Club. He used to manage the club while his bossy mother oversaw everything and vetoed his decisions at her whim.

Now he's in charge. Which has run Trent out. Not that he spent much time there in the first place. He thought it was a waste of fucking time.

"You could ask Phoebe if anything happened," Nova

suggests, reopening his comic book with force. "You know, *talk*. With words."

I roll my eyes but end up muttering, "We're working on it." I can't let anyone touch her. I can't handle the impact of Trent coming as close as he did at the Alps.

He had his cock out. He got naked and crawled in the same hot tub as Phoebe. If I hadn't shown up . . .

I trade my phone for Nat Sherman cigarettes. I don't want to relax. I'd rather be buzzing with nicotine than unwound with alcohol. Leaning against the fridge again, I smack the pack of Nats on my palm. "Did she ever tell you what happened at the Alps? Or Carlsbad? The Fiddle Game?"

"No." Nova looks up at me. "She told you?"

"Yep." I light a cigarette and hold one elbow while I smoke. "The last time I felt this in the dark with Phebs, she'd been hiding something traumatic."

"The Fiddle Game?"

I nod once. "Yeah." *The Fiddle Game*. The job in Carlsbad is what sent her here.

Nova's nose flares, his olive skin turning pallid. He looks murderous and ill. Training an unblinking stare on me, he asks, "Was she raped?"

Nitric acid might as well coarse through my bloodstream. "Not exactly."

"What the hell does that mean?"

I suck hard on the cigarette, then blow smoke downward. "It means you need to ask her. I'm not sharing her personal shit."

"*Fuck*," he curses roughly under his breath, then holds the side of his head in his hand, unable to concentrate on the comic book anymore, though he tries.

I have that lovely effect on people.

The door blows open. Not the one I wanted, unfortunately. Bathroom still shut. Oliver appears through the front entrance with Jake only steps behind.

"Took you long enough," I tell them.

Oliver steals a pear out of the fruit bowl. Then tips his head toward Jake as he says lightly, "Il a la trique pour Hailey." *He has a hard-on for Hailey.*

I blink in annoyance. "On sait." *We know.*

Nova isn't fluent in French, so Oliver said this just to aggravate me. Mission accomplished. Did not ask to be in the middle of whatever the fuck this is with Oliver and Jake and my little sister.

Oliver smiles into a laugh, tosses the pear in his palm, then sinks his teeth in the fruit.

"Ol." Nova stands and fists his brother's black linen shirt. He pulls him toward Phoebe's bedroom. Probably to talk alone. Privately.

What friends do, apparently.

I'm left with Jake in the kitchen. Truthfully, I don't hate it. I almost can't believe I'm at this place with the moral crusader.

"I don't get him," Jake says with a heavy breath, like he's been in a stairwell triathlon with Oliver.

Oliver Graves will race circles around him and eventually tire him out, which makes me feel a *little* bad for Jake.

"Ignore him," I advise, pushing off the fridge to grab a beer out of a six-pack from inside. I hand him the cold bottle.

He's still cemented on Oliver's shadow. "What'd he say in French?"

"You have a hard-on for Hailey."

Jake chokes out an irritated sound.

"*Ignore him*," I emphasize.

"Is he trying to get under my skin?"

"No, but you're making it apparent that he is, sweetheart."

Jake rounds my body to rummage in the drawers for a bottle opener. "Then, is he trying to intimidate me?"

"Doubtful." I raise and lower my brows.

He pops the bottle cap. "So he doesn't care that I'm with Hailey?"

"Oh, he definitely fucking cares," I say into a drag of cigarette.

Jake leans on the counter across from me. He's flummoxed. "Then he's trying to scare me away from her?"

"No, because he also cares about what Hailey wants."

Jake shakes his head way too hard. "I . . . don't understand."

I exhale a rough, deep breath, knowing I should save him from this mind fuck, but I've never had to explain even one layer of Oliver to another person. It feels wrong to expose even the surface of him, but keeping Jake in the pitch-black feels crueler. "You're looking at Oliver all wrong," I tell him.

His frown deepens. "What do you mean?"

"You think he sees you as a threat. He doesn't. He won't even let you be an annoyance, because Oliver so very rarely lets anything irritate him. What he and I do—what we've *done* for a job and what we've seen—"

"What have you seen?"

I blink harder. Thinking about the job that Phoebe never names. New York. Manhattan. "He watched a mark slap his sister across the face. I punched the mark. Oliver couldn't help his sister. Couldn't run toward Phoebe. Couldn't yell at the mark. He had to *comfort him*. He was pretending to be the mark's friend, and the job comes first. Our lives depended on Oliver maintaining the performance, and he doesn't ever break."

"Would you have broken?"

"No. But to cope, you either become me: cynical, angry, hating everything and everyone, or you become him. He doesn't waste emotion on things that could hurt, and he's not wasting emotion on you. So you're just there. You're someone he knows will eventually go, and he will stay. He will *always* stay for Hailey. Because that's what we do. We're here. We don't leave the people we love."

Jake slumps back a little, staring off at the fridge behind me.

I don't know how he feels. But I'm trying to make him understand the truth. "He's irreplaceable in Hailey's life. You can't catch Oliver's horse in this race when he's basically on fucking Pegasus. Flying instead of running."

"And Oliver already knows this," Jake realizes, nodding to himself. He looks very hurt for a guy who said he can't be with my sister in any serious capacity. I'm about to caution him in a not-nice way, but he nods at my hand. "I've never seen you smoke."

"Because you've never seen me fuck. I like a cigarette after sex." I tap ash over on the butcher-block counter. "And, no, I didn't just fuck Phoebe, so this is a new habit."

"It's not a good one."

"Well, I'm not a good person." I force a smile before putting the cigarette between my lips.

"I would disagree," he says quietly. It hits me too strong, but I can't respond. Phoebe and Hailey finally emerge from the bathroom.

My pulse jumps, but I don't shift a muscle. Except for my arm as I take a much longer drag. I scrutinize Phoebe. How she tucks a piece of her midnight-blue hair behind her ear. Moisture bubbles up on her forehead, and she lets go of my sister's left hand as they join us in the kitchen. My eyes race over Hailey's clammy skin.

I can't tell if they just washed their faces or if they're not feeling well.

"You puke your guts up?" I ask Phoebe.

"Intestines. Stomach. Ovaries. All in the toilet bowl." She jabs a thumb behind her. "You want to go check?" Her haughty attitude is normal.

"I'll pass." I skim her up and down, then notice Jake's overly concerned eyes following Hailey. My sister reaches the stack of letters beside the coffeepot. Tension thickens the air as they stay silent.

"You sure?" Phoebe pulls my attention back. "It's quite a grotesque sight." She hangs out in front of me. Her gray baggy sweatpants ride low on the curve of her hips, and her tits push against her strawberry cropped top. I crave to slide my hand against her waist, but as she inches closer and closer, I sense her trying to seduce me.

So I don't touch my girlfriend. "You love grotesque things," I say, reaching for the beer bottle I'd abandoned. I offer it to her.

"Pass."

Alarm drills coldly in me. "Still feeling queasy?"

"Around you? All the time." She threads her arms together.

I stare her down. She grips my gaze with the same molten intensity. Leaning closer, I whisper, "*Liar.*"

This would typically draw a smile out of Phoebe, but her lips noticeably flatline. I see her intake a subtle, sharp breath. Hardly even combating me, her brown eyes strangely soften on the cigarette between my fingers. "I'll just take a smoke."

My stomach clenches, but I slip the cigarette between my

lips, then seize her hips with two hands. "Come here," I mumble, drawing her into my chest. Her arms break apart, her body releasing a deeper breath, especially as she rotates and rests her shoulders against my sternum. Her back to me.

I brace myself against the fridge. Because Phoebe sinks her entire weight into me while I wrap my arm around her chest. I cage her to my body, holding her to me. With my free hand, I pluck the cigarette out of my mouth and keep it pinched between two fingers. I bring it down to Phoebe's lips.

She sucks in, blows out, but I can feel her body tense more than relax. She reaches upward and clutches my forearm with two hands like she's gripping a life vest.

I stare down at her and see her eyes shut. Observe her slowing, easing breath pattern. I dip my head closer to her ear. "You feel okay?"

"Horrible."

"Seriously, Phebs," I snap.

"I'm fine, Rocky," she murmurs softly, heat extinguished. "Really, I'm okay."

She's never lied to me before, and I don't believe she is now. But she's not being completely honest either. I can't make sense of this. I keep thinking she's scared, but what the fuck is scaring her? There is so very little that frightens Phoebe.

I grit my back molars. It feels like an animal is crawling out of my rib cage, but I just hold her as tightly as she's clutching on to me.

I look up.

Hailey is watching Phoebe with wide eyes. She startles when she catches my gaze. I mouth, *What's going on?*

My sister shakes her head stiffly, then flinches at the sound of a door opening. Oliver and Nova return to the kitchen.

"The whole gang is almost here," Oliver says, staring around. "Where's our little psychopath?"

"On his way from the boathouse," I say.

I've been renting the two-bedroom boathouse for almost a year—and we've outgrown it long before then. Trevor has been sleeping in the fucking wine cellar on a cot. Not ideal, but our lives have been more stable here than when we crash at Four Seasons and multimillion-dollar penthouse suites for weeks at a time.

We're not burning through cash at a vicious rate. So we're not in dire need of pulling short cons for quick payouts.

Nova slides back on a barstool. "Are you sure that's where he is?"

"*Yes*," I force out. "He should be here in five minutes, and if he's not, you can lay into me."

Not even a second later, Trevor strolls through the unlocked front door. My lanky dark-haired nineteen-year-old brother looks nothing like the Caufield University student he's supposed to be posing as in Victoria.

No collegiate tee.

No collared polo that the preppy nepo kids would sport around here.

He's wearing shit that makes him appear older, more sophisticated. Crisp black button-down, black slacks, shined loafers, white-gold rings. If it weren't for the hoop earring and shaggy hair, I'd say he wouldn't fit in with his peers.

But this is Trev. This is what my brother likes to wear. If I pulled that at his age, Everett would've told me to change *immediately* and reminded me of who I was supposed to be in this town. I'm not doing that to my brother.

He's more used to being himself. His role as a kid was to remain in the shadows and use sleight of hand. He wasn't trained in face-to-face manipulation, even if he wanted to be right beside me.

"What's up, losers?" Trevor greets.

Oliver bows forward, elbows on the counter, pear in hand. "You're very confident for someone who slaughtered a feeble old woman."

"She wasn't *feeble*. She was the mark."

Jesus.

Nova shoots me a hard look, like *Get your brother in check*. Trev has felt like my responsibility, my kid, for I don't know how long. He's also proof that I'm not equipped to be raising another fucking human being.

"Remember Jake?" I question. "Claudia's son? He's right here, shithead."

"Hi, Jake. Sorry," he deadpans, sounding not remorseful at all. Wonderful.

"It's fine," Jake mutters, more attentive toward Hailey, who flips through the envelopes.

Oliver straightens up. And that's how I know he cares that Jake is interested in my sister. Body language. I would do stupid things to bury my head back into scalding desert sand if I could. I hate being this perceptive over shit regarding my sister's sex life. I want *nothing* to do with it.

"Is that a hickey?" Phoebe asks.

Yeah, Trevor has four massive red welts on his neck. And now I'm thrust into my brother's sex life. Perfect.

He's been dating Sidney Burke, a rich college student who's lived in this Connecticut town her entire life. She's using him to get back at her rich dad, and since she's the writer behind Victoria's most popular gossip column, Trevor has been dating her to influence what hits the press.

He'd been at the boathouse.

"Whoa, whoa, whoa." I point at him, cigarette scissored between two fingers. "You did not bring your girlfriend to the boathouse." He specifically told us he wouldn't.

"For less than seventy minutes."

"So an hour," I state. "For fuck's sake, Trevor."

"We keep fakes in there," Nova reminds him.

"Yeah, *stashed away*." He stares into me, thinking I'll understand. I can't. He did another thing I said not to do.

"And *guns*," I add.

"Like that one? Just lying out in the open?" Trevor motions to the Glock beside Nova. Which causes Nova to holster the gun at his waist.

Phoebe mutters, "I'm not going to prison because of Sidney fucking Burke."

Trevor kicks off his loafers angrily. "She can be trusted."

"No," almost all of us say together.

Jake wavers. He's on the fence because Sidney Burke was his sister's best friend. He's known her since she was in diapers. Like I feel responsible for my little brother, I know Jake feels similarly toward Sidney.

"She could've been *snooping*," Phoebe combats. "She's an investigative journalist."

Hailey sifts through the letters. "Is that what we're calling a gossip columnist now?"

"Trust *me* then," Trevor says to everyone.

Oliver shares a small look with Nova. They empathize with Trevor wanting to be trusted, but he's also the one most likely to make a mistake at this point. He's already made a *massive* one. So, unsurprisingly, we're all more keyed on him.

"Sidney isn't trying to play any of us," Trevor professes. "All she cares about is pissing off her dad. Hence . . ." He yanks his collar to expose the trail of hickies down his chest. "She wanted him to see it."

Phoebe snorts. "Is she part blowfish?"

"Like you've never had a hickey before, PG," Trevor says. "Your whole body has been a Twister mat."

What the fuck? "*Trevor*," I grit out.

"She started it." He gestures to Phoebe. Everyone waits for her scathing comeback, but she's abnormally quiet. Her limbs go slack as she releases her grip on my forearm. Her hands dangle at her sides, and I crane my neck to the left, trying to inspect her face, her eyes, while she's leaning up against me.

My muscles are on fire.

"PG?" Trevor says uncertainly. "Phoebe." Rare remorse flickers in his gray eyes. He looks over at me with confusion and an apology.

Because Phoebe is staring off at the seafoam cupboards. Unblinking, dazed, haunted.

Her brothers notice. Oliver starts to round the bar counter, but he stops as Phoebe mutters out a soft "Not anymore." Louder, she says, "I'm not going to be that girl anymore. I don't want to be."

Hailey's lips tic in a tiny smile.

I exhale a long breath through my nose.

Her focus clears. "You want my role, Trevor. It's all yours."

"Let's not go that fucking far," I caution my brother, but as Phoebe sinks back against me, I wrap my arms around her like a vise. She lifts her chin to look up at me, her gratitude pooling into warm affection. It melts the embers of aggravated heat she constantly carries in her eyes.

We've spent our childhood and adolescence working together. Being paired on jobs. We've pretended to be everything anyone could ever be to someone. It might seem like we're toxic fumes. Like we can't possibly make *us* work out, but all we've ever done is pull each other through the fires we've set.

So we're going to get through this.

Whatever's going on with her.

Whatever happens with Trent.

Whatever happens with her dad—the man who killed my family.

We're getting through it.

There is no end without us together. I can't even remember a beginning without Phoebe Graves.

SEVEN

Rocky

None of us say a word after Hailey passes out the letters, and we all rip them open.

Dear Mr. Grey Thornall,

I'm formally inviting four well-to-do families to my beautiful home on the sea this summer. The Konings, the Bennets, the Thornhalls, and the Smiths. If you'd do me the highest honor in coming to summer at Stonehaven, it will be to your utmost benefit and my utmost gratitude.

As you know, I have no living heir. I'd love the chance to get to know each of you better, as I'd prefer to leave the Wolfe fortune to either a founding family of Victoria or new residents who've certainly made their mark.

There are no games to be played. I'd simply like to spend time with you over the summer in a more personal setting. My doors are open, and if you accept this invite, please meet me on *The Ithaka* (my yacht docked at the harbor) on the first

Saturday of May at 4 p.m. with your bags packed for the long-extended stay.

No RSVP required.

Sincerely,
Varrick Wolfe

Oliver and Nova switch letters, probably to ensure they say the same thing. I've already peeked at Phoebe's and know it's identical except for it being addressed to *Ms. Phoebe Smith.*

"It's a setup?" Oliver asks Hailey.

"It's a possibility."

"How?" Jake questions.

"We don't know if he actually wants to name an heir, or if he's luring us there for another purpose," Hailey explains.

"We should accept," I say, my throat scorched with acid. "At the very least, *I'm* accepting."

The only thing I've wanted more than revenge is Phoebe, and I doubt I'd lose her by summering at Stonehaven. Considering she also wants to skewer Varrick like he's a Christmas ham. Being closer to him will give us information. Leverage. We've had so few interactions, and I need this to change.

Even if he's trying to trap us, I know how to walk around one and push someone else in.

Jake rubs his face too many times. He's wincing.

I shoot him a harsh look. "What is it?"

He sighs out, "This might actually solve a problem." One he clearly isn't excited about sharing, and I realize why when he informs us that Trent is getting this fucking loft.

Great.

Oliver rotates his pear. "Looks like we're all going to be

sleeping in the spider's nest." He bites out a chunk, and he's right. There's no big discussion because it's just known.

We're better when we're all together.

"Rocky, can I talk to you for a sec?" Hailey asks, her eyes glued to her letter.

"Yeah." Pulling away from Phoebe, I follow my sister into her bedroom, and I shut the door with my shoulder blades while she sinks onto the edge of a checkered quilt.

"What's going on, Hails?" I ask, thinking this might be about Phebs, but as soon as she starts speaking, I know I'm wrong.

It's about me.

"I've realized the most advantageous position for you to be in when it comes to Varrick, and I hate having to ask you to do this . . . so you can say no."

"It can't be worse than befriending Trent Waterford."

Her eyes glaze, and that's all I need to know it's going to be so much worse.

"I know you hate him. I know he did monstrous things," Hailey whispers. "But you have to get him to love you like a son."

The man who ate his way through the foundation of this house.

The man who murdered my siblings. My parents.

The man who stole from me the ability to even know them.

I have to get *him* to love me. My stomach roils and flips in on itself. I rake two hot hands through my hair. "What if he's not capable of loving anyone but himself? It's likely he's in the dark triad, and he's also a con man. He'll be trying to manipulate me while I'm trying to manipulate him."

"He doesn't know you though. Not really. He just needs to

believe you trust him more than you've ever trusted our parents. You have to give him what he wants."

"Which is?"

"Us."

I have to play into his hand. "Okay." I nod a few times. "I can do it." I can do anything to see this through to the end.

"One more thing," she says. "And it's the *most* important thing . . ."

"What?" I ask.

"You can't love him back."

I start to laugh hard, but her gray eyes contain real fear. The noise dies in my throat. "You're serious," I say, pushing off the door with raised brows. "In what world would I love that man, Hails? Huh?"

"We don't know how good he is. How charismatic. Convincing."

"He can't manipulate me. *He won't*," I assure her. "Don't be afraid of that. Okay? It's not an outcome. Don't let it plague you."

She nods repeatedly, blinking too much. Staring off too much. Chewing her lip too much. *Christ*. I'm about to ask how much sleep she clocked last night when the door cracks open behind me.

Jake apologizes for interrupting. "I'm about to go." His phone is in the pit of his hand. "I just wanted to say bye before I head out to deal with this party Trent is throwing." His eyes veer from me and stay on my sister as she waves a hand at him.

"See you tomorrow?" she asks.

"Yeah . . ." He trails off, like maybe he wants to ask something.

Let me guess. I roll my eyes. "Is Oliver spending the night with you?" I ask her. "Not that I give a shit."

"Maybe," she tells Jake more than me.

Jake nods slowly.

I feel like I'm in a two-mile-an-hour car crash. I just want it to make fucking impact already. "I'll go with you," I tell Jake.

"What?" Jake asks.

"To the fucking party," I snap. "I need to make an appearance anyway. Your brother has been up my ass all night about it. Let me just tell Phoebe first."

Keys to my McLaren in my hand, I head down the stairwell with Phoebe. "You sure you're okay?" I ask her. "Because I'm about to leave for fuck knows how long."

"How will I possibly survive without you for fuck knows how long?" Phoebe laments dramatically. "In that case, I might as well just throw myself down the stairs."

"Yeah?" I skim the length of her.

"All the way down."

"Let's see it then," I challenge.

Phoebe, stubborn as always, isn't relenting. "Here I go."

"I'll help you." I seize her waist, then push her so she careens forward.

"Rocky!"

I never let go, and I pull her abruptly back into my chest. Her sharp breath is a slight moan as she presses against me. I see her lips crawl into a smile, one she's trying to hide.

My smile feels less bitter. "Adrenaline junkie," I tease.

"You are, too," she snaps back.

I don't disagree. When she spins around, one stair below mine, her eyes cradle more questions. "You sure you want to do this?"

"Want? No, but I need to be at this party." I slide her hair tie off her wrist.

"I meant with Varrick. My dad." She lets me run my fingers through her blue hair, collecting the strands. "You understand what this means?"

"It means I have to make nice with a sick, malignant tumor. What else is new?" I tie her hair into a high pony. "This has been my life since forever."

"It doesn't have to be your life forever," she whispers into the echoey stairwell.

I search her eyes at rapid speed.

Phoebe so rarely talks about weeks from now, let alone a *forever* from now. I wonder what she wants—if she's even figured that out when she's spent so long being told what to do, when to do it, and who to do it with.

I look her over. "You want me to quit grifting with you?"

She shrugs. "I mean, it's an option."

Now I'm on unsteady ground. "I love the control," I remind her. "You can quit, but I can't. I'm not going to."

She nods a few times, staring at her feet, then the wall. "Yeah, I get that."

"I'd believe you more if you weren't talking to the stairs."

She glares right at me. *"I get it."*

I stare into her, my muscles cramping. We've always been the same, me and her, but I can't forge an identical path to the one she is now. I've never imagined a life without deceit, but I also can't lose her. "This doesn't change us."

"You said befriending Trent is testing your limits. I'm just worried about what this might do to you on a visceral level. Varrick isn't some random tech boy billionaire with sadistic tendencies. What's new is that he has history with all of us."

"What's the alternative?" I ask, my voice flaming like the

end of a match. "We hand over the reins to the godmothers? We run from this town? I want to be in the driver's seat, Phebs. Not our moms. Not my dad. I need to be behind the wheel."

She crosses her arms, nodding, understanding. "Control freak," she teases with a slight smile.

"You love this control freak."

"Barely."

"Tell me more lies." I wind her pony around my fist.

She makes a breathy noise and fists my button-down. *"Rocky."* It's a warning as much as a plea. I pull her pony, wrenching her head backward. Her chin up. She tries to look away from me, and I cup her jaw with my other hand. Not letting her move at all.

Her body flushes with aroused heat. Radiating against me. "You like this," I whisper over her lips.

"No," she lies, her knees nearly buckling.

When I share her stair, my legs thread through her thighs, and I bear my weight against her, pinning her to the wall with my build. She tries to move forward, but I press harder into Phoebe.

Her breath shortens.

Hot blood drives straight into my cock. "You want me to kiss the fuck out of you?"

"*No*," she says, too breathlessly. "I want you"—she licks her lips, stares me down in challenge—"to fuck off."

"Keep lying," I whisper-hiss against her ear. "Tell me how you don't love my cock deep inside your tight cunt. Tell me how you haven't been thinking about me pounding into you all night."

"I'll tell you something," she contends in a panting breath. "You can't have me."

I grip her face tighter. "Bad girl."

She lets out a strangled whimper, one that morphs into a

high-pitched cry when I cage her hands above her head. Stretching her arms high. "Fuck . . . *off*."

"How about I just fuck you instead, little nightmare?"

"No, *stop*." She's out of breath. I skim her features urgently. Her hips arch into me. Okay . . . she's fine.

I resist even kissing Phoebe, the strain obliterating me as much as it does her. Tendons shriek in my arms and neck. My cock is yelling at me to ram inside her, but I go nuts inside this overwhelming, mind-altering, unhinged feeling.

"Let me go," she tries to growl, but it comes out breathy again.

"The biggest lie of all."

Her lips part into another soft moan. She tries to push against me. I push against her. Her heady, loving gaze clings to mine with hot depth I could burn inside. It's a blistering tug-of-war with no release. I'm high on the edging as I nip her bottom lip, as she tries to take more while simultaneously yanking her wrists against my hold.

I don't let her go.

I smother her. I'm asphyxiating *me* in our gathering arousal. She mutters out quick, "Stop, stop, stop, *no*, *Rocky*," as I suck the base of her neck and grind my hard confined length against her. As her voice escalates, I cover her mouth with my hand.

I swear to God, if Nova hears her, he just might shoot me. This needs to end here. We're both breathing hard, and I really don't want to tear away from her glare, more than anything, but I step back, check the time on my watch.

She knows I need to go.

Jake is waiting outside for me.

Phoebe tightens her loose pony. I peel an escaped strand of hair off her lips. She catches more oxygen to ask, "What are Trent's parties even like?"

I motion her to follow me down the stairwell. "I could tell you, but then I'd need a couple Advil and bleach for the brain rot."

She stops at the base. "It can't be as bad as that one party in Manhattan where there was a literal dick-measuring contest."

"Worse."

She's disbelieving. "It ended with a fratty asshole *peeing* on his girlfriend."

"Worse."

Her eyes tighten like she can't picture the events. "Promise you'll text me if you need backup."

I arch my brows. "From you?"

She glares. "Fuck you and yes."

I smile a little bit, and I nod to her. "I promise. But don't wait around for an SOS."

"Scared to look desperate and in need?" she taunts.

"More like I'd rather rupture both eyeballs than see Trent anywhere near you." I force a dry smile and skim her flushed cheeks. I wish I could prolong this with her for another hour or five.

"That's sort of hilarious because I'd rather rupture my eyeballs than look at him, too."

We share a serious expression. The easier thing would be to put Victoria in our rearview mirrors. What we always do, but this was my home once upon a time.

And I'm not going anywhere.

EIGHT

Rocky

I hate horses. Yet I've been corralling panicky Thoroughbreds for the past hour, guiding them in hay-strewn stables at the Koning estate. Most would think I give a shit about them, and maybe I honestly give a little one.

These animals didn't ask to be a part of Trent's petulant rebellion against his younger brother.

Some jackass spray-painted them the colors of a rainbow, as if they've been plucked off the set of *The Wizard of Oz*. Then they proceeded to let them loose. The horses neigh and buck as fireworks shoot off. Strobe lights graze the night sky. A DJ remixes eardrum-splitting eighties songs beside the Olympic-sized pool.

It's sensory overload, and I've gripped a dozen reins and ushered the animals away from the cacophony at the mansion. It's a miracle I haven't been trampled tonight. I can't remember the last time a horse trusted me to get this close. I've never led a horse *anywhere*. But maybe they smell the hero beside me.

Tall, preppy Jake has rolled up the sleeves to his button-down like he's a rugged Montana native and not born of New England privilege and clambakes. We're sweat coated and heavy breathed as we work together to lock up the remaining horses.

"Shhh, shhh," Jake coos, stroking a pink-painted horse as he settles her in a stall. She calms against his touch.

I padlock a blue-streaked Appaloosa in the neighboring stall. "Sue your brother for destruction of property."

"I can't." Jake shuts the stall gate and secures the padlock. "These are his horses. I had mine taken off the estate yesterday to the other stables."

My brows jump while I wipe a drop of sweat off my temple. "We've been manhandling *his* property?"

"I don't care if they're legally his. We couldn't leave them out there." He slips into an adjacent stall and heaves a leather saddle off a Thoroughbred. The word *Pussy* is spray-painted red on the horse's torso. I'm suddenly reminded that I hate people.

He places the saddle down. "These aren't normal parties."

"What gave that away?" I say dryly.

"I can't stop the absinthe from flowing or the drugs, but I can stop this," Jake professes, "and too many people are already *plastered*."

"Yeah, some drunk fuck will try to climb on one and get bucked off. They'd learn a great lesson. Don't fuck with horses."

Jake shushes the Thoroughbred as a firework booms. Hooves trample the hay as the horse scoots into the corner with a pitiful sound. Jake side-eyes me. "You want to let them back out?"

I roll my eyes in a harsh arc.

No. I don't.

Before I met Jake Waterford, I'm not sure I would've cared this much about helping out a horse. Excuse me, *fourteen* horses.

"Trent could have *you* arrested for touching his shit," I tell him. "Emphasis on *you* because I'll talk my way out of it as his friend, just like I plan to talk my way out of helping you now. But I can't save you, man."

"I'm not asking you to save me." Jake comes out of the stall with the confidence of a firstborn.

He might be the thirdborn on paper, but he does deserve to be sole heir. In more ways than one. He has boundaries he won't cross and virtues he upholds. He genuinely cares about the people in this town, and maybe this means more to me now that I know I'm a Wolfe. My family founded Victoria with his, and the need to safeguard it has been intensifying inside me.

Still, of all the wealthy circles I've infiltrated, I've rarely seen men like Jake rise to the top. He has the pedigree to claim billions, but not the teeth to protect it. Not when others are more cutthroat and will do what he won't. Manipulate, sell their souls, fuck over anyone to line their pockets and succeed.

I will give him *some* credit. Jake isn't beyond cutting deals with devils. Or else he wouldn't have enlisted our help to take down his family.

Using his bicep, he wipes sweat off his brow. "You have a responsibility to protect your siblings and Phoebe and the rest of the Graveses, but you don't need to worry about me like you do them."

I narrow a look at him. He's exuding "older brother" energy toward me right now, and I'm not sure I love it. But I also don't hate it. Probably because he's right. I don't have a responsibility to him the way that I do the others.

Ever since we included Jake in the family business, it's been an odd change—but not a bad fit. Feels more like packing an extra gun at the hip.

I lean on a wooden post where rope is hung. "I'm not worried about you. *For* you, maybe. I doubt you'd do well in jail."

"I'd survive," he says simply. "And I promise you'll get paid once my funds are untied. Whatever I have." He owes us all a million each for the job that killed his mother, but that was under the stipulation that he inherited everything.

That never happened.

The only one scrambling for that payout is Everett Tinrock, the godfather. He believes it's owed, no matter the outcome, but we all would rather finish the job before squeezing Jake.

Trent is a disease on this town. On Jake. On Phoebe. On me.

It's personal. I don't even care about the money. I'm not sure I ever really did.

"Don't rush to the bank" is all I say.

He nods, understanding. His gaze softening.

We hear a loud *bang*, and our heads whip to the left. "That was a shotgun," I say.

"Skeet shooting," Jake guesses. "It sounds like they're hitting clay pigeons, or we'd hear screams." We're both more tense.

Claudia Waterford laid out an extremely messy division of assets in her will. One term: Trent and Jake were to *split* the Koning estate. She must've fantasized about her sons living together in harmony under one roof.

There is no harmony here. It's mayhem and debauchery most nights. What's become of the estate would make a frat house look civilized. And I've had a front-row seat to the temper tantrum. Jake refused to sign over his half of the estate to

Trent, so Trent did what any big brother would do. He threw a party. And another. And *another.*

His attempt to annoy Jake into giving away his rights to the mansion and land—it's juvenile. Laughable. And highly *fucking* irritating.

I push off the post. "He wants you gone, sweetheart."

"I'm not leaving. I'm not selling him the estate, and he's not accepting any offer I make so I can buy it from him." They're at a cold standstill, and Jake was advised by his legal team to live at the estate full-time.

So he's been sharing a house with Trent. Albeit, twenty-five-thousand square feet of space, but space nonetheless. Trent already told me he was invited to summer at Stonehaven, and if he accepts, then Jake will, too.

I don't want Trent at Stonehaven. I don't want him anywhere *near* Phoebe, but it might be better to have him around Varrick. He's like gangrene, and I want Varrick to deal with this infection.

"If Trent keeps throwing parties here, you need to start playing as dirty as your brother," I counsel. "Or else he's going to do something that you won't survive."

Jake is frustrated. He pulls at the drenched button-down that suctions to his chest. "I can't be like him, Grey."

"Your moral backbone isn't going to win you the estate, *Jake.*"

He scrapes a hand through his light brown hair. "What should I do?"

"Make his life hell, for starters. Cut the Wi-Fi. Have construction workers banging outside his bedroom window. You could be doing reno while he's sleeping. Instead, all week you've been letting him pass out all day and party all night."

He considers this. "I wish I could just call the cops."

It's not a solution when Trent has paid off the sheriff. They've shown up before, said a casual "Keep it down" and turned around.

Jake shakes his head slowly in pained thought. "You said he'd do something I won't survive. What'd you mean by that?"

"He knows you love animals, and he had someone fuck with the horses, Jake. What else do you love?"

He stares off with tightened eyes. "What or who?"

I swallow tar. His reddened gaze lifts to mine, and I wish—I wish, more than anything—that he never got attached to the only two women I'd go to hell for. "He thinks you loved Phoebe. He doesn't know you have *any* feelings for my sister. Keep it that way. Or else she'll be the rope you're wrenching back and forth in your tug-of-war. And it's one thing to have Phoebe in that role, but Hailey has *never* been in that position. Ever."

It's why I've been so very fucking careful of acknowledging my sister whenever I'm with Trent. I barely say *hey* to her. The more interest I give her, the more interest he takes.

And I want him to forget she even exists.

NINE

Hailey

"Toss or pack?" Phoebe holds up a bright neon-green spatula, the side clearly melted.

I've never been attached to *things*. Not like Phoebe, who has a sentimental collection of strawberry paraphernalia. Letting go of a rare green-cloth binding 1894 peacock edition of *Pride and Prejudice* was as easy as forging a signature. No effort. No second thoughts.

So I'm surprised that I'm even contemplating keeping a spatula that looks like it was a Popsicle caught in the Arizona sun. But I remember melting down marshmallows on the stove for Rice Krispy treats. I remember leaving the spatula too long in the frying pan because Olly and I started chatting about Mary Mallon, commonly known as Typhoid Mary. Time passed and I didn't notice the utensil melting until I *smelled* it.

We laughed over the deformed spatula, and Oliver told me I couldn't trash it. "It has too much character to let the garbage claim it," he said with a classic Oliver wink.

Now in the loft, it feels like an easy choice. But one I wouldn't have made a year ago. "Pack," I tell Phoebe.

She startles. "Really?" She squints at the spatula. "I know we're not 'throw money up in the air' kind of flush, but we can afford a new spatula."

"I like that one," I confess. "It has memories."

Phoebe smiles at me, and I give her my best look to *drop it.* But she says, "Hailey Tinrock—"

"Stop." I point a finger at her as her smile blossoms.

She presses her lips together for a split second before she caves. "Being sentimental over an object. I never thought I'd see the day."

"*One* object." I rip a piece of packing tape. "If you find me hoarding deformed kitchen utensils, I give you full authority to initiate an intervention."

Phoebe carefully places the melted spatula on a layer of bubble wrap like it's a fragile porcelain doll. The dramatics of my best friend are nothing new. Watching her fit household items into a box, however, is so new and foreign it feels like we've entered a parallel dimension.

Is that what happened when we came to Victoria? We stepped foot into another universe?

Stop thinking about that, Hailey. One of my worst mental spirals was when I started a deep dive into quantum mechanics and string theory.

Three days have passed since lunch with the godmothers, and I haven't missed any chunks of time since. Not remembering the phone call to Carter or how I ended up in Rhode Island scared me enough to try hard to get better sleep. So far, so good.

I don't need to fuck it all up by restarting an old obsession.

We have enough issues trying to pack for a move to *nowhere*. We're relocating some of the household items—utensils, toaster, bedding—to a small storage unit while we pack our clothes for the summer stay at Stonehaven.

I know Phoebe isn't a dreamer. She barely can see what next month looks like, let alone the next five years. But I hate to say that I dreamed about this loft. Dreamed I would one day have enough money from the Koning job to buy it and the little bookstore underneath. Silly dreams. Wasted dreams. Just more for the trash bin.

While I struggle stuffing decorative pillows into a box, Phoebe asks, "How's the morning sickness?" It's just us two in the loft today, or else she wouldn't be asking so openly. It's still a heavy secret. One that grows heavier by the day. Literally and figuratively. My baby is the size of a grape now, but before I know it, it'll be as big as a pumpkin.

"Better," I tell Phoebe. "Carter sent me some prescription anti-nausea meds that have been helping."

Her eyes go wide. "Should you be taking medication from someone that only has *fake* MD credentials?"

"He did his research before he forged the scrip." I use my elbow to wedge a pillow deeper into the box. Having Carter know that I'm pregnant has been surprisingly helpful. He even sent me prenatal vitamins yesterday.

Phoebe's brows furrow. "The family doctor here already knows you're pregnant. Can't you just ask her for them?"

"I don't trust her." It's as simple as that in my head. I rarely trust *anyone* outside our closed circle. That includes medical professionals. It took an ungodly amount of courage for me to just go get help for my insomnia.

Phoebe comes closer with a permanent marker in her grip. She scribbles *Pillows* on the side of my box. Her eyes flit up to meet mine, concern doubling. Tripling on me. "You will have to eventually go see an ob-gyn for the baby, you know that, right?"

"Right," I say stiffly. "But I can do that in New Hampshire."

"Hails—"

"I don't need any other people in Victoria knowing I'm pregnant. Not yet." I'm not ready to confront the questions. *Who's the father? And are you even fit to be a mother?* I've thought a lot about my own mom. How she'd be thrilled if Phoebe and Rocky became parents. But me . . . I know the first thought in her head will be *Are you even mentally well enough to carry a child?*

I want everyone to see that I am better than I was. And that means putting time between this baby announcement and my breakdown at the storm shelter. It hasn't even been a month. I just need more *time*.

Phoebe helps me manhandle the frilly pillow, and I clamp the flaps down while she tapes the box shut. "I can keep your secret, Hails. You know I can. I will."

Guilt is not a foreign monster. It's one that sleeps with me in my bed. I can't shake the feeling even now. "You don't need to go to great lengths to keep this one for me, Phebs."

"I'm a trained liar. These aren't great lengths. I'm swimming in a kiddie pool."

"My brother is one of the most perceptive humans on the planet. Lying to him can't be qualified as 'kiddie pool' material." I try to catch her eyes. But she's drawing a strawberry on the flap of the box.

"It's not lying. It's evading the truth."

My heart skips. *Don't choose me over my brother.* But I worry she will. I worry she has.

Phoebe has been keeping Rocky so far in the dark that I can tell he's starting to think she's keeping something from him. And I know Phoebe—she will play it up and purposefully mislead him to deflect the attention off me.

She's already slyly laying the groundwork to make it seem like maybe *she* could be pregnant. It's what she does. She's being my best friend. One who throws herself in front of a moving vehicle to make sure the eighteen-wheeler doesn't slam into me. Even at the risk of losing her very real relationship with the man she loves.

I want her to stop.

But I don't know how to make her stop.

I should say the words *Tell Rocky the truth.*

My throat swells, knowing how agonizing it'd feel if my brother knew the news before Oliver or Jake. But letting Phoebe take this one for me crushes me in a different, still painful way. "M-maybe he should just know," I stammer. "I can tell him."

To avoid her eyes, I pick at the edge of the tape with my fingernail.

"In due time, Rocky can know," she says. "But I sense that isn't *now.*" Phoebe and I finally meet each other's gazes and hers is steeled—ready to fight me on this.

I open my mouth to start the argument, but the front door swings aggressively open as someone barges inside. We both snap our heads toward the firstborn heir to the Koning estate.

Trent Koning Waterford.

He struts into the loft with his white leather bucks, white chino shorts, and matching Brunello Cucinelli polo, like he just stepped off a croquet lawn. I'm almost certain he has. He lifts his designer sunglasses to the top of his head and pushes back the longer, fluffier strands of his brown hair, two shades darker than Jake's.

I loathe Trent just as much as Phoebe does, but I've been coached to lay low. *Do not engage*.

Trent only has pettiness in his bones when it comes to his younger brother. What Jake has, Trent wants. It's why Phoebe's been a prized possession ever since Jake dated her. Plus, she's quite literally the definition of a vixen. A real-life siren. Anybody with a pulse could be seduced by her with a flit of her eyelashes, and unfortunately, she's been known to catch strays.

Trent just happens to be the rabid alley cat with fleas.

I try to remain disengaged while Phoebe's eyes flame, her fingers curl into fists at her sides. "What the fuck are you doing here?" she sneers.

He shakes a set of keys. "Stopping by my new place. Is that a crime?"

"Yes, your presence on this Earth is a fucking crime to humanity," Phoebe shoots back.

He laughs. "Just tell me you want to fuck me, Phoebe, and we can get this whole hate-flirting done with."

Phoebe growls, literally *growls*. I step in front of her. "She doesn't want to fuck you."

"The freak speaks—"

Phoebe slips beside me. "Can you go? Seriously? You're not welcome here. Jake said you two agreed you wouldn't do anything with the place until we moved out."

Trent touches a hand to his chest. "And I am keeping my word." He veers toward the kitchen. "I won't be doing anything to the property until you girls are gone, but that doesn't mean I can't inspect it." He runs a finger over the stove. "We'll need to get a Miele induction in here, for sure. And the shades—what are those, paper blinds?"

"So, you're metaphorically pissing on your territory, we get it." Phoebe points to the door. "Exit stage left."

Trent crosses his arms over his chest and leans back against the counters. "There's no need to be so hostile. I know you dumped my brother—"

"It was a mutual breakup," I cut in. Okay, I might feel protective of Jake's reputation. He wasn't the dumpee or the dumper.

When Trent glances at me, Phoebe snaps her fingers. "Hello? *Leave.*" She whips out her phone. "Or I will be calling Jake to let him know his asshole brother is here harassing us."

"So, now talking is harassing?" Trent's brows shoot up. "What are we, *five*?"

"No, but you're thirty-fucking-two and should know the definition of the word *leave.*" She puts the phone to her ear.

Trent rolls his eyes dramatically. "All right. All right. Don't do that." He lowers his hand in the air in demonstration. "Put the phone down."

Phoebe's nose flares.

Trent's lips lift into a wider smile, and I can clearly see Phoebe's fire turns him on. So I interject again, "What's ten days to wait for inspections? We're going to be gone by then."

He barely breaks eye contact with Phoebe to glance at me. He squints. "What's your name again?" He knows my name. He's just being annoyingly obtuse.

Phoebe still has the phone to her ear. "Hey, *Jake*—"

Trent rolls his eyes. "Tell my little brother I said hello." He stuffs his hands in his pockets and casually saunters back to the door.

Phoebe and I watch as he leaves, and as soon as the door

shuts, I make sure to flip the dead bolt. Not that it will help. He has a key.

She sets her cell on the counter and hits the speakerphone. "Your brother just left the loft."

Jake lets out a low groan. "Fucking hell. I told him not to go over there." I imagine he's pinching the bridge of his nose in the way he does when he's at the end of his rope. His brother hasn't just been a thorn in his side, but the entire pricker bush. "Are you two okay?"

"I want to stab something, but other than that, I'm fine," Phoebe says hotly.

"Hailey?" Jake asks. The way he says my name with concern and care in his deep, masculine voice sends a heat wave through my body. I try not to blush. The man has licked the most intimate parts of me; I shouldn't swoon over something so simple. So mundane. And yet . . . here I am. *Swooning.*

"I'm good."

He lets out a deeper sigh, but this one sounds relieved. "Okay, I'm going to stop by the hardware store and get a chain bolt. It's not much, but hopefully it'll give you both peace of mind until you move." He pauses. "And I'm sorry."

"Please don't apologize for your egotistical, skeezy older brother," Phoebe says. "You're not the bad guy here, Jake."

"But I am your landlord."

"For ten more days at least," I say.

After that, who knows what the future is going to hold?

TEN

Rocky

Stars speckle the dark sky in town, but I'm not looking upward on this cool start-of-summer night. Leaning on the brick siding near Baubles & Bookends, I gaze down the lamplit street as people exit the local movie theater. Couples arm in arm. Kids hop excitedly in front of smiling, doting parents. An old man brushes popcorn kernels off his shirt.

Cute.

Bitterness isn't simmering. Something else grips my insides.

For a brief, heavy second, I imagine Christian and Josephine Wolfe coming out with two little boys skipping ahead of them. My older brothers Evan and Griffith. With tacky '80s jean jackets and shaggy hair. Josephine pregnant with me. Maybe the marquee spelled out BACK TO THE FUTURE or THE BREAKFAST CLUB.

I hate that I googled movie releases in '85.

Strangely, I like picturing them on the same street where I wait for Phoebe. I'm not grieving what I lost—because I would never trade my sister and my brother for a life that's not mine—but I am being a fucking fool by romanticizing a place and a family I never knew.

And in the next beat, I think, *I won't leave them behind.*

I blink away the image of my birth parents. I can't remember the last time where my mind drifted this far away from me.

I blame Jake. For telling me everyone loves summers in Victoria. I told him, "I've never loved a season, let alone a place, so good luck getting me to love the hottest months of the year."

"Game on, jackass," he said with a smile.

I rolled my eyes.

But I feel the smallest smile toy at my lips now. *The fuck.* I scrape my hand through my hair, about to dig out my phone and call Phebs. She's taking literally forever, and the only reason I'm not waiting for her in the loft is because I'm guarding the apartment from Trent.

Like hell is he going to step one fucking pinky toe into the stairwell.

If he knew me, like *really* knew me, he would be terrified to pull what he did last week. The fact that I can't put the fear of fucking God and every disciple in him is bludgeon-my-head-against-concrete levels of frustrating.

Apartment door opens, and I kick off the brick wall as Phoebe takes her sweet time slipping out, securing strands of her blue hair back with strawberry clips. I bet she struggled to choose an outfit.

"Were you writing a thousand-page memoir in there?"

"Yeah, and every word was *Fuck Rocky*."

I laugh. "Nice way to make everyone realize you're obsessed with me."

"You're more obsessed," she flings back.

I tip my head. "Yeah." I nod. "As always, I'm willing to take that W."

Her red-hot glare and middle finger nearly draw a smile out of me tonight. Then she finishes fixing her hair. "Ex-husband."

"Ex-wife."

"What's the rush?" She tugs the hem of her pastel-pink minidress farther down her thighs. I'd say the dress is going to fucking kill me tonight. It scoops low over her tits, and her gold necklace drips between them. But it has nothing on the rest of her. The temperature she burns at is my real undoing. "We're just getting ice cream, right?"

"Maybe I'm just an impatient fuck when it comes to spending the night with you."

She chews her lip, trying to subdue a stupidly big smile. *"Quit."*

"Yeah, I'm not going to quit loving you."

Her normal scowl vanishes. She's melting.

I laugh harder.

She growls through a bright smile. "Fuck you." She pushes my chest lightly but clings on to my shirt for an extended beat. Her smile oozes into deeper affection. I wrap my hand around her wrist for even longer. We stay frozen for a second, consuming each other with a tunneling look, and I almost forget where I am.

Not good.

Not detrimental either. The town believes she's single and I'm single, and while we're giving her breakup with Jake some room to breathe—so as not to tank her reputation here—I'd much rather the *wonderful* citizens of Victoria still think I'm actively pursuing my ex-wife.

So people like Trent can back the fuck off.

"Ready?" I nod toward the ice cream parlor. She nods, and we walk side by side, keeping our hands to ourselves. It still ratchets up heat between us.

"I couldn't decide what to wear," Phoebe admits. "That's why I took so long."

"I figured."

She bunches her long hair on one shoulder. "How do I look?" She's not asking sweetly. Her tone is biting.

I glance over at her combative eyes. "Like my Phoebe," I answer.

Her brows spring. "No 'You look like crap, Phoebe'? No 'I can't believe I even married that hideous clown'?" She is so far from ugly, it's laughable.

"You look like crap, Phoebe."

"Hmm, B-minus. For Barely Believable."

The corner of my mouth tics up. "Could that be because I wasn't trying for you to believe that bullshit?"

"Or because I'm immune to your tricks."

"Or because I *never* trick you."

Her scowl teeters in and out, and an unknown emotion flickers in her brown eyes. I'm unable to read the sentiment; she doesn't let me as she skips ahead of me too quickly.

My muscles flex while my mind spins through assumptions I don't want to make. Phoebe peeks back to see if I'll follow her.

I haven't slowed my pace.

I'm at her side in seconds. She seems relieved, but she has nothing to fear. I'm not going to abandon her.

Thirteen years old, fourteen, fifteen, sixteen, all the way to her twenty-four and my twenty-seven—we've been tethered together. Only we're not pretending to be cousins or coworkers or college dormmates anymore.

What we are now feels like the finale. When I know it can't be fucking true. Because I *will* keep grifting. I will keep going.

I can't stop like her.

It's shocking she even can. I always believed this was ingrained in both of us. Part of me still does. Part of me hopes she's not picking up a new boring book when we've been on the same page, the same thrilling story, our whole lives together.

It's hard though, because I really, *really* just want Phebs to be happy. It does something to me, seeing the edges of her scowl soften by millimeter by centimeter by inch.

I look over at her now as she smiles around at the parked cars and families milling across the sidewalks. Drinking slushies. Ordering hot dogs from a little pop-up cart. Laughing, chatting, lost in the mundane ordinary.

She grins wider at Chelsea Noknoi, a fellow VCC server, who cuddles on the fountain's stone ledge with her fiancé, sharing embarrassingly chaste kisses.

My face contorts in a cringe. "They're pecking like birds."

"Romance Scrooge."

"That's not a thing." I sweep her smitten features. "You love it here."

Her smile goes gentle. "It surprises me how much I do," she admits, breathing deeply, and I don't want to say Jake is right—that maybe there is summer magic in Victoria. But it's hard to discount when Phebs looks so at peace in this second. In ways I've rarely seen.

"What do you love about it?" I ask.

"The normalcy, I guess." Her eyes meet mine as we walk. "It's almost exactly what Hails wanted for me when we moved here. A life with no danger zones. Which I guess ends tomorrow when we board Varrick's yacht."

We're less than twenty-four hours away from spending the summer with a murderer. *Fun.*

She shifts closer to me to speak quietly. "It feels like the start of a job," she says.

"Because it is one." We share a strong look, and I nod at her, silently telling her we're in this together. Like we've always been.

"I always like the in-between," she says. "The before and the after of a job."

"I can't say I've enjoyed anything other than being with all of you," I admit. "Sad?"

"Loser material. You need to hand me back the W."

"You'll have to fight me for it with your dinky little biceps." I lift her slender arm as proof.

She pumps her muscles to prove me wrong at the same time that I pinch her waist, tickling her. She squeals and laughs, trying poorly to maintain a scowl. She pushes me lightly. Laughter rumbles out of my chest. Oxygen fills my lungs, and for a moment, we're fifteen again, about to pack our bags for the next big city, and I'm falling in love with Phoebe for the first time.

Like clockwork, something repositions us into stoic stances. Impassive faces. This time, it's her phone ringing.

She digs it out of her purse, flashing me the caller ID: **Isla Rivers**. Her mom's alias. We slow our pace while she puts the phone on speaker. "Hi, Isla."

Magical summer nights don't exist.

If this were one, Phoebe would answer her mom's call and the first thing Elizabeth would say is, *Varrick is sobbing in a corner* or *Varrick just shit his pants*. I don't wish him dead. I want him to *suffer.*

More painfully than that, but at this point, I'd take a festering papercut to ruin his fucking day.

So, when Elizabeth opens the call with a casual "What are you up to?" I have the sudden urge to chuck the phone in the Atlantic.

"I'm in town," Phoebe says. "Out with my ex-husband for a walk. We're getting ice cream." To me, she adds, "I'll probably get salted caramel." It's a surface-level comment to indicate to her mom that we're in public.

"Can we talk in private?"

"Yeah." Phoebe checks left and right for a spot. I catch her hand and lead her to the only decently secluded place off the main street. A dark alley behind Gulp Seafood & Lounge. My narrowed eyes graze the cement where I once found my brother . . . stabbed and bleeding out on Halloween.

EDM songs boom from the bar, which'll muffle our conversation from passersby. I face Phoebe while she tells her mom, "You're on speaker, but we're out of earshot."

"Good." Elizabeth expels a taut breath. The kind that would curb anxiety or stress. That's unlike Elizabeth.

I stare hard at the phone. An uneasy feeling tightens my ribs.

"I don't know how much communication we'll have while you're at Stonehaven," she starts. "The Wi-Fi is spotty there."

"On purpose?" I survey our surroundings casually while we talk.

"Uncertain. The mansion is surrounded by water, nowhere near a cell tower, but I'm sure he takes advantage of the fact."

He could shut off the Wi-Fi and blame bad service—which will be a headache if we can't communicate through our burner phones. But it's not like we haven't encountered these issues before.

"We won't be trapped there," I remind Elizabeth. "We'll still be taking boat rides into town. Phoebe works at VCC.

We're essentially just spending nights and mornings at his residence."

"Right, but before you leave, I think you should know something." Her voice is shaky and hushed. "He's aware you two are together."

"Wait, me and Rocky?" Phoebe tries to stay calm, but her eyes grow. "Together like . . ."

"Romantically together, bug."

My brain is a screeching car crash. "Excuse me?" I shift my weight, glaring at the phone in my girlfriend's hand, then out at the alley's entrance.

Phoebe goes motionless. "How does he know?"

"It doesn't matter—"

"It *does* matter." She presses for more from her mom. I like this new side of Phoebe. The one that won't take scraps or vague responses from the godmothers.

"He assumed based on how often Rocky has spent the night at your loft and how often you've spent the night at his boathouse. He's been watching you, and he's noticed that the two of you were almost always together in various situations. Pair that with your backstories of being divorcees—it reminded him of what we would do."

"We?" Phoebe asks.

"Me and him."

I'm *not* Varrick, but I can't say it. Because I don't know him—other than he's capable of murder. And that is in me, but I can control my fury. I swim inside it every fucking day and night, and you don't see me on a killing spree.

I rub my mouth as bile scorches my throat. *He knows I love Phoebe.* Could he use this against me? Would he? She's his *daughter.* For the first time, I'm hoping that means something sentimental to him.

At least we have some information going into Stonehaven. We're not five steps behind.

Phoebe must be thinking the same thing. "Thanks for letting us know."

"Rocky," Elizabeth says with strain, "look out for my bug, *please*."

I swallow a knot and give a dry response: "I don't know how to do anything else, Elizabeth."

ELEVEN

Rocky

Waiting in a heinously long line outside for ice cream, I contemplate putting my arm around Phoebe. To feel her lean into me. She's jutting out a hip toward me, like she wants to, but she might be thinking, *It's too soon.*

Too soon to go public.

Too soon to risk cheating rumors spreading throughout town. I know that would hurt Phebs. Being deemed a cheater in a place that's supposed to be her permanent life.

"What are you thinking about?" Phoebe wonders, keeping her voice quiet as the line grows and we barely inch forward.

"You."

She weaves her arms together. "In what context?"

"How you're loyal to the people you love." I hold her blistering gaze. "You'd even sacrifice yourself for the sake of my sister. That's what scares me. Your literal, insane interpretation of 'ride or die.'"

"Not *that* literal."

"Pretty literal."

"It's just called being a good friend," Phoebe reasons. "And Hailey did all this"—she waves around town to emphasize the move here, defying our parents, quitting all they've known—"for me. Not the other way around."

I speak under my breath. "Did you come here for her or because you wanted to be here?"

Phoebe goes quiet.

I lift my brows. "Point made."

"She came here for me, too, so that makes us both willing to do what's best for the other person."

"Well, now I'm so *very* reassured," I say dryly.

Children squeal as they race around lampposts with chocolate-smeared cheeks and half-eaten waffle cones, drawing our gazes to them. Phoebe has a faraway focus. I skim her features.

"Do you want kids?" I ask her.

Her head jerks to me. "Where is that coming from?"

I give her an intrusive look. "Kids. You. Staring. *Duh.*"

She makes a scrunched face. "I remember the caveman talk is why I divorced you."

"Funny." I look her over, feeling her dodging the topic. "I suddenly remember you being allergic to 'future talk' is why I divorced you."

She snorts, but then winces a little in real hurt.

"I'm joking, Phebs," I whisper.

"Yeah, I know." Does she? Phoebe looks deeper into my eyes. "I don't know what I want for breakfast tomorrow, you think I've thought about procreating?" She doesn't give me a chance to respond as she quickly asks, "Do you want kids?" She searches my face like I did hers.

I don't want to influence Phoebe by answering. I hate that

I worry I will. I raise my shoulders, and she lifts hers back in a similar constricted shrug.

Yeah.

We drop it.

"What flavor are you getting?" she asks while canvassing the street, left and right. Everywhere the kids aren't. "Let me guess. *Rocky Road*."

Fucking really. "Let me guess, you're getting strawberry."

"Salted caramel. Which I already told you." Her grin briefly meets me. "Look who's the bad listener."

"I was too busy reading your body to hear your lies."

Her mouth forms a cute scowl. "I *am* getting salted caramel." She gives my chest a light shove.

I hardly budge. "I'll believe it when I see it."

"Then watch and believe . . ." She trails off, gaze caught on something behind us. Across the street. She squints at the entrance to Gulp Seafood & Lounge. The door is propped open, and a twentysomething bouncer texts lazily on his phone.

Phoebe suddenly pulls me out of the line and tells the family behind us to skip ahead.

"What's going on?" I ask her as we reach the curb and she squeezes between a parked BMW and Mercedes.

"I swear I just saw your brother."

Shit. "My brother?" I jog across the road with Phoebe.

Reaching the other sidewalk, she says, "Trevor. Nineteen. Skinny. Wears cashmere in the dead of summer. Loves to pretend he's Nosferatu and acts like he's a psycho-killer, which turns out was never an act—"

"Keep your voice down," I growl.

"I'm whispering."

We're both glaring. Heat ramps up between us. I watch her

gaze drip down my muscled frame. Her tits rise with each inhale, especially as she crosses her arms underneath them.

I have the sudden urge to push her against the brick wall and fuck her until she can't stand.

Flush ascends her neck. She releases a short breath to say, "We all promised to keep a closer eye on Trevor. We shouldn't be relaxing with ice cream while he's at the local nightclub. It should actually be the other way around. He should be innocently eating sherbert, and we should be getting drunk."

"I'd rather be stabbed than get drunk." Being so inebriated my vision blurs, time slips, and my body can't be controlled—*no*.

She groans. "That's not the point, Rocky."

I put my lips closer to her ear as I whisper, "What he did—it won't happen again."

Her cheeks flame at my closeness while others who know of us—Grey Thornhall and Phoebe Smith and our contemptuous relationship—pass.

Phoebe waits for Lola, a bartender from VCC, to stroll out of earshot with her girlfriend.

"You don't know that," Phoebe counters, eyes rising to mine. "You said it wasn't the only time. But you won't even tell me how many times it's happened before."

"You don't need to know." I'm not making her a fucking accomplice to his crimes.

"What if he . . ." She waits for an older couple to walk past us on the sidewalk. Once they're out of earshot, she whispers, "What if he offed *Boyd* Delacy?"

Trevor's stalker from Halloween last year. "There's been nothing in the news, and I trust that Trev would tell me."

Phoebe eases slightly. "We all need to be more proactive. We should at least figure out what he's doing in there."

"He's not a dog we need to put on a leash."

"No, he's your brother that we kind of need to babysit. At least right now, Rocky."

She has a point. I've been so hands-off, in fear of treating him like a liability the same way our parents have, that I haven't properly guided him. If I had, maybe he wouldn't have taken matters into his own hands and killed Claudia.

"Okay." I motion toward the entrance of Gulp Seafood & Lounge. "Ladies first."

She flips me off with both middle fingers, then spins toward the bouncer, Jerry Caldwell, who barely pries his attention off his phone. Until he stares at her ass as she goes inside.

Jerry catches my dark glare and shrinks backward. "Uh, hey, Grey." His face reddens. "You think you could get me Phoebe's num—"

"No," I cut him off. *Don't piss on my territory* is a warning I'm writing on his forehead with a fucking knife.

His expression drops. "Yeah, yeah." He coughs a little. "Have a fun night." He goes back to his phone.

Five feet inside, where it stinks of sweat and oysters, Phoebe stops dead in her tracks. I bump into her back, then grab her biceps to keep her from falling forward.

It's instantly clear my brother isn't alone.

He cups a glass of amber liquor while sitting stiffly at the bar. A silver cross around his neck. The top buttons undone on his black shirt. Pieces of his sweaty hair hang on his forehead, like he'd been dancing at some point.

His demeanor right now isn't casual. He's tensed. Barely blinks. Narrow eyed and angled toward a man who's *not* seated.

This fucker encroaches on Trevor. I can't place him. Not from the back. He's wearing a nondescript gray sport coat, appears of average height, average build. He seems older. Maybe forties.

Varrick.

It's all I can think. Varrick just sought out my brother the night before we're supposed to board his yacht.

I whisper quickly against Phoebe's ear, "Follow my lead."

She nods.

Pulling her behind my back, I stride forward. A new popular EDM song, "Levels" by Avicii, thunders in the nightclub, so I slip closer to the bar to better eavesdrop.

"I don't want your money," Trevor says flatly. His eyes shift covertly to me. He notices me down the bar, but he's trained well enough to hide it.

"You're going to regret this," the man warns.

I recognize that pretentious fucking voice.

Weston Burke.

One of the rich widowers who frequents Victoria Country Club and the father of Trevor's girlfriend. He likes my brother about as much as he likes me. Which is to say, he'd throw us overboard any chance he gets. I haven't given him the opportunity.

Shifting closer, I see Weston grip the lip of the bar near Trevor. "I can make your life *very* difficult here." He careens into my brother's space.

I feel Phoebe bristling behind me, but I wait to see how Trev will handle this.

He doesn't flinch. "Like you make hers?"

"Stay away from *my daughter*."

"She's not your property, man."

Weston rips the liquor out of Trevor's hand. I explode forward, grabbing a fistful of his sport coat. I yank him backward off my brother, then I shove him hard into the bar. He relinquishes the glass as I pin him.

Trevor snatches the alcohol off the counter. "Nice talking to you. Now you can deal with my brother." He lifts the rim to his lips just as Phoebe steals the glass out of his hand, liquor sloshing onto the grimy floor.

"What the fuck, PG?" He gapes.

"You're underage."

That's not why Weston tried to take it from Trev. It was a silly fucking power move to make my brother look weak.

"*Get off me*," Weston snarls at me.

I release my hold on him, just so he can turn around. When he does and his back presses into the sticky bar, I get in his face like he got in my brother's. "I don't care who the fuck you are," I sneer, "or how much money you have or how many friends you've bought around here—you *ever* corner my brother like that again and you'll wish the only thing you see are my fucking lawyers."

He works his jaw, fixes his sport coat, and tries to straighten up. As if physical violence is beneath us, but I have no issue knocking him out. The only reason I don't is because I'm trying to set an example for my brother, and I don't want him to beat people to shit.

Weston fixes his gaze on me. "Tell your degenerate brother to never speak to Sidney again, and you and I won't have a problem, Grey."

"This isn't *Let's Make a Deal*. Your daughter is a grown *adult*. She can make her own choices."

"You tell him, Rock," Trevor pipes in.

I bite my tongue from snapping at him to shut the fuck up. He's not making this any better or easier.

Weston is seething. He sees he's not winning, and so this prick seeks out what he believes is my weakness. He tilts his head toward *Phoebe.* His gaze drips invasively down her body, like he's stripping her in front of me. I sidestep and block his view of her, but it's too late. He shoots a sickly smug smile at me, as if she's just a pawn he can move between us.

I know Phoebe is fuming. I don't even need to look to feel her wrath. It sears through me.

Weston starts, "Your brother screws with my daughter, don't expect me not to do the same—"

"Think carefully about what you say next," I cut in with malice. "Because my wife wouldn't touch you with a hundred-foot pole even if she were on her deathbed. So the only way you could get her is by force, and if you even fucking *dare* force yourself on her, you will regret ever knowing who I am."

He falters, patches of red on his cheeks. He's having a hard time coming up with something to say, but I have plenty to add.

"I've seen so many of you," I sneer lowly, nearly under my breath at him. "You're all the same cowardly pieces of shit. When the debt piles up and the liquor stops numbing the hatred you feel for yourself and your outsides curdle like your insides, try phoning a friend. I'd love to see who answers a bastard like you."

His expression is that of distaste and disgust. "Look in the mirror."

"Oh, I have. Trust me. I know exactly what I am." I stare him down. "And you and I—we aren't the same. Not even close."

Unleashing on Weston feels like ripping through a brick wall—one that I've been banging my head against for too long. But it's not enough. Because he's not the number one person I want to rattle and slam into the floor.

I would love to go feral on Trent Waterford. Jake's older brother.

But I can't. He still has too much leverage and power in this town to turn into an enemy.

Weston fixes the collar of his white button-down, his rage mounting. "If you had a daughter," he says tightly to me, "you'd understand the lengths you'd go to protect her."

I flash a dry smile at him. "Well, I don't have one."

"Thank God for that."

"Is that supposed to hurt me?" I let out a blistered, acidic laugh. Then I say, "Go fuck yourself, Weston." I wave him toward the exit.

"Likewise." He marches out with a curled lip and snooty attitude.

I rotate to my brother, eyes skimming him head to toe. "You good?"

He's not blinking. His intense glare is skewering the shadow of the widower, even as Weston disappears out the door.

Phoebe's bugged eyes are pinging to my brother, to me, then back to my brother. Like this is an oh-shit moment.

Oh shit, what if Trevor kills anyone he dislikes or deems a threat?

Truthfully, I'm not as worried as she is, because I didn't just learn this "fun fact" about him. I half expect her to down a swig of liquor. She even brings the glass to her mouth . . . then thinks against sipping it.

Fucking weird.

She's been actively avoiding alcohol the past couple weeks. I haven't seen her drink any beer, wine, or liquor, but she did share my cigarette in the loft. So, no, I couldn't have gotten my sister's friend pregnant. She wouldn't have smoked if she were.

Phoebe can't be pregnant.

There is a fucking way she could be, sure, but every time I've come inside her, I've used a condom.

I smear a hand across my mouth, trying to focus more on my brother and not the gnawing sensation in my chest. He hasn't snapped out of it.

For fuck's sake. "*Trev.*"

"I was supposed to meet Sidney here for drinks." He's still fixated on the last place he saw Weston. "He read her texts. He forbade her from coming, and he tried to pay me to stop seeing her. She hates him, Rock."

"We've known she's hated him. It's why she's dating you—to get back at him." What's changed?

Trevor intakes a staggered breath. He's been spending more time with Sidney than necessary. It's easy to say he caught feelings, but for my brother, that'd be *incredibly* unusual. He empathizes with very few people, but it's becoming clearer he's growing more attached to her.

I tell him, "Weston is insignificant."

"Not to me." He hops off the barstool and slips on sunglasses in the dark. "He constantly threatens to take away Sidney's trust fund when she doesn't comply with his rules. He won't let her live in on-campus housing. He won't let her choose her own major. He won't let her stay out past curfew without having to text five-minute updates. Sidney told me she was friends with Kate because they bonded over how their parents tried to control their lives."

Kate Waterford—Jake's little sister.

I drop my voice. "Weston is a small fish right now. We'll deal with him later. And what you did . . . what you can do—

not a solution. It makes everything worse, and we need to do this together, as a fucking team."

"Okay," he says fast. "*Okay.*" He combs a hand through his damp, shaggy hair. "And the big fish?"

"The triplets' dad." *Varrick.*

He nods slowly, then glances over at Phoebe, who's bumping up to the bar to order a drink. "I don't think she liked you mentioning her dad."

I watch her mime a water to the bartender. "He's not exactly a fun topic."

He cracks his neck. "I can take him."

I stare harder at Trev.

He adds, "With your help, I can take him."

"That's the way, shithead."

A smile pulls the corner of his mouth, but a serious thought draws his lips downward. "I know I can't suck you off, being pseudo-related and everything, but just know, I can do more for you than Phoebe. Don't bench me."

I shake my head at his vulgar comment, decide to hop over it, and say, "You're summering at Stonehaven with us. Does that sound like a bench?"

"No," he mutters, then he says he's going to meet up with Sidney at the docks. She was planning to sneak out, apparently.

I clasp his hand and pull him into a short hug. Then he's gone, and I slip beside Phoebe at the bar. She's waiting on the distracted bartender, Gretchen, who's busy serving her college friends at the other end.

Nearly a year in this town, and I know almost everyone by name.

"You okay?" I ask Phoebe under my breath, setting the whiskey near her.

She avoids. "Yep. Never better."

"Liar," I say casually.

I catch her smile, especially as her eyes drift back to me. "Be honest, you'd love my heart less if it wasn't made partially of deception."

I look her over, and I'm not sure if that's true. Still, it's hard to deny. Phoebe and I—we're built at the foundation to deceive. Yet we've never spent a real moment pulling the wool over each other. I can't tell if that's changed.

"Honestly," I whisper back, "I love your heart at its best and its worst."

Her gaze softens, and I just barely hear her quiet, tender reply. "I hope it's the best here."

TWELVE

Phoebe

At seventy-two meters in length, *The Ithaka* dwarfs all other yachts in the harbor, and I was shocked I never noticed it all these months in Victoria. To which, a steward kindly told me that it just came out of the shipyard after a yearlong refurbishment.

How convenient that as soon as Varrick needs to showboat his wealth, his superyacht appears out of thin air.

I'm not impressed by the infinity pool, the lavish staterooms, the massive saloons, or even the outdoor cinema. If I could spit on each one, I would. But I suspect there might be hidden cameras in every crevice of this vessel.

The sundeck has loungers and a bubbling Jacuzzi behind me. It overlooks the expansive main deck, where the couches, outdoor dining table, and pool reside. The Bennets, Thornhalls, and Konings politely mingle and chat with the illustrious host of the invitational. *Barf.* My brothers and I, the Smiths, have sequestered ourselves to the sundeck like rebels.

Really, we're just trying to talk Nova down from his mood

so he doesn't act recklessly. He's not like Oliver, Rocky, and me. He has a hard time *pretending* to be anything other than what he is.

Grumpy.

Protective.

Guarded.

Pissed the fuck off.

And right now, he rests his elbows on the steel railing, drilling daggers at Varrick from above.

To his credit, Varrick hasn't glanced up here since the yacht left the harbor five minutes ago.

"I think we have his ears," Oliver says like an absent-minded thought as he casually sips his champagne.

Nova turns his glare on our brother. "Seriously?"

"Seriously," Oliver says. "We have to share some traits with him. It's genetics, man."

Cupping my glass of iced seltzer water with lime, I squint harder at Varrick. He's listening intently to Damian Bennet, carrying himself with casual stoicism. There's no strict, uppity air about him. It's as if he'd be as comfortable on this multimillion-dollar yacht as he would in a local dive bar.

It's quiet, magnetizing confidence.

His dark brown hair tucks around his ears and brushes against the collar of his shirt. I find it hard to place his exact age, but he shares that in common with Addison, Everett, and Elizabeth. Able to blend between late thirties and early fifties. He has well-groomed facial hair—goatee and mustache—and he looks so . . . familiar. It hits me. "He looks like Christian Bale, right?"

Nova grimaces. "Jesus Christ."

"I think he looks like Christian Bale over Jesus Christ." Oliver slips me a grin.

I send a smile back.

Nova runs a hand over his buzzed head. "You both are going to kill me." He turns his back to the main deck and leans against the railing to face us. "*The Dark Knight Rises* doesn't come out for another two months, and it's sufficiently ruined. Thank you for that."

I touch a hand to my chest. "I didn't say he was Batman."

"Just the actor who plays Batman."

Oliver glances around the sundeck. "You think he's recording us? Going to learn his kids think he's Batman?"

Nova grumbles another curse under his breath before he says, "I can't believe I'm missing *The Avengers* for this shit." And *that* is where his crappy mood originates. He had tickets tonight to the movie he's been anticipating since it was announced. It'd been a source of pure joy for Nova's comic-book-loving heart, and summering at Stonehaven snuffed it out.

We argue for three more minutes over whether we share any characteristics with Varrick—only concluding that Oliver and Nova might have his jawline. When I see our father slip away from Damian Bennet, I say, "He's on the move."

Sure enough, I watch him bypass a steward and aim his sights on the staircase to the sundeck. None of us had a chance to greet him when we boarded the boat, since we hightailed it to the top deck. A part of me hoped I could power through this voyage without interacting with him. Those chances just slipped down the drain.

"Don't push him overboard," Oliver coaches, his hand squeezing Nova's shoulder in brotherly affection.

Nova crosses his arms. His olive-green shirt pulls tight around his muscular biceps. "You don't need to worry about me."

The three of us take a collective, readying breath as Varrick climbs the last stair, and we rotate slightly to face him, Nova never loosening his arms over his chest, Oliver bent casually while sipping his champagne, and me—one hand on my hip, the other fisting my glass.

My brain hums like static on a television, words lost to this strange, morbid reality. What do you say to your long-lost father, who killed your boyfriend's entire family?

That question sinks in my gut when he approaches.

His leather loafers tap softly along the teak deck, hair blowing in the soft wind. That quiet confidence I observed from above feels more intimidating up close. As if he knows he could own us as easily as he owns the vessel beneath our feet.

Though, maybe I only feel that way knowing who he really is. What he's capable of.

A warm, charismatic smile pulls his lips. "The Smiths," he greets. His champagne flute dangles casually at his side like an afterthought. "What brings you up here? Attracted to the isolation or yearning to be different? Introverts or mavericks?"

Nova glowers at the question.

I struggle to form an adequate response that isn't *Fuck you*. Truly I thought I'd have more decorum once we were face-to-face, but my blood is set to high heat.

Oliver waves a hand toward the sea. "Just admiring the view," he says.

"Ah, yes." Varrick takes in the landscape, the colorful buildings in town, melting together as it becomes a distant landmark across the water. "Your mother loved this view, too."

His words are a calculated slingshot. Nova stiffens and drills a harsher glare into Varrick. I'm sure he's seconds away from telling him to keep our mother's name out of his mouth.

I say quickly, "*Loved*. Past tense. Are you referring to when you knew her in the eighties? Was this even your boat back then or did it belong to your mother-in-law, Emilia Wolfe?" While my words are casual, it's hard not to smother the flame from my eyes. My gaze is full of accusations. I hope it screams, *Murderer. Sinner. Fraud.*

I might be the latter two, but I've never killed for what I have.

We are not the same.

Varrick slips his free hand into his pocket while hoisting his champagne flute. "Very sharp." He sounds . . . impressed.

I cage my breath, waiting for the punch line.

He tips his head slightly to the left, and his eyes pass over me so quickly, so indecipherably that I know for certain—he's reading my body language. He's reading me.

"I'm not making a joke," he says. "You're asking all the right questions. *Yes*, this was the eighties. *No*, it wasn't Emilia's boat. It was her husband William's. I would say *may he rest in peace*, but he was a wretched old man who beat the shit out of his wife and daughter. So may he rot in hell." He lifts his champagne to his lips and takes a casual sip.

Oliver glances nonchalantly around the sundeck, and I follow his gaze with the same indifference, but I'm checking for eavesdroppers, wondering how Varrick can talk so freely. Is it sheer egotism keeping his confidence unchecked?

"We're alone up here," Varrick confirms like he's inside our heads. "But I have no qualms with repeating those words to the stewards or bosun. They know I have little love for my late father-in-law."

My fingers grip tighter on my water glass. "Seems like you have little love for the entire Wolfe family."

He shakes his head. "Not all of them." And in case we couldn't follow the insinuation, he adds, "I have nothing against Brayden."

Nova narrows his gaze. "And you think he can say the same about you?"

Varrick laughs, light in his eyes. "Of course not." He stares down at the honey-colored liquid in his glass. "No, he knows the worst pieces of me." Varrick looks at us. "So do all of you. This summer, in part, is about changing that. I'm not the Big Bad Wolfe I've been painted out to be by Everett, Addison, and Beth—because I'm sure they had plenty to say."

"News flash," I snap. "You painted yourself that way with the creeping around. You snuck up on my car outside a grocery store. Real great Michael Myers impersonation, by the way."

He leans against the railing, forearm on the cool metal, and his eyes trail down to the other guests on the main deck. "Most people wouldn't have noticed me, but the fact that you did was a testament to how well you were raised." He turns his attention back to me. "It's why I've invited you all here. I'm not willing to work with just anyone."

"We're not working with you," Nova says.

For the first time today, this catches Varrick by surprise. It's a split second. Nearly unreadable, but I see the shock cinch his eyes before he eases it off his face completely.

Oliver lets out a deep exhale. "Nova—"

"No, I'm not entertaining this bullshit," Nova growls. "He just wants to use us."

Varrick scans him. "And you can use me. That's what a team is. Mutually beneficial."

Nova pushes away from the railing. "You can take your mutual benefits . . . and shove them up your ass." He stomps away toward the staircase, descending it out of sight.

Oliver winces. "He's, um . . . yeah." My brother tilts his head, then raises his flute in cheers before sipping.

Varrick arches his brows at us. "I'm guessing he was never a principal."

My blood goes cold. He's using *our* terminology like it's his. Then I realize . . . it could have been *his* before it was ever ours. I don't love that we could share more in common with him than half his DNA.

Varrick's eyes flit between Oliver and me. "That's what you still call the lead in a job? Addy and Beth created a whole lexicon that we used. It was quite clever, to be honest."

I try to bury my interest.

I didn't think he had leverage over me, but I realize now *this* is it. I ache for information. *History.* I've never been able to paint a clear picture of the past. Our moms kept it vague and hazy on purpose, but maybe Varrick can fill in the holes.

Immediate regret pummels me. I shouldn't want a single thing from him. Not even the fucks he pretends to give.

Oliver's curiosity doubles mine. I can see it in the way he bows forward slightly.

We don't have time to dig any deeper. Varrick checks the time on his watch and tells us *The Ithaka* should be docking at Stonehaven in the next ten minutes. He says to make our way to the main deck when we're ready, but Oliver and I watch him descend the stairs with an unconcerned, confident gait.

As soon as he's out of earshot, Oliver lets out a weighted breath. His eyes catch mine, and they say the same thing: *He's good. Maybe too good.*

Oliver raises his champagne flute to his lips. Before he finishes it off in a heartier swig, he says, "This is going to be a long fucking summer."

THIRTEEN

Jake

On my sixteenth birthday, my eldest brother called me on his way home from college, promising to hand-deliver a surprise present. The best a big brother could offer. I contemplated driving to Concord, pretending I was sick with the flu, breaking my own leg, and spending the day in the hospital.

Anything to get me out of whatever surprise Trent had up his sleeve.

But Kate, my eight-year-old little sister, ran into my room with a handmade birthday card. It said, *You have permission to ride Bowie all day—today only!*

Her face lit up like she'd given me the world. Her prized horse was never to be ridden by any of her brothers, including me. I didn't want to disappoint her, so I spent the morning at the stables. There was no avoiding Trent once he arrived. No denying him. I tried at least.

I said no when he pulled me into his brand-new Lamborghini Murciélago.

I said no when he drove me to New York.

I said no when his friends showed up and dragged me into a strip club.

I said *fuck no* when Trent paid for a VIP room for me. He grabbed the back of my neck, his fingers digging into my flesh. "Don't be a pussy, Jake," he whisper-hissed. "Most little brothers would be on their knees in appreciation for this gift. Take it. Thank me the fuck later." He pushed me off the couch so forcefully I stumbled into the stripper, having to grab her around the waist before she fell back into the hard edge of the stage.

He laughed.

His friends laughed.

I just wanted to leave, and I realized Trent at least gave me a way to escape *them*. So I stayed in the VIP room all night, talking with Destiny and learning that she was a grad student at NYU studying microbiology and dancing at the club to pay off her student loans.

It was that night that I realized my brother did not understand the word *no*.

It's why I don't say it today while he ransacks a closet, tearing my button-downs and polos off the hangers and tossing them like garbage to the floor. Barely an hour at Stonehaven, and we're already at odds. But I expected as much when the yacht docked at the three-story mansion, and Varrick explained there weren't enough bedrooms for everyone to have their own. He made arrangements for the brothers to room together.

Not a problem for Damian and Sandon Bennet, Grey and Trevor Thornhall, or even Oliver and Nova Smith.

But Trent and I—we have a massive fucking problem. We can barely share the same air. Sharing a bedroom might as well be asking him to sleep inside a coffin six feet under the earth.

Instead of politely telling me to gather my things—things that were meticulously folded and placed in drawers and closets by the Stonehaven staff that unpacked our luggage—Trent has decided to go nuclear.

I'm half expecting him to take out a match and just light my shit on fire.

It's not beneath him.

I lean against the doorframe, arms crossed, the door shut on Trent's request. "Is this really necessary?" I ask.

He takes two hands to scoop my boxer briefs out of the drawer and dump them on the rug. "You weren't going to do it."

"If you gave me longer than thirty fucking seconds—"

"You've always been slow at everything. I doubt you'd have this handled in thirty minutes, let alone seconds." He thrusts open the next drawer. "Just thank me and be done with it."

"What am I thanking you for exactly?"

"Solving this fuckup." He tosses my shorts onto the pile of clothes.

"I'm sure Varrick Wolfe would love to hear how you believe his arrangements are a massive failure—"

"Twisting my words already." Trent shoots me a glare. "You shouldn't even be in this room. My lawyers advised me not to be alone with you."

I laugh. "Is that why we haven't been alone together since Mom died?"

"Obviously. I actually listen to my legal counsel."

Yeah, right.

He shuts the last drawer and tips his chin down to my clothes littered on the ground. "Take your shit and leave."

I don't move off the doorframe. "Where?"

"Don't know. Don't really care."

"And if Varrick asks why I'm sleeping on the couch? Should I let him know my big brother kicked me out of the room?"

"Tell him whatever you want, Jake. *I'm* the one sleeping in this room. *I* didn't lose. That speaks louder than your useless words."

He's trying to impress Varrick, which surprises me. I'd thought Trent agreed to summering at Stonehaven for the novelty of it. A rare look inside the inner sanctum of Victoria's most noble family.

I didn't think he was interested in being named heir.

"You actually want the Wolfe inheritance?" I ask with a frown.

Trent's face contorts like I've lost it. "Who the fuck wouldn't? The Wolfes have double our wealth and more passive income to their name. Varrick is a lucky prick. He's hired staff to manage all of his properties. Barely lifts a finger. While I'm wasting my life in a boardroom trying to please investors." He looks me up and down. "But you wouldn't know what that's like. Mom never let you in the big boy chair."

"I own half the assets now."

"Half doesn't give you the majority, baby brother." His phone vibrates, and he rolls his eyes when he checks the message. "Fucking Jordan. Still bitching he didn't get an invite."

Mention of our brother tenses my body. Jordan called me when he found out about the invitation. He was a mess. I could barely make out what he was saying. I talked to his wife for over an hour trying to convince her to get him help, but she insisted he'd leave her before that happens.

"Jordan needs rehab," I tell Trent.

My eldest brother groans loudly. "Not with this again." He runs an annoyed hand through his hair. "Jordan is pathetic. He doesn't need rehab. He needs a *backbone*."

"Says the guy who supplies him with Percocet."

Trent laughs lowly. "Everyone pops pills. It's not my fault if he has no self-control. It's a personality flaw."

It's an illness, I want to say. But I've been through this toxic merry-go-round a thousand times before. I pinch the bridge of my nose. Over this. We've never seen eye to eye on our brother. It's the same argument I've had with our mom. They'd rather look down on Jordan than admit that they failed him. As a mother. As an older brother.

I'm the youngest of my brothers, and I am *trying* my best to keep this shit together without bandaging our family's legacy with a bloodstained cloth.

"Since when do you care so much about Jordan?" Trent asks me. "You hate him. Unless you forgot that he also sells Perks to caufers." *Caufers*: students at Caufield University.

I haven't forgotten that.

I do hate him for that.

But I can want him to get help and hate him at the same time. Multitasking isn't a foreign concept for me.

I don't give Trent the satisfaction of a reply. Veins pop in his neck; he's unnerved. He motions again to the pile of clothes. "Collect your shit."

Barely blinking, I say, "No."

He laughs shortly. "You don't want to do this with me."

"Why?" I say with an easygoing shrug. "Can't handle someone pushing back on you?"

His smile never wanes. "You've always thought yourself big and tough. But it's just *so* easy to hurt you. I barely have to try." He walks to the closet and finds my empty suitcase. He slings it to the floor, and it splays open next to the mound of clothes. "Pack up your shit or else I will be happy to find another room to bunk in. I heard your ex-girlfriend is sleeping on this floor. Three doors down."

Phoebe.

He doesn't break eye contact.

I know he has it in him to try to enter her room without permission. My joints loosen enough for me to leave the doorframe and kneel beside my suitcase.

Trent doesn't gloat. He steps around me and opens the door, making my embarrassment a public display for any passersby. "You," I hear him call out. "Come here." I think he's flagging down staff until I see the platinum-blonde hair peek into the door. *Hailey.*

Her lips turn down when she catches my eyes.

Trent snaps his fingers at me. "My brother needs help. He's woefully incapable of this task. Hasn't packed a suitcase in all his life."

"I'm fine," I snap. But I don't mention how he's right about the last part. I have people that pack for me. So does Trent.

My brother waves me off. "He's being obnoxiously humble. Please help him." He just wants to shame me, but there's no judgment in Hailey's eyes. She walks farther into the room and kneels on the other side of my suitcase.

Trent sinks onto the bed, kicking his feet up on the mattress. He scrolls on his phone and lets out an impatient sigh as if I'm a nuisance in *his* room.

I start tossing shirts into the suitcase, not bothering to fold them. Hailey's gaze flits from Trent to me, anger growing as she puts the pieces together.

"You can stay in my room, Jake," she says, loud enough for my brother to hear. Defiance pulses against her gray eyes, and I lose myself in them for a second. There aren't many people in this world willing to stick up for me against Trent. Until the Graveses and Tinrocks moved to Victoria, I would have said there were none.

It still feels unreal. Like maybe one day I'll wake up from this dream and live my inherited nightmare.

"So cute," Trent deadpans, his eyes still on his phone. "The freak has a charity case."

She opens her mouth to reply, but I reach out across my suitcase to grab her wrist. Her lips snap shut. Her shoulders slump in defeat, and we share a silent look of agreement. *No provoking.* Trent gets too interested in the push and pull, and if he showed any interest in Hailey, I'd lose my fucking mind.

We return to my clothes, and I watch her fold my black boxer briefs. Her lips quirk in a sly smile as she places them gently into the suitcase and pats them. I try hard not to smile, especially when she reorganizes every shirt I attempt to fold. She does sorcery on it because the collar ends up on top. Her lips keep rising and rising as my expression turns more awed.

I can't stop looking at her. Even though better judgment says I should.

Trent doesn't know it, but he did me a massive favor today. I'm the real winner because I get to spend all summer rooming with Hailey Tinrock.

Thank you, brother.

FOURTEEN

Hailey

The belly of the beast looks more like a fantasy sprung from my head than a monstrous lair. Floor-to-ceiling shelves full of antique hardbacks occupy my guest room. Dark velvet drapes shade the arched windows, and a reading lamp is fastened to the wooden headboard of a regal four-poster bed. It makes me question how much Varrick knows about *me*. About all of us. Did he assign me this particular room because he's aware of my love of books?

No. It has to be a coincidence.

A happenstance.

I can't ruminate on hypotheticals. My brain is already fogged from last night's measly three hours of sleep. A record low since the storm shelter, which has festered a new wave of guilt. Especially after my prenatal checkup in New Hampshire two days ago.

The baby is healthy.

The baby is the size of a date.

But Dr. Perez reminded me three times to get my insomnia

under control. That stress and lack of sleep could cause a myriad of issues, like gestational diabetes, preeclampsia, preterm labor. The list seemed to be endless. "But don't stress," she insisted. "Stress will just make it more difficult to sleep. And right now, you need to focus on sleeping. If normal methods don't work, I highly recommend seeking therapy to root out the issue."

Therapy isn't an option for me. I'd have to omit too many facts or lie my way through it, and so I'm back to my own strategy. My own tools. Last night was a bad blip because I slept alone. *I know this.*

I also know I don't have to worry about that this summer. Not when Jake is currently moving his luggage into my guest room.

He shuts the dresser drawer, then spins toward me. "Are we okay to talk?" he asks, his eyes flitting around the walls like he's in search of eavesdroppers.

"All clear," I say. "I checked for bugs already." It was a tedious task, flipping open each book on the shelf, checking the pages for wireless bugs. Running my hand along windowsills and picture frames for hidden cameras. For anyone else, it might take an hour, but I was able to do it in ten minutes.

Finding any kind of surveillance would have been definitive proof Varrick doesn't trust us.

But I came up empty.

I plop on the springy king-sized mattress, the thick comforter a shade of plum, and the chain on my cargo pants jingles.

Jake grips the bedpost like he's keeping himself from fully committing to sitting beside me. Veins spindle down his forearm as we silently check each other out. *We are sharing a room this summer. A bed. You can't run from him after a sensual fuck, Hailey.*

I can't tell if I love this fact or if I'm terrified of it.

His eyes stall on the two silver hoop piercings on either side of my bottom lip. Ones I take out for work at the country club.

"Snakebites," I tell him. "That's the name of the piercing."

"I like it."

"You do?"

"That surprises you, why?" Skin pleats between his brows. "We've had sex."

"I've slept with guys who didn't like my piercings or my lipstick or my face."

"Your face?" He sounds more heated.

Rocky calls Jake a white knight, and I'd have to agree—he seems like someone who'd go to war for those he cares about far too easily.

"The guy didn't say I was ugly or anything. It was an assumption on my part. When he threw his T-shirt on my face mid-act."

"And you didn't care?"

"It was a quickie. I didn't care if he found me appealing," I admit. "I just wanted to get off. It's not like I was sticking around. It was between jobs, so I was in St. Louis only for the night."

Jake processes this, then nods, glancing at my snakebite lip piercings again. "I like them," he says, this time more firmly. "They're cute. Like you. And I find you more than just appealing."

I start to blush. "I, um . . ." I feel more bashful around him when we aren't fucking, which is weird. I nod a few times. "The feeling is mutual, so yeah." *Smooth, Hailey.*

He nods back to me, drinking in my mesh black top and cargo pants. "Have you always been this alternative?"

"When I wasn't told I had to dress a certain way, then yeah. I liked grunge when I was younger. Then later, more heavy metal."

He smiles, leans a shoulder on the bedpost. "How young?"

"Maybe like twelve, thirteen, I was listening to Nirvana. 'Come as You Are' got me through a whole lot of teenage angst."

"I know how that is." He lets out a laugh in thought. "I used to run ten miles before dawn on Faust's track." Faust is the all-boys boarding school he attended in upstate New York.

"What'd you listen to?" I ask.

"The sound of my feet hitting concrete. My heavy, angry breath. The rustling trees."

I clutch either side of the bed as my mind drifts with the image. "I can picture it. Teenage angsty Jake running down his feelings."

"I can picture it, too." He recaptures my gaze. "Teenage angsty Hailey head-banging out hers."

I smile a little. "I did do that a lot. Even with Phoebe." I soak in his white button-down, the pressed navy-blue slacks, the brown leather belt on his towering athletic frame. He could be in a J.Crew catalog holding the bow of a sailboat. Pensive and masculine and blatantly handsome.

It feels strange that he's in my bedroom. In front of me. "Have you always been this preppy?"

"Yeah. My style wasn't anything I ever questioned changing." He steps away from the bedpost and finally sits beside me.

My face bakes at his closeness. Too shy to meet his gaze, I focus on my toes skimming the velvety moss-colored rug.

"This is a Tibetan rug. Silk or silk blend," I say absent-mindedly.

He glances down at our feet. "How can you tell?"

"The knot structure gives it away. Plus, the wool. It feels buttery soft in a specific way because of Tibetan sheep. The extreme cold climates make the sheep wool denser and longer than other sheep. So when it's hand-knotted, it enhances the quality of the rug."

Jake's gaze bores into me as if I'm rehashing some action-packed story.

I bite my lip piercing. "Anyway, it's not that interesting. Just a mundane fact about a rug."

"Everything about you is interesting to me." His eyes cradle me tenderly, and heat ascends the base of my neck. Concern washes over his expression. "How much sleep did you get last night?"

I nestle my hair behind each of my ears. "Your observational skills are getting better."

Laughter catches in the back of his throat. "Yeah, no. I'm still average at best. Except, I guess, when it comes to you . . ." His gaze sweeps me again. "Did you get *any* sleep?"

My fingers skim the spine of the hardback I'm holding. "Three hours. I spent the night reading."

He sees my book. "Did you bring that with you?"

I nod and show him the spine: A HISTORY OF WOLVES. "You know it's ironic that Rocky chose the name Grey when he was born a Wolfe. A gray wolf. *Canis lupus.*" I draw my finger over the title. "Most people think of penguins when they're asked what animals mate for life. I think of the gray wolf. My brother." I pause in thought. "A pack animal that can only be temporarily alone before searching for another pack." I hug the book, then glance over at Jake. "Rocky can't survive alone. If he could, he would've left us years ago. Unburdened himself with the resentment he carries for our parents. But he never did—he won't. He found his mate with Phoebe, and his pack with the rest of us."

Jake extends a hand.

I place the book in his palm and then watch him thumb through the pages.

"I see the connection," he says, "but why keep reading it if it keeps you up at night?" He slips me a look like he's trying to unpuzzle me. "Do you think it could help with the job?"

"Not really, no." I lift my feet to the bed and sit cross-legged. "It's just another fascination, an obsession, to keep me from thinking of the job and the risks and all the ways I'm putting the people I love in positions that hurt them." My throat swells. Emotion barreling into me. I toy with the chain on my pocket. "Easier to think about wolves than Oliver snorting an obscene amount of coke up his nose."

"He's still doing that?" Jake frowns.

"He went to Collin's last night."

"Maybe summering here will be good for him, too. Get away from that guy."

"Maybe . . ." I'm unsure. It feels naïve to think this isn't trading one viper's nest for another. He slides his hand over his lips, the thick tendons and muscles a real turn-on for me. I love the veins tracking up his knuckles. I remember following them one night with my finger. Our bodies sweaty and spent after an hour-long fuck.

Jake watches me watch him. It's like a book catching you reading its pages.

I smile.

His lips lift.

"Can I blow you?" I ask bluntly. A sudden desire to watch him come shoots through me. Desires. Wants. Aches. They're so easy to share with Jake.

As I turn to him on the mattress, he leans forward. His fingers thread through my hair, cupping the back of my head. "I can get you off first—"

"No, I want you in my mouth." I'm already sliding to the floor. My knees dig into the expensive carpet between his feet. The bed isn't too high, thankfully. He stays seated while my hands rest on his thighs in practiced patience.

When I first asked him to fuck me, I was tornadic winds full of starved kisses and ravaging hands. He captured my wrists to try and slow me, but I kept kissing. The edges of his lips. His neck. His collarbone. "Hailey. Hailey. *Hails*. Heyhey-hey. *Slow*. Slow down." He cupped my cheeks, guiding my face back to his. I was breathless. Confused. Then he said, "There's no rush." He tucked a strand of hair behind my ear. "Can we try it slow?"

Slow.

I'd never had slow.

But with Jake, sex is a slow-building four-section, hundred-musician orchestral performance. A grand symphony.

Here, now, in the guest room, a wanton breath escapes my lips when Jake unbuttons his navy-blue pants. He studies me, his Adam's apple bobbing as he swallows. I pull his slacks to his ankles—too quickly for him. He catches my hand when I grip the hem of his dark gray boxer briefs. "Slow," he reminds me. My pussy throbs just hearing the grit to his voice, and our eyes latch in an aroused beat.

The command both infuriates and electrifies me.

Desire is impatient. It aches for release.

Unhurriedly dragging down his boxer briefs, I free his erection from the fabric. His cock is already thick and hard. I pulse just imagining Jake inside me. I really love him there.

Blow job.

Don't rush.

I nod to myself and grip him at the base, then I skate my tongue along the shaft. The pace is agonizing. My thighs quiver as I study his face while he studies mine.

His mouth parts. His hand clasps a fistful of my hair. I'm slow to take him in my mouth. Slow to fit him between my lips. Slow to ease him to the back of my throat.

When he's inside me as far as he can fit, he commends me with a husky "Good girl."

Wetness soaks my panties, and I make a concerted effort to breathe through my nose so I don't choke. I begin to suck. Ease in and out. My whole body thrums as I watch him. Veins spindle through his neck, his breathing irregular. His pinpointed eyes darken in headier desire.

It feels so good not being inside my head.

It feels so good laying waste to these feelings instead of being tangled inside my thoughts.

A gentle creak sounds behind me, and before I can turn around, Jake mumbles out, "What the fuck?" I quickly remove him from my mouth and glance over my shoulder.

Jake's hand tightens on the back of my head as he follows my gaze.

Oliver. It's just Oliver.

Relief quickly spins into tension.

Oliver shuts the cracked door. Confusion lines his brows. A hairpin is pinched between his teeth, a book under his arm, and his gaze pings from me knelt on the floor to Jake's legs on either side of me, quickly processing the erotic position.

And in this moment, I remember I asked Oliver to come to my room tonight. But that was *before* Jake was kicked out of his room. *Before* he became my roommate for the summer.

The error is mine. So I take responsibility for the building strain.

"I . . ." I start to say, but I realize Jake and Oliver aren't looking at me. Their attention fixes to each other.

"You break into Hailey's room often?" Jake questions, his tone protective. Accusatory. All while his hand still cups my head in tender affection.

Oliver slips the hairpin out of his mouth. "I hardly would call it B and E when I was invited." He leans his shoulders against the closed door, and his gaze lowers to mine. He winks at me. Then his eyes lift back to Jake. "You want me to leave or stay? I don't mind either."

"You wouldn't mind staying?" Jake asks in disbelief. Oliver confuses him, and with Jake's inquisitive nature, I'm not shocked he's fueling questions rather than ordering Olly out.

Oliver shrugs. "Call it curiosity. I've never seen Hailey give head to anyone else but me."

He's always been a playboy, until recently when he promised he'd only sleep with me. It was a big promise, considering I couldn't offer the same. But Olly assured me he wasn't looking for mutual exclusivity. He just felt it was something he needed to do while I was . . . *am* trying to sort through my mental state.

On the surface, it seems like Oliver might be interested in voyeurism. Staying here to get off. The truth is, he wants to stay because he's just as protective, and he doesn't know Jake very well. He's seeing how he'll react.

My neck aches, and I turn back to face Jake.

He contemplates. He considers. He's . . . curious, too.

I suddenly realize, we might all share this one trait in common.

A fuck ton of curiosity.

Jake isn't breaking from Oliver. "Hailey, it's up to you."

The weight of this call bears on me as heavy as their gazes. I don't want to choose wrong, and it does feel like maybe there is a *wrong* choice. I care about their feelings, but tonight I feel reckless. Selfishly, I want both of them. Realistically, I know that ends once they learn about the baby.

Stupidly, I decide now is not the moment to tell them.

My curiosity is too heightened. My arousal built.

I want to drive this speeding train into the ground. Fling it off course. Risk it all. I can't play it safe in bed. I never could.

"I don't mind," I tell them. "Oliver can stay."

I worry Jake might be upset at the choice, but intrigue must supersede all. He nods, accepting this strange road.

He's so confident and assured in his own body, he hasn't even hidden his cock away. His hand remains firm on my head, and I dip down to gather him in my mouth. I restart where we'd left off. Sucking in and out, licking and tantalizing. I watch him, but he's not watching me.

His gaze careens over my shoulder, pinned on Oliver at the door. He studies him in the way that he always studies me. Unpuzzling. Unpeeling the layers. But Oliver has too many, and Jake only grows more restless. His nose flares, and he lets out a low groan when I suck harder.

Jake looks at me. "Slower."

A moan scratches against my throat. The command pulses the spot between my legs. The awareness of Oliver hearing it behind me stimulates me in a deeper way. I obey, until Jake bends down to plant a kiss on the top of my head. He whispers in my ear. "Stay still."

I do as I'm told.

"Good girl."

He moves his hips in and out. In and out. Fucking my face in slow, deep thrusts. His tip hits my throat, but I stifle a gag. Then he releases into me with a low, throaty growl. I wait for the spasms to end before I lick him up slowly.

Oliver rounds the side of the bed as Jake lifts the elastic of his boxer briefs back to his toned waist.

"That was enlightening," Oliver says casually, offering me the book under his arm. I take the thick hardbound copy of Walt Whitman's *Leaves of Grass*. Still on my knees, I sink back against my heels to flip through the collection of poems.

Jake scrutinizes me. "Late night reading again?"

Oliver cocks his head. "Do I hear judgment?"

"You hear *concern*." Jake buttons his pants and gets up from the bed, facing Oliver eye to eye. "She stayed up reading all last night."

With my eyes planted on the book, I feel the heat of Oliver's gaze descending on me. "How many hours of sleep, Hailstorm?"

"Three," I say honestly. I flip the next page, reading quickly. Nerves mount the longer they watch me. My brain buzzes too much to focus on the text. I don't do well with *new*. And this—both of them in my room tonight—is a bucketload of new. I don't have a plan. No blueprint.

It's unexpected. Not unwanted. But I don't know what to do other than . . . read. Or pretend to read.

"You'll try for more than three tonight?" Olly asks. He sinks down to the floor beside me, sitting with his back against the bed.

"Yes." I flip a page.

His hand skims the rug. "Tibetan silk." He whistles.

"Should we take it with us when the summer ends? You think he'll notice it missing?"

Jake rubs his palm against the back of his tensed neck. "I'm guessing rugs were a part of your Billionaire Bullshit School?"

Oliver blinks slowly, confusion crushing his face. "What?" He shifts the hairpin in his mouth with his tongue, then loosely holds his bent legs. It's about the only casual movement he's able to make.

Jake frowns from him to me, then back to him. "Hailey said you came up with that name. It's what you call all your lessons over expensive brands and objects. So you knew which marks had real money . . . is that . . . not right?" He glances to me for confirmation.

I didn't lie to him.

Oliver is just caught off guard. Olly won't look at me, but I can see hurt pulsing against his brown eyes. "No, that's right," he tells Jake. "Did she also tell you why she chose the name Hailey?"

The question jolts me like whiplash. I know Oliver so deeply. Like a story I've read over and over and over since I was a little girl. Pages I've memorized. I can practically see his thought process, and my breath lodges in my lungs.

"It was a fake name for a job when she was six," Jake says. "She kept it because she liked the little girl she was pretending to be. A bookworm who'd been placed in advanced classes."

My pulse pounds in my ears. "Olly—"

"And Trevor? Did she tell you about his name?" Oliver asks.

Jake rubs at his lips, his hesitation landing on me.

I breathe out, "Don't lie to him."

Oliver bites a little harder on the hairpin. He still won't meet my eyes.

"He's the third child in the Tinrock family," Jake says, still wary as he can see the emotion building in Oliver, too. "So, when he was little, he went by Tre for *three*. Then Trev . . . and finally Trevor."

"Phoebe and Rocky?" Oliver asks him.

"They named each other. You named yourself after Oliver Twist, and Nova after a comic book character."

"Everyone then," Oliver murmurs. "She told you about everyone." His expression fractures into a rushing cascade of emotions, most of them bordering on pain. Deep, deep hurt.

Carter spilled the origin of Oliver's name first to Jake, and Oliver never cared. But me leaking information is different, because I once told Oliver I'd rather cut out my tongue than expose the truth behind our names.

Oliver swallows and tries to collect himself, but when he faces me, his gaze rummages through mine like he's trying to make sense of this.

Nothing breaks Oliver Graves. Except me locked in a storm shelter.

And now, I'm terrified maybe this has, too.

"Are you okay?" I ask.

He lets go of his bent legs, just to sweep nonexistent dust particles off his kneecaps. It's not helping him appear indifferent. Not when muscles strain against his neck, when his shoulders won't unbind, when the normal sparkle in his eyes drowns in a dullness I hope to never see again.

It's agonizing knowing I'm the cause.

"Olly," I whisper, our backs to the bed.

He turns his head to mine. "I miscalculated . . ." His voice is tender, soft comfort. The opposite of his gaze. "I miscalculated what he means to you."

My heart lurches. "B-but you knew I was talking to him?"

His eyes redden. "I didn't know you were telling him *our* history. *Our* secrets."

"She hasn't told me everything." Jake defends me, his stance full of warning. He's telling Oliver not to get angry with me.

Oliver would never.

He glances up since Jake remains standing, and yet, there's no power imbalance. Even on the floor, Oliver appears as tall as Jake. No puffed chests or mock display of male dominance. They're both too comfortable in their skin to put on airs.

Oliver slips the hairpin out of his mouth. "You misread me, Koning. I wasn't asking Hailey to take every secret of ours to the grave. I wouldn't punish her for sharing cons we pulled, aliases we made, or even our deepest, darkest fears. I'm just shocked she found anyone, even *you*, worthy enough to know them at all."

Jake nods slowly in realization. "You thought it was just sex."

Oh God.

"But it *is* just sex," I say, and their heads whip to me so fast that my pulse skyrockets. Confused lines crease both their faces. "It *is*. Jake, you've made it clear you can't date anyone because Trent seeks out your girlfriends like a prize. Olly, you've never done relationships. And I would be a disaster at them. So, yes, it's just sex. This isn't serious." My exhale comes out winded.

"Okay." Oliver points the hairpin at me. "But I don't typically talk to the guys you 'just have sex' with. No more than you make conversation with my flings. So, what's this . . . ?" He twirls his finger around the room.

"This is different," Jake explains more to me than to Oliver since they seem to be finding the same track.

I'm the one off course.

Oliver analyzes my expression for a second. "You have to know this is different." I do know I've been telling Jake too much. I do know why. "You aren't fooling yourself, are you?" He tips his knees into mine lightly, like we're teenagers sharing a clandestine moment again, but he is so much more a man now. It's almost distracting. Time and age.

"No," I whisper. "I'm not."

"Then why are you so afraid to like him?" His eyes graze over my furrowing brows, my flushing cheeks, my parting lips. "Or were you just afraid to tell me?"

His words pummel me. Emotion swells my chest. My throat is raw. "Both, maybe," I say so softly.

Oliver nods a couple times, letting this sink in. Then he elbows my arm, recapturing my gaze to say, "I'm glad I know."

"Don't go. I don't want anything to change," I say rapidly, panicked that Oliver thinks I'm falling so deeply for Jake that I'd rather be with him. And it's not—it's not true. I don't think about the baby. How this life inside of me *will* choose for me anyway.

We're not there yet. We're *here*. Right now, and I selfishly want to maintain our status quo.

Oliver wraps an arm around me and angles his body so I can see his face. He dips his head down like we're sharing a quiet, furtive corner that no one can invade. "I don't want you to be afraid to live, Hailey. Not because of me. All we have is now. Tomorrow is never guaranteed."

I make a concerted effort not to snake my arms around my belly. "I'm more afraid to live without you," I whisper back.

"Am I going somewhere?" He tilts my chin up, and I meet his reassuring eyes again. Sparkle has returned to them.

Then Oliver rolls up to his feet and holds out his hand to

Jake. "Let's try this again, shall we? I'm Oliver Graves. I'd say *at your service*, but you're going to be at mine." It's the same line he used on Jake months ago. This time, there is no smirk or accompanying wink.

Jake shakes, tension in both their forearms.

My widened eyes ping back and forth between them.

"How am I at your service when you just watched Hailey blow me?" Jake questions, releasing his grip. "Seems like you're at mine."

"Should we discuss power dynamics? I was invited here. *She* invited *me*." He bites back on the hairpin and rests his shoulders on the bedpost, crossing his arms loosely. "I can keep helping jog your memory, Koning boy. Mine is bulletproof."

"Yeah, I'd like that." Jake nods, his arms threading more tensely over his chest. "Help jog the part where you got hard while you were watching us."

I don't move.

Oliver smirks with a light laugh. "I was about sixty percent sure you were staring at my slight erection. I appreciate you making it a one hundred percent certainty." He golf-claps. Not mockingly, just somewhat entertained.

"Slight erection, okay." Jake nods harder. "Sure."

"You want me to whip it out so you can measure it, too?" Oliver teases the hem of his khaki slacks. "I look better in the nude anyway."

Jake slides a frustrated hand through his hair, then gestures to him. "Are you flirting with me?"

"I flirt with everyone." He shifts the hairpin with his tongue. "It's my biggest character flaw."

I look up at him. "That could be a true fact if it weren't an opinion."

"Subjective opinions," Oliver laments. "My least favorite." He sinks back on the bed. "We prefer facts, don't we, Hailstorm?"

I'm just openly watching them stare each other down, and I can't recall ever seeing Oliver this confrontational outside of a job.

"Jake likes facts, too," I say unhelpfully.

"I have one for you," Oliver says to Jake, bowing forward. Elbows on his thighs, hands cupped. "I came here to fuck Hailey to exhaust her enough so she can sleep. Just like I have most nights."

"*Olly*," I groan, bringing the pages of my book to my forehead.

Jake expels a harsh noise, a deep frown forming. "Like a sleeping aid?"

"Exactly like a sleeping aid." Oliver slips the hairpin behind his ear, then rests his hands casually backward on the bed.

Oh my God! I touch my fingers to my temples. *This isn't real*. But I feel the soft rug underneath my knees, grounding myself. This is no hallucination.

I lower the book. "It's not as bad as it seems," I interject quickly.

Oliver sizes up Jake. "You're angry I'm helping Hailey—"

"At *how* you're helping her," Jake retorts, running two hot hands through his hair. "Have you consulted a professional?"

I cut in. "I did tell my doctor I use sex to sleep. She didn't say to stop."

Oliver motions a hand to me. "Healthy."

Jake glares. "She should consult another doctor."

"Is it the fact that she's having sex to sleep or having sex with *me* to sleep and *not you* that's an issue for you?"

Jake intakes a heavy breath, and he shakes his head like maybe he's unsure.

Oliver leans forward again. "Look, I'm pretending to be a licensed therapist. I'm not actually one. Maybe it's not healthy. Maybe it is. We'll never know because we can't divulge our entire pasts to professionals. We live in the bed we've created for ourselves." He opens his arms. "We're all fucked-up. Either accept it or move on." I hear *Move on from her.*

I can't breathe.

Jake and Oliver talk through their eyes. I can barely read where their heads are at, which only heightens my worry. I never wanted to hurt either of them.

Oliver nods toward me. "There's a reason she told you the origins of her name but didn't tell you I was giving her orgasms as a sleeping aid."

Jake looks to me for answers.

"I didn't think you'd approve."

"I don't," Jake says. "But I'm obviously not going to stop you."

"How is that obvious?" Oliver asks.

"Because I'm not going anywhere. As long as Hailey wants me here, *I'm here*."

"Something we have in common then," Oliver declares.

I close my book with a loud *thud*. "And if I want you both here?" I look between them. "What happens then?"

FIFTEEN

Rocky

And then there were three," Varrick says after the Bennet brothers have left for bed. He passes me a crystal glass of rare Dalmore whiskey, and he hands another to Trent Waterford.

"Agatha Christie fan?" I wonder. (Not that I really care.)

Varrick slouches back into a dark leather club chair. "Murder mysteries have their charm." He's a comedian. His eyes gleam at me; possibly he's entertained by the fact that we can so easily see through each other's bullshit.

"I do love the macabre," I say with a raise of my glass.

He raises his, too, then takes a sip. I don't drink mine yet. I meander around the intimately sized smoking room, acting like I'm so fucking fascinated with the towering bookcases, the marbled bust of a Roman god, and the ornate gold-framed mirrors—about five of them. My calm, self-assured reflection follows me.

What I don't do—I don't let myself wonder whether Christian Wolfe, my birth father, shared a whiskey in here with his own dad. Whether he played on the green tartan carpet as a child and listened to old men prattle on about stocks and real estate while indulging in cigars and bourbon.

What I actually do—I check for two-way mirrors and tiny red lights with each passing glance.

I'm highly aware he's studying me like I'm a mouse in his maze.

Trent kicks back in the club chair beside Varrick. "Now that the children have gone to bed, I'd like to know a few things about your . . . summer proposal." He slouches, ankle propped on his knee, getting comfortable. "Starting with this invite list."

"My reasonings were stated in the letter," Varrick says simply, but I've been enjoying Trent's constant barrage of questions and ridiculously shallow comments that Varrick has had to swat away like gnats.

"Dalmore aged in an oak cask is much better than whatever that is on your shelf."

"Why is there recessed lighting in here? Is that a can light?"

"Your housekeeper definitely doesn't know what a feather duster is. I have the numbers of staff who'd completely turn this place around if you want them."

It's also kept Varrick partially distracted from his interest in me and the Graves siblings. I've seen him try to rest his gaze on us, only to be pulled by Trent.

Why he hasn't told him to fuck off yet, I don't know. Other than he wants something from the firstborn fuckbag.

"I read it. You invited the founding families and families who made their mark on the town," Trent says into a sip of whiskey. "But if you asked anyone who's been here, they would've told you the Bennet brothers aren't worth your time. Damian is *terrible* with money. He purchased a winery that couldn't grow grapes."

That's not necessarily true, but not entirely inaccurate either. Damian won the winery in a poker bet against Jake. Not only was the property worthless but a bad investment that Jake had stressed to me he needed to get rid of.

"Put the winery in the kitty, Jake," I prodded during the poker game.

He resisted screwing over another guy, but I don't think Jake is fond of Damian, because it didn't take a ton of convincing.

"And Sandon Bennet," Trent laughs, "he's *twelve*."

"Fourteen," Varrick corrects, sounding nonchalant.

"Same thing."

It's not.

"And what's with the Smiths?" Trent wonders. "They're trust-fund kids from out of state. Who've been here for less than a year—"

"Grey." Varrick cuts him off for the first time. "Why don't you take a seat?" He tips his head to the empty one across from him.

"I prefer being on my feet." I come closer, just to relax against the bar and not pace around.

"Afraid the house will catch fire?" he banters.

"We're surrounded by open water. So no issue there."

Varrick motions to the chair again. "I insist."

"I kind of like Grey back there," Trent teases. "Under the god-awful lighting, you almost look fuckable. I'm starting to sense why Phoebe might've had a thing for you." He laughs at his own humorless joke.

"She still has a thing for me," I say. "What do you call that?"

"Delusion."

I laugh hard at the irony of *him* calling me delusional. He believes I'm laughing at his joke, so he chuckles. Varrick smiles down at his whiskey, then up at me, as if he's admiring this moment we share together.

The truths we see.

My stomach roils.

"You're going to make me ask a third time?" Varrick wonders, his tone friendly and light.

I'm about to respond when Trent says, "He can stand. The Thornhalls aren't any more prestigious than the Smiths. In fact, they're less than—no offense, Grey."

"None taken." I raise my whiskey. I am uncaring of the Wolfe fortune. Unthreatening. Just here for a good time this summer with my *worthy* best friend.

Varrick taps his finger to his glass, staring between me and Trent. "Please. *Sit*," he orders me, asserting dominance over Trent.

"He might look part pit bull, but he's not a dog." Trent is basically saying, *He's not* your *dog*.

"He is my guest, and I'd like him to join us over here."

I straighten and walk away from the bar. "Don't fight over me all at once." I finally take the chair, placing my whiskey over on the end table beside me. "TK is right though. The invite list could've been shortened. The chances of you leaving your fortune to one of the girls has to be low. They're servers."

"And that would discredit them because . . . ?"

Trent huffs out a laugh, drawing our gazes to him as he loosens the collar of his button-down. "Because they're of no social standing to amass a fortune of *this* size. What are they going to do with it?"

Varrick rests farther back in his chair. "You're both intelligent men." Now he has to be feeding Trent's ego. "You can understand my need to appear generous and benevolent to this town. I'd prefer not to be seen as the monster out at sea."

Trent frowns. "So, you invited Phoebe and Hailey to appear charitable?"

"I didn't just invite Hailey. I'm making her my heir."

What . . . the fuck . . . is going on? "My sister?" I question with a tsunami of confusion crashing against my brain.

"Your sister," Varrick confirms.

"Wait, wait." Trent abandons his whiskey on a coffee table to hold up his hands. "The twenty-year-old goth girl?" Hailey will be twenty-five in July, but I'd never expect Trent to remember anyone's age.

"It's just for appearance's sake. Smoke and mirrors." Varrick lifts a finger from the crystal glass and points at our reflections. "Naming her my beneficiary will appeal to locals, and unlike Phoebe, she's also compliant, easiest to control. So when she marries a Koning, it'll unite the two most powerful families in Victoria. A legacy I'd like to leave behind."

I can't move a muscle. What the fuck is his endgame?

I stare him down, trying to extinguish the visceral heat in my eyes. "You want my sister to marry Jake?" I question.

"Not Jake." He points at the vile prick sitting beside him. "Trent."

I almost black out. Only to be reawakened by Trent's shrill laughter.

"This has to be a joke." He cackles and takes a sharp breath. "Good one, Varrick. You fucking had me." He applauds, but the noise dies out when Varrick shakes his head.

"Not a joke. I've set up this whole summer so you can get to know each other better here at Stonehaven. All under the guise that I don't know who I'm choosing as my next living heir, but it will be Hailey Thornhall. My fortune through wedlock is still a fortune. How do you think I came by it?"

Marriage and death.

I need to talk to my sister. Like right now. I check my phone at my side. No cell signal. *Shit.*

Trent is grimacing. "It's a piece of paper. What money will she see while you're still alive?"

"I'm giving Hailey a sizable trust. It will be yours if you marry her, and then we can talk about divvying up the Wolfe properties around town."

Why? Why the fuck would he do this? It's not adding up in my pounding head.

I force myself not to run my fingers through my hair. Can't be on edge. Can't appear like I want to slit his throat. I'm a mixture of confusion and intrigue. "Who else is going to know about this plan?"

"It stays between us three."

Like hell.

He can't actually believe I won't go rat him out to my sister in a heartbeat.

"Hailey?" Trent keeps repeating with a disgusted expression.

I love that he's repulsed at the idea. Varrick doesn't. He's rapidly skimming Trent like he's searching for a way to influence him.

I'm not going to let him sell Hailey to this fucking asshole. "This seems flimsy."

"How so?" Varrick asks.

"My sister will never agree to it." Nor would I fucking want her to.

Trent downs his whiskey. "What about Phoebe?"

My whole body catches fire. I should've been more afraid of burning alive. "We're working on our marriage—"

"You got divorced for a reason, Grey, *come on*." He makes a face like I'm being pathetic thinking I have a chance with my ex.

"No." That's Varrick, not me. "It won't be Phoebe. Locals would prefer she marry Jake, and like I said, she's *not* malleable. You need to marry a woman you can control. Someone who will do whatever you say so you won't have to sign a prenup. Her money will be yours. Her property, yours. Her body—whether you want it or not—yours."

I want to strangle him. To calm down, I take a breath and fixate on the weight my Rolex is bearing on my wrist. The cool leather of the chair beneath my bare forearm, my sleeves rolled. Another breath.

I still want to strangle him.

Trent crashes backward, his hands on his head. "I have to think about this."

"You have all summer." Varrick stands, his glass only half empty. I've barely even had a sip—or else I'd need to go puke in a toilet. I don't trust him pouring my drinks. I am that paranoid here.

Once Trent heads off to bed, me assuring him I'm not far behind—because to Trent, I'm not important enough to be alone with just Varrick—I seize Varrick's shoulder and keep him in the smoking room for another second.

"We need to talk," I whisper between my teeth, my blood coursing hotter and hotter.

"Later. Five a.m. in this room." He speaks furtively and motions me to follow. The vein in my temple is pulsing too hard as I track his footsteps. When he twists a statue of an onyx wolf on a bookcase, the shelf swings open to reveal a hidden sitting room. "Five a.m.," he repeats. "Bring the others."

"You're calling a meeting?" I stare into him, wondering why he thinks we'd *ever* work with him.

"Five a.m." He keeps a cautious eye on the door while

unpocketing a skeleton key. "This is to Phoebe's room." He's speaking more hurriedly. "Use it to stay with her."

"Why?" I ask, even knowing I can't believe anything he says.

"Trent has made me aware that he plans to win Phoebe over by the end of the summer, and I don't trust what he'd do in the middle of the night while my daughter is sleeping. I can't tell him off. It's better if he believes he can say anything to me so I can use it to my advantage."

He called Phoebe his daughter.

He's feeding me sincerity. It sounds like he's being honest, but I'm scavenging for areas of manipulation. He's just saying what I want to hear.

As if he sees what I'm thinking, he says, "I won't lie to you. That's how this works. We never lie to one another."

It's the playbook we were raised on. "Yeah. That's what your old friends always said to us," I tell him bitterly. "And look how that turned out."

Varrick nods, his gaze so empathetic, I question whether he is in the dark triad. His understanding tries to reach me. "They lied to me, too, Brayden." Because Elizabeth never told him she was pregnant with triplets. He checks the door again. "You need to go now." He shuts the hidden room. Bookcase back in place. "Trent will want to make sure you're following him."

He's not incorrect.

But before I go, I make him very aware of one thing. "If you think we'll let you run a con where you force my sister to marry that fucking prick, you've got us pegged so *fucking* wrong."

"Five a.m." is all he says.

SIXTEEN

Oliver

Anything can happen. I've told myself that since I was a teenager struggling to maintain a Glaswegian dialect for a job. Gain trust from the mark by also being born from the same city—in this case, Glasgow, Scotland. *Easy*.

Eh, it was challenging. It challenged *me*. So, naturally, I loved every second. I loved being so close to failure that I had to push myself to the brink of what I believed I could do.

Anything can happen.

I've stopped being surprised at what can go right and what can go wrong. At curveballs. At breaking balls. At fastballs. I'd like to believe I can hit every single hundred-mile-an-hour pitch out of the park. Until tonight with Hailey.

I don't know what she threw at me. I just know it struck me in the face.

I get a reprieve from this whole thing with Jake when he takes his hands off the wheel, says he'll shower, and leaves me alone with Hailey. He's not a dumb dude, so he knows I'm going to help her sleep.

He cares more about her well-being than fighting with me. I'd have some major issues with him if he didn't put her first, and if Hailey fell for this guy—like actually, truthfully *fell*—then I already know he's more good than bad.

I just always imagined *Carter* would be the threat to my relationship with Hailey. Then he popped in less and less over the years, and our wandering forger felt more like her fantasy than a serious reality.

This, with Jake, is real.

It's stirring new feelings in me. Fears I didn't think I'd encounter. I'd rather be on an acid trip than tripping over insecurities.

"Hey. Olly." Hailey clutches my cheeks with two palms, questions in her gaze about where I'm drifting to, apologies, but she has nothing to be sorry about.

Anything can happen.

I like a focus. A goal.

Tonight, I want to ensure she sleeps more than three hours. "Hailstorm," I whisper sensually against the pit of her ear, then I lift her in my arms. Carrying her to the bed with her legs wrapped around my waist, I nip her bottom lip, then kiss her with a famished hunger. Loving her cold metal piercings against my mouth. Her arms swoop around my shoulders, and her kisses are passionate, deep, familiar.

She warms my blood in ways no one else ever has. There's quiet comfort in being with Hailey that I can't get when I fuck other girls. There always has been, and for me, it's why I've kept returning to her again and again.

It's not long before we're under the silk sheets and heavy comforter. Not long before I've ripped off her mesh top and she's slid off her cargo pants. Not long before she's drawn my black shirt over my head. Not long before we're buzzing, sweaty naked messes of skin and muscle and too much heart.

My heart bleeds all over Hailey. She's the only one who's ever had all of me, the real me, in my entirety.

Her gasps of pleasure sound thunderous in my ears as I keep her tucked close to my chest. She's hiked her slender leg over my waist, facing me on her side. My fingers build friction inside her swollen pussy. My thumb teases her clit. I watch her breath shorten and shorten like she's fighting for each intake of oxygen, and I don't slow my raid inside her.

Hailey tries to squeeze my erection, tries to consume my arousal as a groan scratches out of my throat, but I love the game we play where I get her so completely lost in the moment that she forgets to make me come.

She's about there when the bathroom door opens. I don't stop. Hailey can't see Jake in the doorway. He grips a white towel low at his waist, water still dripping down his carved jawline, his eyes darting to the dresser, where I'm guessing his clothes lie.

Her back is to him, her face buried against my chest. She's clinging on to me while I finger-bang her under the sheets. I watch Jake consider making the trek to the dresser until Hailey releases a whimpering, gasping moan, and his attention falls back to me.

He's more interested in what I'm doing to her. Which I get, seeing as how I watched her blow him with a similar caution and intrigue.

Heat expels off her trembling body. The two of us, slick with sweat. She's let go of my hard cock. She's clawing at my flexed abs. I can't tear my focused eyes off Jake. Not while Hailey cries out like the intensity, the unrelenting speed and pumping inside her, is blissful pain—and normally I'd cage her noises.

We're very efficient at sneaking around, after all.

But something in me wants Jake to see me summoning her climax. To show him what I can do to her, to show him that I'm necessary. He locks in on my challenging gaze, not backing down or shying away.

My muscles pull taut with each intense second he's fixed on me. I breathe through my nose, my jaw grinding down, blood pooling in my cock. I want to break through his stoicism.

Another goal.

I need to finish this one. Hailey's cries sputter into sharp breaths, and while I stare at Jake, I whisper to her, "Come for me." Her hips arch into my hand, and I feel her pulsate around my fingers, then I rub her clit. She spasms violently into my chest, and I hold her tight while I overwork the sensitivity.

Her orgasm is like an exploding battery. It drains her. She has nothing left when she comes undone.

Jake has held strong on my gaze. My body is burning. Her high-pitched cries become soft aching whimpers. Her limbs go slack, and I tell her, "Good girl."

His jaw tics. She liked it when he said it, and he should know by now, I'm a trained imitator.

He finally leaves the doorway to retrieve clothes from the dresser. I concentrate on Hailey, peeling damp pieces of platinum hair off her cheeks. Her eyes stay closed, her head sinking into the feather pillow, and her breath slowing.

She murmurs my name as she drifts off, and my ribs constrict around my lungs. I don't want to lose her. I never thought I could until tonight. She knows settling down hasn't been in my blood. It's why she envisioned a future with Carter and not me.

Just sex.

Maybe it never really was just sex. Hailey has always been a constant for me. Now I'm more afraid Jake is going to stick around and be one for her.

Carefully, gingerly, I slip out of the bedsheets. Buck naked. I'm at half-mast, but Jake isn't staring at my dick. Confusion fills his face while he steps into boxer briefs. I glance downward.

He's huge and also at half-mast.

I feel my body tighten. I'm a shaken soda bottle with the cap too tightly screwed.

"I'm not leaving," I whisper, hopefully answering his silent question. "I'm spending the night with her." Then I push my shoulders into the cracked bathroom, trying to relax. I grab the door so it won't slam and quietly shut it.

I go to wash my hands. *Please be a decent hand soap.* I read the ingredients label on the black dispenser and cringe at the synthetic fragrances. That'll dry out my skin.

I wash my hands anyway.

Then I towel my palms off and inspect my jawline, the skin rough with stubble. Hailey likes it, but I think it's because she knows I obsess over shaving. My features sometimes feel ever-changing. I haven't had my natural dark brown hair since I was a kid. Haven't held a tan the past few years to distance myself from the last job when I did.

My olive skin lacks blemishes after I lasered off a mole on my bicep and thigh. This is the longest I've gone without changing my eye color. Still thankful I didn't wear colored contacts when I came to Victoria. (I don't need to pretend to be blue-eyed for over a year.) This is, without question, the longest I've ever maintained one appearance.

Don't freak out, Oliver.

I crack my stiff neck, then glance down at my grip on the sink. My knuckles have started to scar. I'll need to figure out how to get rid of those for the next job.

Don't freak the fuck out, Oliver.

I squat down to the cupboard. Let's see what the dear old homicidal dad keeps stocked. I rummage through a basket of toiletries. Happy to find a straight razor and shave cream. Ingredients—*Not bad*.

I rise and warm a hand towel under hot water, press the damp cloth to my face, then rub in some cream along my jaw, and I begin to shave. It's not even close to my normal skin-care routine, but my body untenses as I slide the razor up my cheek.

"Hey."

I swing my head at Jake's abrupt appearance, but I don't move the razor. I wince as I accidentally slice my own cheek. *Shit.*

Shit. There's blood. *What a night*. I'm very much off my A game.

"Fuck," Jake curses, hurrying farther in the bathroom.

Quickly, I throw the razor in the sink, seeing droplets of blood on the white porcelain. "Show-and-tell just for you, Koning," I banter. "Con artists *do* bleed."

"Here." He presses a warm towel to the side of my face. I stifle the urge to wince. His large palm sheathes my cheek with extra pressure and force like the cut might be deep. Tension stretches; I'm all too aware of his caring act toward me. His eyes flit over me. "I didn't think you could be snuck up on," he says.

"My beauty is a powerful thing. It even distracts me." I bear the back of my skull against the dark striped wallpaper, staring into him while I reach up to my face. He lets go of the washcloth when I take over, our fingers brushing in the exchange.

I hold it to my stinging cheek and try to relax my muscles. I try not to care about this fucking cut while I'm sharing his company. Don't care that he sees my dick, but I care about a grotesque scar.

I'm hooked on his sky-blue eyes. "Distracting you yet?" I ask, hoping he's thinking about me making Hailey come.

Jake nods slowly, ramping up the heat in the bathroom, just to say, "You'll have to try harder."

"Hmm," I muse. "I am a try-hard." I wink, but even that slight movement pulls the throbbing skin of my cheek.

"Stop flirting," he advises.

"He wants me to be *good*," I bemoan dramatically, like it's more wounding. *"Never."* I stare under my lashes. "You can't make me. But it's not too late for you to be bad. Come over to the Dark Side. You'll survive longer if you do."

His arms cross over his bare chest. "Is it about survival for you?"

I like how quick he is. I'm sure Hailey loves his Ivy League brain even more. "You know what they say? All the good die young." I tilt my head. "So at this rate, I will outlive you."

His concern veers to my face. "You're bleeding through the cloth."

"You don't say." I breathe out a tensed breath, watching him crouch down to the cupboard. Probably in search of a first aid kit or bandage for me. "You care too much about people you shouldn't."

It disrupts his search for a solid second before he continues. "Not all of us can be carefree."

"I'm not free of caring. Just selective in how hard I care." I avoid glancing at myself in the mirror. "Care too hard and you'll strap ten-pound weight plates on your chest." I don't tell him I'm certain I picked up at least two twenty pounders tonight.

He's rigid while digging out boxes of Advil. "How hard do you care about Hailey with me?"

Uh, fuck. I have the urge to lie, but he's a part of the family business. I had no problems bringing him into the fold—the more we can trust, the merrier—but that was also before I knew Hailey had feelings for him.

"Now," I say, "too hard." I mutter more to myself, "I didn't see it coming." Suspected that Trevor might do something disturbing again—*check*. Suspected that Rocky would finally make a move on Phoebe—*check*. Did not account for Hails swerving in the Jake Koning Waterford direction with actual emotion.

"It surprises you that much that she could like me?" He must've heard me.

"You're a silver-spoon polo-playing rich boy. The kind we dupe. If she fell for anyone, I thought it would've been another grifter."

"Like you," he points out.

I laugh into a painful smile. Literally painful. "Keep following my train of thought, it's like *so hot*." I layer on the vocal fry.

Jake rips open a box. "You're a character."

"Many characters," I amend, peering at myself in the mirror. *Shit*. The cloth is very bright red.

"Which one does Hailey love?"

"All of them. All of me." I lower the washcloth and inspect the four-inch cut a little below my cheekbone in the mirror. Blood trickles down my jaw the instant I remove pressure. I'm barely breathing, and I find myself glancing down at Jake.

He's quickly pulling out antiseptic and bandages. I'm in a slight lunge against the sink, and while he's squatting, his face is far closer to my pelvis than should be comfortable.

I seize this distraction. "You like giving or just receiving?"

His eyes catch my cock, then rise to my face as he stands, about an inch taller than me. "You asking me to blow you?"

"You always answer a question with a question?" I counter.

"Like you just did?"

"Oh, see, we're on a roll now. You don't want to stop, do you?"

"Oliver." He's staring at my face.

I wipe the blood off my jaw. "Koning." I look at myself in the mirror for only a second before staring at him through it.

He tears the paper off the bandage. "I don't think you'll need stitches."

I just barely ease. "What'd you come in here for anyway?"

He hands me the bandage. Butterfly tape. Let's just hope this keeps the cut closed. "To ask if you planned to sleep on the floor."

"Not unless you push me off the bed." I concentrate on adhering the tape to my cheek. *Finished*. "Which is very charitable of me, if you think about it." I round his body and reach for a towel on a gold rod.

He shifts his weight. I notice his abs flexing. "How?" he asks.

I tie the towel around my waist. "The fact that I'm even allowing you to sleep in the same bed as me and Hailey."

"Maybe we *should* revisit the power dynamics here." Jake clutches the sink. "Because I was invited to stay in this room with Hailey *all* summer long. You were invited for one night."

"One night always turns into two, which turns into three, four, five thousand—"

"Five thousand," he states firmly.

"You look tired on your feet. I didn't want you to stand there while I count to infinity."

Jake nods a couple times with intense, challenging eye contact. I'm enjoying this back-and-forth more than I should. If it weren't for the stinging on my cheek, maybe I'd even smile.

Especially as Jake says, "Don't care too hard about my body."

"I haven't. I won't." At this, I round his tall frame again and feel his eyes tracking my movements. I push quietly into the bedroom with my shoulder. I wink at him, then tense more when I'm in the room and the distraction of Jake Waterford is gone.

I lightly run my fingers over the butterfly-taped cut. Then I freeze. Hailey is fine. Asleep under the sheets where I'd left her, but the brass doorknob—the door to the second-floor hallway—is twisting.

Jake sidles next to me. "Is something wrong?" His voice is a whisper.

"Stay here." With silent footfalls, I approach the door, then rest a shoulder on the frame.

When Rocky breaks in with a bump key, the first thing he sees is my face.

I swing my head back to Jake. "*That* is breaking and entering."

Rocky double-blinks hard when he sees Jake and me in his sister's room. "Jesus Christ," he mutters. "What is this?"

"Slumber party for the wicked," I whisper, barricading him from entering with my arm across the door.

He glares at me. "Then why's Jake here?"

"Corrupting him by the minute."

Rocky rolls his eyes hard, then steps forward to intimidate me backward. Our chests meet. "Move."

Yeah, no. I'm not going to budge. He's about to bulldoze toward the bed. I put my hand on his sternum. Stopping him.

"Get out of my fucking way," he snarls under his breath. "I need to talk to Hailey. This isn't a joke."

"I'm not laughing." I walk him out the door.

"Oliver." He rips my hand off his chest.

He clashes more with my brother than he does with me. I can swallow the rough, acidic pill that is Brayden Tinrock. I would've said nothing can hurt me, but I know that's not true. I've always known there was a chance Hailey could.

I quietly pull the door closed. In the quiet hallway, Rocky glares at me like he's either going to deck me in the face or shove me into the wall.

If Nova learned he did either, Rocky would have a black eye by tomorrow afternoon, so he won't attempt it.

I guard the door. "You really want to deprive your sister of a beautiful deep slumber right now?" I absorb the guttural fury in his eyes. I can't tell . . . if it's his usual kind. "What's going on?"

He suddenly notices my bandaged cheek. "What happened?" His head whips back to the door, like maybe Jake hurt me. Rocky has his moments. Even the core of a rotten apple is soft.

"Accident," I say. "I doubt Jake would step on a spider, literal and figurative."

Rocky doesn't untense. "Get Nova to look at it."

"That was my plan tomorrow morning." My brother has the most medical training out of all of us. He'll know if it'll scar.

Rocky scratches at the collar of his shirt. "*This*, with Hailey, can't wait. I would prefer she knows what's going on now."

I frown. "We agreed not to turn to her every time we're looking for a solution." She's the mastermind, a moniker we made up as kids, but she's also just *Hailey.* She feels too much responsibility when things go wrong, and I want this to change for her so not every fuckup and error drags her down into the rabbit hole.

"I'm not looking for a solution, man. This is *about* my sister." He tips his head closer to me, his lips against my ear as he whispers most of what Varrick Wolfe told him in the smoking room.

Hailey marrying Trent?

It doesn't compute. She's never taken a role like this in any con. She would never. "There's nothing to worry about," I whisper. "It won't happen."

Except I know, in the back of my brain . . . anything can happen.

SEVENTEEN

Phoebe

I don't need coffee. Both Rocky and I are wired on paranoia and rage. Three a.m.—two hours before my dad's proposed meeting time—Rocky shows me the secret hideaway in the smoking room behind a bookcase.

"It looks like no one's been in here for years," I say, slipping inside the dark parlor. Painter's cloth drapes over a long couch and what I assume are chairs. Moody damask wallpaper peels off the plaster. Weathered cardboard boxes are stacked in every corner. More canvas cloth covers up who knows what.

Rocky flips on the lights, and the cobwebbed chandelier rattles a little. "We check everything."

"Yep."

Rocky and I go to work searching for cameras and recording devices in angered silence. At one point, I even climb on Rocky's shoulders to check the air vents. He holds my thighs as I reach up to peek through metal slats.

"All clear," I tell him.

He grabs my hips and brings me down on my feet.

It feels like old times. Only our tension isn't from refusing to be together, from a yearning so suffocating we both could barely breathe.

Our tension is from impending doom, which really just makes me crave slipping into his embrace. For Rocky to hug me so tightly that if all goes to hell, then at least we're going to hell together.

Can't waste time hugging. Out of all things you really crave to do, Phoebe. Hugging?

I check behind hung mirrors, trying to focus and not think about Hailey and Trent. Trent and Hailey. Varrick hard-launched a scheme without us. I can't even wrap my head around what it means other than *Fuck him.*

Some of my fury sputters out when Rocky whips off a cloth, uncovering framed portraits sitting against the wall.

"Is that . . . ?" I glance from Rocky to the oil canvas. It's a family portrait. A family of five. In formal wear, they're seated on a couch—the same baroque patterned wallpaper of this musty parlor is behind them.

A honey-brown-haired woman with kind, gentle eyes holds a tiny rosy-cheeked baby on her lap. He wears a little tux, but it's his laugh, shared with the two young boys squished beside the woman, that pangs my heart.

On the other end of the couch is a man who I'm now certain is Rocky's father. I look between my boyfriend beside me and the man in the frame. They're the spitting image of each other: the razor-edged jawline, the tunneling gray eyes, the slender nose, even the commanding way he sits, the protectiveness as his arm reaches behind his sons.

I can't even say this is an older version of Rocky. Christian Wolfe looks around his late twenties. About the same age.

I wait for Rocky to speak.

He just crumples the cloth into a ball and tosses it aside. I'm about to prod, but the walls creak. A mirror suddenly slides off its nail.

Rocky catches it before it can shatter on the floor. His superstitious self must be breathing an internal sigh of relief. Externally, he looks ready to punch a fist in the wall. "This place is definitely haunted with the ancestors of my past."

I'm . . . unsettled. "That's really creepy."

"*This* is seriously too creepy for you?" He raises his brows at me. "The girl who likes possessed dolls?"

"Possessed dolls are cute with their single tufts of hair and droopy eyes." I go to a stack of cardboard boxes.

"Cute," he deadpans, then sees me ripping off tape. "We don't need to go through those."

"Scared to find a black cat?" I tease.

He gives me a middle finger. "Seriously, don't waste your time, Phebs."

"What if there's a photo album in here? You wouldn't want to find baby pictures?" I motion to the portrait to indicate that *baby* in the painting is *him*.

He stares harder at me. "It's not the family I'm trying to protect." He points at the oil canvas. "They're gone. But my sister, my brother, your brothers—they're still here." He points at me. "*You're* still here."

It swells my lungs. "And Jake," I add.

He rolls his eyes. "Oh my God, and Jake, whatever the fuck."

That is as good of an inclusion as any from Rocky. I let out an abrupt sneeze. "God, this dust." We keep stirring it up.

Rocky skims the length of me. "You okay to breathe this shit in?"

Do not tense. "Why wouldn't I be?" I pat the tape back on the box.

He rakes a hand through his dyed black hair. "Come here for a sec." He goes to the couch. Cloth already off them, the green floral cushions are exposed. Rocky sits and extends his arm over the back . . . like his dad in the portrait.

I blink away the image, then find myself instinctively beside him. Turning toward him, I lift my stiff shoulders. "We shouldn't be hanging out. We only have an hour left—"

"Phoebe." He collects my hand in his.

My stomach is in knots. We've been on the precipice of this conversation. The one where he nudges deeper for answers about why I'm acting so aloof. Weird. Standoffish.

I don't know what to say anymore. Because I can't tell him Hailey's pregnant. I can't even *allude* in that general direction without feeling like the worst friend on planet Earth. Which is why my default has been to deflect suspicions from her.

It was an instinct. A knee-jerk reaction.

Now, deflecting is beginning to feel like deceiving.

I regret throwing suspicion toward me to begin with. I shouldn't have acted like I could've been ill in the bathroom with her. I shouldn't be avoiding alcohol with her. But I feel like I'm in so deep, and I don't know how to get out without sharing news that's *not* mine to share.

I suck. *I really suck*. Maybe I'm not meant to be anyone's real girlfriend.

"Look at me," Rocky breathes, his voice quiet and more caring.

"I can't."

"Why?"

I squeeze his hand, staring at his knuckles. *"Please."* It comes out agonized.

"Whatever's going on with you, you can tell me."

I can't. I open my mouth, then close it. I swallow a boulder in my throat.

The dead quiet hurts my ears. So I finally look up at Rocky.

He works his jaw, his eyes full of apprehension and rage. "Is it Trent?"

"What?" My stomach curdles, realizing where his brain might be. I . . . I didn't think he'd jump to *that* conclusion.

"Did Trent corner you? Like at the Alps."

"You don't think he would've gloated to his best friend, i.e., *you*, if he did?" My frown deepens.

"He also knows you're my ex-wife."

"Greater reason to shove it in your face—"

"Did he?"

"No," I answer quickly, then try not to cry, realizing how patient Rocky has been with me. He didn't want to force me to open up if I wasn't ready. Because he thought maybe I was assaulted. "No, it's nothing with Trent."

"But it's something." He knows.

I cup his hand in both of mine. "I'm okay. *I'm okay.*" I hold on to his reddening gaze. "You believe me?" It's the truth.

He nods. "I don't believe you're lying to me, but I know you're not telling me something that's been bothering you. And honestly, it's starting to worry the shit out of me."

"Don't be worried. Just . . . trust me." My raspy voice almost cracks. "*Please.*"

He rubs his mouth back and forth, searching my features. "You've been avoiding alcohol for weeks. If you're pregnant—"

"*Rocky.*" I want him to drop this right now.

"I need you to know, the things that scare you, I want to face *with you*. You don't need to do this alone."

I love him. My love for him slams abruptly, powerfully,

against me. He thinks I'm terrified to have a baby, and so naturally, I'm pushing him away. It's a decent guess.

Affection bleeds through my gaze, and I know he can see it. He laces our hands, and I whisper, "Typically, when I'm scared, all I want is you."

I feel terror. The next thing I think is his name. My Rocky. He's my security, my safety, my shelter.

He nods, letting this sink in. "You want me to drop it?"

I'm tormented with this whole ordeal. I can't hide my twisting, contorting face. I can't muster any sort of reply.

He sees. "Anything that hurts you like this is a plague to my fucking system. I can't look away."

"I'm not your problem." I cast him an apology in my eyes.

"You are my problem. And not because you're my sister's bratty best friend."

I release a tight breath, and I wonder if he knows. If he's assumed now that I'm protecting her and shooting my own foot in the process, but I'm too afraid to ask.

"It's because I love you, Phoebe. I'm *in* love with you. Do you understand that?"

I nod strongly, quickly. "I love you, too. I hope you know how much."

He bows forward and cups my face. "It's not too late to tell me." His lips inch higher. "Better yet, scream it."

I grind away a stupidly dopey smile. "So all the ancestors of your past can hear?" I skim his lips. "Phoebe loves Rocky." I try to taunt, but it comes out all too truthful.

"That's all you've got?" He skims my lips.

"Phoebe loves Rocky." I say it deeper.

His eyes devour all of me. *"Rocky loves Phoebe."* We're a hot second from colliding into a devoted, desperate kiss when the bookcase swings open.

Nova has arrived. My oldest brother immediately diverts his gaze from me and Rocky. "Is this really the time for that?"

"We're just talking," I defend.

Nova is disbelieving.

I send a bug-eyed look at Rocky. "You're not going to clear our names here?"

"Am I guilty of something?" He checks the cell signal on his phone. "I don't care if Nova thinks we were about to fuck."

"That's my sister," Nova warns.

"Nooo," Rocky says dryly, widening his eyes. "I had no clue. Thank you for the family tree."

Nova sends me a look. "Your boyfriend."

Yeah. I smooth my lips together, trying not to smile. I chose Rocky, and I do love his serrated edges, even if they unfortunately really aggravate Nova.

"You're early," Rocky says to him. "I told you to come at four thirty."

"It is four thirty." He stays wedged in the doorway. He kicks up a foot against the spun bookcase wall, keeping a lookout. "Phoebe." He calls me over, and when I'm at his side, he digs out a sheathed knife. It's already strapped to a leather band.

"Is this for Trent or our dad?" I whisper.

"Whoever."

"Okay, but you know I'm not going to stab Rocky."

"*I know*," he emphasizes slowly, speaking hushed like me. "Still doesn't mean I think he's good for you."

I crinkle my nose. "It might be the other way around." I peer back as Rocky searches for any cell signal in the hidden parlor. "He's a better boyfriend than I am a girlfriend."

Nova frowns. "I don't believe that."

"You don't want to believe it. It doesn't make it any less true, Nov."

"When have you been a bad anything to any of us?"

I cradle this compliment close to my heart, easing a little. "This relationship is just new territory for me, I think." I'm trying to balance being a good best friend to Hails and a good girlfriend to Rocky. He deserves the same loyalty I give her, but it's been conflicting.

Nova shoots Rocky a harsher look, then asks me, "Did he tell you you're a bad girlfriend?"

"*No*. No, it's just my insecurities at max level."

"Fuck them." Nova nods to me.

I nod back. "Yeah, fuck them." I intake the power in those crude, simple words. He wraps an arm around me in a stiff Nova hug. It makes me smile.

I love my brothers. One of which is still MIA. "What time did you tell Oliver to get here?" I ask Rocky on my way back to the couch. I plant my foot on the armrest and hike up my light gray cotton shorts, exposing more of my thigh.

"Ten minutes till." He pockets his phone, then takes the knife from me. I let Rocky wrap the leather belt strap around my thigh. He positions the knife on the outer side of my leg.

As he tightens the buckle near the inside of my thigh, a flush coats my body. My pulse picks up speed, and I have a sudden flash of Miami.

His hands against my thigh.

His eyes meeting mine behind his lashes like now.

Ten minutes till. I shake out my feelings. "Why that late?"

"We agreed to let Hailey sleep."

"He was with Hailey?" My brows spring, and I smile excitedly over at Nova. He acts far less interested in our brother's romance.

"*Yep*." Rock finishes holstering the knife to my thigh. "And so was Jake."

My face falls before scrunching. "Wait, what?" Like, I know Hailey is having sex with both of them, but . . . not together. "Like all three were in the same room or the same bed?"

"I didn't fucking ask, nor did I want to." Rocky glares. "Let it go."

"The *juiciest* part of tonight?" I make a face at him. "How am I just now hearing about this?"

"I'm sorry, I was a little more preoccupied with the fact that your dad is trying to set up Trent to marry my sister."

"Mistake forgiven."

He pushes my foot off the armrest.

Asshole. I stifle a smile right as Trevor arrives. He rubs his sleepy eyes, wearing expensive black joggers and a matching tee. "Get that thing away from me," he mutters, recoiling from the gun noticeably sticking out from Nova's slacks.

He tucks it farther behind his back.

Trevor collapses tiredly on the couch. "Wake me up when it starts."

"You'll know when it starts, shithead," Rocky says, smacking his legs off the cushion so he can sit beside him. The countdown to five a.m. becomes more apparent.

My insides tighten. We stop having mindless banter. It's quiet and uneasy until Oliver appears.

"Open sesame." He knocks on the bookcase wall. It's already swung open. Nova still guards the entrance, so as soon as Oliver tries to pass through, our brother stops him.

"What the hell?" Nova mutters.

My back goes pin straight at Oliver's *face*. He has on dark sunglasses, and the side of his cheek is sliced red, the cut barely held together with butterfly tape.

"Was that not the passcode?" Oliver quips. "Abracadabra? Alakazam?" He waggles his fingers.

"Who cut you?" I question.

"Myself. Shaving." He shows more of his cheek to Nova. "Stitches?"

Nova inspects it. "No. It's not too deep."

Oliver subtlely releases a breath. Not far behind him are Jake and Hailey. She aims right for her brothers.

All she says is "Tinrocks on the couch." It's a perception thing as much as maybe a comfort for her to be beside Rocky and Trevor.

Varrick will notice how we position ourselves in the room. It's probably best if we just stay close to our siblings.

She sits beside hers. Nova isn't budging from the doorway, so us Graveses end up spreading out. Oliver leans a relaxed shoulder on the wall. I choose a buttoned chair and tug down my shorts to hide the knife that peeks against my thigh.

"Jake should sit in the other chair beside Phoebe," Hailey says. "Varrick already knows you dated."

I think my mom was likely right that Varrick is also aware Rocky and I are together for real. He gave him a skeleton key to my room tonight. It's kind of proof, isn't it?

Still, I keep my distance from Rocky.

Hailey and I exchange cautious looks. Especially as she holds a one-eyed, floppy-eared lilac bunny. Her ugly bunny from Easter.

She stitched her prenatal vitamins into the back cotton. If she didn't leave the stuffed animal upstairs, then maybe she's afraid Varrick corralled us all down here to search through our rooms. Or to have the housekeeper do it for him.

I didn't even consider that until now.

It's fine. I don't think I left anything important in mine.

"Sixty seconds." Nova counts down. We have all considered the possibility of being stood up. We've considered how this could be a trap. We've considered *everything*.

We even contemplated storming Varrick's bedroom to hold this "meeting" there, but we agreed it's better if he believes we trust him enough to agree to his time and location as we would've done for the godmothers.

If it weren't for Nova propping the secret door open, I'd be more panicked our dad planned to gas all of us. Take us out in one blow. But he really has no reason to kill us. It's not like we plan to turn him in to the Feds.

We've been cooperative.

Nova crosses his fingers at his side, indicating to us that he sees Varrick. I really did believe this was a setup. Because I'm more shocked when my dad saunters into the dimly lit parlor.

He smiles back at Nova after slipping past him. I detect notes of appreciation . . . admiring Nova's forethought? Guardedness? Caution?

He picks up a wooden stool. Places it in front of us. Then takes a casual seat. "Now. Let's get started." He nods to Nova. "You can close that, Son."

"I'm not your son," Nova says, but he does shut the secret door, enclosing us in this musty space.

"Biologically, you are. In every other way, you can blame your mother for that."

Nova glowers at the ceiling to stop from retorting.

"She kept your existence from me," Varrick says in a softer tone, but it's also clear he's disgruntled with my mom. Could this really just be his revenge plot? Take us as assets from the people who deceived him?

Hailey stares at the purple bunny in her hands. Okay, what my mom did is *not* comparable to Hailey keeping her pregnancy a secret now. Hailey hasn't lied for twenty-five years about a baby, and my mom only did that to protect us from Varrick.

Supposedly.

She did. He's a murderer.

Jake and Oliver are *good* guys. Hailey will tell them eventually.

"Yeah," I cut in snidely. "She did keep us from you. I wonder why that was."

He opens his palms. "I don't know what she told you, but I'm sure she felt she couldn't trust me, even if I'd told her *exactly* what I planned to do and when I planned to do it. I never lied to Elizabeth. Unfortunately, that trust wasn't reciprocal."

Rocky leans forward. "Could that be because you planned to kill children?"

"You mean you and your two brothers," Varrick says as easily as if we were discussing the stock market. "I didn't plan to kill Christian and Josephine's kids. The three of you weren't supposed to be in the backseat when I ran your parents' car off the road. I only realized the kids were with them *later.* Everett and Addison were tailing me, which—how do you think they were tailing me in the first place?"

We're trained not to fill in the blanks.

So no one says a thing.

He nods to himself, staring around at each of us. "They knew the plan to eliminate Christian and Josephine. They got cold feet. But you can thank them for pulling you out of the river, Brayden." He locks eyes with Rocky.

I can't believe Varrick is admitting, out loud, to murder.

He cups his hands together, elbows resting on his thighs while he slightly manspreads. "You can thank them for a lot.

They taught you well." He studies our postures, likely the same way we're examining him.

Hailey blinks out of a stupor. "They were on vacation," she says. "Christian and Josephine. They were leaving for a family trip. Of course they'd have their children in the backseat."

The insinuation is clear.

He's lying.

Varrick eyes her for an extra-long beat. "Correct." He smiles at a thought. "You really are Addison's daughter."

"Not biologically."

"But in every other way." He speaks quickly, likely sensing Rocky about to interject. "Christian didn't enjoy traveling in the car with his kids. He planned to have the nanny drive them separately. That was until she came down with the flu. Which I didn't know at the time."

It's a convenient twist on the story our parents told.

Rocky sits backward, reaching an arm behind Trevor, who's been staring Varrick down without blinking, like a real psycho.

At least he's ours.

"Let's say you're being honest," Rocky decrees. "You never planned to kill children. How does that change the fact that you premeditated the murder of Christian Wolfe?"

"And Josephine Wolfe," I add.

"William Wolfe." Hailey includes Rocky's grandfather.

"Daphne Wolfe," Nova says. Rocky's aunt.

"Brent Wolfe," Oliver finishes. Rocky's uncle.

Varrick loosely threads his arms together. "It doesn't change the fact. I did kill them."

I'm flabbergasted. "Are you . . . ?" *Out of your fucking mind?* I want to spit out, but I swallow the words and back down.

Varrick laughs into a wider amused smile at some of our reactions, then grips his knees. "You all could be wearing a wire, and I'd be screwed. But trust does need to go both ways. You're here, even though I could've rigged this entire room with surveillance equipment. Though, given who raised you, I'm assuming you already checked."

I glance over at Rocky.

He scrutinizes Varrick. "Why kill them?"

"It was the best way to take their fortune. William was unscrupulous. His children, lazy and entitled."

"That's not what we do," Rocky states plainly.

"Isn't it though?" Varrick motions around the room. "Please, share with me how you all are so different? You've been eating through the Koning dynasty with the help of the thirdborn"—he gestures at Jake—"and you've killed to do it."

No one admits to Claudia's death out loud.

Trevor shifts uncomfortably.

Varrick notices, and Rocky shoves his little brother back into the seat, pressing a protective hand on his chest.

"Varrick," Oliver muses, drawing his attention off Trevor. "The name. It's fake. Old Germanic or Dutch."

Our dad begins to smile. He likes Oliver. I can already tell how much.

I catch myself imprisoning a breath. Nova and I exchange a subtle look of concern. I knew Oliver longed for a father figure as a child, but I just don't want him to desire our real one now.

"It's either derived from Frederick," Oliver continues, "which means *peaceful ruler*. Or . . ."

"Or . . ." Varrick grins.

"A location."

"Van Rijk," Hailey says in a daze. "Which means from the rich or from the powerful."

Oliver props a hand on the wall. *"Power."*

"Clever, you two." Varrick scans us again. "The main manipulators." He motions from Rocky to Oliver, then his finger aims at me. "A honeypot, like your mother."

I take full offense that I'm not being considered as a *main* manipulator. Even if I shouldn't want him to see us so fucking clearly.

He shifts direction to Nova. "A lookout." Then Hailey. "A mini Addison. You puppeteer." He lingers on Trevor. "You." He wags a finger in thought. "You're . . ."

"Your worst nightmare," Trevor concludes.

God, I want that to be true.

Varrick laughs. "You're the youngest. The baby."

"I'm *nineteen*, fuck-face."

My lips curve upward. *You tell him, Trevor.* Rocky is less enthused at his brother's responses.

"Nineteen and desperately in need of more training," Varrick notes.

"Back the fuck off," Rocky warns him.

He raises his hands, says he meant no offense, then he finishes by nodding to Jake. "The new recruit."

"Okay, you think you know us," Rocky says. "We get the idea. What the fuck do you want?"

"To work with you. As you might know, Elizabeth tried to bribe me to leave town. I'd get a cut of the Koning job if I helped you finish it. In return, I'd flee Victoria. We don't need her. You don't need to work with the three of them *ever* again. I can help you take Trent out of the picture."

Jake chimes in, "You're *not* killing my brother."

"I don't plan to. We can get him to sign his assets over to you."

His ploy.

The one with Hailey at the center. I didn't think it was to help us complete the Koning job. The guys seem more tense than they were. I keep blinking. Probably too much.

"What do you want in exchange?" Hailey asks.

"A partnership. We pull jobs together wherever, whenever. It is my deepest pleasure to take from Elizabeth, Addison, and Everett what they took from me." He spreads his hands out in a wide semicircle. "All of you."

Revenge. I understand the desire well.

Rocky even more so.

He barely moves a muscle. I highly doubt he wants to replace the godmothers with Varrick. Not when he's wished to get out from under their control his entire life.

Rocky arches his brows. "There's a problem with your little job you already set up here at Stonehaven."

"And what's that?"

"It's not *fucking* happening," he finishes.

"You don't want the details first?" He's asking all of us.

"I'd like them," Hailey says so softly. I hope his eardrums are crammed with wax and he can't hear. I'm already tempted to know more, and I'd rather this be shut down before he dangles a carrot. Working with the devil to take down another devil—it's not the most ludicrous thing ever.

Varrick focuses on Hailey. "Trent has to want to marry you. Make him think it's his idea." He explains the job in greater detail, including how we'll pull the rope and Trent will end up giving Jake everything.

My head spins a hundred miles per hour. My pulse accelerates to faster speeds. On one hand, I'm enticed enough to admit it's a well-constructed job. One I could see us taking under different circumstances.

On the other hand, I don't want it to be her.

I don't want Hailey in this position.

This is my role.

It always has been.

"The marriage has to be as real as it can be," Hailey says, doesn't ask, as she stares off in thought. "If he thinks it's fake, it all blows up."

"Everything hinges on the marriage being believable," Varrick agrees.

"*Hailey.*" Rocky forces out her name.

I haven't seen her blink in a solid five minutes. I'm gripping the armrests of my chair. Even Trevor has shifted forward, trying to catch his sister's eyes, but she's not here. She's obsessing over this job in her head.

"We're not entertaining this," Jake states, looking at Rocky, then at Oliver.

Oliver hasn't taken off his sunglasses. His hand, still planted on the wall, tenses more than it should. "This isn't what Hailey does," he explains to Varrick. "As you pointed out, she's not a main manipulator. She's rarely been a principal."

"She's been a shill, hasn't she? Surely, they taught all of you how to be actors, even if only a little bit?"

That's true.

Trevor whispers too loudly to Rocky, "If it's a real marriage, doesn't she have to consummate it?" *She's pregnant. She's pregnant.* It's all I can think.

"*Hailey*," Rocky sneers.

Jake runs a taut hand through his hair. Oliver just watches Hailey closely.

I cut in hotly. "She's not having sex with *Trent*."

Not only is he a disgusting piece of shit, she's with my brother and my fake ex-boyfriend. Okay, she is *taken*. Doubly so.

Hailey thinks aloud, "He won't want to have sex with me. He thinks I'm weird."

Nova scrapes his hand back and forth over his buzz cut. He turns his back to us, his expression so tightly wound, I know he's swallowing a furious scream.

"Don't kid yourself," Rocky tells her sharply. "He'll want to fuck his wife."

"Not me," Hailey says.

"That's a big *if*, Hailstorm," Oliver says lightly.

Jake shakes his head repeatedly. "If you don't put out, Hailey, he won't want to marry you."

"Maybe he still will." Her glazed faraway eyes haven't come into focus. "This will work."

Varrick smiles.

No.

She's pregnant.

"I'll do it," I interject as I spring onto my feet. I avoid Rocky, or else I might break down and cry.

"You can't," Hailey breathes.

"I'd rather you not, Phoebe," Varrick suddenly says.

My face contorts. "So, you'd want Hailey to marry a sleazebag but not me?"

"You're my daughter."

Like that means something? My stomach somersaults. "This is what I was trained to do." It hurts even saying it. "And doesn't it make more sense to be me? Trent is already trying to get with me this summer."

"*To fuck you*," Rocky emphasizes so it drills into my head.

The pain in his narrowed eyes is eviscerating. "There is no avenue where Trent marries you and won't want to fuck you, Phoebe. Do you understand that?"

I understand helping my best friend.

I understand completing the job.

I've understood sacrificing my body time and time again to do it, and this town—this place was my fresh start.

My new start.

"You gave up this role for a reason," Hailey says, her gray eyes lifting to mine. "You can't go back."

I know she's right. I just don't know how to help her if I'm not the one taking the stray bullets. "Hails . . ."

"I can do this," she says to me. "You've all put yourselves at risk every time I've placed you on the board. I think it's time I put myself in the game. It's only fair."

Not now.

"Inertia," I tell her, my eyes welling with burning tears. "*Inertia.*" I'm invoking our childhood pact that sent me here to Victoria, that changed the course of our lives.

An object will continue at its current motion until some force causes a change in its speed or direction.

I'm that force this time.

Hailey rises from the couch and comes closer to where I stand. "It's a piece of paper. A marriage certificate. It's nothing."

"It's *Trent.*"

Hailey wraps her arms around me. I wrap mine around her in a tighter hug, and it feels like we're alone in the parlor. Just the two of us with our lifelong friendship and love. She whispers against my ear, "I need to do this. *Please*, Phebs. Take it back."

Take the inertia back.

I didn't realize just how much guilt she's felt over past jobs.

Especially for the Fiddle Game, the con she constructed in Carlsbad. I want her to feel absolved, but I wish it weren't in this way—putting herself at risk like she's put us at risk over so many years.

"Now's not the best time," I whisper to her.

"It's just a summer job."

Her baby isn't due until December.

Very quietly, she whispers to me, "Can you imagine if it all ends here? This could be it, Phoebe. I-I know I haven't been well, but I need you to believe I can be. I need you to believe I am."

I have the utmost faith in her. I really, really do.

"I need to do this," she pleads. *"Please."*

"I take it back."

EIGHTEEN

Rocky

As if Trent wasn't a lesion festering on my skin enough—now this. With my sister. I want to reject it on the pure basis that Varrick set it up. I want to reject it because Hailey really shouldn't be taking lead in this type of role. But she's right when she says, "It's our bread and butter."

It should be easy for us.

This job is typical Tinrock-Graves fare. Phoebe has been engaged to dirtbags. I've been married to marks. Legally, sure, under the name Cal Creighton. So *fake*. I can't even count my marriages to Phoebe. Some lasting five hours for a short con, some lasting months for long ones.

Now I'm Grey Thornhall. Legally divorced from Phoebe Smith. Thanks to Carter for gouging me for those papers. Hailey's marriage will also be fake in the sense that she's not really Hailey Thornhall, but it is a name that she wanted to be hers for longer than a job.

Then again, most jobs like this have been challenging in a

different way. The emotional ties we have to each other make this type of deception feel like quicksand.

I'm used to fighting the grip against my legs.

Oliver, also a professional.

Jake, not at all.

He's the one shaking his head before Varrick is even out the door.

I'm the first one to speak once Nova confirms Varrick has left not only the hidden parlor but the attached smoking room. "I don't like that Varrick is dictating shit," I tell my sister. "If this were *your* choice to start, it'd be different, but it feels like he trapped you here."

"I'd already considered marriage as a possibility," she admits, sinking back onto the couch beside me. "I know . . . I know feelings are . . . involved." She shies from Oliver and Jake.

I shoot Oliver a deadpan look, like *Oh, but I thought it was just sex*.

He waves at me like I'm sending him a gift basket and not an *I told you so*.

Hailey continues, "But this really is the best shot we have at finishing what we started. We'd be smart to take it. We'd be stupid not to."

We all process in a quiet beat. Jake is careened forward, his fingers steepled to his lips. His eyes ping around us, as if expecting one of us to shoot this down.

He zeroes in on me. "What happened to 'it's not *fucking* happening'?"

"It's nothing we haven't done before."

"If it were Phoebe—"

"We've been through this," I snap at him, my blood igniting just picturing Phoebe springing out of her chair and trying to take this from Hailey. There is no fucking scenario where she could take this on without major *irreparable* consequences.

There must be a God, because I don't have to talk Phoebe into walking away. She did that on her own.

I can live inside excruciating pain, but not a world where Trent has her. That would've fucking killed me.

If she didn't back down, I would've manipulated Phoebe into not taking this role (being brutally honest). I would've done *anything* so she'd drop this bomb.

It's not that I don't love Hailey. It's that the risks are much different. So are the desires, but just to be certain, I ask Hailey, "Do you *want* to do this?"

"*Yes.*"

I nod hard. "The second Trent puts a hand on you, this is *over*," I warn her. "The job is off. I'm only agreeing to it on the flimsy fucking notion that he'll see you solely as a piggy bank to Varrick's inheritance and not a pair of legs he wants to slide between."

"O-okay, *Rocky*." Her widened eyes dart over to Oliver and Jake.

"You're embarrassing our sister," Trevor tells me.

Oliver's lips quirk.

Jake's eyes soften on her, but he intakes a sharp breath through his nose. He's acting like we're throwing her into a pit of vipers. He either thinks Hailey can't handle this job like Phoebe can—because *Jake* did not show this same level of worry for Phoebe—or he's just very much in love with my sister.

Hailey's cheeks are still splotchy red. Yeah . . . she must really like them if she's getting this bashful. I'm just glad she's not so deep in her thoughts that she can blush from this.

She manages to sit up and face Jake. "I want to prove to myself, and maybe to all of you, that I'm better. Every day, I'm getting better. I can handle this mentally. I can take this on. I-I know I've been a burden to the team lately—"

"Hailey Tinrock," Phoebe chastises, "you are *not* a burden."

"I haven't pulled my weight."

I scrunch my face at her. "You literally figured out I'm a Wolfe."

"I just need this, please." She's beseeching Jake. He's the only one digging his heels in the sand. "It's not like I'm pretending to be someone I'm not. I get to be the most *me* there is. The girl that Trent finds off-putting. Who knows? It might actually be fun." She looks to Phoebe for encouragement.

Who, of course, is going to dole out a Mack Truck–sized one: "Fucking over Trent *is* fun."

I cut in. "Being around Trent is the opposite of fun."

"When has Rocky ever had fun?" Oliver teases.

"You can't seriously be okay with this?" Jake asks Oliver with actual blazing heat. Jesus, are they in a real fucking love triangle?

Oliver pushes off the wall. "Running scenarios with Hailey to prep her for a high-risk, epic showdown? It sounds better than a summer blockbuster."

Hailey smiles over at him.

"You mean that geeky little movie Nova missed the premiere of," I pipe in.

"*The Avengers*," Nova retorts, "probably headed to be one of the highest-grossing movies of all time."

"Dork."

"Asshole."

We're share a subtle smile, which seems to pull one out of everyone else. Everyone but Jake. Until Trevor says, "We are pretty much the Avengers. Just less G-rated. More badass. Like Dark Avengers."

"That's not a thing," I say.

"It is, actually." Nova smiles—*really* smiles in a way I haven't seen since we were young, a time before his mom dated dickhead after dickhead mark—and he laughs to himself, his tough brown eyes rising to meet us. "They're a group of villains who impersonate the Avengers."

"So . . . frauds." I raise and lower my brows.

Phoebe has an all too smitten smile. She does love the counterfeit. It makes my lips rise higher.

Oliver grins. "If the shoe fits . . ."

"Wear it," Hailey finishes.

He winks at her.

I've never seen myself as a vigilante, but for Jake, imagining he's this summer's hammer-wielding superhero might keep him from wanting to rip his hair out. Trent isn't just a mark; he's the older brother Jake despises, so this is another level of fucked-up for him.

If this isn't an initiation into our world, I don't know what is. "Welcome to *my* magical summers," I tell him later that night. "They've always been very unhinged."

I can honestly say I've been enjoying working alongside Hailey. It's new—her taking huge pointers from all of us, listening and following what we have to say. The hot, sticky summer days feel cool as fuck knowing Trent is being bamboozled at every turn. Friday, we attend Victoria's movie night on the green, and he's loosening his tie and curling his lip as Hailey stretches out on a blanket beside Phoebe. Both girls digging into a bucket of popcorn purchased from the outdoor vendors.

"I know she's your sister, Grey, but what the fuck is on her face?"

Hailey put in all her piercings at one time. Septum, both eyebrows, bottom lip, studs on her earlobes, and hoops in the cartilage.

"She's alternative, man," I say. "A little weird. I don't know, we're not that close."

"Yeah, I've gotten that sense." Trent cringes while we wait for gourmet sliders from a burger food truck. "I don't know about this."

"You want to ditch the movie?" I nod toward the opening of *The Sandlot* playing on the giant projector screen. Families and couples hunker down on the lawn space with Fizz sodas and boxes of candy: Junior Mints, Skittles.

"I meant Varrick's idea," he whispers, eyeing me seriously. "I was already married once. I'm a *widower*." A title he wears with pride. "Getting married again, while I'm in a legal battle with Jake, to your . . ." He makes a sour face at Hailey. *Good.* "Her." He motions to Hailey as she picks chewing gum out of her mouth and sticks it to the side of the popcorn tub. (Phoebe's idea.) "What the fuck?" he mutters, then grits out to me, "There's nothing in it for me."

"Really?"

"I *really* don't see it." He gives Hailey another once-over from afar.

"He's basically handing you a cash cow. It's the *Wolfe* fortune. They were building railroads and shit. Wasn't one of them friends with the Rockefellers back in the day?"

"Carnegie, I think."

"Old money," I say. "Loaded for generations. You and all your degenerate offspring." The quip comes out far too lighthearted to be real from me.

He laughs, then grimaces again. "And *her* degenerate offspring." He narrows his eyes from her to me. "Thornhall. I can see how you'd like this, being her brother."

Deep, sudden laughter rumbles out of my chest. "Yeah, *yeah*, I would. Who wouldn't want to be one degree from probably a billion, maybe more. But I'm not telling you it's worth it so I can bag a fucking dime. I don't have to be from around here to know the depth of money from the steel industry." I nod to him. "To be honest, the chances she accepts any kind of marriage proposal from you is *low* anyway. You probably shouldn't bother—"

"Whoa." He catches my arm before I turn back to the food truck. "You think I can't get *her* to marry me?" He laughs even harder than I did, a little pissed. "Are you high right now?"

"Man—"

"I'm a twelve. She's a *two*. Most of this town would *pay me* to be Mrs. Trent Waterford."

I stomp out the urge to roll my eyes halfway across the Atlantic. "I don't think my sister cares about your pedigree."

"Wasn't she sleeping with half the staff at the country club?"

Yeah.

Hailey did do that.

"Exactly." I focus on the chef flipping burgers off a griddle in the truck. "My sister isn't the marriage type. It's not you. It's her. The one thing I do know about Hailey, she's not going to settle down. It'd be a miracle if you could even get her in on this. Especially since you don't need to sleep with her. You just need to be legally married." I collect my blue cheese sliders from the chef, letting Trent ponder this on his own. I hand him his paper tray of mini burgers. "You good?"

"You want to bet on it?" He extends a steady palm, staring me straight in the eye.

"What exactly?"

"That I'm going to be the richest man in Victoria."

Too easy.

Manipulating him has never been hard. He's just ego and vanity. Withstanding him has taken untapped patience, but things are changing this summer.

After I shake his hand, accepting this bet—we put twenty grand on it—he chooses to watch the movie on the blanket beside Hailey. I gladly take the spot beside my ex-wife. Phoebe grinds out a smile at me, leans her shoulder into mine, and most of the town can see.

We're steadily moving from "exes who are friends" to "exes who might be dating." Trent—he's hating every second of this movie.

Hailey is whispering to him about baseball. From the physics, velocity of pitches, to the material of the balls, to the twenty-seven times the Yankees won the World Series. To the point where the vein in his temple throbs. He side-eyes her like she's an insect crawling inside his ear canal.

When he steals my attention, he points at my sister like she's a defective toy he can't play with, and I shrug at him like *Told you it's impossible, man.*

Trent loves to chase after what he can't have. He never listens to the word *no*. He hates being told, *You can't*. His entitled response in every scenario is *I will*.

I can see his brain circling over the words now: *I will get Hailey Thornhall to marry me.*

The movie on the green is just the start of me stoking his desire for the Wolfe fortune and Hailey playing hard to get. By Wednesday, a sunset cocktail cruise has Trent downing whiskey shots to entertain Hailey's rambling energy.

I'm never far. Trent likes when I appear and cut in on their conversation. I take pleasure in his twisting scowl and annoyed glances. He's short with Hailey, then tries to apologize. Poorly.

He can't pretend to like her. Not even with billions and his pride on the line. At the end of the night, he ditches Hailey to go flirt with the stewardesses.

"I'm losing him," she whispers to me.

"No, you aren't," I say into my sip of bourbon. "You aren't supposed to sleep with him." Even uttering the words makes me want to empty my stomach over the bow.

"He's going to get tired of the chase."

"He won't. Trust me, don't act like you want him, Hails."

She still hasn't noticed Oliver keeping an eye on her from the upper deck. He parties with Collin Falcone and Trent's laundry list of part-time friends. The two of us being so ingrained in Trent's social circle isn't just helpful; it's vital.

In town, Oliver, Collin, Trent, and I are still dubbed the Fortunate Four (stupid). Trent acts like he's far above the moniker but will bring it up to bag out-of-towners everyone calls "skunks" (also stupid) like we're wealthy celebrities.

We party late into the night.

I stay away from the girls. From the booze. Trent would prefer I partake with him, but I cite work. He believes I'm employed by the CIA.

The real reason, of course, is Phoebe.

It's not the first sunset cocktail cruise Trent invites Hailey to. The second and third, she rejects.

He's never been shot down by someone who's slept with the VCC bartender, valet, and not to mention, "That ugly fuck, what's his name?"

"Clark," I tell him. "The pool guy."

I hope this is making him toss and turn on his sweaty fucking pillow every single night. He storms into Stonehaven most evenings and drowns his failings in Varrick's liquor cabinet. He's never been such a loser (he's always been a fucking loser), and I twist the knife inch by inch, reminding him he should've never bet me.

I'm going to win.

"You're sadistic," Phoebe tells me when I sneak into her bedroom.

"It's turning you on."

"Not even."

"I'd believe you more if you weren't the Cheshire fucking Cat right now."

She crosses her arms on the bed, barely able to hide her smile with a scowl. "You're taking so much enjoyment from tormenting him." Phoebe teases me every time I rehash Trent's bitchy little breakdowns.

It's a great summer. (So far. I'm not getting ahead of myself.)

Bolstered by the fact that Trent knows, actively *knows*, I'm pursuing my ex-wife, and I remind him he doesn't want Phoebe anyway. He should be going after the billions.

Trent isn't tossing in the towel. His fragile little ego is now at stake.

Since Hailey won't integrate herself in his social circle, he begins showing up to hers. He attends the quirky town events he so very much detests, bringing me, Oliver, and Collin along. The town is buzzing as *the* Trent Koning Waterford becomes more of a day bird instead of an elusive night owl.

Could he have his eye on a girl?

My little brother gets Sidney to publish theories about Trent looking for love in her gossip column. He's ready to move on from his late wife and the grief of losing his *beloved* mother as he becomes more active in the community.

At the lobster roll fest, Trent asks Hailey on a formal date.

She crinkles her nose. "I don't date."

He lets out an incredulous laugh. "What does that mean?"

She pops a piece of lobster in her mouth. "I like to just do my own thing."

"She's too good for you, Trent," Phoebe notes.

"Oh, is that right, Phoebe?" Trent mocks back.

I shoot him a glare from behind his head, then mouth to Phoebe, *Knock it off.*

She's drawing his attention in the wrong direction. Hailey licks her thumb and just leaves his side to go read her book. She finds a seat on a bench, places her lobster roll down, and cracks open the paperback.

He shields the sun with his hand. "Why don't you put a good word in for me with your friend Phoebe?"

"Why don't you go choke on a twelve-inch lobster roll?"

I rub my lips to keep from smiling. She notices it and smiles over at me. Trent spins to open his stance up, eyeing me and her like he's missed something. That's not good. He must never be the butt of a joke. Me and her—we're getting a little sloppy.

It becomes more apparent during the Cardboard Boat Regatta—a fundraiser for the science college at Caufield. From the harbor at the Mariner's Club, Trent and I watch makeshift cardboard floats head into the sea with students voraciously paddling, and he tells me, "I don't think Phoebe's good for you."

I'm casual, interested but not concerned enough to be suspicious. "You'd rather she date Jake?"

He slips me a *Be serious* look. "You should just be single with me this summer, Grey."

"You're trying not to be single," I remind him. "How's that working out for you?"

He casts a real glare to shut the fuck up.

"I'm joking." (I'm not.) "Relax, man. Maybe the easiest way to get Hailey on board with this thing is to actually tell her the plan. Bring her in on it. She could want the money, too."

"I don't trust that she won't tell Phoebe or Jake's staff at the fucking club. My baby brother finds out, and he might be able to use it as leverage against me in some of this legal shit. It's too much of a risk."

Gradually, Hailey begins integrating herself in Trent's friend group at my insistence as his best friend. I've done him a solid. He's happy.

Hooray.

Oliver stops snorting so much coke. He's not high when he's around Hailey during the several midnight yacht parties she attends with us. He pretends to do several lines with Collin. No one notices he's faking but me and her.

"You want some, Hailey?" Oliver offers her the coke while we're seated around a coffee table in the main saloon.

To which she declines. "I'll pass."

He blows her a playful kiss, and this is where shit goes a little sideways. Trent sees Hailey gazing at Oliver for an extended beat. He sees the crimson ascend her neck to her cheeks into a noticeable flush.

"Do you like him?" Trent laughs like it's a schoolgirl crush.

Oliver grins at her. "You have a thing for me?"

"Not really, no." She picks at the label on her beer and chews her pierced lip. Her nervous eyes shift to me.

Hailey.

My muscles burn as I actively ignore her. I bail her out another way. "We should do a round." I grab the tequila off the table.

Hailey clutches the neck of a beer. One she hasn't taken a real sip of. I'm aware of how she's been refusing all alcohol this summer. Like it's better for the job if she stays sober.

Maybe that's true. Or maybe it's something else.

Collin smacks Oliver's chest. "Dude, she's *so* into you. Look at her."

Oliver plays it off with a trained laugh and smirks at Hailey like she's just another girl at another party we all attend. No one special.

Hailey bursts into sudden tears.

Fuck.

Oliver's smile vanishes in an instant. Because those are real tears. Real guttural emotion.

"I-I can't be here," Hailey stammers, and I rise with her at the same time as Trent. He's shooting me looks to back off. This is his time to intervene while my sister is vulnerable. I am not to intercept him.

"Hailey!" Oliver calls after her. "Wait!"

She swings back around, dabbing at her contorting face as heavy tears keep streaming. Smudged mascara streaks her cheeks like rubbed charcoal. "I . . . s-sorry," she hiccups.

"Come here, my little freak." Trent opens his arms to her in preparation for a bear hug, and he'll swing her around in a circle like they're best fucking friends.

My stride is lengthy to my sister, especially as she recoils at Trent. Mesh sleeves in her hands, she raises them to her face. And thank God she says, "Grey."

I bypass Trent and tell him, "I'm going to bring her back to Stonehaven. Don't wait up for us."

"I can come—"

"N-no," she sobs.

I mouth to him, *Let me talk to her.*

Trent crosses his arms but nods. "Hey, Hailey. You need anything, you have my number, yeah?"

"Double fudge," I tell him. "Her favorite ice cream."

Trent says he'll pick a pint up for her, and as I swoop an arm over Hailey and help her off the docked yacht, we trek along the harbor. Sailboats, catamarans, dinghies sway lazily in the bay. Moonlight sparkles on the water and brightens our path to the private dock. The one we use to go to and from Stonehaven.

I keep my arm around my sister, and the only time she somewhat calms down is when she says, "D-double fudge. That's your favorite."

She's still crying.

"Making him my errand bitch is my third-favorite thing about this summer."

Hailey sniffs harder, her reddened eyes lifting to me. "First one is Phoebe."

"Yeah," I murmur. It's always Phoebe. Being with her in any capacity. On the job or off the job, real or fake—I love it all.

Hailey rubs her fist on her mascara-smudged cheek. "What's the second?"

"Spending more time with my sister."

Her head jerks up at me in surprise.

"Yeah, *you.* It's not often we run jobs this closely, and you're making my time being that fucker's friend a vacation."

Her chin quivers. "Even if I screwed up tonight? M-maybe I'm not cut out for this after all."

"You've been doing great." I stop her near a racing sailboat named *Sunny Daze* so she can catch her breath. Her back to the sea and the moon, she keeps scrubbing at her cheeks and muttering, "Stop crying, *stop crying*."

I almost wish Phoebe were here to comfort my sister in ways I know she needs.

"Hailey, just breathe," I say, not nicely. I smear a hand down my face. My phone is buzzing in my pocket. I check the text off my burner at my hip.

(OLIVER): she ok?

I send him a thumbs-up. "He's asking about you."

"Olly?"

I nod and raise my brows at her. "Is it complicated now? You and him and Jake?"

She nods more vigorously. "Yeah." She chews her lip again, then stares out at the twinkling light reflecting off the water. "I'm not used to Oliver pretending with me. Back there"—she motions to Trent's yacht—"I just lost it when he acted like I meant . . ."

"Like you meant nothing?"

She breaks into another sob.

I clutch her arm. "Hailey, it's *pretend*. Exactly what you just said. It's not how he really feels about you."

"Phoebe always said the lying is like foreplay and exciting, but this was just . . . this *hurt*."

I pinch at my eyes, then let go, and use that hand to bring her into a hug. She's very emotional over this. Her tears won't let up.

As my sister cries into my chest, my head almost goes numb with the realization of what's happening. Until now, I've *never* seen her struggle this hard to contain her emotion. I've *never* seen her reject alcohol for more than a couple weeks. I've *never* seen her be nauseous more than a few times.

I've felt as if Phoebe was hiding something from me.

Now I know why she let me draw those conclusions. There is only one person Phoebe would go that far to protect. Only one girl she loves this much to where she'd even attempt to deceive me.

It's been for my sister.

Hailey is pregnant.

And I'm guessing she's hormonal and upset and carrying a secret from Oliver and maybe even Jake. One so heavy that it's making tonight harder. All I care about is making sure she's okay.

Bringing up I've figured out what she has *clearly* intended for me not to know—not fucking helpful. I can keep my mouth shut until she's ready.

I am . . . *petrified* for her.

I'm relieved it's not Phoebe. Because the truth is, I never want children.

"You're not failing, Hails," I whisper to my sister. "You're really doing better than you even realize." Now, knowing what she's been dealing with, I feel it even stronger.

She calms down a little, her hiccups receding.

"You think tonight is bad?" I ask. "I can name about five different scenarios Phoebe, Oliver, and I have been in that'd make this look like a victory lap."

She pushes back her platinum hair and stares up at me with raccoon eyes. "I-I don't know if I can believe that."

"Believe me," I profess. "I wouldn't lie to you. Even if it'd make you feel better if I did. You know that."

She nods.

"Did Phoebe ever tell you about Nashville?" I ask her.

"The Melon Drop?"

"That's the one." My throat tries to close.

"She just said that it really sucked. Bad night, but those aren't that hard to come by."

I nod a couple times, my gaze daggered too violently to place on my sister. I look out at the glittering sea before I can soften my eyes on Hailey. "It was one of the worst nights of my life," I say to her. "And Phoebe's."

NINETEEN

Phoebe

FOUR YEARS AGO
THE MELON DROP
Nashville, Tennessee

"Yeeeeee-haw!" Oliver howls and tucks a cowboy hat on his head full of natural dark brown hair. "This round is on me, boys." He barrel-chest-bumps the bachelor, Bradley Wheeler, who's a city boy from Toronto and looking to experience Nashville's nightlife before the big wedding day.

Bradley is also loaded.

Like flew a private jet here loaded. Buys the most expensive liquor at the bar loaded. Wears a Breguet Swiss luxury watch loaded. That's probably fifteen million just on his wrist.

Lucky for him, he just so happened to run into three "Nashville locals." After striking up great conversation, Oliver, Rocky, and I offered to take his bachelor party on a honky-tonk bar crawl. To show Bradley and his groomsmen the *best* music, the *best* drinks, and the *best* time.

Bradley is all grins, pumping his fist as he follows his new friend Oakley (ahem, Oliver) to the packed bar.

"Tequila with lime, Penelope?" Shane, the best man, asks me on his way to the bar, too. He's bought me shots at the past three stops. I drank two Jäger bombs, then dumped the third when no one was looking.

"Just a water!" I shout after him, my Tennessee twang more subtle than Oliver's. Per usual, my brother is going above and beyond. Just hopefully not too far.

"Aw, come on!" Shane shouts back. "Don't be a Debbie Downer! I'll get you a tequila!!" He disappears into the sweaty throng with the rest of the bachelor party, not giving me the opportunity to decline.

"He wants in your pants," Rocky says huskily, a toothpick between his lips and his elbow perched casually on a wooden barrel. He's Rhett. My college friend. Same with Oliver. We all supposedly met freshman year at Vanderbilt.

Rocky hangs back with me, and I'm momentarily hooked on how hushed and deep he speaks. Like we're slipping clandestine notes to each other.

"He'll have to try a little harder. I'm waiting till marriage." I thicken my twang. "Thank the good Lord."

Rocky almost smiles at my lie. *Almost*. "Praise be."

"Praise be," I joke, too, but Rocky looks straight into me. He's holding my gaze for longer than any man ever does. It's more intimate than a full-body once-over. Flush tries to roast my cheeks.

If attraction is a scorch, then Rocky is the only one who gives me third-degree burns. I'm hooked on more than just the photogenic planes of his cutting jawline, more than his annoyingly perfect hair as a few tendrils lightly brush his forehead. More than his toughened stance that commands, *You fuck with her, you fuck with me*, to the rest of the bar. More than how he wards off other men from approaching me.

More than how I feel safer when he's close.

I'm hooked on the entirety of him. How he's choosing to be at my side. How his real coarse nature flickers across his striking features for only me to notice. For only me to see.

His dark, smoldering eyes still transfix me in a vise I'm not readily escaping. Not now. Maybe not ever.

"Rhett," I warn half-heartedly, not wanting him to stop staring.

"Penelope." He bites on the toothpick, never tearing his gaze away. My heart thumps harder, faster.

Last thing I need is for Rocky to believe a falsehood—that I'm *infatuated* with him. I'm not some obsessed puppy about to slobber on his lap and beg for a fucking pet. I don't want to be petted. I want to be *ravaged*.

I'm simply a twenty-one-year-old woman with a high libido. And I can admit to myself that it's highest around him. I can't help that my hormones go haywire in his presence. I can't help that I *love* the feeling of my racing, skidding, flyaway pulse when he's inches from me.

It's human nature, and these are just *biological* problems.

Gathering my bearings, I face forward. The fun part of tonight is the best distraction from Rocky.

Live country music booms from a stage. Blue lights bathe a guitarist and fiddler along with the dance floor. Girls in cheeky Daisy Dukes and cute leather boots are line-dancing with belt-buckle-clad guys. Most are bachelor and bachelorette parties. I see Barbie-pink bedazzled cowboy hats, sashes that say LAST RODEO, and penis straws.

I'm trying to enjoy tonight, especially since it's our last one in Nashville.

"Do you think Hails will come out?" I ask Rocky more quietly. I've already texted his sister. She can pop in as a college friend who's meeting up with us for a drink. It'd be an easy ruse to pull off.

"The godmothers specifically told her no, so no. You both don't break rules."

"That's a good thing," I point out.

"Being good gets you stepped on." His deep voice sounds even more gravelly with his twang. "You must love looking at the bottom of your mom's heels."

"We all can't be anarchists wanting to *burn it down*."

His lip twitches into a slanted smile. "Does it look like I'm burning it down?"

He's not setting fire to our lives. We are a well-organized machine of deceit. "You aren't lighting any matches," I observe, resting my forearms on the barrel in a casual lunge. It doesn't draw his attention to my ass or my breasts. His focus remains on my face as he reads me.

It's intrusive. Intimate again.

In a hot blip, I imagine Rocky moving behind me, sliding his possessive hands against the crook of my hips, and fucking me *hard* against the barrel. I brick-wall my expression so he can't read those desires, but he has all the tools to knock me down if I'm not careful.

I don't want to be careful with him. That's the exhilarating, yet terrifying, part.

I skim his features. "Why not try to usurp them if you want to so badly?"

"Y'all don't want me to try." He eases out a sexy drawl and moves the toothpick with his tongue.

He might as well be saying, *Because I love y'all more than I hate them*.

My heart swells and pangs, and I should probably distance myself from Rocky—I should go entertain the bachelor party instead of sharing his company. I have a job to do, so does he, but neither of us moves.

I wonder when we became a vortex together. Exiting the EF5 winds takes hellacious effort, and I'm not fighting against the force of nature.

"Y'all?" I ask in a tight breath. "As in . . . ?"

I want him to say, *You. Mostly you. I love you more than anyone I know, Phoebe.*

He shifts the toothpick again. "You know who."

Right.

His siblings: a younger sister and brother. My siblings: two older brothers—granted, older by minutes.

I nod and say out loud, "You love Hails more than you hate the godmothers."

"Astute," he says. But he's not adding me into the equation. He's not putting me before his sister, and why would he? I'm just her best friend.

I'd put Hailey above myself, too.

I bend a little more. "I've been known to be perceptive."

"Not more perceptive than me," he says thickly. I'm unsure if it sounds like a challenge or a come-on.

I open my mouth to combat him. Instead, I intake a strange, shortened breath of arousal. I hope he doesn't comment on it. And he doesn't, not as his own muscles flex, as if controlling something carnal within himself.

We are perceptive. I think we both know attraction exists, thrives, *terrorizes*. Tension thickens at the unsaid things. Our bodies are mere inches apart, and still, neither of us shifts away or nearer.

I breathe hard.

He does, too.

Feelings are thorns we let puncture us. Sometimes I believe Rocky and I like bleeding out together.

I finally straighten up, and he slides his darkened gaze off me. If he had a beer, he'd likely chug it right now.

I wouldn't say the tension snaps. It's buried in my core, and I try to ignore it by checking my phone.

No new text from my best friend. I frown, wishing Rocky were wrong—that his sister would sneak out. Which is a funny phrase: *sneak out*. She's in her twenties, too. Sneaking shouldn't be a thing for us, but I guess it's more like being held up at work. She's clocking in overtime since she's helping our parents preplan the next long con.

After this, we're heading to Miami.

I shove the phone in the front pocket of my frayed jean shorts. My ass peeks out. Each bar has been burning hot, so I've loved my skimpy outfit for comfortability. Plus, the matching bejeweled jean vest is seriously cute.

"She wanted to be here," I remind her brother. "The original plan was better."

Hailey had concocted a Bar Bill job. It would've taken at least a month, if not two, to pick out a mark and for one of us to be hired as a bartender, but our parents rejected it. Now we're just passing through Nashville with this short con.

Last night, when we were told the change of plans, Hailey looked so defeated and said, "I just wish they gave me better constructive feedback over why they axed it."

"They said it wasn't personal," I told her. "It wasn't a bad con or setup."

Hailey fell flat on the bed, dejected. "I'm pretty positive they don't think I'm ready to plan a job of that level yet."

I lay back with her and held her gaze consolingly. "It's probably just timing."

Hailey's Bar Bill job would've meant she'd be having fun with us at Rowdy Rooster's Watering Hole tonight. We could've even ridden the mechanical bull.

Now she's stuck alone at the Ritz, which—*yes*, it's not a Super 8 or an RV park, but seeing Hailey's devious dreams get shot down offends me as her best friend. The universe should be better to her.

Hailey ended up taking her blues out on a pint of Moose Tracks. Rocky had gone to the nearest convenience store last night to get her the ice cream. I imagine she's finishing off the last of the container while we're here.

"The original plan," Rocky says under his breath, not dropping the subtle Tennessee accent. "Did you like it because your best friend came up with it? Or because it involved her being here?"

"Both. And because of Nashville." I watch the line dancers. "I'm not ready to leave." The catchy tempo from a fiddle is invigorating. "Are you?"

I feel him studying me. "I could stay."

I try to pry my eyes off the rhythmic bodies, but I'm latched on to the heel-toe taps of cowboy boots as I say, "You finally fell in love with country music?"

"Yeah," he deadpans. "It's growing on me like a cold sore."

I snort. Why would he even want to stay here for longer? "I bet it's the toothpick," I tease. "You've always wanted something to gnaw on."

He flips me off.

I laugh, and I see the start of his smile before I'm entranced by the dancers again. Girls smack their heels and hop-jump to the beat. Guys tip their cowboy hats as they shimmy to the side.

Rocky pushes off the wooden barrel and suddenly captures my hand. Leading me to the dance floor. My pulse rushes ahead of me.

I pick up speed with glee. We slip into the line dancers, and side by side, we mimic the moves in seconds, sharing smiles at the ease of our inception. Shuffle to the right, toe forward, heel back, clap our hands, spin, twirl our hips.

Rocky looks like a skilled country boy from *Footloose*. I'm captivated for a heady moment. In how effortlessly he becomes someone else—and in how deeply I still see him through the veneer. In a way, this is all of him, and this is all of me.

We're every skill we've learned, every lie we've created, every secret we've shared.

Even dancing, he's still attentive, observant. His eyes land on me, then the bar as we rotate—where Oliver hands the groom a shot. Then back to the fiddler on the stage.

We glide closer to each other. With the music blasting, we can have a private enough conversation, so I ask him while we dance, "What would you be doing tonight if you weren't working?"

"Is it work?" He claps, then we spin side by side.

Our eyes are fastened with our movements. "It's called a *job*."

Rocky passes close, his lips brushing my ear. "It's a *lifestyle*." My skin vibrates with electricity, especially as he whispers, "Think about it. Have you ever gone out and not done it?"

It.

As in, lie.

Scheme.

Con.

Hailey and I got tickets to some underground heavy metal band she loved, and even at that concert, we fucked over this raging dick who purposefully spilled a drink on his girlfriend's head. The girl was mortified. Crying.

So we stole his wallet and his phone (unlocked) and found his passcodes typed out in a notes app. Including his ATM pin.

We emptied his checking account.

It was impulsive. Unplanned.

And I rode that high all the way to our hotel, where we ordered the entire dessert menu from room service.

"I usually do it," I answer Rocky, knowing in little instances and bigger ones, I've always cheated my way through a day. "I can't imagine *not* doing it."

We shuffle back together and dip forward.

"Same," he says with the raise and lower of his brows.

My pulse skips. I stumble over my boots on a side step, and before I can brush off the momentary lack of coordination, Rocky rotates out of sync with the dancers and catches my hips. He spins me into his chest.

Breath evacuates my lungs.

His arms, around me, are familiar, devoted, protective, powerful.

And he says, "I'd still be doing this. It's not work to me." His gunmetal grays dive deep into me, and I imagine his hands rising to my cheeks. I imagine him possessing me with a forceful, agonizing kiss.

It's not work for him.

Rhett could have the hots for Penelope.

Penelope definitely has feelings for Rhett, even if she

shouldn't. Even knowing this'll all end when the job ends. Because Rocky *does* clock out.

He's still never kissed me outside a job. Practicing when we were younger doesn't count.

Just when I think he's easing in, he veers to my ear and whispers, "I'm getting you a water."

"Yeah." I nod assuredly a few times, forcing down the aggravating flush. "Okay." We both see the bachelor party at the bar. They're searching for us.

Get the job done, Phoebe.

Rocky is likely going to try to keep them at the bar, away from me. He leaves after a deep "Be careful." And I don't need to imagine his dark gaze lingering on me. I feel the heat of it stroking the length of me in a red-hot caress before he peels away from my side.

I struggle to intake breath. It's like he took my oxygen with him.

In the next minute, I miss his presence. It's hard to have the same energy dancing alone.

I slide to the brick wall for a breather.

"Was that your boyfriend?" a girl in a disco cowboy hat asks me, her face full of glitter.

"No, he's just"—*Rocky*—"a friend."

She gasps. "Oh my God! Is he single?!" She's about to flag down her friends to share the *terrific* news.

My face burns, heat gathering in my lungs. "No," I lie fast. "He has a girlfriend."

Her shoulders slump. "Really?"

"Yeah, she's not here. She's super nice, too."

The blatant side-eye she gives me is deserved. Penelope was a little too cozy with a taken man, but I want to brand him with the name he gave me. I want him to brand me with the name I gave him. *Phoebe. Rocky.* Deep, thick, bleeding scars visible over our thrashing hearts. More permanent and painful than ink.

I shut my eyes, my breath deepening, and I picture the bloody mess as his lips crash against mine, as our limbs tangle. I picture how everyone can see who we are to each other—ingrained, embedded, entrenched.

And I wonder how long I've really been in love with him.

TWENTY

Rocky

THE MELON DROP (CONTINUED)

The mark's bachelor party hasn't migrated away from the bar. I'm waiting on a water for Phoebe and talking Shane's ear off about bull riding.

"Man, you've gotta come out and see the Stampede. It's worth another trip here." I clasp a friendly hand on his shoulder and block out the violent urge to wring his neck.

He's bobbing his head but losing interest. His attention swerves over to the dance floor. To Phoebe, as she stands off to the side in her Daisy Dukes and claps to the gasoline-fueled beat of "The Devil Went Down to Georgia." She hollers, cheering on a few girls who tear up the floor with a complicated line dance.

"Huh?" Shane asks me.

I force myself not to stake him with a glare. It's only easy because I fixate on Phoebe for a long beat. She's cupping her hands to her mouth and cheering even louder for the talent on the floor and stage.

A smile almost crawls across my mouth. I *almost* push

away from the bar and pull her back into the line of bodies just to dance with her again. It's a craving—being beside her. It'd be an addiction if I didn't have this much fucking self-control.

Seeing Phoebe having a good time is actually making me have one, but she's also making tonight harder. Because Shane is practically busting a nut in his fucking pants, and there are about three, four, *six* other salivating fucks checking her out like she's a prize.

Phoebe is so captivating that she's catastrophic. A siren who'll drown men as they try to board her ship, but I can't even stand watching them try to climb.

She doesn't want these guys around her.

And I can't pretend that it'd be different if she did. I'd *still* want to shove them into eight-foot swells and hope they choke on salt water as a riptide wrenches them under.

"Penelope can really hold her liquor," Shane says to me. "A girl that size, I would've thought she'd be on the floor by now."

Then why the hell have you been feeding her more shots, you fucking dipshit? I post my elbows back on the bar and chew on the toothpick. I remember what Phoebe said about me gnawing on the thing. Yeah, sure, I like taking my aggression out on it when I can't deck him in the face.

"You should've seen her freshman year." I let out a long whistle. "Girl drank half a keg and could've walked a perfect line. Penelope never gets drunk."

"She puts out though?" Heath, the groom's younger brother, pipes in with a laugh. "I'd fuck her."

"After me," Shane laughs, then he catches the raging heat barreling out of my body and eyes. "We're joking, Rhett. Lighten up, man." He pats my tensed shoulder now, but he's still drooling over Phoebe while she jumps to the tail end of the song.

"You can't be talking about my friend like that," I warn.

"Yeah, yeah." He's fixated on her bouncing tits.

My ribs are on fire, and my knuckles throb as the desire to punch his lights out overwhelms me.

I laugh hard and block his line of sight, then pat his chest. "We should get another round." I draw him closer to the bar, farther away from Phoebe, and I scan the bachelor party to find her brother. "Oakley!" I call out to Oliver, who's currently entertaining the groom with alcohol. "You like Jäger bombs, don't you?" It's the code for tonight to pull the rope.

Let's screw them over now.

"What was that?" He feigns confusion and swoops over to me with a bottle of Koning Lite. He wraps an arm around my shoulders, drawing me away from Shane.

I whisper, "You ready?"

He angles his head to me, lifting his cowboy hat up some. "We could try now, but it'd be better at the next bar." He looks ahead at the groom, who talks animatedly about wintering in Monaco like it's out of fashion. He'll be in the Maldives this year. Oliver has no facial inflections, no noticeable reaction, but under his breath, he murmurs, "No one should have that much."

"Then let's take it from them," I whisper back.

Oliver contemplates.

"I'm getting her a double," Shane says loudly from the bar. He's flagging down a bartender who still hasn't handed me a water.

"Getting who a double?" Oliver asks me.

"Who do you think?" I whisper back with a dark look. I can't exactly say, *Your sister*, out loud, but we've been doing this shit long enough that all it takes is one serious glance.

Oliver's brows jump and freeze, his lips in a flat line of

concern. He sees Shane is trying to get Phoebe drunk. To get laid. "Jäger bombs, now." He dips his cowboy hat, and mirth replaces his concern—a grin breaking over his face. He hollers and slips back to the groom.

I convince the bartender to give me a water before Shane catches anyone's attention. "Rhett!" he calls out, but I pretend not to hear him or notice his plight.

Water in hand, I join Bradley's cluster, and the groom motions me over. "Rhett, did you know Oakley is a savant?" He laughs, touching Oliver's shoulder like he's an *aww shucks* hillbilly windup toy he found on his trip.

Oliver pretends to be oblivious as Bradley makes him the punch line, but let's be clear, Oliver is very aware they're a bunch of pricks.

"A savant of what?" Heath chuckles into a swig of beer.

"Time and tech," Oliver says, very seriously.

They snicker.

I couldn't stand them an hour ago when they mimicked Oliver like he was a hick. Now I wish this were a job that'd end with them believing they're getting arrested. Something that'd make them piss their pants at the very least. I swig the water, do a quick check on Phoebe, who's still on the dance floor. *She's okay.* Then back to Bradley, the groom.

"His daddy is also a tech whiz," I say plainly. "He lives in Belle Meade."

"Belle what?" Shane laughs.

"No, I've heard of it." Bradley grows more interested. "Famous people live there, don't they? Country singers?"

"Politicians, too." I jerk my head toward Oliver. "If you're lucky, Oak might show you the prototype his daddy's been working on for years. The tech is worth more than you've ever seen."

"Doubt that," Bradley laughs, but his intrigue flits over Oliver. "You have the prototype on you?"

"Just for today." Oliver shrugs like it's no big deal, and before long, the groom and his closest friends gather around as Oliver shows off a watch with phone technology.

It doesn't really work, but the tech industry is already projecting that watches will have the ability to make phone calls. It'll likely be a staple in years to come.

Right now, the prototype is just a flashy tech advancement that we pretend to have thanks to my little brother. Trevor made this dupe. It can't do anything but show the time. It looks fancy as fuck though, so when Oliver passes the watch to Bradley, I can't let him actually play around with the thing.

I shove into Heath as I rotate to the bar.

Heath falls forward into Bradley.

"You all right, man?!" I shout, trying to help them up, but I trip over their legs, spilling water—adding to the confusion. I bring them down to the floor. Oliver has already dropped the watch. I hear the *crunch*. Because I step on it.

"Fuck, fuck!" Oliver shouts, shoving Bradley and Heath off the pile, and I stand and slide backward. "You broke it!" He accuses Bradley.

"I . . . what? No . . ." He's slightly drunk, his glazed eyes drooping to the busted watch screen.

Oliver taps it. "It won't even turn on anymore. *Fuuuck*. Fuck. Do you know how much this costs? Do you?"

"Man, man, shhh." He puts his hands on Oliver's shoulders. "I can pay for it. Don't worry."

"You don't have it," I cut in, shaking my head, then I scan my surroundings. Where the fuck is Shane?

"I have it. *I have it*," Bradley assures, pulling out his wallet. "How much?"

My pulse is in my ears as soon as I see Shane chatting with Phoebe against the brick wall. He's in her space with two more of Bradley's friends. Her job is to distract the groom's party, which she's doing well.

I know this isn't a task she loves tonight, despite being great at it, and I've been keeping most of them out of her reach. She's holding the double shot of tequila he bought her, and every time they look our way, she skillfully draws their eyes back to her.

Go to her.

The instinct slams into me.

Don't leave her.

"You don't have a quarter mil," Oliver retorts.

Bradley pales. "Uh, not on me, but I can get you enough." He's either afraid of looking poor or what he offers next is chump change to him. "I'll write you a check for three hundred."

"Grand?" Oliver clarifies.

"Of course."

"That'll bounce," I say angrily, accusing him of scamming us.

He glares. "Where's the closest ATM?"

And there we go. Oliver and the mark depart with the promise that they'll be right back, and then I rush over to Phoebe. One of Bradley's friends—Pete—cuts off my path.

"Rhett! Man." Pete swigs his beer, and his shit-eating grin sets every shrill alarm off in my head.

I sidestep.

He follows.

"*Move*," I sneer.

He's taken aback. "Chill. We're cool."

I see through him. I know why he's separating me from Phoebe, and I don't hide the fact that I know exactly what he's fucking doing. My gaze is a hacksaw of lethal judgment.

Fear flickers in his eyes. "We're cool?" His breath is uneven. "We're not doing anything wrong."

"Yeah?" I get in his space. Bump up against his chest. He stiffens as I growl against his ear, "You drug her, you piece of shit, and you won't walk out of here on two fucking feet." Then I thrust him out of my way, and he's too startled to fight back.

His reaction sends me into overdrive. It's the dread of someone who's already committed the crime.

I'm not slow to reach her. Shane and some other ugly fuck are crowding Phoebe. She's careened as far back as she can. Her shoulders are mashed against the brick wall.

I tear through the guys, sloshing their glasses of whiskey.

"Hey!" Shane yells.

"We're getting out of here," I tell Phoebe in a hot Southern drawl, then I see her empty plastic cup. "You drank the double?" *Tell me you didn't drink it, Phebs.* Each tight breath scorches my lungs.

"Yeah . . . ?" Her face falls as mine hardens. "Is something . . . ? Did he . . . ?"

I can barely nod. My neck is scalding, burning steel.

Shane tries to wedge himself beside me, and I shove his chest with a furious hand, keeping him away from her.

He stretches his arms out at me. "What the fuck, man?" Then to Phoebe, he shouts, "You're really going to let your friend control you like this, Penelope?!"

Her horrified eyes are giant saucers. She spins on him. "Did you spike my drink?"

"What?" He acts offended.

"Did you?!" She raises her voice with real fury. I know just how real because involuntary tears glass her eyes. The bachelorette party starts to stare.

"No, I didn't *spike* your drink." Tiny creases form along his forehead.

He's lying.

Phoebe nearly crumples against the wall at the realization. Blistering rage erupts inside me, and I unleash on him, throwing a right hook into his jaw. My violent pulse hammers in my ears. I hear nothing but my heartbeat for a split second.

Then the commotion slams back at me as he stumbles into a wooden barrel and the crowd *ooohs*.

I spit my toothpick at Shane. "You like to roofie girls? You like 'em unresponsive? You wanna see how it feels, motherfucker?" I kick him in the crotch with my steel-toed boot. He yelps into a wail and rolls into a fetal position.

The bar lets out a collective wince.

I bend down very, very close to him, and against his ear, I sneer in a whisper—one void of my fake drawl, one entirely, completely real—"Guys like you shouldn't have a fucking cock. You're lucky I can't cut it off."

Shane chokes on air in mounting terror, as though believing I'm a sociopath. He pisses himself, his jeans darkening at the crotch. Well, at least I got that tonight.

His friends panic, and even though they didn't hear my last threat, they shy away from me. They'd rather leave him to the monster than risk being torn apart. Let the white-collar elite fight with checkbooks and backhanded, petty insults—I'm not doing it tonight.

They're already waving the bouncer over to come escort me out.

Some locals applaud me as I rise, and they even try to shoo the bouncer away. The fiddler entertains everyone with another high-octane song.

I'd say I grab Phoebe's hand first, but that might be a lie. She's pulling me out of the bar as much as I'm pulling her.

Broadway is packed, and we're pushing through the drunken commotion. "Hey, *hey*." I try to stop Phoebe, but she's tearing through the masses like she can outpace the drugs in her system.

"Text Oakley," she tells me while I have my phone out. "Tell him we're around the corner."

"Jesus, slow down, babe."

She halts suddenly and crushes into my chest. She shoves my arm. "Don't call me that. I'm not your *babe*, I'm your . . ."

Phoebe.

My chest collapses. "Penelope. I say this as nicely as I can—you're going the wrong *fucking* way."

She blinks, then notices we're heading into the most congested part of Nashville's night scene. "Where . . . that way?" She points back to where we came.

"Yeah."

Phoebe lets me lead, and in a matter of minutes, I bring her a few blocks from the bar we left. Then around the corner. To a narrow alley.

She squats beside the brick siding and gathers her hair with one hand. Again, she tells me, "Text him." *Her brother.*

I shoot both of her brothers a text.

Phoebe sticks her finger down her throat. She gags. Nothing comes out.

This is killing me. I crouch behind her.

Tears have pooled in her eyes. Sweat built on her forehead.

"Phoebe," I say gently and hold her hair for her. I wrap the brown strands around my fist.

She wipes at her watery eyes with a groan and a growl. "I should've known. *I knew.*" Her pain is mine. Her hurt, *mine.* "I knew they were the type to slip me something." A strained, wounded sound escapes her. "What was that about me being perceptive?"

"*Us*," I correct.

"This was on me. It's my body. I should've . . . I could've—"

"No, this isn't your fucking fault," I cut in harshly, even as guilt ransacks me. I didn't reach her fast enough. I should've been there sooner.

"Then why does it feel like it is?" Her voice cracks, and she keeps wiping at her eyes, uncontrollable tears falling. "I shouldn't have drunk it, but they kept pressuring me. I couldn't figure out how to convincingly get rid of it. *I* took that risk."

"*They* spiked your drink," I breathe angrily against her ear. "Don't let them make you feel like shit."

She's nodding a ton, squeezing her eyes shut.

I press my lips to her temple, almost kissing her. I'm holding her from behind. She's gripping on to my forearm like we're about to tandem-skydive and free-fall to the ground together. She's never been drugged before. Being roofied has been one of her biggest fears since she learned what it meant. I know that.

I saw how eager they were to get Phoebe wasted. They wanted her incapacitated. To take advantage of her, likely to rape her, and they wanted me out of the way to accomplish it. I should've sent her a signal. *She was too far away.*

I should've texted.

I should've run to her.

All night, I'll be replaying what happened and torturing myself with what I could've done to prevent it. Too close—they were too fucking close.

Phoebe rubs at her cheeks.

"Try again," I urge, not sure how long she has before the drugs take effect.

She tries to make herself puke with her middle finger. Nothing. She's shaking, too upset. "Rocky." She's scared.

With one hand, I hold her hair, and with the other, I stick my finger down her throat. Not letting up until she vomits, and she covers the pavement with what she drank tonight.

"Fuck," she cries, spitting out saliva. "Do . . . do you think that was everything?"

"I don't know." I help her again, and she throws up more. When her stomach is emptied, I grip my black shirt, pull it over my head, and let her use it as a towel. She wipes at her mouth. Then I help her to her feet.

She's woozy, more emotionally spent than physically.

No one pays us much attention. She's just another drunken mascara-smeared girl on the street, and I'm just another person taking care of a wasted friend.

Soon, a black Land Rover with tinted windows slows to the curb. Sliding into the back, I brush aside newer-looking *X-Men: First Class* comics off the seat and an older issue from the '70s titled *Nova*.

"Careful with those," Nova says from behind the wheel.

I pry another comic book out from under my ass. "Guess I don't need to ask what you were doing this whole time."

Nova twists around, probably to tell me off, but he sees his sister's clammy face. "Phoebe?"

"Where's Oliver?" she rasps.

"I'm picking him up next." He puts the car in gear but checks on her through the rearview. "Polar bear?"

She blinks a few times, battling tears. "Platypus."

It's a triplet thing. All I know is *platypus* means she feels like shit.

"What happened?" Nova asks when we're on the road.

"She was roofied," I say with bite, still furious. Partially with myself for letting it get this far. I failed her tonight, and she is the *last* person I ever want to fail on a fucking job. Her role puts her in some of the riskiest positions with outcomes that I can't . . . I can't let happen. Ever.

I smear a hand over my mouth, feeling sick to my stomach. Acid rises in my throat, and I swallow the burn.

Nova's fists tighten on the wheel. He says nothing. Doesn't ask if she's fine. I'm positive that's what *platypus / polar bear* is for.

Once Oliver is in the front seat, he puts his cowboy hat on the dash and shows me a check. "Daily limit at the ATM is five grand. I got him to write me a check for three hundred. But . . ."

It might bounce. "Cash it in the morning."

Oliver salutes me, but the gesture dies out when he catches sight of Phoebe. She's slumped down and still has my shirt balled in her hand. His face falls on me. "Don't tell me . . ."

"He roofied her," I say again. "Probably GHB." The date rape drug.

Oliver is not Nova. He reaches back and squeezes his sister's knee in comfort. "Phoebe? Are you hanging in there?"

She buries her face in her palms and groans, "I'm so stupid. Mom will be so upset. She's told me . . . *so many times*. To not . . . to look out for . . . to watch . . ."

"Breathe, Phebs." I tuck my arm around her shoulders.

"You're not stupid," Oliver reaffirms. "You're savvy and sly, and those pricks had it coming."

"We didn't do anything!" She sounds wounded. "Five grand? That's it? And I did *nothing*. I should've dick-kicked him."

"I dick-kicked him," I remind her.

"It should've been *me* . . . I was just stuck . . . in shock." Her eyes redden. She presses the heels of her palms to her watery gaze. "*Stop crying*," she tells herself. *"Stop it."*

I wrap both of my arms around her. It takes her a second, but she nestles her face in my bare chest and grips on to my bicep. She breathes deeper, her body gradually loosening. I clutch the back of her head, feeling her heartbeat start to slow.

It's helping me, truthfully. Feeling her ease. Feeling that she's here in my arms. In no one else's.

To be honest, I never want to let her go.

"Mom won't be upset," Oliver consoles. "She'll be happy you're not passed out in some guy's hotel room."

I clench my jaw. "Thanks for that mental image," I say dryly.

Phoebe doesn't respond. Her breath is shallow, and her eyelids go heavy.

"Phebs?" I whisper.

"I feel . . . weird. This isn't right." She's panicking. "It must still be in my system. It's still in there."

Shit. Fuck. I try to untense—for her sake. She's on me. She can feel my muscles flexing beneath her. "Take deeper breaths. I have you. Your brothers are right here, too."

Nova tries to peer over his shoulder, but he slams on the brakes as a group of sash-wearing girls jaywalk across the road. "How much did he dose her with?"

"I don't know. I didn't see him slip it in her drink."

Phoebe tries battling the effects. "Rocky." Her voice pitches in fear. "Everything is getting hazy. I can't . . . see . . ."

I pull her more across my lap, holding her in a cradle against my chest. She blinks slowly, like she's already consumed five vodka martinis past her limit.

I cup her face, and her hooded eyes fight to stay on mine. "You're going to pass out," I tell her. "Nova is going to drive to the nearest motel. He's going to rent a room, and you're going to wake up on a bed beside me."

I can't carry a limp girl into the Ritz. Sure, I can talk my way out of it if anyone asks. I can say she drank too much, but the elevators have cameras. So do the hallways, and I can't be sure if more management will ask questions in the morning, if I'll have to convince them I'm not the one who drugged her.

Our aliases aren't helping. The three of us aren't related to Phoebe in Nashville. We're all just college friends. It's safer to spend the night somewhere else.

"A motel?" she repeats.

"A motel." I nod. "I'm going to carry you out of the car and to bed."

Tears squeeze out of her eyes. "I hate this. *I hate this*." She tries to lift her arms, but they're deadweight at her sides. "Don't leave me."

I dip my head toward hers. "You think I'd let you out of my sight?"

She eases.

"The whole time you're out of it, I'll be with you, Phoebe."

"We'll all be there," Nova inserts.

And I try not to be rigid. Try not to wish it were only me that Phoebe needs. It's good she has her brothers. I'm not trying to replace them. I'm definitely not a sibling to her—I've never wanted to be her brother. I think it's very clear we've been something else to each other.

I thumb away her escaped tears and whisper against her ear, "I have you in my arms. I'm not letting you go. You're safe tonight." I repeat the sentiments a few times. "Then tomorrow, we pack our bags and we're leaving this shithole."

She shuts her eyes, her breathing slowing. "You wanted to stay in this shithole, too." That was before Nashville became the place where I failed her.

The truth is . . . I'd only stay in this city for her. I'd stay anywhere Phoebe is.

TWENTY-ONE

Rocky

NOW

I rack a shotgun. As I aim, a loud *bang* fires off on my right, and the quail drops from the sky, thudding to the grassy earthen floor.

Nova Graves lowers his gun before I even put my finger on the trigger.

Quail hunting is apparently Nova's fifth talent. Every time he shoots down a bird, his narrowed gaze finds Varrick among us. No love spared for his dad this summer. He sends him blatant threats every now and then.

And still, Varrick seems more impressed by his son's firearm skills than offended by his brusque attitude. It puts me on edge, but then again, I haven't been relaxed around Varrick since we moved into Stonehaven.

The Bennet brothers invited us to these private hunting grounds. A gentleman's outing of tracking and killing easy prey. This is Damian Bennet's way to try and ingratiate himself with Varrick since he believes the inheritance is still undecided. He whistles at his English setter, and the dog skips ahead of us to locate more quail.

"Nolan, goddamn," Trent says to him as we all follow the sniffing setter. "Save some for the rest of us."

He's begun calling Nova by his "legal" name ever since a dinner at Stonehaven, when Trent declared, "Nova is a girl's name, you know. Whoever nicknamed you must've hated you." He looked to me when he laughed, so I had to share in his ugly snicker. He pointed his butter knife at Phoebe's brother. "You should go by your real name. Nolan. It's stronger. *Better.*"

Nova didn't care to correct him.

"A name is what you make it," Varrick piped in, cutting his rib eye with a fork and knife. "You only believe it's a girl's name because that's all you've heard and seen. But now you know a man who's being called Nova. Your perceptions will change."

"Doubtful."

Trent has a pasta colander for a filter. He's not a suck-up. He was never admonished by his mommy and daddy for being rude. He believes he's above reproach, that no matter what he does, he will still be handed the golden goose on a silver platter.

So I wasn't shocked when he added, "The name makes the man, and anyone who calls him Nova is saying he's a pussy."

"*Trent*," Jake snapped.

"Jacob." Trent smirked back. "Don't be such a prude."

Phoebe almost threw her dinner roll at Trent. "The only *pussy* at this table—"

"Is who?" Trent taunted.

"The strong man makes the name." Varrick intercepted the

conversation right before I could. "The weak man would let the name make him."

"Don't quit your day job of leisure," Trent said into a strong sip of merlot. "I don't think you're going to make it as a poet, Varrick."

That "family" dinner was only a few days ago.

Varrick hearing Trent call his son *Nolan* has him slipping an unsubtle glance of annoyance across the grassy field. Then he checks on Nova, who slings the shotgun on his back. Either Varrick is ensuring he's okay or he wants Nova to see that he cares about him.

I wonder if he's been trying to appeal to each of us. Now his oldest son. He's attempting to find a connection. A way to reach him.

See, we both can't stand that prick. I'm on your side. I have your back, son.

To manipulate him?

I'm naturally skeptical. Always mistrusting of others. It's near impossible for me to believe Varrick is so genuine in his outreach toward us.

His desires feel thin yet sticky enough to make me question myself. He wants to get back at the godmothers. *Revenge*. He wants to use us to pull more cons. *Power.*

Still, I can't shake how easily he's handing everything to us.

We want Trent to be taken care of? *Done*.

We want the father figure we've never had? *Done*.

We want pure, relentless honesty that the godmothers didn't give us? *Done*.

This stinks of raw manipulation to me.

On the flipside, could he just be this fucking caring?

Yeah.

He's definitely up to something.

"I've been thinking," Trent says quietly to me, and I track his gaze over to Oliver, who strolls lackadaisically on the far left side of the field. He chews the end of a twig he pulled off a branch about a half mile back.

I have a great sense of where this conversation is going, and I already hate it. "Yeah?" I act more interested in my gun.

"You think they've fucked?" Trent whispers. "Oliver and Hailey?"

He can't get over her blushing at Oliver. It's starting to become a stupid fixation. I grimace at him, toning down what I want to be a threat. "She's my sister, man. I'm not contemplating her sleeping with anyone."

Trent groans, "*Please* don't be a stick-in-the-mud like my baby brother. Having Jake everywhere I turn this summer is bad enough. I don't want my best friend becoming him, too."

"No worries there." I lower my shotgun while we hike toward a meadow of wildflowers. "What does it matter if they've hooked up anyway? Hailey seems free-spirited. You like to do your own thing, not be tied down. Maybe you can make a deal with her." I scan the cloudy blue sky. "An open relationship or something."

Trent is fixated on Oliver. Barely listening to me. Great. "It's almost hard to picture her fucking anyone."

"Can't say I've ever tried to picture it," I note more harshly.

He laughs to himself, under his breath, then tips his head toward mine. "If Hailey is as amenable as Varrick *says*, then I should be able to get her to do anything I say." His eyes glimmer at the idea.

My blood is on fire. I raise my brows at him. Waiting for him to look me in the *fucking* eye. When he does, he asks, "What?"

"High standards. I thought you had them." I know he

doesn't. "You've slept with models. You called my sister a *two*, and you want to watch her have sex? That's a little . . ." I cringe at him.

He tears his gaze off Oliver. "You're probably right." He pats my back. "Always keeping me in check, Grey."

Not nearly how I'd *love* to.

We exchange a brief smile, and he drops his arm. "Speaking of the prude," Trent says as Jake comes over to our shooting zone. We're in a walking line.

Jake ignores the comment. "Varrick wants to talk to you about something, Trent."

"You bore him already?" Trent tries to reach up and pat Jake's face, but Jake bucks backward to avoid the belittling gesture.

"Bye." Jake points him over to Varrick on the far left.

"Sorry you have to suffer with Jake," Trent says to me, then adjusts the strap of his shotgun on his back. "Be back soon." He pats my shoulder blade again. We watch Trent head over to Varrick.

"*Bye, bitch*," I say under my breath to Jake. "I think you dropped the second word. I picked it up for you, your moral highness."

He smiles, one that's a little too fleeting. Then he casts a quick glance backward. "Should he be behind us?"

Trevor left his zone in the walking line about fifteen minutes ago. About ten feet behind us, he's sulking, kicking rocks, and holding the shotgun like a barbell behind his neck. It's unloaded. He made me empty the tube and confirm there were no shells *four* times.

Knowing Trevor's rap sheet, I can see how Jake would be nervous my brother would put a bullet in Varrick or Trent's chest.

Honestly, I'm more worried about Nova.

"He's fine," I whisper to Jake. "He was accidentally shot in the foot as a kid. He just doesn't want to be near any of us in case we fuck around and he finds out."

Jake's brows jump in surprise.

"It still shocks you"—I read him easily—"what we've been through, even knowing who we are?"

"Your past lives are endless." He keeps his gun at his side, like I do. "I'm not sure I could ever uncover everything." He's staring at Oliver, but in a much different manner than Trent just did.

It brings me back to the night of Hailey's onslaught of tears. When the two of us finally made it to Stonehaven, I figured she would beeline for Phoebe. Seek comfort from her best friend.

We found Nova, Phoebe, and Jake seated around the stainless-steel kitchen island. They were eating leftover seafood paella that Varrick's private chef made the night before. The instant they saw Hailey's runny mascara and tear tracks, they shot to their feet.

She ran straight into Jake's arms. No hesitation. No question. No pause.

He wrapped his arms around my sister with a wall of empathy. Erected to protect and defend to the absolute death. I'd never liked Jake more than in that moment.

"What'd my brother do?" he asked me, his hatred for Trent so visceral. I could feel the same scalding ember burning through me.

"Where's Oliver?" Nova questioned.

"Go get him," I answered Nova first. "He's still at the party." Nova was already grabbing his utility jacket off the barstool. Out the door in a flash. I learned Trevor was in the tower room trying to get cell signal to talk to Sidney. Safe and accounted for.

After I explained what happened, the girls decided they'd crash in Phoebe's room together. Phoebe took out pints of Moose Tracks for the night in, Hailey's favorite ice cream.

Jake wanted to wait up for Oliver. He was stewing.

Someone is getting punched tonight, I thought. My money was on Nova decking Jake for when Jake would attempt to swing at Oliver.

So I stayed up with Jake to play referee.

I wanted less bloodshed for my sister's sake. She was dealing with enough, and she didn't need two guys literally fighting over her. I doubted they knew she was pregnant.

We waited in the main living room. The antique grandfather clock ticked in our silence.

"He didn't do anything wrong." I defended my girlfriend's brother, a guy I'd known my *entire* life. "Oliver had to act like she was just another girl at a party."

"He didn't *have* to be a jerk. He didn't *have* to treat her like . . ." He shook his head, his anger bringing him to his feet.

I watched him pace. "You're blowing this out of proportion."

"All Trent does is objectify women." He outspread his arms. "I didn't think I'd have to worry about *Oliver* joining in on that with *Hailey*."

"First off, he was flirting with her like he flirts with *everyone*, and then he brushed her off. She started crying. That's it." I understood Hailey's reaction made this seem worse, but I wouldn't lie to the Knight of the Moral Round Table. "Secondly, I guarantee you it's going to be worse from now on that Trent knows Hailey is even semi-attracted to Oliver. He was doing what he could to protect her from your egomaniac brother without sacrificing his position in the job, which *is* important. She can't be around Trent in any setting like that without us there. Trust us, this is all we've *ever* done. We know what we're doing."

Jake inhaled a sharp breath. Not even a minute later, Oliver and Nova showed with urgent strides and concerned eyes, drenched like the boat ride had been rough.

First thing Oliver asked was "She okay?" He shrugged off his windbreaker and noticed Jake on his feet.

"She'll be fine," I told him. "I can't say the same about him."

Oliver pushed his wet hair out of his face, assessing Jake's heated stance. "You okay, Koning?"

"No."

Nova rested his ass on the armrest of the couch, positioning himself to where I knew this was going to get ugly.

I edged up on the end of the sofa. Did not want to catch a stray punch to the face, but I prepared myself for the inevitability. Because my dumb ass was going to insert myself in this drama. All I could think was Phoebe was going to be pissed she missed this.

"Something I did?" Oliver asked, approaching him without fear. Unafraid of towering apex predators since he's also one.

"Hailey" was all Jake said.

"Yeah." Oliver lifted his foot, just to pry off his soaked leather loafer. Right one, then the left. He chucked the expensive shoes aside. "One of us is good. One of us is bad. And after tonight, you're scared that I'm bad *for her*."

"You don't *have* to be—"

"You don't want to change me." Oliver stepped closer in challenge.

Jake tensed, his arms uncrossing and hands clenching.

Nova rose slowly off the armrest.

I had to follow suit, standing, but my brows furrowed the longer I observed them. How their gazes danced over each other. How Jake sheltered too many breaths.

"Because deep down," Oliver said, "you know I'm exactly what she needs. And it drives you *mad*."

"Is that your specialty then?" Jake rotated as Oliver circled him, their eyes fastened together. "Driving people insane?"

"You tell me." Oliver inched closer and closer, testing how near he could get. His chest pressed against Jake's. "How far down the rabbit hole have I led you, Koning?"

Two pulsing beats passed.

And then Jake fisted Oliver's wet shirt and shoved him hard against the wall.

Nova sprung forward, and I caught his bicep, yanking him back. He tore out of the hold too easily. He just had to be the fucking Hulk when it came to protecting his brother. Reaching out again, I restrained him from behind.

Jake hadn't thrown a punch yet. He white-knuckled Oliver's shirt, and Oliver had his head braced against the wall, staring straight into Jake with challenge. Egging him on. Their chests were rising and falling too hard.

Oliver had a glimmer of a smile in his eyes. "You going to kiss me or hit me, Koning?"

At this, Jake released his clutch and stepped back.

"Neither," Oliver tsked, giving him a once-over. "Well then, I have somewhere to be." He moved around Jake. "I plan to go remind Hailey what she means to me."

Nova had already stopped fighting against me. We both stood still as Oliver left a very tense Jake in his wake.

Then Jake spun around to ask, "He's straight?"

"He's straight." Nova nodded but then looked to me to see if I knew any differently.

Oliver is a flirt, but it doesn't mean he's attracted to everyone. He's kissed guys before. Said it did nothing for him. I've kissed guys. Definitely did do something for me, but that is a past life. In this life now, my sole attraction is Phoebe.

"Straight," I confirmed.

Jake let out a deep noise of vexation. "And he knows I'm bi. So he's messing with me."

Nova frowned at the hallway where Oliver disappeared. "I've never seen him do this with a guy." *Me either.*

Jake rubbed the side of his strained neck. "I'll see you in the morning." Oliver was right. He was absolutely driving Jake mad, and by the way they were looking at each other, I think Jake liked it.

I think Oliver liked it, too.

Jake left, and Nova scraped a hand over his buzz cut. "What the hell are they doing?"

"Being fucking messy." I thought about my sister being pregnant. "Be grateful it's not for us to figure out."

So while we're hunting for quail—as Jake stares at Oliver in the walking line—I know now it's not just fascination drawing him in. It's deeper attraction.

Add in the fact that my sister is allergic to commitment as much as Oliver and Jake are, and this is going to be a rude awakening when the guys learn a baby is on the way.

I have literally *zero* desire to be the one to unleash this news. But there'll be a point where I might need Oliver to know. Just to better protect her on the job. We're constantly around drugs and alcohol, and he should know Hailey can't consume either to save face or to gain social influence or to appease Trent.

Oliver would want to know.

But so would Jake.

Way too complicated.

The English setter startles birds off a thorny shrub. I raise my gun as several quails flush into the air.

Nova shoots one. I manage to hit another. After the birds fall, Varrick claps for me. It reads as genuine applause.

I believe he wants me to like him.

Why wouldn't he?

I tip my head in appreciation. Showing he's growing on me. He knows I've never trusted Everett, Elizabeth, or Addison. I've said as much.

Our gazes hold for too long.

He smiles a little more. He likes me. Maybe he does. Maybe he's enjoying this. Maybe he likes toying with us. Maybe he likes that I can see through his bullshit like he can see through mine.

Because how could he ever think I'd trust him after he admitted to killing my birth family? I'm good, but tricking a grifter isn't the same as duping a run-of-the-mill narcissist. We're both using the same playbook.

I just don't know who's ahead in the game.

TWENTY-TWO

Phoebe

Living at Stonehaven has its benefits: made-to-order meals by a private chef, free rent, a million-dollar view, and *Rocky*.

He's been slipping into my room to spend the nights with me. A perk we didn't have when we were split between the loft and the boathouse. There are even days I try to convince myself that summering at the mansion in the sea is worth living three doors down from the ever-deplorable Trent Waterford.

But this morning is *not* one of those days.

I squint into the rising sun, watching *The Ithaka* float away toward the mainland. "This is getting ridiculous," I growl out and toss my purse into the dinghy.

This is the fifth morning in a row that Trent has beat us to the boat. We *all* agreed the yacht would leave the dock at seven a.m., and he's consistently woken up earlier each and every day this week just to convince the crew to give him a private charter to the mainland. Leaving us all to cram into the small dinghy, which is about as fun to ride in as one of those old water coasters.

My ass goes numb. My hair gets knotted to hell. And I will undoubtedly have a see-through white blouse by the end thanks to the rough waters.

Damian Bennet grimaces, equally annoyed, and his nose curls up at the dinghy as Hailey squishes in beside me. He removes his Persol sunglasses and nods back to the mansion. "I'm going to wait for *The Ithaka* to return."

"Ditto." His little brother, Sandon, follows him up the dock toward a set of winding stairs cut through the rock. They lead to the stately front door, complete with a bronze wolf knocker. Sometimes I remind myself that this is one of the most famous properties in Connecticut and not just a fun little vacation at a B&B.

"Anyone else coming?" Jake asks, standing up in the dinghy. He balances effortlessly, and I have to wonder how many sailing lessons he took as a kid.

Nova scowls, his face already turning a shade of green. "I puked last time. So it's a pass."

Oliver unpeels a piece of gum. "I thought you had that fancy-pants art dealer coming into the museum this morning."

Nova and Oliver have been keeping up their fake personas as museum curator and small-town therapist.

My oldest brother groans, running two hands atop his head. "I'll get Angela to fill in."

Last week I asked if Angela was cute, and laser beams might as well have zapped out of Nova's eyes. She's apparently *eighteen* and an intern at the museum. *Oops*.

Oliver slips the gum into his mouth and checks his phone. "I can't miss my eight o'clock appointment."

Jake appraises the sky. "We need to beat the storm." He

makes a quick gesture. "Hurry." Clouds darken ominously above us, and Oliver hops on board while blowing a bubble and popping it with his tongue. He's as steady as can be, and I'm not shocked he squishes on the other side of Hailey.

Her nose is buried in a paperback.

Oliver slides on sunglasses, then slips a casual arm down Hailey's shoulders, his hand hanging across her chest. She never pries her eyes off the pages, not even as she reaches up and touches his knuckles, his wrist, as if to ensure he's really there.

Their fingers lightly brush and hook.

Jake keeps looking away, then back at them. Away, then back. Each time, his muscles flex more.

I think it's safe to say my best friend is in a full-blown love triangle. The real kind. Not like the manufactured one between Rocky, me, and Jake. Emphasized by her admission they've been sleeping in the same bed this summer.

"We just sleep," she explained. "I mean, they do things to help me sleep." I'd known one of them was rocking her world to bed when she admitted it to her doctor. I did not know it was *plural*.

"They?" I almost choked on my pancake that morning. The two of us were eating breakfast alone in the dining room before our shift at the club. I swigged some cranberry juice. "Like together? At the same time?" I hesitated to ask further, because one of the guys is my brother. But curiosity can really kill since it did not stop me.

"No." She stirred brown sugar into her oatmeal. "But maybe . . . I don't know. Sometimes one will watch me get off, but I think they're watching each other, too."

"Like a stare-down?"

"Kind of, yeah."

"Hailey motherfucking Tinrock." I practically sang her name. I stood up and applauded. "Two guys are getting off fighting over you. You know what this means?"

She smiled a little. "I'm a mess. To never be replicated."

"You have swiped your V-card."

"Swiped that a long time ago, Phebs." I still can't believe Oliver was the one who did the swiping.

"*V* for vixen," I clarified. "And you say you're all brains. You are a very hot, very desirable catch that two men are trying to pluck from the sea."

"Which might be why I'm in this predicament." She pointed her spoon at her flat belly. No bump yet. "It is kind of nice though," she said in thought.

I sank back in my chair. "Getting off times two?"

"Being cared for . . ." She swirled her oatmeal again. "Being loved."

It was then that I realized this wasn't some wild summer fling, a romance meant to last one dizzying season. "I like that part, too. Of being with Rocky," I said quietly, and we shared a smile.

Her *Mystic Pizza* life in Connecticut is turning out to be as drama filled and complex as mine, but maybe it's how it was always supposed to be for us. Twisted, messy, and so far out of the ordinary.

On the dinghy, I catch Oliver looking over at Jake. He stares at him for even longer than I think Jake realizes. I know they both want what's best for Hailey. Beyond that, I really have no clue what they're thinking.

Jake ensures no one else waits for the dinghy ride, then unties the rope from the cleats on the dock.

Trevor Tinrock sleeps until noon, so he's not boarding, and Rocky always manages to have his BFF tell him the yacht's "amended" departure time. He'd clue us in if it wouldn't blow brownie points with Trent.

Hailey flips a page in the paperback. Reading is her go-to boat distraction. This bumpy, ass-numbing ride can't be easy while she's sixteen weeks pregnant. But to keep her secret, she hasn't made it a big deal. So of course, I try to at least help my best friend where I can.

"Jake?" I call out as he starts the motor. "Could we try to keep this gentle, perhaps?"

He looks at me like I've lost it. "We're going to be lucky we make it before the skies open up."

Great. *Awesome.*

I locate the nearest life preservers and hope for the best.

Arriving at Victoria Country Club in a soaked blouse from seawater and rain can't be demeaning if the owner of the club arrived in the same fashion. Half the guests and staff drool over Jake's carved abs, on full display as his wet shirt molds to his chest.

He's too hurried to even notice, disappearing toward the men's locker room in a flash. With the women's locker room out of order due to some mold issue, Hailey and I end up in the bathroom trying to dry out our blouses under the hand dryers.

She bites the end of her thumbnail.

It's hard to tell what's distressing her when it could be so many different things, and I ache to just take *one* thing off her plate. I can't, obviously, carry the baby for her, so that leaves the thing I'm good at. The thing that I'm trained to do.

"Hails," I say over the *whoosh* of the hand dryer. "What's the fruit this week?"

She glances down at her stomach. Still no pooch. "An avocado," she tells me. "I-I think I'm going to start showing in a couple weeks. According to the internet at least." She removes her lip piercings in the mirror, then tucks them into her pants pocket.

"Let's talk work."

"Work or work-work?"

"Work-work." I refer to the con job, and I twist my head a little just to triple-check no one is in the stalls before I ask, "What part is stressing you out?"

"Trent keeps asking me about Oliver. Like . . . *teasing* me about him." *Asshole.* "And Rocky said I need to show disinterest in the whole conversation, but it's hard." She sighs at the hand dryer. "Even if I pretend to read a book, I still feel my face get red. I can't turn that off."

"You and my brother hid a romance from us for *years.* You're experts."

"We hid that we were hooking up," she counters. "What's happening now feels different . . ." Her cheeks redden. "I'm blushing, aren't I?"

I shake my head. "No. You're ghostly."

"Liar. There are mirrors all around us, Phebs."

"I can't help myself. Lying is in my DNA," I say, and we both smile together.

Hers vanishes into a wave of nerves. "I worry Trent won't even want to propose if he thinks I'm in love with someone else. Then I worry that if he does propose, he won't believe I want to be his wife if I'm in love with another man."

"You're way overthinking this."

"It's what I do." The *whoosh* suddenly stops, and Hailey slams a hand at the button to restart the dryer for me. Her platinum hair frizzes around her face.

"Not anymore," I declare, keeping my shirt under the dryer. "You need to stay in the moment. Not bunny-hop twenty steps ahead of us and obsess over all the different outcomes. Okay, think about Trent having gangrene on his penis when you're around him. That is your *mission*."

"To visualize Trent's decaying dick?"

"Yes." I nod heartily.

She laughs. "That might work." After a deep breath, she sways back into the sink with a faraway smile. She's blushing again.

"Oliver?" I ask.

"Jake." Hailey grips the sides of the sink. "You know that two-tenant rule he had for the loft? The one he was adamant about us obeying when we first moved in?"

"I remember." Jake had been a major stickler for the rules upon our arrival.

"Apparently, he didn't really mind if we had a third roommate. He was just enforcing it a ton because when he first saw Rocky with us, he thought he was an abusive mark who stalked you here. He didn't want him staying with us for that reason." She tucks a piece of damp hair behind her pierced ear. "He was protecting us before he even knew us, Phebs. I didn't think men like him even existed. I thought they were imaginary."

My lungs swell. "He is a really good one, your Jake."

Her face is fire-engine red when I call him *hers*. "He's not mine." I hear the uneasy tone.

"Sorry." I shift uncertainly, seeing her get a little weird about it. "Would you rather be with Oliver then?" I love that for my brother, but this whole situation just feels too complicated to aggressively root for anyone.

"I don't want to make the choice, and maybe the answer is no answer at all."

My fingers slip off my blouse, letting it hang. "I don't follow."

"No commitments. No ties that bind. They can go fly free. I'm releasing them from being devoted to me."

There is no way my brother can stop caring about Hailey in the same way that she can't stop blushing at the mere *mention* of him. And Jake—if Jake didn't love her, he wouldn't look so tortured every time she has to hang out with his dickhead brother.

She plucks some luxe paper towels from the basket by the sink. The ones Katherine has told us explicitly are *for members only.* She uses them to squeeze out the water from the damp ends of her hair. Her eyes mostly on the floor.

"Hails," I whisper. "I think you're just scared. Maybe the next step is finally telling them what's going on? I'm the *only* person who knows you're pregnant, and that pool should open up, especially while you're a principal on this type of job."

"Carter knows," she reminds me. "He's been telling me to loop in the whole team."

I raise my hands to the air. *Thank you.* "Yes, I agree with our beloved forger."

"Of course you do. If you were me, you would've already told Rocky. You would've told your brothers and Trevor and Jake. You would've let them help you." Her eyes well. "You're so much braver than I am."

I used to assure her that she's smarter than me in comparison, but I don't think it's what she needs to hear anymore. "You're just as brave." I say the truth strongly. "Braver even."

Her chin tries not to quake.

"You're doing a hard task out of your mastermind wheelhouse while dealing with an unexpected pregnancy and a romance with two eligible bachelors. All in a town that gossips about literally everything, including a restaurant's supposed shrimp burglar, which turned out to be a *cat* stealing prawns off the patio."

She lets out a laugh, the sound softening into a smile. "I love it here."

"Me too," I murmur with the same tenderness. "Good thing we technically don't have to leave."

"Technically, yeah, we can stay if all goes to plan."

We have to execute this job. "We will." I nod, my ribs tightening.

I won't screw up.

But I'm not a main player on the board. I've chosen to sit this one out. This isn't going to come down to me anymore. All I can do is help Hailey. "You ready?" I tuck my decently dried blouse into my black slacks.

She crumples the paper towels. "I'm going to tell them."

"Wait, what?" I have whiplash. My jaw slowly drops to the floor.

"I'm going to tell Jake and Oliver about the baby. *Today.*" She throws the paper towels in the trash. "They deserve to know. They *need* to know. I'm going to be brave."

I nearly start crying at the strength in her voice, and I hug my best friend. Again, I remind her, "You already are."

Tighter than tight, she hugs me back.

I wish we could spend the day together, but Katherine Rhodes sends me a rude text about mimosa duty. Soon, we go our separate ways. Hailey to serve the ladies at the pool and me to man the sunroom.

After I deliver four palomas and one Corona to Jake loyalists (aka the awesome ladies who wake at the ass crack of dawn to hit plastic balls), I enter the very empty dining room.

I can't believe I'm saying this, but I miss the midday rush.

I miss being pulled every chaotic direction. I'm actually *pissed* so many decided the Mariner's Club is "trendier" when VCC is ten times better. Even with the elitist undertones.

At least we're not harboring a misogynist named Trent Waterford.

It annoys me that the town is still determined to pick sides between the Koning brothers, and it's translated to them talking with their pocketbooks. Team Jake versus Team Trent has become Victoria Country Club versus the Mariner's Club.

It's a petty feud, but bored townspeople aren't beneath *petty*. If I weren't so completely and wholeheartedly Team Jake, maybe—*maybe*—I'd find entertainment value in the drama. The reality is that I want to stab anyone who tells me they're leaving VCC for the Mariner's, which is why I am staying away from knives.

It's also why I am throwing extra love to those who have stayed. In the form of pleasant smiles.

It's not hard to maintain real ones when I've grown fond of so many people here. Like little old Meara O'Neil, acting like Fizzle royalty while slurping soda and asking for help with the *New York Times* daily crossword. I do get excited every time I see her rosy-cheeked face.

I bend down behind the bar to restock my tray with Evian from the mini fridge.

"The pool chairs are for *guests*." Katherine's voice grows loud as she walks into the room. "Not staff."

I freeze in a squat behind the bar. Hidden from view. *Ugh.* I didn't intend to accidentally eavesdrop on my boss today.

"Hailey is on a break. It's one hour." And that's Jake talking. Make that *two* bosses.

"We have a standard to uphold here," Katherine tells him.

"A standard your mother set, whether you appreciate it or not. Membership dues are down by fifty-five percent. We've had members . . . *drop out*," she whispers as if the bubonic plague is spreading. "How do you expect anyone to return if they see servers using guest spaces? They're not paying members, Jake. It's not fair to those who are."

"It's one hour," Jake says carefully, gently. "Just today. She won't hurt the reputation of the club, and if she does, we can discuss ways to fix it together."

He's so in deep for Hails. Because there's no way in hell he'd let *me* use the lounge chairs. He told me to stop stealing peppermints from the front desk last week.

Katherine lets out a resigned sigh. "Just today."

The room goes quiet, and I wait a solid minute before standing up. Sure enough, they're gone. My stomach overturns as I process what Katherine said. I knew membership had dropped, but I didn't realize we were at half capacity already.

Between *this*, the ragers Trent is throwing that are slowly destroying the Koning estate, and the ongoing legal disputes, Jake must be under a lot of stress.

I don't think "baby news" will be a lovely addition to his issues. Hailey wants to tell him today . . . It'll be fine.

I empathize with her hesitation now. I'm sure she hasn't wanted to front-load this baggage onto him.

I pull my hair into a high pony. "Could this day get any worse? Signs point to . . ." I trail off, just smiling as I think of Rocky. He'd totally be giving me shit for even floating the question in the air. His superstitious soul would say I just jinxed myself.

Good thing I don't carry the same belief.

Heading back to the sunroom, I make my rounds. Not one

but *three* of the ladies give me compliments on my morning brunch recommendation after I tell them to steer clear of the lobster eggs benedict and go for the duck confit hash.

Sipping on her soda, Meara O'Neil watches the news on the only television in the sunroom. An ornate gold frame surrounds the screen like it'll hide the fact that it's a TV.

Meara waves me over, which is a departure from her usual intense eye contact to get my attention. When I approach, she asks hurriedly, "Phoebe, turn this up, dear?"

The remote is already secured in my back pocket for this very purpose. I smile—at least I am excelling at something. But when I turn the volume up and focus on the television screen, my lips begin to drop. "Meara, this has been playing for weeks. It's *old* news."

She shoos me with a hand. "They might be saying something new."

Unlikely.

The news anchor repeats the viral headlines. "As we've been reporting, Lily Calloway, daughter of the founder of Fizzle, is a sex addict. She has slept with over fifty men. But today we have breaking news . . . It's been *confirmed* she hired male sex workers."

Meara gasps.

I almost gasp with her—we have a shared love of tabloid drama. The entire sunroom explodes in a wave of whispers. I stare at images of a thin brunette, her posture a little awkward and her green eyes downcast like she's camera shy. *Well, someone is having a worse day than all of us*.

Honestly, I feel bad for this Lily girl. No one should have their sex life blasted on national news, especially if she does have a problem, and I wouldn't be shocked if she's being harassed by the media if this is *still* airing on TV.

Meara side-eyes her glass of Fizz soda like it's somehow diseased. *Dear God.*

I slip the remote into my back pocket and escape toward the state-of-the-art gym to see if any of the members need an Evian or cold towel. I get as far as the windowed rotunda when a postman arrives with a stack of newspapers fresh off the press.

"I'll take those," I say like a dutiful employee. I am nothing if not *helpful*. Doing menial tasks. Not at all nosy.

"Just sign here, ma'am." He passes me a clipboard along with a few envelopes addressed to the Konings' LLC.

I consider signing Jake's name. Or even Katherine's. I've memorized their signatures out of habit. I should be a better version of myself and simply write, *Phoebe*, but self-preservation takes over, and I do a slightly immoral thing.

I scrawl an illegible curly signature that could read as *SpongeBob*. I hand the pen back with a smile. I'm going to hell.

At least Rocky will be there. It morphs my fake smile into a flush-inducing real one.

I've started thinking maybe it's okay to not be honest *all* the time. Is it possible to give up the pieces of grifting I hate, but not reject everything I learned? Or will I have to hang up my con artist cap for good?

Questions of the future seem too far away to grasp when I can barely predict what'll happen when everyone knows Hailey is pregnant. *Today.*

God, I can't believe that's happening today.

I'm nervous *for* her.

The postman leaves, and I slip the envelopes in my back pocket. (Will give those to Jake later, I'm not a total asshole.) I set the newspapers beside a glass dispenser of cucumber water, and I pluck a *Victoria Weekly* off the stack. Immediately flipping to the gossip column written by Sidney Burke.

SIDNEY SAYS

Entries for this year's Victoria's Sweetheart are now open. New residents = new competition this year?

Trent Waterford seen out with Hailey Thornhall once again! This time, a stroll through the park with Phoebe Smith and Grey Thornhall. A double date, perhaps?

Looks like a romance between Phoebe and Jake isn't being rekindled anytime soon. Sad news for the Watersmith shippers.

Varrick Wolfe's quest for an heir continues with the Konings, Bennets, Thornhalls, and Smiths summering at the infamous Wolfe property: Stonehaven. Sources say he'll be naming the heir in the coming months. Be sure to watch from the pier to catch a glimpse of their comings and goings from the mansion.

Sidney has been covering the Wolfe drama since it began. Trevor told her the reason we're all summering at Stonehaven. Gossip abounded. I've overheard some ladies at the pool putting bets on the outcome. The attention is good. It pulls people's eyes off the growing discontent between Jake and Trent.

I keep reading, glazing over lines about a florist dating Mr. Ortiz and college students forking the dean's yard, and then the warmth of a figure prickles my body.

Someone is behind me.

I see a male arm reaching inches away from my hip to grab a *Weekly* instead of politely asking me to move.

I whirl around on him. Not my boyfriend. Not any guy I would want within five feet of me. Could today get any worse?

Signs point to *yes*.

Because it's Weston fucking Burke. Sidney's dad. He wears all-white attire as if he's posed for leisure sports like croquet or golf.

I can't tell what I hate more—his self-satisfied expression, like he one-upped Rocky just by finding me alone, or the fact that he's not budging backward and offering me much-needed space.

"Phoebe," he greets. "Beautiful afternoon for a *Cognac*. Isn't it?"

The fact that *Cognac* has become a sexual innuendo between us is nauseating and partially my own doing. At times, I wish I was never the new girl who flirted with the widowers to "appease" them during my shift. I wish I never felt like I had to.

Still, I am glad.

I'm glad that in almost a year, they haven't checked out another server's ass. I'm glad they've fixated on me. I worry if Jake hires a new girl, their attention will divert to her, and for what? It's not like they're tipping us.

I look away from him.

"Why don't you go get me one, sweetheart?" I feel his gaze drip down me. "I'll wait." He unfurls the paper.

I don't respond. I don't entertain him. I don't ask why he's still a member at VCC when he should be flocking to the Mariner's Club with the other widowers. I don't care if he's a rat come to spy and snitch. Or if he can't leave the delicious tomato bisque served on Mondays. The best way to crush his superiority complex is to deem him *irrelevant*.

I promised Rocky that I wouldn't engage if this were to happen. So I sidestep away.

Weston matches my movement.

I do my best to holster a glare.

"I have a question for you before you go," he says casually. "If you've broken up with Jake Waterford, why do you continue to serve here? Doesn't it make it a little awkward?"

Fire flames my insides. "Get out of my way. Please and thank you." My pleasantries sound excessively snide. *Sorry not sorry, Rocky.* I have the ability to contain a glare, but I don't want to. I want to explode on this rich prick until his flesh bubbles and melts off his bones.

"It's a simple question," Weston says with heat. "No need to be rude."

"Why are you such a perv?" I retort. "That's a simple one, too."

He lets out a disgusted noise. "Excuse me?"

Yes, I'm *so* unbecoming. I will gladly act my age—younger even—and be exceedingly *uncouth* if it even marginally turns him off. When his seedy gaze crawls over my body, I only see a man wanting to *take*. Like I'm up for grabs. Like my voice means absolutely *nothing* in every single power play.

Fuck him.

"You know what I believe, Phoebe?"

"Like I care." I try to push past him without making physical contact.

He blocks me against the refreshment table. His hands on the wooden edge on either side of my waist. Confining me. *Shit.* I glower as he adds, "I believe you love being ordered around—"

I knee him in the dick.

He buckles forward with a pained grunt, and I slip so far out of his reach, my pulse skipping away from me in abrupt panic, but fury still sears my veins. Fury still grows, vaporizing my flight response. Fuck him. "*Fuck you*," I snap as I breathe harder and harder. "For thinking you can just trap me and make me listen to whatever sick thought crosses your mind. Fuck you for thinking that's at all *okay*, and, *no*, I will not get you a Cognac. Get it yourself."

Weston is red in the face from me crushing his family jewels and from . . . anger. I'm supposed to serve his every desire, and definitely without the hostility or the attitude.

His tightened eyes veer to the security camera near the crown molding. There are very few in the club, and none capture sound. Since day one, I've been aware of the ones that exist and precisely where they're located.

"You'll be fired for this," he threatens into a cough. "This is *assault*."

Fuck him five *billion* times over. "You harassed me."

"I was grabbing a newspaper to read my daughter's column." He straightens up, clearing the wounded knot out of his throat. "You were in my way." He fists the paper and smacks the wrinkles out of it on his thigh.

"Then ask me to move," I growl out, just so ready for men like him to feel a deep, unrelenting sting. To be singed long enough to be *scarred*. "Jake and I might be broken up, but we're still friends. He won't fire me. So go ahead and try." Weston has no authority over me here. Not with Claudia gone.

I ride the high of my burning rage, and I flip him off with two fingers. Hoping he detests *this* juvenile behavior.

He grinds his jaw. Quietly seething.

This feels way too good. I pocket the small victory, internally smiling in vindication. I move to find Hailey so I can rehash everything to her. When I take a single step toward the dining room, Weston follows me.

Ughhhhh.

"About that Cognac," he says.

I stop in place. "Shut up about your stupid *Cognac*," I

retort. "I will *never* serve you. Not on my hands, not on my feet, not on my back or my fucking deathbed."

He releases a biting laugh, then gazes around the windowed rotunda as natural light streams onto the white marble. "You think I was planning to stay? I've already sent in my application to the Mariner's Club. Where the service respects *decorum*. This place has gone downhill fast. Hiring any whore who comes into town."

His words don't pierce me. I outstretch my arm toward the long hallway that leads to the main entrance of the country club. "Hated to have you here. Glad to see you go." I force the fakest smile alive. "Byeeeee." My overly feminine, high-pitched tone and joyful shoulder shrug cause his face to sour.

Good.

But he passes too close to me. I try not to visibly stiffen at his nearness. He sneers, "You're a *child*."

"I am decades younger than you." I glare. "Happy you finally noticed." I swat the air like he's a pest I'm shooing out the door. "Go—" He seizes my wrist midair, and I tug back, but he clamps harder. "*Get off me*," I grit out.

"Weston Burke, isn't it?"

I go motionless at the smooth masculine tone as casual footsteps clap toward us from the long hallway, and Weston immediately releases his painful grip at the sight of Varrick Wolfe.

My father.

TWENTY-THREE

Phoebe

I jerk away from Weston, my heart skipping several beats as Varrick nears him. *Why is he here?*

Varrick *owns* the Mariner's Club. There's no reason he should be milling about on enemy territory. Plus, he's made a point to keep us all in the loop on his comings and goings from Stonehaven. I know he has lunch with my mom on Thursdays. I know which barbershop cuts his hair. I know he hates the smell of Gulp Seafood & Lounge and will walk one street over to avoid it.

He's been suspiciously *open*, considering before this summer he'd been as secretive and elusive as Ghostface. Oliver thinks he wants on a team so badly that he's trying everything to gain our trust.

I'm not so sure.

My suspicions only mount with him showing up here.

Varrick comes into spitting distance of Weston with a steady, confident stride, like he's made to withstand an inferno. Like he's the one who starts them. He wears a tailored blue sport coat, casual white tee, and khaki slacks. No strand of his slicked-back dark brown hair tickles his temple or is ruffled out of place.

"Yes, I'm Weston Burke." Weston's eyes narrow into pinpoints on him. "I don't believe we've met." He's gauging the temperature of the situation.

Varrick hasn't approached with hostility. There are no fiery footprints left in his wake. He's nonconfrontational. Friendly. He might as well be outstretching a hand before he takes it out of his pocket. Yet he says nothing in response.

To which Weston adds, "You must be Varrick Wolfe."

"Must be." He cranes his neck toward me but keeps his eyes on Weston. "There's a word we use for someone who puts their unwanted, unsolicited hands on a woman."

Weston balks. "I didn't—that was a misunderstanding."

"A misunderstanding implies *I* misunderstood what I saw—"

"Varrick—"

"Mr. Wolfe." He corrects him nonchalantly, like Weston is simply a schoolboy in Varrick's world. A child. A novice. Someone who needs to be taught a lesson. It's a casual display of dominance. Especially when he adds, "The next time I catch you touching someone without consent, you will have a nice little visit from Sheriff Latham. How does that sound?"

Ire consumes Weston's glare, but he remains surprisingly quiet.

Varrick smiles warmly. "And if you had any notions of joining the Mariner's Club, I'd rethink those plans."

Weston lets out a sharp, brittle laugh before he turns to me, his gaze half softening in a silent plea. "You will let Jake and Katherine know this *was* a misunderstanding." I hear a hint of desperation, but it's not enough to wash away the past ten minutes. Hell, the past ten *months* of serving him and his leery, too-prolonged stares.

My smile carries exactly *zero* warmth. "I will recount the events in great detail."

Anger flashes over his eyes.

Varrick clears his throat.

Weston intakes a tighter breath before he says to me, "I hope you'll be honest then, Phoebe." He ignores Varrick before exiting the rotunda in loud, irate strides.

The silence he leaves in his wake does nothing but ratchet up my pulse. Varrick tilts his head to me, hands still stuffed coolly in his slacks, and I feel as if he's *waiting*.

"If you're looking for a thank-you, you're going to be standing here all day," I tell him. "I had that situation handled." False confidence is better than having no confidence at all, and I'd rather eat dirt than let my dad think we're friends after this.

He came in and helped me with Weston. It's not like he performed a resurrection and brought Rocky's biological family back to life.

He nods, not disagreeing with me. "Sometimes it's nice to have an assist though. I've missed that aspect of working with others."

I'm no longer shocked he talks so openly. He feels powerful enough to navigate any situation, even one where Weston is lurking down the hallway and eavesdropping.

"Is that why you're here? Checking in on the team?"

"Something like that. I came to talk to Jake—"

"He's living with you this summer; I don't think you need to stop by his place of work to find him."

"True. But Trent also lives with me, and he tends to get his feathers ruffled if I so much as glance at his brother."

That checks out, at least.

His gaze drifts back down the hallway where Weston disappeared to. "Your mother had the same trouble with men. They see her and think they can take. It's why I always wanted her out of that role in the business."

"That's nice of you," I say stiffly. "Caring so much about her. Must be why she left you and spent twenty-plus years not telling you about your own children."

He sighs heavily, a disappointed frown drawing down his face. "It's not how I would've wanted things to turn out. If I'd known she was pregnant, I would have been in your lives."

"To puppeteer us."

"No, to be honest with you. Beth took a misstep when she raised you. Like I've said, we don't lie to each other."

I cross my arms over my chest. "So, if we're being so honest, what do you need to talk to Jake about?"

"His horses." Varrick unbuttons the third button of his sport coat. "I was just tipped off that someone reported the abuse to the authorities."

"Wait, the horses that have been spray-painted? Those are *Trent's* horses."

"They're in Jake's stables. He's going to be charged today unless I can get him on the phone with the district attorney to smooth it over."

My blood runs cold. "Did Trent put someone up to this?" I can see him making up some phony report and citing Jake as the culprit.

"No clue," Varrick says. "But I'm trying to keep him out of trouble as best I can."

"Thanks," I say without thinking. The word sours in my mouth. I glance around the rotunda, feeling the weight of our conversation. We've been talking freely for *way* too long for my comfort.

He watches me in intrigue, not carrying an ounce of panic. "I assume your mom never trained you in sensory deprivation or saturation."

My throat dries. "It was optional." I want to ask if he trained in it and whose idea it was in the first place. His? My mom's?

Locked in a pitch-black room for hours on end, made to distinguish even the smallest of sounds. Only later to be in the same room with a cacophony of garbled noises and instructed to piece apart each one. Not all of us loved it.

I hated it.

It was the only exercise I ever refused to do. I hated myself for giving up, which might've been why I never did again.

Seeing Rocky enter and exit that room day after day without me hurt more than even being inside the darkness. Can Rocky hear if someone sneaks up behind him? Most likely, *yes*. But it's not as if he gained superhuman hearing. He can't hear someone approaching from the other end of the building.

Varrick's confidence lives in risk, but maybe that comes with decades of grifting and never being caught. I assume he thinks he can hear an eavesdropper before they even get too close.

Even living at Stonehaven, I've refused to ask him questions about the past. About his relationship with my mom. I don't want to be influenced by his answers, but the hunger to know more about the past gnaws the weak parts of me.

I cave. "Did you train in it?" Immediate guilt accompanies the question. *This means nothing. I still hate him.*

He doesn't gloat like he won something over on me. He nods casually. "Yes. All of us did. Your mom, Addison, and

Everett. It was Addy's idea, most things were." He tilts his head. "Hailey doesn't fall far from the tree in that respect, I've seen."

My chest tightens, not receiving the relief I expected from an answer. I just feel more exposed.

Varrick reads me too well because he doesn't wait for me to trudge up a conversation ender. "I should go speak with Jake," he tells me before he leaves the rotunda.

It's only once he disappears that I remember Hailey's baby news. *Today.*

I groan into my hands. And I thought I was having a shitty day.

Jake Waterford is about to take the prize.

TWENTY-FOUR

Jake

"Whoa, whoa. Backtrack." Oliver's feet drop off his desk and hit the floor in a loud *thump*. "You almost got arrested tonight?'

"Charged—not arrested." I run a tense hand through my hair. Oliver's office is quiet since his last patient left an hour ago. Never thought I'd be making a visit here unless I was drunk, high, or otherwise incapacitated. "And major emphasis on *almost*. The charges were dropped." I lean two hands on the club chair that faces the desk. Mid-lunge. Trying my best to unwind my muscles, but I'm not sure I can relax.

Oliver props his elbows on the mahogany desk and watches me. "You don't look like someone who just dodged a stain on his spotless record."

"You do know you're not a real therapist?"

"Wrong, Koning. I am a real therapist. I provide very real services to my clients." He tosses a glass paperweight between his hands. "I might just be lacking the real credentials."

I let out a low groan. "I shouldn't be here. I don't want to be complicit to whatever *this* is." I wave a hand around his office. The warmly lit room has camel leather chairs, a full shelf of self-help books and scientific journals, a box of tissues on the oak coffee table, and a con artist sitting behind the desk.

Oliver wags an unserious finger. "You're okay with the death of your mother, but you draw the line at me actually helping people?"

I shoot him a glare. "You know that's not it."

"I know that your moral code is Swiss cheese when you act like it's Gruyère." He leans back, the paperweight soaring up in the air in a higher toss. "Lucky for you, I love both Swiss and Gruyère." He winks.

"Lucky for me," I repeat, meeting his confidence head-on. The intensity of Oliver should make me let go. *Walk away.* He's like a monster under a bed, but instead of being scared, I just want to peek underneath and he just wants to play.

Then I think, *What the fuck am I doing?*

What are we doing?

Oliver is with Hailey. Even after the night she came back to Stonehaven crying from the brush-off on the job.

I'm with Hailey.

Oliver and I are . . . enduring each other? Circling each other? Competing with each other? Some days I feel like he's trying to get under my skin to run me off, but most days, I feel like he's the distraction I need.

I can understand why Hailey is drawn to him. And he's right. If I really thought he was bad for her, I would want him to change. But they've known each other for as long as they've been alive. The way they interact, their silent touches and quiet care, is built off history I will never know. Even if Hailey spends hours sharing with me.

His gaze tracks down my chest. Which confuses me more.

I squeeze the top of the chair harder. "Can we not? Not today." I wouldn't even be here if Hailey didn't send a text to meet her at Oliver's office after work.

Oliver catches the paperweight and studies me harder, his humor settling into something more serious. "Is there more to it than the charges being dropped?"

"Varrick was the reason they got dropped," I explain. "Took him five minutes on the phone with the DA. Threw Trent under the bus at the same time."

Oliver lets out a low whistle. "Dear old Dad with the high-up connections." He tips his head, impressed. "He's good."

I've had conversations with Nova and Phoebe about Oliver, about their fears that he might be more suspectable to Varrick's manipulation, which makes me remind him, "He's a killer."

"He's good at being bad," Oliver rephrases.

"He's a *killer*," I emphasize. "Of children."

"I don't throw stones. Or else I'd have to launch one at our little psychopath." He tosses the paperweight again, and I can't read him. But he reads me with one stroke. "Don't fear for me. My heart isn't melting over that imposter. I'm not a fourteen-year-old boy yearning for a father." He rolls into the desk. "But you got out of the charges?"

I release my grip on the chair in a large exhale. "Yeah . . . It was a close call." *Too close.*

I can't shake the stress of learning I could've been charged for a crime my brother committed. Now more than ever, I need him out of my life.

I meander toward the bookshelf and slip off a hardback on attachment theory. Flipping open the dense text, I draw my eyes back to Oliver. "Have you read these?"

He sweeps me in a quick up-down. "Of course. You think they're all for show?"

Maybe. *Probably not*. Oliver wouldn't half-ass his research before turning into a character, but it dawns on me for a second. How much he must know. How intelligent he must be to have become hundreds of different people with different professions and skill sets.

I turn more pages. "Did Hailey give you any other info about this news she has?"

Oliver leans forward to remind me, "We were in the same group chat."

She did text us together. Just a simple I have news. Meet at Oliver's office at 7pm.

I rotate toward him. "You're actually admitting you don't have a secret text chat with her?"

His forearms lie on the desk, hands cupped lightly. "And why do I need to secretly text her when I can talk to her face?" He locks eyes with me. "Slip my hands down her back. Underneath her shirt. Snap off her bra—"

"We get it."

"The royal *we*. Fitting for a king." He relaxes back, then spins in his chair to face an ornate mirror on the wall and fixes his hair. "No, I don't have any other details about her news." He catches my gaze through the reflection. "Do you?"

"No. I just hope it's good news." I tense more. "Today has been full of shit news."

"Like?" He spins back to face me, and I almost believe he's interested in my problems.

I lift a shoulder. "The club needs new members, or I might have to start firing some staff. I can't choose favorites and"—I exhale roughly and shove the book back on the shelf—"Hailey and Phoebe were the newest hires. They'll most likely be the first cuts."

"And why haven't you asked me to join your club?"

I give him an intrusive look. "Do you have the money for that? Initiation fees aren't cheap."

Oliver puts a hand to his chest. "I'm a trust fund baby who didn't lose his inheritance, unlike my wonderful sister, Phoebe." *His alias*. He doesn't explain further, and I wonder how much money from his past jobs he still has at his disposal. But I let the temptation to ask go.

"I don't want your money," I state firmly.

He looks me up and down again. "Power dynamics?"

"Something like that." I walk over to his desk. Closer to him. "I've seen your cock. I don't feel like taking your money."

"I could put it under your pillow like the tooth fairy if it'd help you sleep at night." He tugs a string to a stained-glass lamp, and it casts a soft glow over the desk and his dark eyes. "I am an expert at helping people sleep."

Flashes of him fingering Hailey until she writhed against him, until she cried, invade my mind. His gaze plants on me in challenge, and I don't break away. He fucking wants me to have that visual, but I'm not going to give him the satisfaction of thinking it makes me uncomfortable.

It doesn't.

We've spent over a month sleeping in the same bed together, Hailey wedged between us. I enjoy the competition more than he realizes. Maybe because I know this is one that's decided by Hailey. Not by him. Not by me.

In the end, we're at her mercy. Which is where we both want to be.

Whatever this is between Oliver and me is just a side quest.

Entertainment. I'm having too much fun for a guy who might lose everything: The family estate. The family legacy. My own reputation.

"It's my night helping her sleep," I remind him. Just a polite way of saying, *I'm fucking Hailey.* I've given in to the idea that it has an added benefit of making her relax and fall asleep.

She's stopped losing time since she started summering at Stonehaven, she's said. Maybe it's been less stressful having me and Oliver with her together.

"I have it penciled in my calendar." Oliver smiles, slipping a ballpoint pen behind his ear. "Thanks."

"You put it on your calendar?" I ask, disbelieving.

"With little hearts around my dates." He draws a heart in the air with his finger. "And little frowny faces around yours." He drops his lips in dramatic fashion.

"Sure," I say, and check my watch. Our arrangement has been working well so far. We've split up the nights we have sex with Hailey. We're allowed to watch, which has been . . . interesting. We don't climb in the bed together until she's fast asleep. So one of us is inevitably standing, most of the time in the bathroom doorway.

It's become a contest of wills, where we refuse to walk away and just let her be fucked by the other one so easily. And there's definite intrigue rooting me. Oliver is so rough with her. The first time I saw him thrust his cock inside of her, I wanted to throw him off. His pace was relentless. He never let up on her, not even when she started crying, and if I didn't know she liked going past the sensitivity, I would've stopped him.

When he wasn't kissing her, he stared at me. He wanted me to either get hard or get timid, and when I didn't do either, his breath staggered and he lost pace just slightly.

So, yeah, it's become a game between me and him. Hailey

seems enthralled by it, often asking me questions in the morning. "Did you come, too?"

"No," I said. "But I didn't mind watching." That's been . . . evident for me and him.

Oliver will act like it does nothing for him. Still, when he's on his feet and I'm on the bed, he's trying to unnerve me. He'll smile, which will flicker in and out. He can't stand how long I take with her. How slow I am just tracking my lips up her body. It drives *him* mad just standing and waiting and seeing her squirm beneath me.

I fucked her so slowly, pulling her against my cock, I thought for sure he was going to come before she did.

He even looked at me like I'd nearly gotten to him. He had to leave for the bathroom. I heard the shower cut on, and I smiled against Hailey's lips in a deeper kiss.

Thinking about our situation together, the three of us, I just keep reminding myself, *It's the summer. It's a heat wave. It's a distraction. It's tranquilizing for more than just Hailey. It'll pass like a haze.*

I thumb through a stack of magazines on his desk. "I regret getting here so early . . ." I trail off at the pictures on a tabloid.

"Who do you recognize?" he asks.

"That obvious?" I pick up the *Celebrity Crush* magazine. Fizzle, a company located in Philadelphia, has been all over the tabloids after this major scandal involving the CEO's daughter. I didn't expect to see him in one of the photos. Even if I knew he was originally from Philly. "Connor Cobalt, or Richard Connor Cobalt."

"Old fling?"

I laugh. "No. He's five years younger than me. We both went to Faust Boarding School for Young Boys." I stare at the photo of his deep blue eyes and confident gait as he walks hand in hand with a girl who's likely glaring at the paparazzi. "He's someone you don't really forget."

Oliver reaches for the magazine.

I hand it to him. "He's incredibly smart. Broke most of the academic records at our school. He was *very* good at getting people to do what he wanted. He understood social capital so well, I figured he'd be a billionaire by thirty if he wasn't already an heir to a Fortune 500."

"Meh, I could take him." Oliver skims the photo. "Could've been our next mark, too bad he's *famous* now." He tosses the magazine. "I'm not risking my face being caught in a tabloid. Some grifters *love* the attention, but that's not a thrill we seek." He threads his hands behind his head, about to kick his feet on the desk, but they stay grounded when the door opens. His fingers unlace, and he's pushing up to a stand.

Hailey has arrived like a speeding train slamming into a brick wall. She suddenly halts two feet into the room. The door bangs shut behind her.

"Hailey?" I take one step, but she holds up her hands.

Oliver and I stay back. Chunky black headphones cover her ears and flatten her platinum hair, and she begins pacing, wringing her mesh sleeves in her hands. Chains jingle on her cargo pants in the silence.

I skim her for any signs of harm. *My brother.* What did Trent do now?

It ravages my brain, until I notice the elastic Calvin Klein waistband sticking out of her pants. I side-eye Oliver. "Is she wearing your underwear?"

"Wouldn't be the first time." He assesses her more than me. "Jealous, Koning?"

I smile to myself. Just happy for the distraction. Even one so brief and fleeting.

Then she stops, takes a breath, and yanks her headphones to her neck.

She must've been blasting the song. It floods the office, and the lyrics and the melody pummel me because this isn't her normal metal headbangers. The first time we ever exchanged music, I sent her this poetic song about love, death . . . and fear.

She intakes another readying breath as "Death" by White Lies plays on high volume, and she says, "The job *must* go on. This doesn't change the job. You need to know that before I tell you something."

Oliver keeps his hands in his pockets. His casual demeanor isn't unspooling the tension in my muscles. If anything, it's making me more on guard.

"Did something happen with Trent?" I ask.

She shakes her head. Her hands grip the headphones around her neck as the chorus blares, and her eyes reach mine as she says, "I'm pregnant." She looks at Oliver. "I've done the calculations a thousand times, and the baby could be either of yours. It must've been around March . . . I was sleeping with you both then."

I can barely think.

Oliver's eyes skim her. "That'd make you around fifteen weeks?"

"Sixteen," she corrects.

"Sixteen weeks pregnant." I shut my eyes tightly. *Four months*. "Hailey—"

"Wait."

I open my gaze on her steady eye contact. Like she's played this moment in her mind over and over a million and one times and seen all our possible reactions. None could surprise her.

Now she's here, and she's confidently saying, "I will have

this baby. I will love this baby. I will be known as a town whore more than I already am. There will be speculation over who the father might be once I start showing, and I don't care. This is *me.* I've never been in a relationship. I've never done anything the normal way. I don't know what *normal* is outside of pretending to act it, and maybe that's okay." She takes the tiniest breath. "And I know you two don't want kids—or at least aren't ready for them. I know anything serious freaks us all out. So I'm releasing you from this situation." She nods several times. "You don't have to be a part of this. I have it under control. Me."

Oliver and I open our mouths at the same time, but she cuts in again.

"One more thing." She raises a finger. "Just one."

"Okay," I say tentatively.

"No matter what happens with us or the job, my child will *always* know the truth of who they are. Who their real mom is. Who their real dad is. I'm not deceiving them. Not for anything or for anyone."

I keep falling more and more in love with Hailey. She stays resolute on my gaze, drinking in my respect for her, my affection for her, my concern for her. Only tearing away when Oliver bridges the distance between her and him.

He swoops his arms around her thin build. Lifts her off the ground. Spins her in a circle round and round while whispering in her ear. As her arms weave around his neck and her ear turns toward his lips to hear more, I can almost picture them as teenagers.

Fourteen and fifteen, embracing as the towns and cities change in a blur around them. And I'm certain—they will never change.

Hailey and Oliver will endure like all the Tinrocks and

Graveses. Even if this job fails, even if they're run out of Victoria, they will be together until the very end. Like they were together in the very beginning.

The only question is me. It's why she was staring at me. I have more to lose. Being associated with Hailey and a baby out of wedlock—especially while the town thinks my older brother is interested in her—it's gossip fodder. Salacious. Reputation damaging.

Not just to her.

I imagine Oliver doesn't care. He's a playboy. No one would be shocked if he knocked up a girl here.

And me . . .

I stare down and almost smile. I'm always revolting against what people want me to be. Had it been up to my mother, I'd be married to a girl from an upper-class family and we'd have four kids by now.

I'm not worried about what people will think of me. Shame is for those who can't be proud of their convictions, and I've never been ashamed of being with Hailey. I'd never be ashamed of having a baby with her.

I'm deathly concerned about her being around my brother now, but that's another conversation. Because when Oliver rests her feet on the floor, when she turns to me, she looks uneasy.

Oliver places a hand on her head and tells me, "I'm not going anywhere."

"I know," I say lightly. "You'll always be in her life. Whether you're the father or I am, you'll still be there."

"Jake . . . ?" Hailey hesitates.

"I wouldn't take him from you," I assure her. "It'd be wrong for you two to lose each other."

Her eyes glass. "I . . ." Her face says, *I don't want to lose you, too.*

It crushes me, realizing she believes I'm going to walk away from her and this baby. Then I breathe deeply, and I see her during wintertime.

Twinkling stars carpeted the night sky while we sat on my catamaran sharing a woolen blanket over our shoulders. She'd been interested in Stonehaven, the history of the Wolfe family, and I'd taken her to my boat since I had a perfect view from the dock.

I didn't think she'd bring binoculars. There ended up being less spying through the windows and more talking. For hours and hours and hours, we discussed her life and mine, from the simple joys of reading to the shared guilt we had over the people we loved. I felt responsible for not helping Kate sooner. I felt responsible for my mother's pettiness and cruelty. She felt responsible for what happened to Phoebe in Carlsbad. She felt responsible for finding answers about all their origins, their birth parents, before it was too late.

She was losing time.

I was losing hope.

And somehow, we found both that night in each other.

The frigid air was almost unbearable, and we'd eventually have to go inside the catamaran, but we still lingered. I didn't want to leave that moment.

I didn't want to leave her.

Then her gray eyes bounced between me and the mansion on the rocky island. Back and forth.

"What is it?" I smiled down at her.

"Being here with you just reminded me of a poem." Her cheeks went flush, and not just from the cold.

"Well, now you have to tell me."

"Forget I said anything. I, uh . . . I'm just thinking too much."

"Emily Dickinson? The poem about the sea and her dog," I guessed. "I don't think it has an official title but I've always called it 'By the Sea.'"

She smiled almost instantly. "Kind of close."

I smiled back. "Theme or year?"

"Both poets were alive at the same time. 'By the Sea' actually rhymes with . . ." She trailed off, her blush spreading as it dawned on me.

"'Annabel Lee'?" I held her gaze while she searched mine rapidly.

"Do you . . . do you know it?"

I didn't just know it. I had recited it as a child for school, and every line was ingrained in my memory.

"'It was many and many a year ago, in a kingdom by the sea,'" I whispered, glancing out at Stonehaven, then back at her. "'That a maiden there lived whom you may know by the name of Annabel Lee. And this maiden she lived with no other thought'"—I watched her eyes pool with emotion, and my heart filled past capacity—"'than to love and be loved by me.'"

Hailey stared into me so deeply, hanging on to these words I spoke like a fairy-tale romance I was bringing to life for her, and I wanted it to exist for me. The haunting, unending love of Poe's "Annabel Lee." That night it felt like it was written for her and me.

We stared at each other for so long, I would've believed time froze. I didn't think. I just felt. And I kissed Hailey for the first time that night, under the stars, with the words of her favorite poem hanging around us like icicle dreams.

I thought they would melt come morning.

But they never did.

I later learned it wasn't just her favorite poem. It was the poem the Tinrocks and Graveses used as a cry for help when one of them was wounded or in trouble. She said it encompassed the undying love of their families.

All Hailey has ever known is a love that's more than love.

And now she's seeking that in me. I want to love someone to the depths of poetic death. I want to love *her* this way, but my home is a place. Her home is an organ pumping through five different bodies. All she needs is them to survive.

I need this town. I can't leave my birthright. I'm still, and will always be, a Koning.

"Hailey," I whisper in the office.

She shifts her weight, nervous. Oliver stays behind her, and she peers from him to me. "I can only give you the information. You have to make a choice, too."

"Are you releasing me?" I ask her. "That's what you said. You want to release me from the responsibility of being a father? The responsibility of caring about you, of loving you?"

"I don't want to," she breathes. "But if it's easier for you—"

"It's not easier to walk away," I interject softly.

"Jake . . ." she draws out. "If we fail this job, I can't stay in Victoria. E-even if the baby is yours, I can't. It won't be safe."

I nod, knowing, and I don't lie to her. "I can't leave this town," I say gently. "I will do *everything* I can to make sure I get the full inheritance, because I can't fathom abandoning you. I'm not scared about my reputation. I'm just scared you won't be able to stay here with me."

She's pregnant. Even picturing her packing her bags with a round belly, carrying my child, and I can't follow is tearing me apart. That's not the man I ever wanted to be.

BURNER PHONE CHAT

(JAKE): Reminder: Trent's biggest party at my family's estate is tonight. I could use help making sure he doesn't set the place on fire. Girls still excluded, sorry. 👑

(PHOEBE): As you've told us a million times already 🍓

(ROCKY): Make it a million and one 🕷️

(JAKE): I don't want you two around him at these things. 👑

(ROCKY): Same 🕷️

(NOVA): Third ⚔️

(OLIVER): Fourth 🦎

(OLIVER): We're missing our fifth? Get in here, batty 🦎

(TREVOR): I'm not against using the fruit as bait 🦇

(NOVA): NO ⚔️

(ROCKY): ffs 🕷️

(HAILEY): We promise we won't be there 🖤

TWENTY-FIVE

Rocky

I've lost count of the amount of belligerent, debauched parties Trent has thrown at the Koning property. Even summering at Stonehaven, he hasn't packed away his inane strategy to piss off his little brother. Every fucking Saturday, we have to babysit the estate like it's a prized jewel and the thief is inside the vault swinging a hammer at it.

Trent's tactic to gain the rest of the Koning inheritance is so harebrained that I lose brain cells trying to rationalize it. Jake will *never* just hand over the other half. Not even if Trent takes a shit in his bed every night.

It's not happening.

And yet, here we are. *Again*.

All the parties vary on levels of depravity, but tonight's is especially unhinged. Trent usually has a guest list, or at least a cap on people roaming the main house, lawns, and pool.

Tonight, I'd bet my soul (if I had one) that there isn't a bouncer at the door.

He's letting *anyone* in, and if I had to make a guess, some stupid prick from Caufield University spread the news of a "Koning rager" because it feels like every face I see can't be older than twenty-two.

One blessing: Trent doesn't know I'm here, or else I'd have to be glued to his hip like a mole.

Second blessing: Phoebe isn't here, or else I'd be going out of my mind. Trent wants Phoebe too bad for him to just casually ignore her at a party.

So, yeah, I'm hanging on to those blessings while Jake and I roam the grounds to make sure no one fucked with the horses again. My shirt sticks to my skin in the thick summer humidity. Sweat beads up against the back of my neck. Jake runs a hand through his hair, peeling back the damp strands that cling to his temples.

A shotgun blast goes off, followed by rowdy applause. Unfortunately, the sound came from *inside* the Konings' mansion.

Jake clenches his jaw and closes his eyes in an exasperated beat. He can't catch a break. I can relate, but my home isn't the one being decimated from the inside out.

"Let's go check the house," I tell him.

We end up trekking back to the mansion. We pass a lewd game of croquet that involves stripping and hitting lines of white powder off hands. Firecrackers pop on the manicured grass, and college students in Caufield tees cheer on a topless girl doing a keg stand.

Jake has shaken his head so many times, he might need a chiropractor tomorrow.

Solo cups and beer bottles litter the backyard, and we don't stay here for long to observe, lecture, or participate. We're like missiles on a critical course inside the debauched mansion to ensure the kitchen isn't up in flames.

Liquor bottles of tequila, vodka, and bourbon are everywhere.

The bottoms of my leather shoes stick to the alcohol-covered marble.

"You want to set off the fire alarms again?" I ask. We did that last weekend.

"I can't waste EMS resources." He's more honorable than me. (But we all knew that.)

The kitchen is intact. Outside of a young boy puking in the sink, and when I recognize him, I nearly groan. "Sandon." Damian Bennet's fourteen-year-old brother and our summer roommate at Stonehaven is being swept up in this shit. "Hey, man, you good?"

Since the Bennets are the third founding family of Victoria, I'm not shocked to see a boy this young with status and wealth at this party. Seen it too many fucking times before. Lack of parental supervision combined with the pressure to succeed and live up to some family legacy, and you have a recipe for underage drinking and drug use.

He hoists a limp thumbs-up.

Jake hands him a rag. "You need to go home, Sandon."

He groans out, "You go home, Jake."

I almost laugh.

"This is my home," Jake says lightly, then tells me, "Call Damian to come take care of him."

I cock my head. "And you can't do that yourself because . . . ?"

Jake scans the opened cabinets that've been raided for snacks. He's evading. "Because."

"That's not cagey as fuck."

His annoyed eyes hit mine. "We had a thing."

Ohhh. I laugh hard now. Jake eyes Sandon as if he's an eavesdropping problem. "He won't remember shit tomorrow," I say. "You had *a thing* with Damian Bennet? And you're just now saying something? We've been living with the guy for over a month." Now that I think of it, I don't recall Jake ever saying a word to Damian. Have they even looked at each other? I rack my brain.

"We hooked up a few times, and it ended in a fight. We don't talk."

I let out a lighter laugh at a thought. "He asked to blow me the first week I moved to Victoria." The party at the boathouse.

Jake isn't surprised. "You let him?"

I think about Phoebe. "No."

"Good call."

"That bad in bed, huh?"

"Not great." His expression says something darker.

Jesus. "I don't want to know." Picturing a guy hurting Jake makes me want to knock them out. Weird. And I'm not psychoanalyzing myself tonight, or the way that Jake cautions, "Just don't sleep with him." Like protecting *me* is the moral of this story.

I glower. Wishing I could just say the fucking words out loud. *I'm with Phoebe.* I grind my jaw. Instead, I say, "You know I'm with someone. Exclusively. I don't fucking share."

He starts to smile at that. I'd say he's happy for us.

We hear a loud crash from above, and we look at the ceiling as the gold pendant lights rattle. Charting course for the second floor, I call Damian to collect his brother, then I shove my phone in my pocket and feel the vibration of my burner cell.

I stop in the curving stairwell with plush carpeted steps, and I dig it out. "Go ahead," I tell Jake.

He waits four steps above me.

I glower. "I love the part where you listened to me."

He tips his head. "I learned from the best."

"Phoebe?"

"Who else?"

I widen my eyes in irritation, then check the message, and my blood runs cold.

(PHOEBE): We're at the party. We have a girl emergency. Don't freak out or try to intervene. All is good. Just looping you in. 🍓

All is good? My stomach churns thick acid. Why the fuck is she here? What emergency?

We all agreed the girls would steer clear of this party. I'm on a steeper edge when I glance upward and see Jake peering out of the circular window in the stairwell. His brows are knotted. Severity hardens his entire face.

That's not good. "What?" I ask him and send a quick text.

EMERGENCY and GOOD don't belong in the same sentence. What the fuck is going on? 🕷

"Come up here."

I'm at his side in seconds. Out the window, we have a perfect view of the east grounds, where curved hedges form the beginning of a garden maze.

"Is that Phoebe and Hailey?" he asks. Apprehension cinches his deep voice.

My pulse skids. "Where?"

There are so many fucking people. Grinding, dancing, screwing, drinking. Glowsticks worn around necks and wrists illuminating bodies. Pops of vibrant color explode in the sky.

"By the fountain."

I spot her.

Her dark blue hair blows in the sticky, humid breeze. Her off-shoulder white linen dress looks beautiful on her, and under normal circumstances, I'd be happy to see Phebs. She has an arm around my sister. I love how she loves Hailey so completely—just not when their bond goes to the extreme to where they would suffer for each other.

Hailey has her platinum-blonde hair in two braids. She wears black cargo pants and a matching mesh black top, standing out like the lone goth in a sea of prep.

Red Solo cups are in their hands, and I'm guessing Hailey has water in hers. Phoebe, no clue. It's just a reminder my sister is fucking *pregnant*.

There's still no one who knows that I suspect it. I think she might've told Jake and Oliver the truth yesterday. A sneaking suspicion based on Oliver's insistence on role-playing scenarios where Trent peer-pressures her. And also Jake asking if we've ever failed a job before.

The short answer: no.

The long answer: it depends on the definition of *fail*. Have we fumbled and had to leave a city very quickly with less money than we desired? Yes. Have we ever been accused of fraud? No.

At least my sister told them.

I push down my thoughts to tell Jake, "Yeah, that's them."

Phoebe and Hailey disappear from our vantage point. Dread tries to wash over me.

Jake fixes his weighted gaze on mine. The same worry coursing in his blue eyes can be uncovered in my grays. We need to find them. Acid is in my throat. In my lungs. In my core.

After I show him Phoebe's text, I try calling, but she doesn't pick up. I shake my head with aggression. "What kind of girl emergency couldn't they solve any-fucking-where else?"

He's dialing a number, then frowns. "Hailey isn't answering."

The window rattles from the heavy bass outside. "Maybe they can't hear the phones ringing from out there." The music is excruciatingly loud when stepping out the doors.

We go silent as male voices grow louder from upstairs.

"No, really. I swear."

"You swear?"

"Dude, he paid him to put it in her drink. I heard the whole thing. TK is planning to fuck Phoebe Smith tonight."

TK as in *Trent Koning* Waterford.

Raw, brutal rage and urgency slam into me. I skip two steps at a time going downstairs to search for Phoebe. Jake is following without hesitation or conflict. We bump shoulders with guests in a narrow hallway, and I ignore the glares.

"Heads up!" a guy yells, cupping his hands up high. A porcelain vase sails through the air and lands in his palms like a football. College-aged students laugh shrilly and continue racing down the hall.

Everything is too fucking loud. It's all piercing my eardrums.

We come upon a makeshift bowling alley with plastic bottles of vodka for pegs. I walk straight across their game, kicking aside the pins.

"Hey!"

"Booo! You fucking suck!"

"Grey looks pissed."

"He always looks pissed."

I entertain no one with a response. I'm gone.

Into the living room.

Out the side door. The remix of "Sweet Dreams" by the Eurythmics hammers into my skull. I can't stand this song. It's toxic fuel in my bloodstream. Feasting on my last fucking nerve.

"Grey!" Jake shouts, trying to catch up to my hurried pace across the patio. "Grey!" I'm not stopping. "Rocky!" And then, "BRAYDEN!"

I feel his hand on my shoulder.

"Don't." I tear his arm off me as my shoes sink into grass.

"Call Trent," he advises in a heavy breath. "Get to Trent first."

"I can't. I have to get to her. If he drugged her . . ." Nausea and ire barrel up my throat, scorching my voice. "You don't understand. You *can't* understand, Jake. I don't lose sight of her in these positions! I don't leave her like this! Not without her fucking brothers!"

His concern for me is so unnecessary and *infuriating*. This isn't about my trauma, my past with her. This is about the stark, merciless present that doesn't care what we endured yesterday, five years ago, or what we'll withstand five years from now.

"You go east!" he yells over the high-octane tempo and earsplitting beat. "I'll go west in case they left the garden!"

Breath tries to reach my lungs, but it's on fire, charring me.

We break apart, and while I'm on a fast-moving hike east, I start calling the cavalry.

"What the fuck?" Nova answers groggily. "It's two a.m., Rock."

"Get your ass out of bed. You need to get here now."

Adrenaline clears his voice. "What's going on?"

"Grey! Come play with us!!" women shout from a beer pong table. I don't waste time acting interested. I'm not saving face. I'm not playing a role.

I'm just trying to find her.

And *fuck* this song.

I fist the phone against my ear.

"Rocky?" Nova growls. "What the fuck is going on? You're still at Trent's party?"

"Yeah. I'm still here. Hailey and Phoebe showed up." I grip the phone closer to my mouth to drown out the music on my end. "Phoebe might've been roofied."

"Where is she?" I hear the slam of a car door. The ignition.

I'm on the east side of the mansion. On foot, this rave is mind-bending chaos as liquor drips down lips, as sweating bodies shift and dance and pack the area. My vigilance sears the pits of my eyes. I'm barely blinking. I'm searching and weaving between people, trying to reach the stone fountain. Not stopping when girls grab my arm and call out my name.

I tear through them.

"Rocky?!" Nova yells when I don't answer.

"I can't find her." I hear the deep, coarse grit in my voice. My flexed muscles are fiery, taut bands of rage and fear. I don't relax. I can't relax.

"My sister got roofied. And you don't know where she is." His fury is palpable, but it's nothing compared to what's brewing inside me. "You better fucking find her, Rocky. I swear to *fucking* God—"

"Who do you think I am?" I sneer back. "Get here."

"I'm speeding." I hear the rev of the engine.

Good. We hang up, and I call Oliver, who's already at this party and going to split apart from Collin Falcone to search for the girls. I call Trevor, who's been at the public beach all night looking for sea glass. He wanted to make Sidney a necklace for her birthday.

I don't have time to ask if he's still there. I just tell him, "Hailey needs you. I need you here."

I hear a car rumble to life. Then I try to call Phoebe again. No answer. I hear Jake in my head, urging me to go find Trent instead of her.

I think I have a good idea where he might be.

It feels like I'm being torn in half. Split in two. But I change course for the Konings' pool.

TWENTY-SIX

Phoebe

Nothing about tonight feels good.

I'm not even five percent as superstitious as Rocky is, but if a crow or a raven or any creepy avian creature flew at me right now, I'd rethink my beliefs.

I didn't expect for Sidney Burke to call Hailey and beg her to come to Trent's party.

I didn't expect her to also say, "You can bring Phoebe, too. I just need help. *Please.*"

There's no way in hell Hailey and I were going to ignore the desperate plea of another girl, even if that girl likes me about as much as an ingrown toenail.

The electronic rave music and thumping bass split my head. I drown it out with a big gulp of whiskey soda from my red Solo cup. The liquor burns the back of my throat, but I'm looking forward to the buzz.

I can't remember the last time I had a sip of alcohol. My days of covering for Hailey are officially over. I'm trying this thing where I *don't* take the fall for my friend anymore.

Though . . . it's hard. But the upside is that Jake and Oliver know she's pregnant. Soon she'll tell her brothers and Nova.

My heel gets stuck in the soft grass of the lawn. "Shit. Hails . . ." I call out.

She turns around and doubles back to me. I use her shoulder for support and unearth my heel. These strappy white stilettos were unwise, even if they are so very cute. I unbuckle them and let them dangle from my finger.

Hailey's gaze pins toward the north side of the estate. "We should hurry. We don't know what kind of trouble Sidney is in."

Sidney wouldn't give details over the phone, but she sounded distraught. Panicked. Enough that we hightailed it over here and broke our promise to stay away from this party.

"What if she's pranking us?" I ask as we head toward the Konings' private beach, the meetup spot. My ears ring as we distance ourselves from the DJ who's going too hard on the reverb.

Hailey slips me a look. "You don't think we'd be able to tell?"

"True." I take another swig of whiskey, practically guzzling the mixed drink, and I can't avoid Hailey's beaming smile.

"You're happy I'm about to get wasted?"

"I'm happy that you've finally started enjoying yourself again," Hailey says, balancing with her arms outstretched, a red Solo cup filled with water in one hand, as we maneuver these slippery stones among the dune grass.

We choose to go off the beaten path since a horde of college students smoke blunts on the stairs to the beach.

She catches my hand as we both wobble. I'm still barefoot, and I try not to spill my drink.

"Just can't believe I'm enjoying myself at *Trent's* party. Gross." I crinkle my nose. The alcohol settles sourly in my stomach when I spot the petite blonde on the small empty beach. Sidney paces back and forth, and her white eyelet dress billows in the warm breeze.

As soon as we join her on the sand, she races to us with bloodshot eyes and tear-streaked cheeks. "You both came?" Her eyes round in shock, mostly directed at me. But it's hard not to notice her shoulders sagging in slight relief.

"We did consider this might be a prank," I admit. "Are your friends about to jump out and throw pig's blood on us?"

She sniffs. "Uh, no. I'm not vile, Phoebe. My friends don't even know I'm here. I just didn't know where else to go that he wouldn't find me."

He.

Hailey and I share a deeply concerned look. *Trevor?* I never even considered he might have something to do with this. I can't wrap my head around it though. Trevor is a lot of things—psychopath, murderer—but I would have bet all I have that he'd never hurt Sidney.

I suck in a tight breath. "If Trevor did something—"

Sidney sends me a sickening glare that stops my sentence dead in its tracks. "Trev is helping me. He's the reason I called you." Her eyes ping to Hailey. "He said that his sister is really good at solutions and getting people out of trouble. And if I ever needed someone, I should talk to her."

Trevor. He might actually really love this girl after all.

Wow . . . I didn't think . . . I honestly didn't think he had it in him. I feel proud, even though I had nothing to do with this growth. I am proud of him, nonetheless, and I think Rocky would be even more so.

Sidney scowls at me again. "So don't drag his name through the mud over this. He doesn't deserve that."

I hold up my hands in defense. Glad to know Sidney hasn't

lost her bite even though she's asking for *our* help. If I wasn't the one being chewed out, I might even respect it.

"What happened?" Hailey asks her. "Who are you hiding from?"

"My dad." Sidney laces together and unlaces her fingers, fidgeting at the mention of him. "He called me tonight and told me I've been unenrolled from Caufield University and transferred to some school in London. A school I've never even heard of. He's moving the entire family to England *tomorrow*."

Weston Burke really is a piece of shit.

"You're nineteen," I remind her. "An adult. You don't have to go where he tells you. Just tell him to fuck off."

"I did. Before I called you. He froze my credit cards and locked me out of my bank accounts. He threatened to take away my trust fund if I'm not on the plane tomorrow morning." She shakes her head, her hair frizzing around her face. "I'm broke, and I don't have anywhere to stay. He already sold the house." Her eyes flash to Hailey in panic. "I can't go with him. Overseas? My college is *here*. I have friends *here*. Trevor"—her voice tremors—"Trevor is here. If I go to London with my dad, he controls everything I do and I'm . . ."

Trapped. Her eyes well with tears, and she glares up at the sky while she rubs her face with the backs of her hands.

Hailey nudges my shoulder, and I can see in her eyes that she's already mentally mapped out a strategy. "The Reynoldses still haven't rented out their boathouse since Rocky moved out."

"I don't have money for rent," Sidney interjects with a hoarse voice.

"Worry about that later," I tell her. "We can front you. Just get away from your dad first."

Sidney swallows hard. "I . . . I can't take your money. You don't even like me."

I roll my eyes. "Do we have to like each other to look out for each other? I do *actually* know how disgusting your dad is. We agree on that at least."

I don't ask why she hasn't gone to her friends. They're all college students living off their parents' money. I'm sure she's worried they'll say no, or she'd have to tarnish her reputation by begging them. Hailey and I—we're not going to judge her as harshly as her peers.

"The boathouse is a longer-term solution," Hailey says more to me. "Until then, we should get her a hotel room down at the harbor. Under your name. Her dad won't think you're helping her."

"Good idea." I pull out my phone to book her a room and see a missed call from Rocky. My gut drops. I must not have heard the phone ring while we were near the DJ.

I know he's worried about us, but we're okay. We're on the beach. No one's even around us. Trent is probably already having a three-way in his pool house.

Sidney rubs at her watery eyes when I email her the room confirmation. She thanks us a million times. "What happens if he cuts off service on my phone tomorrow?" Real fear drains the color from her face.

"One step at a time," Hailey says before Sidney's phone rings.

She glances at the caller ID. "It's Trevor. Maybe he can give me a ride to the hotel." She answers the call, thanking us again, before she heads toward the stairs.

Hailey and I watch her disappear up them. We're both silent. Moonlight shimmers across the rippling ocean, and rough waves lap angrily against the sand.

It's quieter here.

"Was that the only good deed we've ever done?" I finally ask, my throat swelling at the thought.

"It might have been." Hailey lets out a weighted breath.

I sweep the desolate shoreline, the umbrellas fallen and chair cushions blown toward the water, and I pluck my phone from my crossbody purse so I can call Rocky back. But when I dig my feet into the cold sand, I feel floaty all of a sudden.

Brain fog gradually rolls over me, and I stare at my drink. Did I pour more than a couple shots' worth?

My phone rings in my palm, and I quickly answer the call from Nova. "Hey?"

"Where are you?" The rawness of my brother's dire concern takes me aback. I figured he'd be pissed I'm here, but not this level of worried.

"I'm at the Konings' beach. Hailey and I were helping Sidney—"

"You're with Sidney?" Alarm scratches to the surface of his rough voice.

"Not anymore. She just left. It's just Hails and me." I feel so off. Physically off. I struggle to keep my arm hoisted and the phone pinned to my ear. Panic tries to reach me. "What's going on?"

"You tell me. Rocky just called saying you got roofied."

"I got . . . what?" I recognize this sensation that heavies my body now. He put a name to it. "Hailey?" I drop the phone on the ground. It slips out of my hand. What the fuck is happening? *I know what's happening.* I know what this is. "I need to sit down."

She grabs my phone from the sand and follows my hurried pace to the teak lounge chairs sunk in the sand. As soon as my ass hits the cushion, my body sags.

"Phoebe?" Hailey catches my arms, keeping me upright, but I'm falling backward onto the lounge chair. No, no, no, *no.*

Nova's voice is muffled in the phone. I try to hang on to Hailey, but my arms droop. "I can't feel . . . I can't control . . ."

Her eyes are saucers. "Lie down. Lie down." She helps me lie on the chair like I'm sunbathing. Like this is a voluntary act. A voluntary position.

I don't want this. I did not ask for this.

I stretch out my legs, but they barely move with my effort. "We bumped into people on our way here, didn't we?" My voice pitches.

"We squeezed through the crowd."

"Enough that someone could've slipped something in my drink?"

Her horror is mine. I struggle to breathe as the terror starts suffocating me. *Rocky.* The urge to cry out for him consumes me, but his name is stuck in my swollen throat. *Where's Rocky?*

"You'll be okay," Hailey assures. "You're just going to take a nap. I'm staying right here. I'm not going anywhere."

A nap.

My nose flares and chin quivers as I fight blistering, enraged tears. "I can't believe this is happening again." Was the whole whiskey bottle spiked with GHB? Are other people passing out right now, too? "You feel okay?" I ask her.

"I'm fine." Her eyes keep widening as she stares into the pitch-blackness of the grassy dune cliff.

"Hailey?" I try to sit up. I can't. I can't do anything but lie here.

My brain drifts too far away. She's so fuzzy. I try to squeeze her hand. I barely sense her squeezing mine, but she's here.

She's here.

As tunnel vision drives me into complete darkness, I form one last unsteady, desperate plea.

"Rocky."

TWENTY-SEVEN

Hailey

I can do this. I can do this. I can protect my best friend.

Just like you did in Carlsbad.

I clamp my eyes closed, trying to erase the worst night of my life, then I open them with a deeper inhale and determination. I can do this because the inverse is being witness to something more horrifying.

I won't let anyone hurt her.

"I'm right here," I whisper to Phoebe, gently placing her limp arms on her abdomen but with more urgency than she can see or feel.

She's passed out, but she looks less lifeless as I carefully adjust her, combing soft blue strands of hair out of her face. A face that I've seen elicit catcalls and wolf whistles, a face that's had poised men tripping in shined leather oxfords, a face that stuns, that incites desire and greed.

My silent tears fall and wet her cheeks.

"Shit," I curse and thumb away the droplets.

I've never once envied the beauty of my best friend. All the attention she drew as we grew older, I sighed in relief when she'd taken it off me.

She never really basked in the gawking. She never liked it. She just loved being able to shift a spotlight off me, knowing I hated the burn.

Phoebe has always protected me, and at each opportunity, I come up short at protecting her.

Tonight has to be better. I brush off sand from her phone, and I see Nova is still on the line. Quickly, I put it to my ear. "We're at the beach," I say in case he didn't hear Phoebe before. "She's unconscious."

"Fuck!" His curse booms so loud I have to draw the phone away from my ear.

In a quiet, shaky breath, I say, "I can't lift her. I can't carry her. I'm not strong enough."

"We're coming to you." Nova's voice is like jet fuel, able to explode everything around him. "Just stay there."

I don't have a choice.

I don't know what's worse—having no choice at all or having too many terrible ones to pick from.

My head whips side to side as I canvass our isolated surroundings. Dune grass dances in the salty nighttime breeze, and relaxed waves roll over the darkened, coarse sand. *Pretty*, I'd considered just moments ago.

Unfortunate, I think now.

It's too lonely. Too sheltered from the mansion party. I can only see so far down the shoreline.

The air tastes more humid. Sticky against my heavy tongue. My ears prick at the tiniest noises. The flapping fabric of a lopsided umbrella. The *whoosh* of the water kissing the sand. The faraway thumping bass from the poolside DJ.

Drunken cackling. Drunken laughter. Is that originating up at the mansion or down below where we are?

Jumbled chatter grows louder. More distinct. I freeze as several figures descend the wooden stairs that lead to the beach. Then they drop onto the sand. Deep husk gravels their voices.

I squint harder. Male figures. Four of them?

As they trek farther into the orangish moonlight, I know for certain. *Four men.*

My pulse shoots out of my chest. "They're coming over here," I whisper to Nova. He really needs to call the others. He's now the only one who knows we're on the beach.

"Who are?"

I'm afraid to talk.

Scenario one: They don't see us. They mind their own business. We mind ours. But does staying silent outweigh giving Nova information? Especially if they see us anyway.

"*Hailey*," Nova forces out. "Who?"

I fight the urge to hang up on him. He's too loud. Nova is always too loud, yet he can be the most silent of us all.

Making a fast decision, I whisper, "Men. They're drunk." As they near, the broad-armed one falls into his lanky friend with hearty laughter.

They could be good men. There's a scenario where they sincerely, empathetically care that my friend has been drugged, and they wait in aid while I call my brother for help.

That percentage lowers due to their alcohol consumption, due to the entitled types that frequent these parties, and due to the fact that this is a group, which could be negatively influenced by peer pressure.

"Is there a weapon around you?" Nova asks. "Anything metal?"

"No," I whisper, "and fighting them isn't a solution, Nova. They're *huge*. I think one is wearing a Caufield jersey." Football players. College students.

Wow, we really did not luck out tonight. There are still several positive scenarios, but trying to crack a linebacker over the head with an eight-foot umbrella or wrestle him to the ground isn't a realistic option.

Nova is thinking like a man.

And unfortunately, in this scenario, I'm a woman, and my options for success are drastically limited.

As they near, their glazed, heavy-lidded eyes come into focus, their hands occupied with bottles of Don Julio, and I'm painfully still, even as the broadest one squints into the dark.

"I-I have to hang up," I murmur.

"No—"

"You need to call the others. Tell them where we are." My voice trembles. "They're going to hear me."

"Can you hide?"

"I'll find a solution." I end his call, and I want to silence the phone but not at the risk of moving.

I wish Phoebe wasn't wearing white. She glows like the arresting moon that dangles over the ocean. I'd rather they fixate on the magnificence of nature and not the breathtaking beauty of her. And I regret ever dyeing my hair a blinding platinum shade. I should've worn my black baseball cap tonight. I should've lain down next to her. I should've shielded her completely from view. The option slips out of my hands—it's too late.

"Hey!" the broader jock shouts. "Who's out there?!" He points directly at me.

I chew on the inside of my cheek. My heart pounds harsher and heavier.

"Is that a chick?" he asks his friends. "You see that?"

"Man, I bet it's that whore Genevive. Fifty bucks she's touching herself."

"Oh God, I hope it's Priscilla. I'd face-fuck her until she pukes."

They laugh, then argue over the repulsiveness of vomit on a dick.

"Who art thou goes there?!" one shouts in a boozy slur. "Julia Kelsey?!"

"Virgin," one singsongs. "I'll pop your cherry, baby!"

"Fuck, I think there's two of them."

"I'd fuck them both."

These are not good men.

"Watch them be goddamn Craig and Bert."

"In that case, you can have them, Timmy."

"Fuck off."

Their footsteps carry more intrigue, their strides lengthier.

I glance backward at Phoebe as she lies like Sleeping Beauty in a dainty white cotton dress awaiting to be saved or be ruined. She's femininity twisted around haunting vulnerability. Her pink-painted toes are speckled with sand. Dozens of scenarios zip rapidly through my head with outcomes that steal my breath, that choke me, but I land on the ones that keep her safe.

"I'll be back," I whisper to my best friend. "I promise. I won't do anything that you wouldn't."

It would scare her.

It honestly scares me.

Springing quickly off the edge of the chair, I sprint toward the four men. "Hey!" I shout. "Hey." I roll to a stop, and instinct nearly causes me to recoil. The pungent tequila stench alone knocks me backward.

Their mops of perfectly coiffed brown hair scream, *Rich!* One sports a flashy A. Lange & Söhne leather-banded watch, another a navy-blue Brioni polo and khaki shorts. Two have on forest-green Caufield Sea Serpent jerseys and hungry glints in their eyes.

I'll be twenty-five in July. If they attend Caufield for undergrad, then I presume I'm older than all four of them. It's wild how I don't feel older.

Not as their gazes roam crudely over me. I do my best to smile and not scowl. "Nice night, huh? How about we go that-away?" I make silly, inoffensive finger guns toward the mansion.

They laugh.

"Whoa, *whoa*," the broadest one says, his jersey clung too tight around his muscled biceps. I watch as he rests an arm on his friend's shoulder and leers toward me. "You're Grey Thornhall's sister, right?"

"Isn't she friends with Phoebe Smith?"

"Man, she is so hot," the preppy one says about Phoebe.

"Oh shit." One stares past me. "Is that her?" They're pointing to Phoebe's unconscious body on the lounge chair.

I step closer. "Let's not go over there," I say. "Seriously. You could just . . . leave us alone? We're pretty beat." I play it nice. It's one of the weakest scenarios, but I'm not against exhausting most of them.

"Aw, did she have too much to drink?" the broadest one laughs.

I layer on the nastiest glare. *"Seriously."*

"Seriously what?" He moves to go check on Phoebe, the predatory look in his eye enough to rattle me. I block him with my body and two outstretched palms.

"You're not going over there," I warn.

"Or what?" He laughs. They all laugh like I'm a weak little twig they can just toss into the ocean and let drift out to sea.

My stomach caves in on itself. What would Phoebe do? I twirl a piece of hair that escaped my braid, cock my hip, and bite the corner of my mouth with dusty seduction. Flirty, I am not, but I try. "What if I want you all to myself?"

I seize their attention enough. I doubt my minimal sex appeal entices them. They're wasted. I bet they'd fuck a cardboard box right now, but if they weren't drunk, we might not be in this situation at all.

"Yeah?" The broader one tips his eyes from my lips to my chest.

"Man, she's the easy one," the preppy guy whispers to the barrel-chested jock. Maybe my reputation as a slut is the real godsend.

"What would you do for us?" the barrel-chested one asks. He likely weighs 250.

"Follow me and find out." I walk backward toward the stairs, drawing them away from Phoebe step by step. This is the last scenario where I get out of this without dropping to my knees.

They're five feet from the twisting wooden staircase when they abruptly stop. My stomach plummets with my pulse.

"I'm not going up there, Callahan," the prep says to the broadest one. "It's too fucking loud."

"Yeah, my ears are still ringing."

Callahan up-nods me. "Come back here."

"It's better if—"

"Nah, come here. Don't be a bitch."

It takes *everything* not to glower. Face-to-face manipulation is not my forte, but I've been working on it this summer. I let out a tiny laugh to cover the disgust. I approach. Inches from them, I peer upward to meet their faces, feeling small. Like a solitary doe among hunters. They've gathered for the skinning.

My mother would loathe knowing I feel like prey. She'd say I've taken a crucial misstep. That somewhere, I've lost the greatest leverage. They should have the illusion of power, but I should always be the one holding the shotgun to deliver the fatal blow.

I motion them to stand where their backs will face Phoebe. "Line up."

"How about we tell you what to do?"

"Yeah, take out your braids."

"I kinda like the braids." One snickers.

I touch one of the two sloppy fishtail braids. It's already come unraveled. "Take off your pants," I tell them, hoping to bide my time.

"You first." Callahan grins.

Phoebe would strip without issue. She was trained for this.

A pit forms in my chest, and I pry my mesh shirt off my body. It was see-through anyway. I'm left in a simple black B-cup bra. "Now take off your pants," I counter.

"We call the shots."

I swallow a grimace. "Or I could just bite your dick off."

Callahan grips my face with one palm, painfully pinching my cheeks together. "You bite us, we will fuck you ragged in this *fucking* sand." He throws my head to the side, my neck aching, but I don't turn back to him right away.

I stare at a divot in the sand. A footprint.

This is not my role, and I hate that it had to be hers. I hate that it could belong to anyone who's perceived as weaker. Isn't this what it is? Perception? I'm smaller. They're bigger. Two simple, important facts.

My brain buzzes with more solutions, scenarios, and possible outcomes until I land on one that gives me more time. That's all I need. *Time.* The longer I can distract them, the better chance Nova will find us before it's too late.

My eyes flit between the four of them, not shying from their gazes. "Have you heard of the term *oral fixation*? It's a controversial theory developed by Sigmund Freud."

"We don't speak freak," Callahan tells me.

His friends snicker.

"The uncomplicated version . . . I want things in my mouth."

That quiets them. They look from me to one another, sizing up their friends' curiosity. I'm a weirdo they've never encountered before. I'm allowing them access to the bizarre, and I'm hoping maybe that's a little more enticing than the beautiful girl passed out behind them.

"So before you put your cock in it, why don't you try something else?" I say. "You can test me. I won't bite. I promise. I get off on this." I open my mouth as wide as I can, convincing myself this isn't exposing the vulnerable parts of me.

I just need *time*.

"Dude." The preppy one slides a look at Callahan. "She really is a slut."

"We'll see just how much you get off on this." Callahan steps forward and grips the side of my cheek again. His eyes lance me in warning before he slips his thumb between my lips. I can't avoid the salty taste of his skin. "Close your lips."

My heart beats heavily as I comply, my eyes pinned to his friends, making sure their attention remains on me. One of them nears just to start slowly untying my braids.

"Suck it like you would my dick," Callahan prods.

My pulse pounds. I lose track of the other two guys as they slip behind me. I try to look over my shoulder.

Callahan's grip tightens, not allowing me to turn my neck. "I said, *suck*."

From behind, fingers tug at the hem of my cargo pants. They're playing with me like I'm a toy that I dangled in front of their faces.

My plan.

It's working . . . a little too well.

My stomach lurches. Nausea spools through me as I begin to suck Callahan's thumb. He grins wickedly. "Aw, she's enjoying this."

More snickering.

I can't . . . I can't do it. Some darker part of me snaps inside.

My teeth clamp down on his thumb hard enough that the metallic taste of blood pools in my mouth. "Fuck!" He growls, pushing me hard into his friend. Hands catch me around the waist. I'm not done. I whirl my head back, hawk up a loogie, and spit at Callahan's face.

Wet, bloody saliva splatters against his cheek.

He growls, "You fucking—"

I shriek—a demonic, unhinged shriek—hoping they'll be so freaked out they'll jolt backward. Instead, Callahan tries to muffle my shrill sound with his meaty hand. Like he promised, he brings me down to the sand. I scratch him with my black-chipped and bitten nails, trying to rip out of his hold, but he's clamped too firmly.

"What did I tell you was going to happen?" he growls in the pit of my ear. Fingers fumble to try to unbutton my cargo pants as I thrash against them. Knees pin my thighs to the ground. Sand gets everywhere. Under my nails. In my eyes. I taste the coarse grit in my mouth and crunch it between my teeth.

I try to kick out when I hear Jake bark, "Get the fuck off

her!! What the *fuck*?!" Now they jump back as though they've been electrocuted.

I claw away, then pick myself up, adrenaline coursing through me, making my pulse race at a speed I can't control. Jake is screaming at them behind me, and their hands are raised in defense like they're little innocent schoolboys.

They make excuses.

They try to laugh it off like it was no big deal. That I asked for it. That I like it rough.

Jake is the second-most-powerful person on this property, and they know it. I don't wait around to see them shuffle away with hung heads and bruised egos.

I only care about Phoebe, and I sprint back to her, tripping in the sand, digging into it to stand back up, and when I collapse next to her on the lounge chair and see she's safe, I dry-heave.

What nearly happened slams so violently into me. I choke for breath.

"Hailey." Jake crouches in front of me, his hands so gentle on my cheeks. "*Hailey.*" His eyes dip to my stomach. "Are you okay?"

I nod and blink through a glassy film. "Phoebe." I rotate my head to her, and he follows and bends over her unconscious frame. Two fingers to her neck, he checks her pulse. He listens to her breath, then comes back to me. "She was drugged?"

I nod rapidly. Snot is dripping out of my nose, and without thought, Jake uses the bottom of his shirt to wipe it, then he cradles my face again with an avalanche of compassion compressing on me.

It has a way of breaking me open. "Th-th-this is what they do, you know?" My splintered voice hurts my throat. I'm crying, and I can't retract the waterworks as they cascade in heavy, anguished waves. "This is what happens to them over and over and over. *This*."

Jake searches my eyes for clearer answers he can't see. "Who . . . ? What?"

"Phoebe and Rocky," I cry. "This is what they were taught to do. Th-this is what happens. She almost . . . and he comes in . . ." I choke out. "Their roles. Their responsibilities."

He casts a hard look backward to where my mesh shirt lies crumpled in the sand. Then back to me with the devastation I feel.

"It's not fair what they had to do for our parents. It's not fair what they gave up for us . . ." My chin quivers as I remember Carlsbad. The Fiddle Game. The mark. His grotesque friend. "I just hear them in that fucking room with her, and I couldn't get in. They wouldn't let me in to stop it . . . I would've done anything to stop it."

I sob, and Jake pulls me into his chest. I weave my arms around his shoulders. As he stands, I'm lifted with him, and I don't have to hang on. He holds me against his muscled, towering build.

His cerulean-blue eyes sweep over me. Into me. Dreamlike. I stare into him, unable to look away. His thick brows harden like his jaw, but he's not severe or stern. Of his many layers, most are soft. Caring. There is only care in his expression now, and it begins to calm the torture in my lungs.

This is a good man.

I gaze longer, soaring inside the summer sky, and I wonder how high I can truly go before gravity brings me down. He tucks a stray piece of hair behind my ear, the soft act a caress to my heart.

We both hear the quickened, urgent breath of someone running toward us. Our heads turn in unison, and I see Oliver.

His eyes sweep our embrace, my lack of shirt, my tear-streaked cheeks while I slide down Jake. I'm shaking. I can't stop the full-body tremors as panic and anxiety crush my windpipe.

"What happened?" Oliver asks with mountainous concern, then he spots his sister passed out on the lounge chair. He *bolts* for Phoebe. "Shit. *Shit*. Phoebe?" He pats her cheek.

I sink on the edge of the chair beside her bare legs.

Oliver sends an alarmed glance back at me. "You need to tell me." It's not a harsh demand. Oliver is never harsh or unkind or cruel. Unless he has to be. But never with me.

"I-I . . ." I watch Jake trek away to retrieve my shirt. "I was here when she passed out. I didn't see who drugged her."

"Did anyone come over here?" Oliver asks, taking Phoebe's pulse on her wrist. "Hails?" He reaches over and squeezes my knee. "Was anyone else on the beach before Jake got here?" It's a gentle ask.

Yet I feel sick.

I puke between my knees. Barely missing my combat boots. *Terrific*.

"Just let it out, Hailstorm." Oliver steps over the lounge chair with his long legs, coming to my side while unbuttoning his white shirt. "Nothing like a regular Saturday night rager. One for the history books."

A strangled laugh is stuck in my burning throat. "I don't want to reread this one." I spit off to the side.

Oliver hands me his shirt to use as a rag and kicks sand on top of my vomit. Then he squats in front of me, scrutinizing my features. I fixate on his hair that curls around his ear. On the curve of his soft kiss-worthy lips. Whether he's a warm golden tan or paler from avoiding the sun, whether he's stubbled or clean-shaven, whether he's shed weight or gained ten pounds of muscle, the glimmer in his caramel-flecked eyes stays the same.

His very existence is a cool balm to my wounds. Soothing, trying to wake me.

I'm not like him. I worry I'm not something that can heal others, but rather, something that will hurt.

He shifts in his squat, his eyes still tracing me. "Well, she seems fully intact. Where are her wits?"

"Lost for a moment," I say.

"Nothing I can't find." His charismatic smile could draw a faraway one out of me, but his is slightly dulled with concern for me and for his sister tonight.

His pupils are also ginormous. I stare right into those big black orbs. He knows that I know he's high. *I wasn't supposed to be at this party tonight.* Without me here and while he's around Trent, he probably thought it was a good time tonight to snort a line or two to assimilate. Blending in as the chameleon comes with its own plights.

I wipe my mouth with his shirt. "Thanks, Olly."

"How many were there?" he asks in one breath. He holds up his hand, and I lower his pinky finger. "Four?"

I nod. "I-I did something gross to bide me time."

His brows rise in consideration. "I'm sure I've done grosser."

My eyes burn. I wish that weren't true. My lip quivers, and Jake returns with my shirt. His dark gaze and visceral heat on both of us. "We should leave."

I nod, swallowing more nausea. "She'll need smelling salts. We promised her . . ." I meet Oliver's eyes, and he exhales heavily into a nod.

"Promised her what?" Jake looks between us, confused.

"If this were to happen, she made us promise to wake her up. Even for just a minute or two." I don't tell him that most medical professionals would advise against it. The smelling salts won't counteract the drugs in her system. They'll just make her alert for a short while, but no one is going to go against Phoebe's wishes on this one.

Oliver turns to his sister. He scoops her up like she's a Disney princess lost in a forever slumber. While he carefully cradles her limp body in his arms, her head slumps against his chest, and his gaze returns to me.

I take the shirt from Jake. Sticking my arms through the mesh fabric, I fight with the material as I roll it down my stomach, and I collect her purse and heels.

Oliver passes me and whispers, "Did they touch you?"

"Please, Olly, I don't want to cry again." I glare at the sand to subdue the wreckage I feel. Jake presses a comforting hand to the back of my neck as he walks beside me, his thumb stroking me, and I ache to grab hold of him.

I try to slow my pulse with measured breaths. Phoebe compartmentalizes, purposefully forgets, but I don't know how to. All I do is remember. My skin still crawls from the meaty hand over my mouth. From the thumb against my tongue. From the hands that I couldn't see but I could feel on my body. "Just go," I breathe. "Jake, call Rocky."

He's likely out of his mind right now.

TWENTY-EIGHT

Rocky

Trent finds me before I find him.

I've led him away from the east grounds, away from any place where I think Phoebe might be. On the stone backyard patio, I step over cigarette butts, deflated inner tubes, and abandoned sandals.

I subtly check my phone to see if anyone found her. No new messages. No updates.

My insides are being shredded ded alive with every passing second I'm separated from her. My eyes are enflamed, and I have trouble seeing farther than ten feet in front of my fucking face.

The unknown is very slowly, very excruciatingly, thrashing through me like an uncaged animal.

I can't produce a friendly smile.

I can barely level my voice.

To force myself from glaring, I concentrate on the sweat dripping down my temple. The sensation quickly grates on me, and I scrape the heel of my palm against the side of my face.

"You need to quit helping my brother," Trent bemoans

again, running fingers through his dark brown hair, then outstretching his arm to the humongous lap pool where the DJ is serving *tinnitus* and an idiot cannonballs off the second story into the red-lit water. Topless women lounging on flamingo floaties squeal as waves rock into them. "You really want to stop this, Grey?!"

"I'm helping *you*!" I shout over the music and pop of fireworks. "Jake could so easily sue you—"

"Please!" he cuts in with a laugh. "My little brother?! He's too fucking *soft*!" Trent has both my shoulders in his grip, stopping us in a puddle of water near the pool. "He's not like you and me! He never will be!" His slanted smile stretches with arrogance I can barely withstand right now. "If he were, maybe he'd still have Phoebe!"

I am visceral rage. But only inside.

"And what if Jake never caves?!" I grimace at the C-rate wedding party DJ as if it's beneath a Koning's status.

"He'll cave! In the meantime, have some fucking *fun*." He rattles my shoulders, and the urge to punch him intensifies. My general disdain for Trent lives underneath a more ruinous emotion that I can't name. It feels catastrophic now.

"You know this isn't my scene!" I yell back. "I find these parties to be too inclusive!" It's a shallow dig. "It'd be better with a smaller guest list!" I check the time on my watch, needing to cut loose from him.

Needing her.

It's a desperation, and I can't let him smell it on me.

"Couldn't agree more! But you have to look at the bigger picture here!" He pats my face lightly, seeing what he can get away with, and I slap his hand off me. It's a warning.

"Don't bust my balls, man! I've had a long, *long* week with work!" I'm in the CIA and he's the only special fucking soul

I've offered this confidential intel to—not even my ex-wife knows. Another check of my Rolex and I tell him, "I need to meet up with my wife!"

"*Ex*-wife!" He shouts back the reminder, testing my boundaries.

But I'm not a beta bitch. He's liked that I'm an alpha who won't let his bottom-feeder friends run all over me, but I am never to run over him.

I'm about to step away.

He shoots out a hand and snatches my bicep, stopping me. "How is Phoebe?!"

I tear him off. Is he stalling me? Alarm blasts shriller than the music, popping the external noise around me. All I hear is my dread.

I stare through him with a daggered gaze. Does he know where she is right now? Did he always know?

I sweep my eyes over the pool, the backyard, but all I see are flashes of Nashville, of our early twenties. I'm gripping her hair in the alleyway while she pukes. I'm holding her in the backseat of the car as she loses consciousness.

She's crying. *I hate this. I hate this. Don't leave me.*

I snap back into focus on Trent. "I thought you knew she was here?!"

"I saw her from afar! I didn't think she'd come tonight! She never does!" At face value, I'd say he's telling the truth. "I might've . . ." He swings his head from side to side with a shit-eating grin.

"You might've what?!" I smile to pull it out of him. We're just friends. He can tell me anything. I even say it. "We're friends, aren't we?!" I smack his chest with the back of my hand.

"We are!" He dips his head toward me. "And you've been

moody *as fuck*, Grey. You need a good release." He pauses, gauging my reaction, and I nod and smile in agreement. He continues. "Look, as your friend, I'd say she's still into you, but she's not putting out without some encouragement. It's going to be a hell of a lot easier tonight."

"Yeah?" *Fuck you*. "How so?"

"I paid that cuck Howie to put a little something in her drink to get her loose." He smacks my chest now. "You can thank me later, but only if I can watch." He laughs as if it's a joke, but his darkened gaze says he's serious—that there better be an invite. He will participate. I will share and thank him for this gift.

My brain is numb. I hear nothing but my raging pulse. I see nothing but my all-consuming, heart-wrenching life with her.

A thousand times I've bit my tongue until it's bled. A thousand times I've crushed my real feelings in a blender for the job. *The job*. There's still an unfinished job. A rope unpulled. I need Trent close.

I can't sever the rope between me and him.

I can't hacksaw it.

But I can't force down the violent surge inside me. All the blistering, untapped anger. The overpowering rage. It amasses. Too quickly.

I lower my head, our foreheads nearly touching as I stare into him. "You think I'm a cuck?"

He sees something new in my eyes. A flicker of doubt reaches him. The music shuts off abruptly to exclamations of "Hey!" and "Turn it back on!"

I step close to Trent, bumping my chest into his.

"Grey?"

I sneer, "You think I'd let you rape my wife?"

People gasp as they hear me.

Distaste writhes across his ugly face. “No one said anything about that, Grey. *You* went there.”

I walk him farther backward. To the edge.

Her voice is in my head again. *I hate this. I hate this. Don’t leave me.*

I erupt. I thrust him in the pool. And I go with him.

Let me be clear, I *want* to go with him.

The red-lit water is freezing cold, but I can’t feel the chill. I grapple with Trent under the surface and above, punching and kicking every time we come up for air. Violent splashes of water slap back at my face. I hammer my fist into his jaw, and he lands one on my mouth. The commotion from bystanders around the pool is muted in my head. I only hear my pounding pulse.

Then I sink him in the eight-foot depths, drag him down. The red pool light glows hot next to us. I rip the collar of his shirt, yank his arm behind his back. He tries to dunk me to propel himself to the surface.

He’s fighting for air.

I wrench him back down like a steel anchor. He thrashes more frantically as I keep him under. He can’t shove me off. I’m stronger and more meticulous and careful in how I cage my breath.

I bet he didn’t have a father strap ankle weights on him and give him a crash course in the water like he was a teenage Navy SEAL recruit. I bet he’s never been this uncomfortable in his life.

I bet he’s never felt powerless.

He screams underwater, bubbles expelling from his parted mouth.

Seeing his unrighteous anger switch into fear—it frees

something inside me. I've never felt this much oxygen fill my lungs.

I don't know how long we're underwater for, but I could last forever. I could kill him. I have it in me. But I never let my base desires dominate me. *You're not in control, Bray.* I hear the woman who raised me.

I'm not in control.

Do I even care?

Before I answer that question in my head, someone plunges into the water. Hands grab at my shoulder, my ribs, and then yank me off Trent. I don't fight them.

Trent kicks toward the surface, battling for his last breath.

When I breach the water and suck in air, I seize the pool's edge and heave myself out onto the stone. I turn my head left and see Jake.

He's pulling himself out, too, and he's drenched. I honestly thought it'd been Nova . . . It wasn't Nova. Jake was the one who jumped in after me.

The weight of this bears down on my chest. Now I feel like I can't fucking breathe. Hilarious.

Trent hangs on to the edge and stays partially submerged in the pool, not having the strength to bring himself to land. He coughs up water, hacks up a lung.

I pay only partial attention to the shocked, inebriated crowd. These aren't the older prim and proper socialites who frequent Victoria Country Club; these are their thirtysomething and college-aged children.

"Holy shit!" A drunk exclamation fills the tense silence.

"Is that Grey?"

"Wait, Grey and Trent are fighting? Aren't they, like, best friends?"

Two social climbers try to help Trent out of the pool. He shoves off the guys, not wanting to appear weak, even as he wheezes.

I push my wet hair back and intake bigger lungfuls of air.

There's a chance Phoebe never consumed the spiked drink. There's a chance Howie never slipped GHB in her cup. It doesn't change the fact that Trent premeditated this, but it changes the outcome of tonight.

Though, if she did get drugged . . .

It slams into me.

Suddenly, unbearably.

I move so fast, shooting toward Trent—I can't see even two feet in front of my face now. All I imagine is stepping on his hand, hearing the bones crack, and then shoving his head beneath the water again.

Jake slips his arms beneath my armpits, gripping me from behind and wrenching me backward. He fucking *lifts* me off the ground to keep me from reaching his brother. "Stop," he says in the pit of my ear, a lot less hostile, a lot more consoling than I'd be. "Stop, Brayden."

Him saying my birth name—yeah, that does it.

I suck in the rage, containing it with one harsh inhale. Jake releases his hold on me while Trent catches his breath enough to snarl, "What the absolute *fuck*?" The venom in his face is tangible.

There is a way back from this. A way to convince him it was a simple misunderstanding. But do I even want him to believe that?

No.

I want to force-feed him the truth until he fucking chokes. "You think you're a god to this fucking town?" Heat expels off my rough voice. "You're a *tumor*."

"Fuck—"

"No, fuck you," I grit between my teeth. "What's mine isn't yours; you don't fucking own me. You never did, you *never* will." I feed off his disturbed expression as he sees me, sees the *real* me and what I am. I've never been his friend. "If it's not fucking clear, *TK*"—I spit out his nickname—"I think you're a repulsive piece of *shit*. I've chosen a side. And it'll never be yours." My harsh gaze flits around the stunned audience, Solo cups crushed in hands and mouths agape. "You all should do the same."

Trent blinks through the mindfuckery of my abrupt betrayal. "Get out of my house," he says coldly.

"With pleasure." I leave the patio with a hot, forceful stride. People back away from me, giving me a wide berth like I might catch them on fire.

I feel someone at my side.

Trevor. He's here. He's been here for I don't know how long. Like a shadow passing unseen through the crowds.

He keeps my hurried pace now. Quickly, I hand him my waterlogged phones. All dead. Useless. But if anyone can bring them back to life, it'd be him.

He pockets them. "You went feral. You said to never go feral."

"It wasn't planned."

This stuns him, then he faces forward. "She's going to be okay, Rock. PG is the strongest girl I know."

A ball lodges in my throat. Did someone . . . ? Is she . . . ? "Where is she?" Right as I ask, Jake reaches my other side.

"Follow me," he says, catching my elbow and tugging me in a new direction.

As Trevor falls back behind us, I say under my breath to Jake, "You could've let me drown him. It would've solved all your problems." He's *wished* for his brother's death. Well, it was right there.

And he stopped it.

Jake's jaw muscle tenses, then he meets my gaze. There is something crushing in his eyes, something that reaches too far inside me. "I wasn't saving him."

He was saving me.

From prison.

Every tormenting thing about tonight piles onto me, and an onslaught of emotion rams into my chest, making it harder to breathe, and I see water, a dark river. I picture the family I lost. I think about Evan Wolfe, my older brother, who likely saved me as we went under, and I can't even look at Jake.

TWENTY-NINE

Rocky

When's the last time I ran this fast? Was it carrying my wounded brother on Halloween? Was it racing toward a storm shelter where my sister was hallucinating?

Now it's for Phoebe.

I want to say this is worse somehow. That the suffering of her is the suffering of me. But it's all hell I've grown strong inside. This urgent, desperate feeling isn't new to me. It's been undying.

I run out of the side yard with Jake and Trevor, coming to the front of the estate. Trent Waterford paid off the security guards. They refused Jake's direction to stay the night, and they've left their posts at the gate so anyone could get through.

Dozens of cars are parked in jagged, uneven, chaotic lines on the edge of the road leading to the mansion. My McLaren among them.

It's not what I'm aiming for.

Nova's olive-green 1969 Pontiac GTO is idling in the horseshoe driveway. He's digging in the popped trunk while Hailey disappears into the driver's seat.

The rear door is open. Oliver is bent inside the car, and I can only guess who he's laying across the backseat.

My lungs are on fire when I reach Nova as he slams the trunk, a trauma bag slung on his shoulder. The glare he shoots me hits a deep nerve. I wasn't careless about his sister; I've never been careless about Phoebe in my entire goddamn life.

I clench my jaw and pass him without a word. We say nothing because we're trained to move and not air grievances when things go south.

It takes an ungodly amount of force not to immediately check on Phoebe. All I want is to hold her, be with her, tell her I'm here.

It's a nail gun to my chest just to avoid the rear door and reach the driver's side.

"Get out," I tell Hailey.

"I can drive—"

"It's not that." As she climbs out, I draw her several feet away from the Pontiac. She's shaking. I can't make sense of why she's trembling or gathering the sleeves of her mesh shirt in her fists. I can tell it's not from anxiety, but the origins are lost on me.

I'm not the person who can comfort her right now. As much as I want that for my sister, it's not going to be me. In this moment, I'm shrapnel. "I need you to be honest with me," I say quickly. *"Hailey."*

She lifts her gray eyes to mine. They're bloodshot and puffy. She's been crying.

My ribs constrict. "When I ask you something, you need to tell me the truth and fast—for Phoebe, for her health." I'm ninety-nine percent sure I know the answer to the question, but I have to ask anyway. I have to be sure.

Hailey looks sick.

I drop my voice. "Is she pregnant?"

"No." She maintains steady eye contact with me. "But I am."

I nod. "I know," I whisper, the magnitude of this trying to combust inside of me.

"You know?" Her eyes well, and she glances toward the car.

"No one told me. I figured it out."

Her nose flares, but she manages to nod back. She swipes at her eyes to stop tears from falling. "Phoebe," she chokes out before I can react. "Go to Phoebe."

I'm being ripped in two directions, and my skull is throbbing as I rush back to the Pontiac. The rear doors are open, both Graves brothers leaning inside the car.

I throw keys to my McLaren at Jake.

He catches them midair, then runs to Hailey as she crumples against the tire, burying her face in her palms.

"Move," I tell Oliver on the rear passenger side. He shifts out of the way, letting me through. I see the way he glances over the car. I see the way he searches for my sister, but I don't linger on it.

Because I just want to be with her.

Phoebe.

Phoebe.

Anger and something deeper amass like an abyss inside my chest.

She's unconscious on the leather bench seat. Her head nearest me. Her feet near Nova. I examine her so rapidly. Her white dress isn't ripped or torn. No dirt or bloodstains. Just sand on her toes. Her arm hangs limp over the seat. Her blue hair conceals her face, and I push the strands aside and cradle her head. I inspect her cheeks, her lips.

My pulse won't stop accelerating.

Nova is bent over his sister and unspooling the tubes for an IV drip. His glare hits me more than once.

"I didn't fucking lose her," I say roughly, climbing into the backseat and lifting Phoebe onto my lap. I have her.

I have her.

I'm not letting her out of my sight.

"You didn't find her either," Nova retorts, then eyes my mouth. I assume my lip is split from Trent landing a punch. I'm also soaking wet. "I hope it was worth it."

"Fuck you," I say weakly, my voice hoarse. Guilt is already killing me. He doesn't need to twist the knife.

Nova must see. He tosses me a rubber tube. "Tie this around her bicep."

I prop her head on my thigh and quickly knot the rubber around her arm. He rests a knee on the seat near her hip. While hovering over her, Nova flicks the inside of her elbow, then sticks a needle in her vein.

We're rushing at a pace that has no room for thoughts or feelings. I don't let them enter while he starts the IV. I hook the saline bag on the car hanger bar above my head.

There is no *We can't handle this*. There is only *We have to handle this*.

It might as well be the Tinrock-Graves motto.

Oliver stands outside behind me, and I tell him that I gave Jake my keys. "He needs to drive Hailey to the marina," I explain. "*The Ithaka* is at the docks. We'll all stay on the yacht tonight."

Oliver bows down closer to me, his hand on the frame of the car. "I'll go with Hails—"

"No, you need to drive us," I say. "Your brother is going to stay in the backseat with me." Nova is already shutting the side door. He's sitting beside me, and Phoebe's legs are splayed over his lap. He digs out a pulse oximeter from the trauma bag.

"Trevor?" Oliver glances backward, but as he scans the horseshoe driveaway, I know my brother is already gone.

I saw him tinkering with my waterlogged phones and walking away about the same time I talked to Hailey.

"He left in the Honda," I say. "He'll meet us at the yacht. Send him a text."

"You don't need to text," Nova cuts in fast. "He's spending the night with Sidney at the Harbor Hotel." He clips the pulse oximeter on Phoebe's finger, then meets my hard gaze. "That's why Phoebe and Hailey were here. For Sidney." He explains what happened in under thirty seconds—information he sourced from Trevor and Hailey.

I stare at the back of the headrest, a migraine hammering against my temple. Weston Burke and Trent Waterford fucking me over in one night.

I try not to replay the downward spiral of events, but this night will get infinitely worse if Weston Burke finds his daughter at a hotel and Trevor is there. I just tell Oliver, "He stays on the yacht tonight. Call him."

"Calling our little psychopath," Oliver confirms, putting the phone to his car and shutting the car door.

I lean against it more, and I pull Phoebe higher up my body. Her shoulders are flush with my chest, and her head lolls against my collar. "Should she be this cold?" I ask Nova while I rub her arms, careful of the IV.

"The fluids should help. I'll monitor her, but if her vitals drop, we're taking her to the hospital." He passes me a medicine bottle. "Here."

I read the label: SMELLING SALTS.

I send him a short look of appreciation. The small exchange

is one of amnesty between us. He could've easily done this himself, but he's letting me take over this part and care for his sister like I usually do.

I'm not going to be an ass and remind him of that or how my love for her hasn't depreciated in the past twenty-four hours. Nothing has changed—not even the fact that he doesn't want me with his sister long term.

I wave the white flag because it's easier when Nova and I aren't banging heads like two stubborn bucks locking antlers.

Oliver slips behind the wheel. "All aboard." He starts the ignition.

Nova casts a toughened glance of concern at his brother. I wonder how much coke Oliver snorted tonight. It's a fleeting thought as he drives us out of the Koning estate. Nova turns back to me to say, "It'll wake her up, but not for long."

I open the childproof cap. The car glides across smooth paved roads and through the iron gates. Phoebe isn't being jostled against me, thankfully, and I quickly pass the bottle beneath her nose.

The ammonia in the smelling salts triggers an inhalation reflex, and she suddenly jerks into a gasp. Her eyes blink open. "Wh-what the fuck?" she curses out with such a biting tone (classic Phoebe) that Nova nearly smiles, and weight releases off my chest.

"I have you, Phebs," I whisper against her ear. "You're safe in your brother's car. I'm not letting you go."

She clutches my forearm that's wrapped around her chest, holding on and registering her surroundings. Her eyes drift to Nova, then upward at me. She blinks hard, her heavy-lidded gaze trying to close as quickly as it opened. "Rocky?"

I cup her cheek with a firm hand. "You're okay. *I'm not leaving you.*" I force this out so she understands the permanence, the promise. Her body slackens. I press a kiss into her dark blue hair. She expels a deeper breath, and I murmur, "We're taking you to *The Ithaka*. That's where you'll wake up again."

Her lips form one word. My name. *Rocky*. Her eyes glass, and I thumb away silent tears slipping down her cheeks.

She shuts her eyes, too out of it to comprehend anything other than my presence—that I'm right here. The comfort and security of this keeps easing her body against me. Soon, the drugs begin to drag her back under.

Now that Phoebe is being taken care of, my mind travels back to my sister, and my migraine strengthens like a screw drilling halfway into my skull. "What happened to Hailey?" I ask them.

"Oliver and Jake found her on the beach," Nova explains in a wooden tone that sends a shot of adrenaline into my bloodstream. I can't relax. "She was protecting Phoebe."

"She was protecting Phoebe," I repeat with a similar flat tone, and an iron taste floods my mouth. It takes me a second to realize I just bit my tongue. "Was she assaulted?"

"I don't know." Nova pulls at his khaki crewneck like he's burning up inside. Anger pulses his narrowed eyes, and he cranks down the window to let balmy nighttime air into the car.

Silence eats at me.

At us.

Oliver has one casual hand on the wheel. "Hailey shouldn't have been in that position. It's not a role she's been trained to handle." He doesn't bring up her role in conning Trent, since she's been struggling with it.

Nova scrapes a palm back and forth over his short brown hair. "The three of you *barely* handle it fucking well. Phoebe dissociates, Rocky has a sensitivity problem—"

"It's not a *problem*," I interject.

"—and you spend three hours organizing the bathroom cabinet, Ol."

"Coping mechanisms," Oliver reasons. "That's what we were taught, Nov. Hailey has *none* of that when it comes to these situations. If it'd been me or Phoebe or Rocky, we would've been able to lead these guys back to the party with promises of a good time that we were *never* going to deliver."

Guys? There were *guys* on the beach. Confirmed.

My brain is on fire. Especially as Nova says, "This wasn't a job. They weren't working a fucking *job*, Oliver."

I grind my jaw. "It's Trent," I chime in. "It's always fucking Trent." He's a malignant growth on this town. We're just the parasite determined to bring him down.

But I fucked up. *Really* fucked up. My friendship with Trent was obliterated in one instant tonight. I lost every shred of influence over the eldest Koning. Our plans to push him out of Victoria just became infinitely harder.

All thanks to me.

THIRTY

Rocky

Just like old times," Nova mutters tightly as he hooks an IV bag to a coatrack we brought from the yacht's main saloon to the primary suite, and I cover Phoebe's legs beneath the comforter.

Like old times. Nashville, our early twenties, the image of a motel, doing this same thing with Nova Graves as I rested his unconscious sister on a bed. Our past strikes me like a flashlight in my eyes. It pierces. Tries to hurt.

I never left her that night. I wouldn't leave her now. I'm accustomed to doing the same things over and *over* again. This twisted merry-go-round is a ride we can't seem to jump off of. We're falling victim to the same patterns. Same behaviors.

There are moments when I wonder if we like it.

If life would be too mundane without these insane highs and devastating lows, then I don't want to believe it. I don't want to believe that life with Phoebe needs to be this painful.

"A time we're not repeating," I say more to the room than

to Nova, and I mean it. I can't do this again. I can't have her in harm's way again and *again*.

After I tuck my passed-out girlfriend into bed, I take a seat on the edge beside her waist, and I unlace my Italian leather boots. My muscles can't unflex. My abs won't untighten. I'm resting at a perpetual state of pissed-off fury.

Nova is also stewing. About what exactly, I'm unsure, but he's not bolting out the door. He keeps watch of his sister, gripping the bedpost like he's forcing himself not to do something rash and stupid. Like hunt down the fucker who slipped her drugs.

There are bigger monsters to stake in the heart than *Howie*.

I don't tell him that. Because, again, can't read his mind. "You can go," I say, my tone not close to sweet. "I'm staying with her for the rest of the night."

Nova also stayed in the motel with Phoebe years ago, but some things have changed since then. I need him to acknowledge this. Like right now.

He's quiet. His jaw muscle twitching.

I pry off my boot, gripping it like he's gripping the bedpost. "What more do you want for her?" I ask him outright. "I would *die* for your sister. I would protect her until my last fucking breath. I love her how she wants to be loved. What more is there, Nova? Because that's all I would want for Hailey."

"I don't want you to pull her back," Nova states, his gaze resting not harshly on mine. He's scared for Phoebe. "I want her to quit this lifestyle *for good*."

I glance backward at Phoebe as she "sleeps" soundlessly. "I'm not actively drawing her toward it, and at the end of the day, it's her choice. What you want or what I want doesn't fucking matter."

Nova glowers. "And what I really want is for my sister to be with a guy who'd never let her be the honeypot. Who'd tell her no."

I would've told her no if she insisted on being the one to marry Trent. But I didn't have to, because Phoebe backed down and let Hailey take the role. But I can't even defend myself because I know this is the *one* exception. I can't be sure I'd tell Phoebe no for anything else.

I meet Nova's piercing eyes. "I'm not going to *dictate* her life. She's had twenty-five years of being told what to do, and she needs to figure out how to call her own shots."

He runs his hand over his head, stressed-out. "So, you just never tell her what you want? You never express what you'd like her to do?"

"I'm not manipulating Phoebe."

"The people who raised us, they screwed with us. I can cop to that, Rock, but you are bouncing too far in the opposite direction, man."

I'm glaring, but I'm listening.

Especially as he says, "Expressing what you want out of a partner—that's not manipulation."

"It'll sway her decision."

"You're making a decision about your future together. She should know what you want."

I raise my brows at him. "You want me to convince her to quit grifting, but you wouldn't be saying this to me if you knew what I hoped."

Nova looks like he could punch me. "You seriously hope she won't quit?"

"I *seriously* don't want to stop lying and deceiving with her. Yeah." I ignore his lacerating glare as I add, "But I do want her to stop being the girl who's two seconds from being assaulted. She doesn't need to be in those positions. Because I know the damage it's done to her."

"Tell her that."

"I have before," I say. "After the Alps, I did." Back when Trent jumped in the hot tub naked.

"What about the damage it's done to you?"

"She knows I hate it, but I hate everything, including this conversation." I chuck the boot toward the dresser, not even in the mood to force an annoyed smile.

Nova doesn't flinch as my shoe thumps onto the carpeted floor.

I grip my knees. "She decided she didn't want to be bait for Trent. That was *her* choice. She's getting there on her own."

I've never wanted to shove Phoebe in the direction I want her to go. I've always thought if she ends up down a path that makes me want to strangle and decapitate someone, I'd just live inside that volatile feeling. It's where I've existed.

But Nova is right in the fact that I don't want to be here.

I want this to stop. I want her out of harm's way for good, and I'm the one who's terrified of having to control the situation. But I might have to.

So I tell him, "I hear you."

He nods, sheathing his swords he loves waving in my face. Maybe I needed him to. I don't know yet. I do know that he's still not leaving.

I watch as Nova pulls out his phone and sends a quick one-handed text at his waist. He sees me staring and explains, "I'm not going into the art gallery tomorrow. I let the owner know."

His job as an art curator has no bearing on his job as a grifter. It's a useless position. But he hasn't given it up and no one has asked him to. Because we all know he genuinely loves art. It's one of the few things Nova Graves does love that isn't Oliver or Phoebe.

He takes his sister's pulse again, and I cast a glance at the door, worried about mine in the next second.

Hailey is pregnant. The thought still pulverizes me, and I hope she'll loop in the last to know, Nova and Trevor, because the easiest way to protect her is if we're all on the same fucking page.

THIRTY-ONE

Hailey

There is no shower hot enough or long enough to erase the memory of a stranger's disgusting sweaty thumb in my mouth. Especially when I had asked him to put it there. The steam makes me uncomfortable. Suffocated. In need of air. I only last five minutes before I exit into the small bathroom. I can't escape the vapor. It fogs the mirror and cocoons me in unpleasant heat.

Where's Phoebe? It's a panicked thought until I remember, *She's with Rocky.*

He carried her to the primary suite. I relax.

I run my fingers through my tangled wet hair. I should know how many hours have passed since we've all arrived on *The Ithaka*, but I don't. Time slips between my churning thoughts. Replaying tonight's events. Where I went wrong. Where I could've gone right. Why had I relied so heavily on someone finding us? And what would have happened if Jake didn't come to the beach at that exact moment?

I think about everything. The reality and the wasted opportunities.

"Stop thinking," I mutter. *"Stop it."* I catch myself picking at my cuticle.

Normally I'd just camp out with Phoebe in her stateroom. We'd eat a melting pint of Moose Tracks and watch some vintage slasher flick. Or she'd put on *Never Been Kissed* for me. A favorite of mine mostly because Drew Barrymore essentially cons the whole student body into believing she's a teenager when she's really an undercover reporter.

Phoebe always makes faces when David Arquette's adult character seduces a high school senior.

"Gross!" she would yell at the TV. "He's not even that hot!"

"He's not even that smart," I'd add. "But he can play baseball."

"Okay, but can he wield a crossbow like a fucking baddie? Unless he turns into a vampire hunter or *is* a vampire and stops creeping on high schoolers, then he's a solid one-point-two on the hot meter, Hails." She'd flip off the screen every time he'd appear.

I'd laugh as each middle finger would get progressively more animated and closer to the TV. My cheeks would strain into an ache.

I want to smile now, just thinking how we decompress from emotionally taxing nights. With junk food and movies that transport us out of our lawless lives.

I love consuming knowledge, but it's not entirely why I love films and books. I crave the escape. To be carried to a faraway place, to visit a thousand different destinations and lose myself among lives so unlike mine.

It's why I also loved being a grifter. Traveling, being a voyeur who slips in and out of cities, never residing long enough to be called "the easy one" or "the town slut."

I don't really care about being labeled.

I don't care about my reputation in Victoria. Because even if it's bad, I like having one. I like being *real*. Most of the connections I've made here aren't forged from fictitious threads I've created. I have more purpose than just being a master puppeteer who's scared of dropping a string, causing harm to those I love. More than just being Phoebe's best friend.

I have the simple purpose of being *me*. Of figuring out who *I* am.

And I'm honestly Hailey, a country club server. Hailey, a girl who has fallen epically hard for *two* men. Hailey, a girl who doesn't know what the future holds. Who, for the first time, can't see that far ahead.

I think I'd want my baby to feel multidimensional. To find simple purpose in life before wading into the deep.

I've done it all backward.

"Inside out, outside in," I mutter to myself, my thoughts spinning.

I blink a few times before I enter my guest cabin in a cotton towel.

The small space only has room for a king-sized bed, two end tables, a television on the wall, and a long button-tufted bench at the foot of the bed. Warm lighting bathes the suite, and it's not empty.

Jake and Oliver sit on the bench. Side by side. Waiting for me.

Their whispered conversation dies as soon as I step onto the soft carpet and shut the bathroom door behind me.

Instead of prying into *that*, I ask, "Is Trent coming onto the yacht tonight?"

"*No*," Jake says, his brows furrowed. "No, he's not stepping a foot on here. Varrick already picked him up in the dinghy and took him back to Stonehaven."

My stomach curdles. Varrick being nice to him, not a revelation. I understand why he has to be. Trent is the mark. It just sours every part of my insides that Trent gets to roofie Phoebe's drink and then walk away unscathed.

Not unscathed if we can complete the job.

Which still relies on *me* getting Trent to marry me. A shiver skates across the back of my neck. "How do I make him want to marry me if I'm going to want to stab him every time I look at him?" I say more to myself than to them.

But they obviously hear me.

Jake grimaces. "You're still thinking about the job?"

"She's always thinking about the job." Oliver rises to his feet, television remote in hand.

"It's easier thinking about that than what happened tonight . . ." I turn to a stack of clothes on the end table. Their eyes trail my body as I tug on a clean baggy Metallica tee and black cotton shorts.

"I know you don't want to talk about it, but Jake said he found you on the ground," Oliver says hesitantly like he's gauging how hard to press his finger into an open wound. So this is most likely what they'd been whispering about before I came in.

"But I don't know how you got there," Jake adds. "Whether you were pushed or kicked or dragged—"

"I don't have an answer to that. It happened too fast." I spin to face them. They look at me with such heavy concern, it nearly steals my breath.

"Do you need to see a doctor?" Jake asks. "For you or the baby?"

I shake my head. "I'm not bruised or bleeding. I think we're okay." I tuck a strand of hair behind my ear, crawl onto the middle of the bed, and glance up at the television screen.

"You want to watch a movie?" Oliver asks, already holding out the remote for me.

My heartbeat hammers in my chest. "I-I have to . . . I have to tell you both what happened first. Because if you think it constitutes as cheating, I think you both should know before we continue the night . . ."

My words drain the energy out of the room. Jake rubs a tensed palm over his mouth, despair already written across his eyes.

Oliver doesn't blink, his hand with the remote dropping to his side. "You were protecting my sister, Hailey. It won't change anything for me."

Jake lifts his head and sends a challenging look to Oliver. A combination of a grimace and glare lances his face. "And you think it'd change something for me?"

Oliver shrugs. "You tell us."

Rising to his feet, Jake faces me while I sit cross-legged on top of the comforter. His expression excavates the vulnerable parts of me. I try my best to breathe when he starts talking.

"I know we said we'd all be exclusive, but you could sleep with a hundred people, Hailey, and I would only care if your happiness was intact. I fell in love with you not because you're mine, but because I don't want a future where I'm not yours."

My eyes well with an onslaught of emotion. "This isn't real," I mutter under my breath.

"This is very real, Hailstorm." Oliver's words come out choked. "He loves you . . . I love you."

I shake my head on repeat. Over and over. Damp hair starting to frizz in my face. I pull my knees to my chest. "Then you both are out of your minds. You should hate me."

"We can't hate something we understand," Oliver tells me.

It touches the most sensitive parts of me. I cry, and they both come onto the bed like I've beckoned them with my tears. Before they touch me, I blurt out, "I told them to put anything in my mouth."

I think this will stop them from touching me.

It doesn't.

Jake wraps an arm around my shoulders, his hand atop my head. Oliver has an arm around my waist, his hand against my thigh. Tears cloud my vision and slip down my cheeks. "I-I let him put his thumb in my mouth." I release the truth.

Jake kisses the top of my head.

Oliver rubs the tears off my cheeks with his hand.

"I sucked it . . ." I wince. "And then I bit it."

Oliver's lips quirk. "Burying the lede there."

"It doesn't change anything." I sniff and curl my knees closer to my chest. "Other than the fact that I had his blood in my mouth." My grimace hurts my face at a harsher realization. "Fuck, I might actually need to see a doctor. Wh-what if he had diseases . . . ?"

"You don't need to worry about that tonight." Oliver wipes off more tears, his familiar affection calming my speeding pulse.

"We can take you to the doctor in the morning," Jake offers. The plan eases my uneven breathing. *Plans*, I like those. Jake rubs soothing circles with his thumb against the back of my neck. "Is that why they pushed you to the ground? Because you bit him?"

I nod. "Yeah . . . they were . . . they threatened . . . they might've . . ."

"But they didn't," Jake tells me.

My eyes well with tears. "Because you showed up. And I keep wanting to be grateful—I do—but all I can think about is the Fiddle Game. When all she had was me. And it wasn't enough. No one showed up to save her."

"Hey, *you* saved her tonight." Oliver nudges my shoulder with his. "*You*, Hailey. Not Jake. Not me. Not Nova. Not even Rocky. We weren't on that beach. Tonight, *you* were enough." His eyes deepen into mine. "I know it feels like things went wrong, but a lot of things went right, too. You have to find a way to focus on that."

This is how they cope. Oliver, Rocky, Phoebe. There's too much darkness in what they do to hang on to the shadowed parts of their lives. It's about driving toward the light. I want that.

More than anything, I want to figure out a way to forgive myself for what happened in Carlsbad. I thought bringing Phoebe here was a start to that, but I know I can't fully repent until Victoria is safe. No Trent. No Varrick. No darkness.

I focus on that future. The peaceful vision of it.

We sit in silence for a few more minutes, and they let me drift off as my breathing slows. Oliver flips on the television and finds my favorite movie on a streaming service: *Mystic Pizza*.

Connecticut small-town charm. Undefined romances. Crisp fall leaves. Sisterhood. It's the first time I've watched the movie with both of them, and I find it a good distraction. When the end credits roll, Jake looks at me. "Are you tired?"

I shake my head. "The opposite actually."

"Do you want sex?" Oliver flips off the TV with one hand.

With his other, his fingers dip to the waistband of my shorts. "I can put you to sleep with mind-altering orgasms." His smile glitters his eyes.

My cheeks heat in a deep flush. I know it's Olly's night to have sex with me. But I'd feel bad having Jake leave the bed just to watch. It feels wrong after all that's happened.

"I don't want to sleep," I tell them, folding my arms over my chest.

They both share a look I can't quite decipher. Then Oliver motions between him and Jake. "Do you want us to make out?" Olly asks.

My lips part in surprise.

Jake glares. "Funny."

"It wasn't a joke, Koning," Oliver says with no playful tone. "I wouldn't offer something I don't fully intend to act on and enjoy."

"You're straight," Jake reminds him.

"This is a good point, Olly," I cut in.

"Yeah. I thought I was." Oliver sizes Jake up and down. "Until I started watching you fuck Hailey every other night, and I don't just watch her, I watch you, too. But you can't say you don't watch me—"

"Of course, I watch you," Jake growls.

"Okay, so does it even matter what I am?" Oliver asks. "I'm attracted to women and to you. There you go. I said it. It's out there now. Are we all happy?" He looks from me to Jake and back to me.

My eyes are wide. "Um . . . yes?"

Oliver's jaw tightens in slight panic.

"Olly, *yes*. I'm happy if you are. If you both are." I grip my kneecaps, caging my breath. I don't know what's going on, but I'm not about to stop it or disturb it. I truly just want everyone in this room to have a boatload of happiness. Isn't that what this is about? Being together should bring joy—not the other way around.

Jake blinks, his forehead creased in deep lines of confusion. His eyes flit from me to Oliver. He expels a breath before he says, "Fuck it. Just kiss me."

Oliver grins, and both of them lean over my lap to clasp each other's faces. Their lips collide in a hard, detonating, hungry kiss. Only I watch the combativeness of it.

Olly pushes for speed and Jake attempts to decelerate the momentum. Oliver slips his tongue into Jake's mouth, and a groan catches in Jake's throat. Not even discreetly, Oliver's eyes flit to me, examining my expression. Jake does the same. My lips have parted between panting breaths.

How am I supposed to react? Unbothered? *Impossible.* They kiss only inches from my face. Not chaste pecks. Their lips grow red under the devouring kisses. Both their fingers thread in each other's hair. They are making out in front of me—and blatantly watching my reaction like it turns them on just as much as each other.

My pulse thumps and drops teasingly low between my legs. Heat crawls up my skin in building arousal. Is this what happens when one of them watches two of us together? Desire spools like a taut rubber band, and I bask in finally getting to experience this side of things.

Oliver pulls Jake in closer, their chests melding together, and Jake rips his lips off Oliver's as he growls out a tortured, "Slow down."

Oliver moves his mouth to Jake's jaw. "No."

"*Yes.*" Jake tugs Oliver's head back by his hair.

Olly grins wickedly, his chin tilted up. "I've watched you fuck so agonizingly slow that I realized, have you ever been with someone that challenged you here? Or do you get to set the speed no matter what? *King.*" The nickname has acidic, sensual undertones that I can't decipher between compliment or insult.

My heart beats faster. "I think we should be nice to each other," I whisper.

"She says be nice." Oliver's brows arch; he doesn't look away from Jake. "What nice thing are you going to do for me, Koning?"

That is not what I meant. But my words stick to the back of my throat in anticipation.

Jake doesn't break Oliver's gaze. "You're going to stroke me until I come."

Oliver laughs. "Weird way to say you want me to give you a hand job."

"Just fucking do it." Jake's already pulling off his shirt, gripping the back of it to tug it over his head. Oliver does the same in a hurried pace like they're competing for who can get naked first.

I'm beyond wet.

Their gazes flit to me as soon as they're both stripped bare.

"Hails, you okay?" Jake asks.

"Please continue." I wave them on. *Ignore me.*

That causes their lips to pull into smiles, and they face each other again. On their knees, they continue to lean over my lap. Jake spits in his own hand. Oliver places his palm underneath my mouth. His eyes pinned to Jake as I do my best to gather saliva and let it drip into Oliver's hold.

Jake watches us with hooded eyes. "Jesus fuck," he curses and then groans.

Oliver wears a self-satisfied smirk, and they both fist each other at the same time. It's another battle of speeds. Jake sliding his large palm along Oliver's erection in slow, sensual movements. His other hand braces the back of Olly's neck.

Oliver rampages in fast, forceful strokes.

They both look undone. Heavy grunts, weathered expressions like they're fighting to stay the course. Curses mix with winded breaths. I squeeze my legs together to stop the wetness from spreading.

Oliver growls, "Just go faster, man."

"No," Jake rasps.

Oliver lets out a choked noise and presses his forehead to Jake's. They stare into each other's eyes, combative. Challenging. Until they both shudder against each other in quaking spasms. They release at the same time, and cum coats both their abdomens. Jake keeps his hand against the back of Olly's neck, and Oliver keeps his on top of Jake's head. Chests heaving and caving with ragged breaths. They both angle their heads to look at me.

I'm full of unspent desire. But really, I have *one* specific want. And I'm not too shy to ask.

"Can I lick up the cum?" I ask bluntly. The craving flushes my face, but I don't want to take it back. Especially not when they both start smiling like I'm the most precious thing on this bed. Oliver even lets out a soft laugh.

Still out of breath, Jake nods.

So does Oliver.

I clean them both up, satiating my wants as easily as they satiated theirs.

I stop thinking about my mistakes, and I start thinking about something more tortuous. More unbelievable.

I start thinking that I want this to last much longer than just the summer.

THIRTY-TWO

Phoebe

Early-morning rain patters the yacht, the only sound between the seven of us in *The Ithaka*'s main saloon.

"Phoebe," Rocky says from the floor, various blankets and pillows strewn around the long curved sofas. Two marble coffee tables, a fully stocked bar, and floor-length windows outfit the luxury boat. Varrick offered to have his private chef board this morning and whip up breakfast for us, but we were all craving the comfort of local food. So earlier, Nova and Oliver picked up takeout from Seaside Griddle.

All the guys are eating their breakfast on the ground. I have no clue who slept where, except for Rocky.

I woke up in the primary suite, and he was there.

He just held me for a while under the sheets and explained the fallout of the worst party imaginable. I couldn't talk. My throat is still scratchy, like I've guzzled a gallon of sand. Might be the aftereffects of the drugs.

I haven't wanted to physically separate from him. I even dragged him into the shower with me.

We had emotional sex against the tile wall, and even though it feels like he's still inside me now, it's not close enough. I want the weight of Rocky. I want him to bear his body against me. I want his arms in a choke hold around me.

I want him to never let go.

He's sitting too far away. I'm on the couch. My wet hair soaks my oversized pink Strawberry Shortcake tee. Hailey is beside me in sweats, too, and we're underneath a knitted sage-green blanket. I have two warring needs—the need to be with Rocky and the need to be next to my best friend.

After what happened to her . . .

"Are you mutilating it or eating it?" Rocky snaps me into focus again, and I glance down at my eggs.

"It's a breakfast scramble," I say with the same heat. "It can't be mutilated any more than it already is." Though, I am stabbing the crap out of the bacon bits. "Why don't you worry about deep-throating your burrito?"

Oliver peels an orange on the floor. "Can he take the whole burrito? That's the question." I just barely catch Oliver looking over at Jake.

"Shut up." Rocky grips his egg burrito with one hand, his forearm on his bent knee, and his intense gaze hasn't left me. I love that desertion is so far off the table, even his eyes refuse to abandon the sight of me.

I intake a sharper breath through my nose. Unfortunately, everyone can hear in the silence. I'm tired of saying, *I'm fine*, when I'm just sort of fine, and instead, I say, "So, some guy named Howie slipped me drugs, but Trent was the one who asked him to. Right?" I turn my head to Rocky.

He's strangling his burrito. "He confirmed it. Yeah."

Heat brews in my lungs, but it's not because of what Trent plotted. It's the fact that Rocky has a split lip and a nasty welt blemishes his cheekbone. I heard he nearly drowned Jake's older brother in the pool. Fists also flew. I hope Trent's face looks like he made contact with several brick walls and cement floors.

During their confrontation, Trevor Tinrock even did a smart, unprompted thing and cut the DJ's music at a great time. Right when Rocky accused Trent of some vile shit. People heard. Chelsea Noknoi and a few other country club servers have texted me and Hailey, asking if it's true.

I know Rocky hates he's lost his connection to Trent, but I'm *elated* he no longer has to buddy up to that prick. Hopefully the town's sympathy toward Trent will wane, and they'll realize he's still a garbage human.

Rocky's little brother really came through in the clutch last night. I'd give him props if I thought he wanted a pat on the back from me, but I'm certain he values my opinion like I'm a tiny rusted cog in this machine of deceit. He wants validation from his older siblings. Which is fine—as long as he's not putting a hit out on anyone.

Right now, he's sitting against the mini fridge, and he's wearing sunglasses indoors, drowning his sweet potato pancakes in syrup.

Hailey picks apart a powdered donut. "And I'm supposed to pretend like I could still be interested in Trent, even though he roofied my best friend." Her eyes darken, and I look around the room.

Nova squirts hot sauce on his breakfast burrito like this *is* the correct path. No one pipes in. Not even to curse out Trent, and I realize that while I was sleeping, they've all probably discussed Hailey's trajectory for the job without me.

They *definitely* discussed Hailey's pregnancy, because Trevor has been asking if he should go by "Uncle Trev" or "Uncle Trevor."

No one brings up the elephant in the room, but I've been thinking about it all morning. Howie could've so easily slipped something in my best friend's drink.

At least it wasn't Hailey.

She's pregnant. At least it wasn't her, but I was incapacitated, a burden to the team, and worse, I wasn't there to protect my best friend from drunken Caufield fuckbags. Instead, she had to switch into my role, and my skin crawls imagining repulsive, *leering* men surrounding her while she feared assault.

Nausea still roils. Is this what Hailey feels when she watches me? Is this why she risked everything to bring us here for a fresh start? Because right now, I would drag her to the Antarctic if I thought it'd save her from a repeat of last night.

I poke at my scrambled eggs. I can barely eat, but I check the time on my phone. "I have a shift in a couple hours." I abandon my breakfast on the coffee table and climb off the sofa.

"You're going to work?" Jake whips his head from me to Rocky, like he's expecting him to stop me. I do feel the eternal hellfire off Rocky's tunneling, intrusive gaze. It silently scorches me, but he's not barricading me from the exit.

For one, I'm still in sweatpants and a T-shirt. I need to actually get ready to serve a dozen mimosas and even more crab cakes on this drizzling Sunday afternoon.

"We," Hailey says. "I'm on the schedule with her." She hops up beside me.

Which causes Jake to stand. "Take the day off. Both of you."

"We don't want to lose our jobs," I remind him, and I catch Rocky rolling his eyes. I flip him off, and normally I'd snark back that some of us (i.e., me and Hailey) have come to enjoy our time at the country club, but I can't dislodge the ball from my throat.

Not as my brothers stare deeper into me, too.

"You might lose your jobs anyway. I'll have to make cuts at the end of the summer if I can't turn around membership," Jake admits into a sip of his coffee.

Rocky's brows rise. "And my sister and Phoebe are first on your chopping block?"

"It's not personal." Jake sighs.

"Obviously, we know that," Hailey chimes in softly. She slips me a *What if?* look. What if we ditch work?

Jake must detect my hesitation. "This isn't a suggestion, Phoebe. I'm telling you you're not clocking into a shift today. I'll call Katherine and let her know you both won't be there. Take this time to process what's happened."

"I think that's a good idea," Nova chimes in, his overprotective brotherly concern like hot coals to the face and not a cozy blanket. Oliver is the comfort, and he's offering me a gentle smile and light shoulder shrug.

I cross my arms, unsure of how I feel, but I start fixating on Rocky. "You aren't going to tell Jake to stop being bossy?" I'm glaring.

His glare is coarser. "You were *drugged*. People saw Oliver carrying you out of the party. Do you really want to spend all day at the club volleying nosy fucking questions from rich old ladies? You don't want to talk about it, Phebs, fine, but you go to work, they will bring it up."

He does have a point.

I'm used to the end of bad jobs when we pack our bags and forge ahead as if we never waded through a toxic spill. I can feel the acid searing my ankles this time. I wonder if it's better to feel something than to feel nothing at all.

I've been either numb or angry for so long. Maybe I do need time to process, because I've never left Hailey in that position before . . . in *my* position. And we weren't even working a con. She wasn't pretending to be someone else. She was *herself*. That happened to *Hailey*. It's awarded me new gnarled feelings I can barely untangle and a brand-new perspective on my life.

I turn to my best friend. "What do you want to do, Hails?"

Her gray eyes travel to the window. "The rain is letting up. It's supposed to be warm today. I could read on the beach."

"And I could suntan and flip through a *Celebrity Crush* mag." We exchange growing smiles, solidifying this normalcy, and it's strange but kind of nice to have this option.

Thanks, Jake.

Hailey is a more pleasant person than me, because she verbalizes her gratitude in a soft "Thank you."

By the early afternoon, the clouds make way for a sunny blue sky. We all end up on the public beach and not the country club's private one, where we'd be able to rent cabanas and chairs. It's a change of pace for the guys, but no one puts up a stink about roughing it with the plebs.

We claim a sandy spot near the lapping sea and away from any screaming children. Much to Rocky's delight, I'm sure. He acted like he had an instant root canal when he heard shrieking in the parking lot. A toddler cried about his sandy feet, and his mom frantically cleaned his toes with wet wipes.

"Are we sure that little hellion doesn't belong to Grey?" Oliver bantered with a smile while carrying the umbrella for me.

Nova shut the trunk, a cooler of beer and sparkling water in hand.

I think Rocky's eyes are still rolling from the asphalt to the beach. I also took note of the tiny glimpse he cast me. Babies. The future. *Our* future. He hasn't asked me again if I want kids. I haven't broached the topic either.

We are stubbornly not discussing what we want months from now, let alone years. It feels like wasted breath when everything could change if this job doesn't go our way.

On the beach, I spread my pink strawberry towel beside Hailey's checkered black one.

I slip a glance back at Rocky while he stakes the umbrella in the brown sand. Tendrils of his black hair brush his forehead, and his aggravated, pissed-off eyes make me smile bit by bit.

You'd think he hates the beach. The scorching heat. Sweat dripping down his jawline. The salty scent of the ocean. Granules of sand going *everywhere.*

And he does hate it all.

Yet, he's here. For me, for his sister, for every one of us. As his narrowed eyes flash over to me, I'd like to believe he's mostly here for me, and when his affection sinks into me like razor-sharp teeth against my tender flesh, I sense that's true. That at the end of the day, I am his first reason and maybe even his last, too.

Eventually, I peel away from Rocky and Hailey to take a walk with my brothers. I'm closest to the water, feeling shorter on the downward slope of the sand.

Nova picks up seashells every time he spots one, just to chuck them into the waves. "You haven't talked to Rocky about last night?"

"He's rehashed the horrible events to me." I fix my twisted baby-blue bikini strap on my shoulder.

"But he said you haven't *talked* about it, so what were you doing all this morning with him?" Off my raised brows and head tilt, Nova expels a heavy sigh and launches another shell into the water. "Do you two even communicate beyond fucking?"

"That *is* communication," I argue, then look to Oliver for backup.

"It is," Oliver chimes in while lathering sunscreen on his cut biceps. "They're communicating with their bodies."

"Exactly. We don't always need *words*." It's deeper with Rocky.

He chucks another shell. "You two need to slow down. One unplanned pregnancy is already one too many."

Oliver squeezes Nova's shoulder. "You're only saying that because you don't like babies."

"I'll like yours," Nova says.

"Might be Jake's," Oliver reminds him, and before we can ask, he says, "The paternity doesn't matter. I just want Hailey and the baby to be healthy."

"Agreed," Nova and I say together.

"Jinx," I add fast. "You owe me a Fizz."

Nova almost smiles, but he just has to reinforce his point: "Seriously though. Slow down."

"Rocky and I are using condoms. We're having safe sex," I assure. "And, no, I'm not *slowing down*."

He glowers.

So I add, "You don't understand. Being close to Rocky is a *need*, especially when terrible things happen, like last night. He makes my body feel like mine, and I don't want to ever lose that."

Nova blinks hard, trying to let it go.

I mentally try to walk away from this conversation, but all I can picture is the last few seconds with Hailey at the party—right before my vision went hazy.

I pull my hair into a high ponytail. "I can't stop thinking about last night. What Hailey went through after I passed out . . ." The sun feels hotter, but it might just be my anger burning me. I snap my elastic tie.

She was using the tactics I was trained to do to bide time. Seduce. Distract. Delay.

Being an ace at seduction, that's been my superpower. It's my greatest talent, but I have a love-hate relationship with my role.

"Carlsbad," I say after I tie my hair and drop my hands to my sides. "I never told you both what happened. I don't know if Hailey or Rocky ever told you, but . . . I let the mark and his friend have sex with me so we could finish the job. That's why Hailey brought me here. So I would stop being in those positions. I don't think I ever would've stopped if she hadn't."

I love her for it.

Releasing this truth now was much easier than the first time, when I'd struggled to pull it free to tell Rocky. I feel like maybe this is what healing is. Slow repair. Sewn up enough to not bleed out with each word.

Nova releases a long breath, nodding to me. "Thank God for Hailey."

I nod just as strongly.

Oliver wraps an arm over my shoulders, giving me a consoling squeeze.

I kick up sludgy wet sand while we stroll along the shoreline. Laughter and chatter blend with sounds of soft, crashing waves and squawks of seagulls.

The beach is fairly crowded as the town relishes the sunny June weather.

We walk past a cluster of twentysomething guys in board shorts. They toss a football back and forth, and their gazes shift over me. As their eyes descend to my tits, my abdomen, and the strings of my swimsuit that peek out of my jean shorts, riding high on my hips, a gross sensation slithers across my skin.

Normally I'd just feel . . . numb.

My pulse accelerates. In this second, I don't want them to look. Oliver is shirtless, so I slip a silent plea to Nova. He's already pulling off his olive-green T-shirt, then hands it to me.

I'm grateful for the cover-up. The fabric hangs big on me, and I let it drop to my thighs.

Oliver checks his phone after it beeps. "Varrick," he tells us. "He wants to know how you're holding up, Phoebe."

Nova rolls his eyes and picks up another shell. "Pretending to be a father?"

"He technically *is* our father." Oliver finishes rubbing in his sunscreen.

Nova glares. "And not only has Varrick killed before, he likely *abused* Elizabeth, Ol."

He still won't call Varrick our dad, just like he's stopped calling Elizabeth our mom. Even knowing she's biologically *ours*, Nova can't easily forgive her for the lies and the lifelong deception. I still struggle, too.

"We don't know that," Oliver says. "Because we haven't asked." His bitterness is noted. But we all agreed to holster our curiosities and not ask our dad to crack open a family memoir. I failed exactly *once* when I asked Varrick a question, and I still regret it.

"Elizabeth *ran* from him for how many years?" Nova asks.

"She never let him believe she was pregnant. She never told him about *us*. She might've done some heinous fucking things with Addison, but she's always tried to protect us from whatever trash she hooked on her arm."

Nova leaves out how he's always tried to protect our mom from them, too. Her husbands were never upstanding men, so the chances of Varrick being a decent guy are slim to none.

Still, we don't know the origins of their relationship.

Oliver lifts his sunglasses to his head, letting us see his eyes. "I'm not making excuses for our dad." Nova cringes as he uses the *dad* title, but Oliver continues, "All I'm saying is that I'd like more of the story, Nov. I'd just be open to hearing what he has to say. Is that a crime?"

I cross my arms. "Not one that will send you to literal jail."

"What? Is there a pretend jail I'm unaware of?" Oliver drops his sunglasses over his eyes. "Monopoly prison—"

"Is that Elizabeth?" Nova asks, stopping dead in his tracks.

Oliver and I follow his gaze, and we spot our mom on the patio of the Lure, a ritzy beachside restaurant where I've gladly overpaid for oysters and melt-in-your-mouth buttery crab. She's at a two-seater table with a half-filled mimosa flute.

Despite our roller-coaster relationship, her warm aura still captivates me in a single instant. Honey-blonde hair cascades over her slender shoulders like rivers of gold, and her dainty diamond earrings match the sparkle in her brown eyes. She's breathtakingly beautiful.

And her smile is pure sunlight on her town bestie, Stella Fitzpatrick.

"Let's go back," I suggest, not aching to confront our mom today, but as soon as the words leave my mouth, her head swings in our direction.

She straightens up, then waves an energetic hand at us.

"What's she doing?" Nova asks under his breath, very baffled. We all are, because in Victoria, Connecticut, her alias is *Isla Rivers*. She has zero relation to the three of us.

I've publicly interacted with "Isla" because Claudia Waterford tried to hire her and Addison to matchmake me and my ex-husband, but that ploy never really came to fruition.

"She's getting up," I whisper in panic to my brothers. What the hell is happening?

Our mom is out of her chair. She snatches her pistachio-green alligator Hermès Birkin, puts a sweet hand on Stella's shoulder as if to say a quick goodbye, then struts down the patio stairs toward the beach. The ones that lead to us.

Her very pretty pale-yellow sundress (Oscar de la Renta, I'd bet) leaves me with fragments of envy, which are much easier to digest than the shards of hurt and betrayal.

"Stella's watching us," Oliver mutters, his lips barely moving.

"Should we just leave?" I ask them, but it's clear our mom is coming to greet us. She's plucked off her heels, then goes barefoot in the sand.

Nova is rigid. He's glaring out at the ocean, unable to even look at our mom.

"It's too late for that," Oliver says, and with a dazzling smile, he waves up at Stella.

Her lips form a soured pucker, but she manages to acknowledge my brothers with a stiff hand while completely ignoring my existence. My social standing is shakier being Jake's ex-girlfriend and working as a server. Luckily, Stella grabs her Chanel handbag and enters the Lure, not sticking around to snoop on us.

"Fancy finding you three here," our mom says, journeying closer to us at the water.

"Some fancier than others," Oliver teases me, since I'm the only one who currently appears like I shop at Old Navy. Nova has on an emerald-green Piaget watch worth over seventy grand, and Oliver exudes preppy yachtie energy with his striped swim shorts and perfectly styled brown hair.

The town believes our fictional backstory where the Smith family come from old money, but my disapproving parents revoked my trust fund when I rebelled and married Grey Thornhall. So it shocks no one in Victoria that my brothers are loaded while I'm serving clam chowder and crudités.

"What'd you tell Stella?" I ask our mom, unable to uncross my arms from a defensive posture.

She peers backward to make sure her fake best friend has left. "She knows I love good gossip—or rather, Isla Rivers does." Her eyes brush over me, then Oliver, then Nova. "I told her I'd pick your brains and find out more about last night's party at the Koning estate. The fight between Trent and Grey is all anyone can talk about. No one saw it coming. Honestly, neither did me and Addy."

"Probably because he went off-script," Oliver says casually.

"Rocky lost control?" She sounds as surprised as she does worried. "Was it something Trent said or did?"

We don't outright gush forth like we're a trusting, unfractured family. A fissure still runs between her and us, and I can't figure out how to fill the crack. How do we forgive our mom for lying to us about our father? Is there really any coming back from that?

She's careful of any passing beach walkers who could eavesdrop, but for the most part, the ocean drowns our conversation. Especially as she whispers to us, "You have every right to be hurt, but *please* don't shut me out. I was just trying to protect you all from him."

Nova launches a shell at the water, and our collective silence fills the air with tension.

"I was scared that he'd even find out you *existed*," she continues. "You can't even know what that was like. I was younger than you are now. Twenty-two. Checking over my shoulder for *years*, hoping he'd never run into me." Her reddened eyes ping between us with a sadness and desperation for us to believe her.

My heart pangs suddenly, and Oliver's must as well, because he asks, "So, then why did you sleep with him, if you were so scared of him? Were you playing him?"

Nova stiffens, his muscles flexing in his arms.

Our mom wears a sad smile. "I loved him. He made it easy to love him. Until I saw him for what he was."

"A stalker," I say.

"A murderer," Nova adds.

"A monster," I continue.

Oliver holds up a palm. "We get it." He swings a hand back to our mom. "How are the date nights going?"

Our mom has been keeping tabs on Varrick in her own way. Using her history with him to have a weekly night out on the town. I think it's the only reason she, Addison, and Everett feel comfortable handing over the reins to us. They have *some* connective tissue to the con.

Her cheeks flush, and her gaze falls.

The same thought seems to be circling my brothers. Nova looks ready to hurl as he says, "You're getting back with him?"

"No." She pushes blonde tendrils out of her eyes, her face contorting in a grimace. "But in the name of being transparent . . . in the event the job doesn't go to plan, I've been using every tool in my arsenal to seduce him out of this town. Which, yes, includes sleeping with him."

I'm speechless.

Nova pinches his eyes closed.

Oliver tosses up his hand like it's just another weekend in our mad, mad world. "What every kid dreams of, Mom and Dad getting back together." The joke almost lightens the air.

Our mom shares a small smile with Oliver.

Nova shifts his weight with aggressive heat. "Varrick isn't leaving, so how's that fucking working out?" he asks her harshly.

"Nov," I retort, defending her, because it must've been a hard choice. "She doing that *for us*."

"I didn't ask her to get in bed with Varrick," he says hotly under his breath, then narrows a dark look at her. "I'd *never* want you to do that for me."

"I know." Her gaze is so gentle on him, like he's fifteen again and not twenty-five. "*I know.* But it's what I'm good at." She has a melancholy yet cheery smile, as though she's accepted all the bad parts of being a seductress and learned to live with them.

Will that be me . . . in twenty-some years? It terrifies me. I've never wanted to become my mom and make the same *awful* choices she does where men are concerned.

I hug my arms around my body, and I ache for Rocky.

Nova scrapes a hand against the back of his neck before gesturing to our mom. "About last night . . ." He starts telling her about the party. The details from the start to the end. It's an olive branch, this offer of information.

Her brows subtly spring upward. She's good at concealing her shock in public, but her exhales sound heavy and pained. "I'm so sorry, bug," she apologizes to me, then frowns in thought. "I didn't think it was real, but some people have been saying Rocky accused Trent of rape . . . Did he actually—"

"I wasn't," I cut in, my stomach in knots. "He didn't touch me."

Nova chucks another seashell. "He got someone to drug her."

She reaches out to hug me.

I instinctively recoil. "*Isla*," I force out, reminding her she's *not* my mom here.

"I'm comforting you. It's something Isla would do. It's also something your mom really would love to do, too. *Please*."

I want to walk into her maternal warmth. Except, some part of me isn't ready. I step even farther back. "I'm fine."

Her hurt flares, but she nods, understanding. I see her twist her Cartier bracelets. A small tell that she's uneasy. One she rarely makes. Then she feels for the delicate gold chain around her neck, and I watch as she unclasps the heart-shaped locket. Jewelry she's had forever.

As a little girl, I used to play dress-up with her heels, her sparkly pink eye shadow, her bangle bracelets, and that locket. She'd put it on me, and I'd crack open the heart to find the inside nearly always empty.

"Why don't you put pictures of us in here, Mommy?" I'd ask. "Or of Daddy!" I'd bounce on my toes, thinking maybe she'd show me a photo for once.

She'd bop my nose and smile. "You think the love I have for you can fit in a heart this small? It's grown *so big* outside of it, bug. And this gold heart is meant for trickery." She wagged her brows playfully.

"And treats!"

"And treats." She'd tickle me. I'd giggle and calm down as she said, "When you get older, you'll see."

I did see her fill the heart with lies. With stock photos of men she'd call "soul mates" who passed tragically. With pictures of us she'd call beloved "godchildren." With Pomeranians she never had.

I loved her heart of lies because it was our cherished secret. Maybe that was the treat, knowing where the deceit was kept, knowing I was in on the truth. She was honest with me.

I'm stunned when she brushes back my hair and drapes the necklace around my throat, clasping the locket. The gold heart thumps over my breastbone. Light and less cumbersome than I thought it'd be.

"A sympathy gift from Isla," she says. "A belated birthday gift from your mom." She squeezes my hand.

My real heart flip-flops. We turned twenty-five last month. "Is May twenty-ninth even our actual birthday?" I ask her.

"*Yes*, it is," she assures, careful of eavesdroppers again before whispering, "but I didn't give birth in a hospital. I delivered you at a beach rental in Pensacola and paid off the midwife. There is no record of you anywhere. Every lie was simply to protect you. It was never meant to hurt you."

But they all ultimately did.

If I were stronger, I'd return the locket, but when I thumb the outline of the heart, I feel the fond memories between me and her, where she'd smile so brightly and twirl me around like I was her beautiful mini-me, and we'd dance to Heart's "Barracuda" and make virgin daiquiris. Days of innocence and childlike wonder.

So I keep it close, protecting these pieces of her I still adore.

When she says, "Keep in touch," and we split from her and head back to our spot on the beach, we're all quiet. Each processing what she's confessed about our father.

THIRTY-THREE

Rocky

If I were to choose to lie on the beach, it'd be at a resort or someplace where my back wasn't being killed on the hard fucking sand. I didn't pack chairs for this little therapeutic outing because we'll be here for under an hour. At most.

Phoebe can't sit still unless she's watching a movie or in the middle of a job. It's why five minutes into being here, she took a walk with her brothers.

While she's gone, I'm on my feet, popping the tab of a beer that Jake just handed me. He shakes melted ice off another can and rises beside me. His eyes are on my sister.

Hailey flips a page in her book, sitting cross-legged beneath the shade of the blue umbrella. She wears a long-sleeve black T-shirt and dark pants. A typical Hailey beach outfit. She burns easily and usually avoids the sun.

His concern has been at a twelve since she got in the car last night. It's impossible for me not to notice how often Jake checks on her. It's so apparent, so in my face that it'd typically grate on my last nerve.

Now—after what happened to Hailey at the Koning estate, after knowing I couldn't be there for her in any capacity, after knowing she might be pregnant with Jake's or Oliver's baby—I like that Jake is attentive toward my sister.

I like that he loves her.

I haven't talked to him one-on-one about the baby or Hailey's pregnancy. I was way too worried about Phoebe coming off of the drugs.

Four years ago, when Phebs gained consciousness in a Nashville motel, she said it felt like waking up underwater. I think this time was easier for her but harder in different ways. We're a real couple, so I could hold her for longer . . . and we had sex. Deep, penetrative, *I will fuck you inside out* type of emotional sex that she's been craving more and more. Over and over. I love fucking Phoebe like I'm staking my territory. Claiming every fucking inch of her as mine. It's euphoric and detonating.

The only downside? This almost torpedoed too far.

She spaced out for a full minute. Not the first time this has happened. I only saw because I'd been taking her from behind while she held the lip of the sink. I could see her eyes glaze in the mirror. I slowed down, then fisted her hair and lifted her head up so she could see me as I thrusted into her cunt.

"Look at me," I gritted in her ear. "I'm the only one who's *ever* going to be inside you. The only one who's *ever* going to fuck you." She regained focus with parted lips and hitched breath as I rammed deeper. "All of you," I grunted out. "*Mine.*"

"Stop," she moaned in a way that said, *Never fucking stop.*

I pulled out. She was about to protest, but I flipped her around and pushed back inside her, just needing her to fully face me. I didn't trust that I could read her well enough with her face obscured. I almost forgot the blip of a moment because our sex is soul ripping. Like Phoebe is trying to fuse bodies, and all I want is deeper, harder, *more*.

While we got dressed in the bathroom, I asked her, "When you space out—"

"I don't space out," she defended.

"This isn't a critique on your performance," I said. "I'm not giving you an F here."

She slowly slipped on her Strawberry Shortcake shirt. "What are you asking?"

"I just need to know if you're coherent enough to actually use a safe word when that happens—when you need me to stop."

We have a safe word in place—*Miami*—because when we fuck, no means yes and stop means go and I need to know when to literally *stop*. I thought maybe she'd be too stubborn to use it when she needed to. Now I'm wondering if it's something else.

She pulled her damp blue hair out from the collar of her shirt. "If I wanted you to stop, I could've said it. But I didn't want you to . . ." She trailed off, then threaded her arms together like she was done. There was definitely more there. That was not the fucking end of her thought.

"To what?" I asked.

She struggled to verbalize it.

I ran a hand through my wet hair. "Phoebe."

"To just pull out and leave," she finally said.

"Come here." I grabbed her elbow, breaking apart her crossed arms. I wrapped her in a tight hug and whispered, "If you say, 'Miami,' I won't scurry away from you like you're fucking diseased. I'll pause for a second, check in with you, and then we go from there. All it does is ensure I don't hurt you." I stroked the back of her head while she clung tighter. "That city doesn't mean *abandon* and *forsake* to you, does it?"

Her face heated. She chose the safe word for a reason. That place holds meaning for her and me.

"No," she murmured. Her fiery eyes met mine, and I wanted to take her all over again.

Phoebe being drugged this time has been harder because she's still unpacking so much trauma. And unlike with the Melon Drop, Hailey was intertwined in this mess last night.

We've all been smacked in the face with so much at once, it's strange as fuck we're leisurely at the beach right now. I take a swig of beer, then press the cold can to my throbbing cheekbone. Because I was *literally* smacked in the face.

Jake sets his consoling blue eyes on me.

I glare. "Redirect that look on my sister." I lower the beer can. "And just so you know, your brother probably has two black eyes and a fat lip this morning. Go send him a sympathy basket if you're dying to comfort someone."

"Me being fake nice to my brother would help us how?" Jake asks in seriousness.

"It wouldn't," Hailey pipes in with a page flip. "Trent wouldn't believe you."

I lift my beer. "She's calling you a bad liar, sweetheart."

"Okay, jackass." Jake has this overprotective expression on me now. "You're not patching things up with Trent."

That wasn't a question. I drill a more aggravated glare at him. "Maybe you should go be a lawyer since you love laying down the law."

"Grey."

"Jake," I retort with the raise of my brows. "To repair the damage that I did with your brother could take months. He's already blocked me on socials, and if I tried calling, I'd bet he's

blocked my number, too. So rest assured, I'm not going to be his best fucking friend anymore." To work my way back into Trent's good graces would involve me bending a knee and sucking his fucking toes, and I'd rather swallow several buckets of sand and salt water than act like his lapdog. "Varrick called and told me Trent is trying to get me kicked out of Stonehaven."

Hailey closes her book for a second. "Really?"

"It's not working. Varrick says he's not playing favorites. So we'll just have to not kill each other in the hallways."

"Jesus." Jake curses into a cringe and looks me over, examining my ticked-off face. "I just thought you'd be happier about it. You've hated being his friend."

"Happier?" I lift and lower my brows. The word so foreign to me. Down by the glittering water, I catch sight of my little brother knee-deep in the ocean with Sidney Burke. He splashes her, and I can't hear her giggle. I just see the sound in the way her lips part and body buckles. His slanted smile grows to rarer heights.

Seeing Trevor so emotive over a girl and not working a con does make me happy. Being with Phoebe for real makes me happy. Everyone I love being protected and safe—*happy*. But that last part isn't a reality. It's a fucking fantasy right now.

Still, it's easy to acknowledge the most happiness I've ever experienced in my life has been in this town in the past year.

I look back at Jake. "I'm happy I don't have to stoke your brother's overinflated ego or bite my tongue in half when he even utters Phoebe's name. But I'm not happy I lost . . ."

I lost control.

And it felt good. I hate how freeing it'd been. The only time I ever feel that wildly undone is when I'm with Phoebe.

Jake frowns. "Lost what?"

I lower my voice. "Being in his ear gave me power. Severing that rope is not good for *any* of us. I have no influence over him anymore, and with Hailey being the crux of this job . . . it just makes it a bigger risk."

I don't know what Trent is thinking. He's not venting to me about what happened. He's not even venting to Oliver. For one, Oliver is Phoebe's brother. For another, Trent views him as a hedonistic, coke-fueled fuckboy. He's a party friend. I'm sure he's not someone Trent would confide in unless it were a group setting and booze were flowing.

My fuckup is just so bad.

I feel like we went fifty steps backward in one night.

The good coming out of this—he now knows I will kill him if he tries anything with Phoebe. But that doesn't even matter if we can't secure Jake's full inheritance. Trent owning half this town means it's not worth it to stay here.

We'd have to leave.

I'm a Wolfe, but I'm also a Tinrock. I've made peace with needing to say goodbye to Victoria to protect my family that's still alive.

Jake takes a short swig of his beer, his eyes flitting back to Hailey. There's now a much greater chance we won't pull this off.

We'll become a figment to Jake Waterford, some twisted dream—one year of his life when six con artists strode in and unsettled his foundation, leaving him in our destructive wake underneath the debris.

We'll find a new town.

New city.

We always do.

Six spiders. Seven, if he decides to come with us . . .

Yeah, why the fuck would I want him to? I put my beer to

my lips, trying not to internally stake myself with a glare. I don't lie to myself.

Of course I know the truth. I like Jake. I would trust Jake with my life and their lives. I don't want to leave him behind. He might even be the father of my sister's *baby.* Yeah . . . complicated.

"So you need someone in my brother's ear?" Jake asks, keeping his voice hushed as a family (not influential) parks their wagon of beach gear less than twenty feet away. "And that can't be Oliver because . . . ?"

"Because it'd be an uphill battle, for one. Also, Trent probably knows Oliver is *here* with me," I explain, "and not nurturing his broken ego like a loyal best friend would."

"I suggested the beach day," Hailey says more to her book. "I wanted Oliver to be seen out with us. I don't think he's right to be Trent's best friend. He goes too far."

She's trying to protect Oliver from going the extra mile to finish the job. The same way she protected Phoebe. It's nothing our parents ever did. Nothing they tried to do. They pushed and pushed and pushed us past our limits. Stretched the boundaries and barriers until there were none.

Because "you have to do whatever it takes," because "you could be caught if you don't," because "don't you want to live lavishly?," because "we're a family."

I'm proud of my sister for not following in Addison's footsteps when it's all she's been conditioned to do.

"So you're . . . benching him?" Jake asks Hailey.

"No," she says. "You can't take Oliver off the board. He's like two bishops and two rooks at once. Four pieces."

Jake glances at me. "What does that make you?"

I open my mouth, but Hailey says, "The queen."

I flash Jake a tight smile before taking a rough swig of beer.

Jake sighs. "So, the queen is off the board?"

"Yep." I nod. Sun beats down on our bare glistening chests, and I rub sweat off my jaw, hating the heat.

He wipes condensation from his beer on his navy-blue swim trunks. "How far would Oliver go?" He's still considering him as a viable solution out of this giant fucking pickle. "He won't do drugs around Hailey."

"He'll hurt himself." Hailey sounds panicked. "*No.*" She shuts her book.

Oliver has punched himself in the face before to escape a jam. So her fears aren't unwarranted.

I don't bring up how there's also the problem of Trent being obsessed with the idea of Hailey having some dumb crush on Oliver. It's been ridiculous how often I've had to *actively* get Trent to stop suggesting the idea of watching Oliver fuck Hailey.

Yes, I have had to shoot that idea down. Five times.

Five.

It's not a miracle he never asked Hailey, "Would you fuck Oliver in front of me?" It was me working my ass off getting him to quit thinking with his cock every fifteen minutes.

Hailey doesn't know this. No one does because not everything needs to be aired when it's understood what Trent is capable of. But this is exactly why I'm more nervous that I'm not a devil breathing down his fucking neck anymore.

Jake shakes condensation off his fingers. "Then give him parameters of what not to do," he suggests.

I arch my brows at him. "You really want to see Oliver be queen fucking bee, huh?"

He side-eyes me as if to say, *It's not like that.* Oh, it is like that. He likes Oliver *like that.* I am too good at what I do not to notice. (Unfortunately.)

Jake says, "I just think he deserves to make the choice himself."

"What role?" Trevor suddenly appears, snatching a nautical striped towel off the stack by Hailey's feet. Sidney is halfway down the beach with a group of college girls. Out of earshot and almost eyesight.

"Be Trent Waterford's best friend," Hailey explains. "Rocky's old position."

"I'll do it," Trevor volunteers.

I glare. "No, you won't, shithead."

He dries water from his pale legs. "I think *I* deserve to make that choice myself." He echoes what Jake just said.

I lift my brows at the Koning heir. "Do me a favor next time and shut the fuck up."

Jake exhales, then looks at Trevor. "If your brother and sister think it's not a good idea, then it probably isn't."

Trevor runs a hand through his damp hair. "Hailey never said it wasn't one."

She blinks a couple times. I imprison a hot breath, waiting for her to decree, *It's a shit plan*. Her mind must be racing, and I can't keep quiet. "He's not ready," I tell her.

Trevor's expression deadens. "Thanks, asshole. I believe in you, too."

"It's not that, Trev." I catch his arm before he peels away, and I tug him back into the shade. "You're too young in Trent's eyes. He's in his thirties. You're *nineteen*."

"Then he can view me as his little brother."

"He knows you're *my* little brother," I retort. "He's pissed at me right now, and he's a vindictive fuck. He might use you to retaliate against me."

"Is it being used if you know it's happening, Rock?" he

questions. I think about his relationship with Sidney. "I could use it to my benefit. I could use him, too."

Hailey's eyes rise to mine. "Trevor might not be able to influence him like you, but he could keep tabs on him. If Trent wants to get back at you, he'll keep Trevor really close to rub it in your face. He could be our eyes and ears, and that's better than nothing."

I grind my molars.

"It's another piece on the board, Rocky," Hailey says. "It's already hard with Phoebe off, and now you . . ."

I don't think Trevor will be manipulated or played. Trent Waterford isn't in the dark triad. But he's so *fucking* unbearable, I don't even want Trevor around him. Let alone kissing his ass. It's not easy.

I'm not ready for my little brother to take my role, but I've never been ready for this. I've *never* wanted this, even though it's part of what he's always desired.

"This isn't the only option," I tell Trevor.

"I want to do this, Rock. *Let me.*" He's pleading.

Christ. I squint out at the sun, then turn back to him. Knowing I need to give him the chance.

Trevor needs to get into Trent's good graces. Quickly. So I tell him, "We're about to have a very public, very aggressive fight. You're going to need to hit me because I don't want Trent to believe you're scrawny and can be pushed around."

Trevor is grinning.

Make no mistake, this next part, I viscerally hate. But the things that torch my soul are just necessary.

I shove my brother toward the ocean as he screams, "Get the fuck over it, Grey!" I stalk toward him with pent-up anger that lives inside me 24/7, and he bumps up into my chest, his eyes ablaze in ways they never really are, and I think, *Keep it up, Trev. Don't let go of the rage.*

Three minutes later, I'm wrestling my little brother to the sand as fury explodes inside me, and I let his fist connect with my jaw. Not once but twice, I push him forcefully off me as my mouth fills with blood. Sidney shouts his name in the distance, and he almost breaks the fake animosity between us to look at her.

I thrust my hands at his chest, and he comes back to land a blow on my ribs.

At that one, I fake cough and fake wheeze.

From down the beach, Phoebe yells, "What the fuck, Trevor?!" Oliver and Nova outsprint her, and soon, they're separating me from my brother.

I spit a wad of crimson saliva onto the sand and shout at my brother, "If you even step near Trent, me and you are going to have a fucking problem! You're *my* responsibility! He's a shitbag. I don't want you around him!"

Trevor lets out a pained laugh. "You think you can tell me what to do?! I'm a fucking adult. I *like* Trent more than I like you right now. So fuck you. I never wanted you as a brother anyway." His own words impale him. He slips me an uncertain look. Afraid he's harmed me.

I spit again and glare. Hoping he stops breaking character. "Trevor." I try to reach out to him, but not so he'll reciprocate. "I don't want you hanging around him, *Trevor*."

Trevor flips me off with two middle fingers like a little punk and walks backward toward Sidney and her friends. When he spins around, he casts one glance back at me.

I can't tell him, *I'm okay. Your lies can't hurt me. I still love you, shithead.*

Because I know the truth. The Graveses do, too, when I give a sign it's fake by rubbing hard at my temple like I have a migraine.

Phoebe plays along, not dropping her shock and horror. I let her draw me away from the water while Trevor retreats into Sidney's consoling hug and her gaggle of friends.

"What the hell was that?" she whispers while we hike up toward the umbrella where I left Jake and Hailey.

I hawk up more blood, spitting one more time. I'm proud of his right hook, but *fuck*. I'm about to explain his new position in the takedown job of Trent Waterford, but I suddenly notice what she's wearing.

The gold heart-shaped locket belongs to Elizabeth Graves. And yet, it's not what's setting off a shrill alarm in my head.

"Is that Nova's shirt?" I narrow my gaze at her.

She glares back. "Yeah, so?"

So, why is she wearing his shirt? Phoebe isn't Hailey. Her normal beach attire is skimpy and barely fucking clothed. What made her feel like she needed to cover up?

Last night.

Being drugged, maybe. I knew it'd affect her, but I haven't been sure to what degree.

"Don't look at me like that." She crosses her arms and raises her stiff shoulders. "I'm fine . . . sort of. But being sort of fine is still *fine*."

"Fine," I snap back.

"Fine."

I scrape a hand across my throbbing mouth, then I reach out and draw my girlfriend against my chest. Phebs untangles her arms to hold on to me. I cup the back of her head and feel her pounding pulse begin to slow. Then I kiss her temple before she says, "I didn't want them to stare at my body."

"Who?" Aggravated heat ratchets up inside me.

"Just these guys on the beach."

I glare out. Wanting to maim and injure. I can only hope this is just Phoebe still processing the night. *She'll be okay.*

The best part of this moment—everyone can see me and her together. There is no more hiding what she means to me. There really doesn't have to be.

THIRTY-FOUR

Jake

I'm struggling.

My Porsche idles in the parking lot behind Baubles & Bookends, and the hardback of *When the Wind Blows* by James Patterson sits on my passenger seat. Book club starts soon, but I'm more likely to melt into the leather than leave the car.

Before this summer, I made peace with the idea that happiness was never really in the cards for me. I grew up aware that any future foretold was one filled with some kind of misery. Even if the Graveses and Tinrocks can pull through and land me the crown, that headpiece is made of thorns. It's a position of power behind a legacy of misdeeds.

Being with Hailey and Oliver this summer has been like tasting the forbidden fruit of happiness. I understand now what it is I'm setting myself up to lose if the con goes sideways.

All I can see is packed bags, waves goodbye, a future where I daydream about what they're up to, and a life filled with what-ifs.

I am struggling with fear.

I'm scared I'm going to lose them—really lose them.

Maybe this is how it was always supposed to be. Maybe they're not meant for me. My future was never destined to carry happiness. Only purpose.

The rev of an engine cuts my thoughts, and I see a silver Bentley Continental GTC pull into the parking spot next to mine. Trent flicks the visor up, and I let out a heavy sigh. He's inescapable.

I check my watch. Can he just fuck off to wherever he's going? I look up and jolt. He's at my passenger door. He taps the window with his knuckles and, sunglasses in hand, points at the door.

Against my better judgment, I unlock it.

Trent picks up the hardback and tosses it on the dashboard before he climbs in. When the door shuts, he tips his chin toward the Bentley. "You like?"

My jaw tics. My judgment really is in the dumpster, because I entertain his bullshit.

"It's new?" I ask.

"Just got her yesterday. An early birthday gift from Jordan."

"Your birthday is in November."

Trent smiles. "Maybe he just wanted to suck up to me then." He passes a hand between us. "He senses blood in the water."

"And which one of us got a chunk bitten out of them?"

Trent runs his fingers through his hair. "The thing with Grey was a misunderstanding. I've never wanted to sleep with his ex-wife. I *definitely* would never force myself on her."

"It's been a week. How many people are buying that story?"

He rolls his eyes. "Can you be a good brother for five seconds and just believe what I'm telling you?"

"Maybe if you told me the truth—"

"Hey, *hey*." Trent holds up his hands like he wants to squash this. "I didn't come talk to you to start an argument."

I growl out an annoyed breath. "Then why are you here, Trent?"

He glances out the window. "To offer an olive branch. I'm tired of fighting with you, Jake. We're both drowning in legal fees and baseless town rumors. They shouldn't have to pick sides between brothers. Aren't you sick of people whispering behind your back?"

"You used to enjoy the whispers," I remind him.

"Well, they're no longer fun." He grabs my hardback off the dash. "You love this town. You love the people here." His eyes lift to mine. "I'm willing to give you all the properties in Victoria for your share of the company."

This is not an olive branch. It's scraps, but it's the first time he's been willing to give me even a crumb.

He's scared.

The fight with Rocky unsettled him. Losing his supposed best friend. Losing the respect of some people in town. It must have hit him.

I try not to smile when I say, "No."

Trent rolls his eyes again. "As expected, you make the stupid choice." He opens the passenger door, taking my hardback with him.

"Trent!" I yell, jumping out of my car as soon as he climbs out. "That's my book."

Trent slides his sunglasses back on. "Thanks for letting me borrow it."

I shake my head. "Trent—"

"See you at book club." He waves me off and heads toward Baubles & Bookends. My muscles constrict knowing Hailey is inside the store.

THIRTY-FIVE

Hailey

"Leave some pickles for the rest of us." George Reynolds means no harm by the comment, considering it's followed with a chortle. He has *When the Wind Blows* tucked under his armpit and tops his plastic plate with rosemary and herb crackers.

My cheeks burn a deep shade of red. Book club has one of the best charcuterie spreads every month, and today I've piled my plate full of tiny cornichons.

In my head, George has just screamed, "THIS ONE IS PREGNANT!"

Pickles have been my latest undoing. I crave them. All kinds. Sweet ones, spicy ones, bread and butter chips, dill spears, even the sour pickles I used to hate. I'm beginning to think this baby might come out a full-blown pickle.

No one is thinking you're pregnant, Hailey. I take that reminder and my plate to a high-top table next to a shelf of horror novels. If anything can calm my sudden nerves, it's being surrounded by books.

I crunch a cornichon and cough. *What the fuck?* Trent just

walked through the doors. I fight the urge to duck under the table or slip behind the bookshelf. Hiding from Trent—not the job. But I didn't expect him to be here. Book club is my sanctuary zone where I get to eat free crackers and cheese and mingle over thrillers with Jake.

My stomach sours, and I barely get the pickle down with a gulp of water before Trent spots me. He beelines for my table.

This is good, Rocky would say. *Use the opening.* I see the opportunity, but improvising has never been my forte.

"Just the girl I was looking for," Trent greets as he places the hardback on the table. "How's it going, Hay-Hay?"

I blink extra hard at the new revolting nickname he just created. "Hailey," I say.

He bites the end of his sunglasses. "Hay-Hay is cuter, no?"

"No," I say into a crunchy chomp of pickle. Other book club members start eyeing us with sudden intrigue. Trent has been the talk of the town, and not so fondly. But this isn't the first time his name has been churned through the rumor mill, and I'm sure he's waiting for the dust to settle and his name to be cleared once again. Guys like Trent always come away from scandal with no more carnage than a wrinkled shirt.

"If you were looking for me," I add, "why not catch me at Stonehaven? We live in the same hall." I don't *love* putting this idea into his head. Like hell do I want him knocking on my door in the middle of the night. But I am genuinely curious why he wouldn't just take the easy route rather than jump-scare me in town.

He flips open the hardback absentmindedly, ignoring the onlookers. "Yes, but we're also living on a big rock in the middle of the harbor. Your brother tried to drown me in a pool. What's to say he wouldn't throw me in the sea if he sees me talking to his little sister?"

I frown. "You're scared of Grey?"

"*Scared*' is a strong word, Hay-Hay. I am reasonably on guard, and if I didn't respect Varrick so much and his competition for heir, I would've packed my bags already and moved back home for the rest of the summer."

I'm sure this has more to do with Varrick's money than respect, but I don't push back on that. In fact, I choose to stay quiet, munching on my pickles while he eats air.

He watches me for a long second. "Phoebe is your best friend, so you two must have *some* similarities."

My forehead wrinkles in a deep frown. Is he trying to pump himself up into marrying me? Figuring out if I'm at all like the girl he can't have? I'm not trying to be his dream girl. That would involve him wanting to marry me *and* fuck me.

"We're very different," I tell him.

"Are you exclusively into men, or are you into girls, too, like Phoebe is?" His eyes don't leave me, as if this is a serious question. It almost feels like an interview, and I don't ask how he knows Phoebe has slept with girls. That's not something she hides.

"Just men," I say.

He lets out an annoyed sigh, and I can almost see his dreams of having his future wife partake in a threesome float away.

I dip my cornichon in mustard. He looks around the room, almost out of boredom. I'm losing him—clearly.

"Did you see Jake before you came in?" I ask, pulling his attention back.

"Jake?" Trent grimaces like he just ate a lemon. "What do you want with him?"

"He always comes to book club."

Trent angles his head toward the door. "There's your answer."

Jake walks into the bookstore, his hair disheveled from the afternoon wind. He's the definition of *preppy* in his designer navy polo and crisp white pants. I don't take my eyes off him. I love the edges of his strong, stubbly jawline. *Heroic*. The kind of face that'd be sculpted and erected in the Pantheon to be worshipped and to last for all time.

Since I moved to Victoria, we've run into each other so often in public. The town square, the bookstore, VCC, the pier, restaurants, and diners. Each time, I had to remain uninterested. He had to appear friendly but detached.

So, for the first time, seeing him in public, I let myself smile.

Truly smile.

Like blinding *I'm so fucking happy to see you* smile.

When his blue eyes hit mine, he halts a little. Stumbles. Confused lines pleat between his brows for a split second before realization hits, and he lets himself smile, too.

We're just smiling at each other across the room for a good thirty seconds before he starts approaching my table.

Trent's gaze flits between me and his brother. "Hay-Hay," he groans. "Please tell me you don't have a crush on my brother."

"He's cute," I whisper bashfully as I swirl my pickle in mustard.

Trent sighs. "Bad taste, going for the uglier brother." He gives me a quick once-over. "Listen, I know all about your proclivities—"

"My what?" I ask, feigning stupidity.

"I've heard you sleep around," Trent says, not bothering to whisper as Jake reaches us and is in earshot.

I swallow my pickle.

Jake is glowering at his brother and snatches Trent's hardback on the table so possessively that I have a suspicion Trent might have stolen it from him. "Did you come in here just to harass her?"

Trent gapes. "Seriously? The accusations are getting a little tiresome. We're friends." He motions between me and him with his sunglasses. "Right, Hay-Hay?"

"Right," I squeak.

Trent smiles. "And I was *about* to tell her that you are a grade A prude. Exclusivity is a nonnegotiable with you."

I stay quiet.

"And that matters because?" Jake frowns.

Trent looks between us. "She thinks you're cute, and I wouldn't want her to get her heart broken."

Jake turns to me, his lips rising in an affectionate smile. "You think I'm cute?"

"I mean . . . yeah." My face must be tomato red. Hot. All. Over. Of course, he's cute. He was in my bed last night, and I was riding him until I could see stars. Oliver was behind me, teasing my clit, sending me to another plane of existence.

They kissed.

They kiss a lot when we're in bed together.

The image sends greater heat through my body. I don't need to be thinking about Jake's cock in me right now. Nope. *No.*

Trent's eyeing me suspiciously, then his brother. We're really walking a thin tightrope here. He needs to think Jake likes me. He wants what Jake has. It's a known fact.

But we don't need him to want me so badly he'd want to fuck me, too.

I'm not sure if I messed this up. All I can do is mumble out an "I think I'm going to get some air." I leave the bookstore quickly, but not before I grab my plate of pickles.

My heart beats quickly. *Did that work?*

I'm not sure I'll have a way of knowing until I see Trent again.

I find my phone in my crossbody bag and call Nova to come pick me up. Within a few minutes, his car is at the curb.

"You okay?" Nova asks me as soon as I'm strapped in the passenger seat.

"I think so." I let out a deep exhale.

He barely removes his gaze off me, and I wonder if I'm doing a bad job at hiding the stress lines in my face. I'm just . . . overthinking. It comes with the territory when I'm not as confident in this role.

He doesn't vocally express his concern, but it's written all over him from the wrinkles in his forehead to the depths of his brown eyes.

He's not as good at hiding his emotions as Oliver.

Apparently, I'm not either.

"I'm fine," I reaffirm.

He puts the car in gear and peels onto the street.

"You're sleeping?" Nova asks.

"I am. I have been." I blush, thinking about my sleeping buddies. "Stonehaven has been good for me. Ironically, spending the summer with the devil has its benefits." I tilt my head toward him. His seriousness never dissolves. "Are you worried I'm one sleepless night away from hallucinating again?"

Nova's jaw tightens. "Maybe," he admits. "But I'm also worried my brother is one drug-fueled night away from an overdose, I'm worried my sister is one night away from getting assaulted, and I'm worried Rocky won't survive if that happens while he's dating her. So don't take it personally. I'm just fucking worried all the time."

I mull this over for a second. "More or less worry than before Connecticut?"

He stares ahead, his brows knitting in deeper thought. "About the same. But it's also different here."

"How?"

"I see my sister changing. I see *you* changing. Hell, even Rocky. In good ways." His hand loosens on the wheel. "I've never wanted to be this stationary, but I can admit being in one place for longer than three seasons has made it easier to reflect on our lifestyle. To stop and think."

I nudge Nova's shoulder with mine. "Nova Graves, are you changing for the better?"

He tips his head toward me. No smile. No mirth. Just a heaviness against his brown eyes. "I don't know how to change, Hails. I'm going to be the same guy until the day I die."

"Relentlessly worrisome."

He lets out a gruff laugh. "Sounds about right."

My phone buzzes in my cargo pants. I dig it out, careful not to rip my black fishnet fingerless gloves.

"Is that Oliver?" Nova asks.

"Let me see," I say as I click into my phone. "*Not* Oliver." I read Jake's text.

Leaving book club early. You going back to Stonehaven? 👑

I send a quick reply. **Yes** 🖤

See you there 👑

"Phoebe?" Nova guesses again.

"Jake," I answer.

"Jake." Nova says his name without much emotion attached.

"I thought you liked Jake."

"I do like Jake," Nova says into a deeper breath. "But I like my brother more."

My nose wrinkles in a scrunched frown. "You don't have to choose one over the other. There's no competition between them."

"Maybe not for you." Nova stops the car at a red light. "But I have a priority list, and Jake, being the new guy, is at the bottom."

"So, if this priority list is ranked by longevity, does that mean Rocky is number one, seeing as how he's the oldest and thereby been a part of the team the longest?"

Nova glares at the street. "No. Oliver and Phoebe are at the top."

"So it's not based on longevity. It's based on familial ties."

"It's my own ranking system," Nova says hotly.

"Where do I stand on it?" I wonder. "You can be honest with me. I wouldn't much mind if I'm at the bottom since your ranking system has an arbitrary structure."

He laughs under his breath. "We should have more of these one-on-ones, Hails. I forget how funny you are."

"I wasn't making a joke."

He smiles. "I know." After a deeper breath, he admits, "Ever since you were fifteen, and I walked in on you and Ol, I tied you together in my rankings."

I wince a little at that memory. We'd been careless, but Oliver's tutor had gone home sick with the flu, so we had an entire day to do absolutely *nothing*. A rare occasion of freedom that we spent tutoring each other in the art of cunnilingus. We didn't anticipate that our moms would send Nova to the house.

I tilt my head toward him. "You know, I didn't sleep with him to gain Nova protection benefits."

"Of course not. You never knew about my 'arbitrary' ranking system."

"I find it fascinating though," I tell him. "Who's after Oliver, Phoebe, and me? Rocky or Trevor?"

He groans. "Why are we even having this conversation?"

"Because it's interesting," I say. "More interesting, at least, than discussing my awkward conversations with Trent."

"I'll cop to that."

"You know what I think?"

"No, but I know you'll tell me."

"Rocky is at the bottom of your list," I say, thinking out loud. "Not because he's the least important but because you've known for some time my little brother is capable of terrible things, and it makes you want to protect Trevor more. It's why you, Oliver, and Rocky named Trevor *the psychopath*. Somewhere along the way, you knew." I glance back at Nova, and his face has gone paler.

His gaze has darkened on the road.

He doesn't tell me I'm right.

But I know I am.

THIRTY-SIX

Phoebe

"Please! Don't kill me. You don't want to do this. I promise, you don't." The final girl on the giant movie screen sobs and pleads for her life while the masked murderer looms over her. He cranes his head in a creepy, sadistic tilt. Then he raises an axe and—*bam!* She pulls out a gun and shoots him square in the head. Blood drips down his temple before he collapses at her feet.

Rocky coughs on a popcorn kernel, and I swiftly hand him a fountain soda. He takes a gulp, then leans into my side to whisper hiss, "What the fuck? When did she get a gun?"

"Ten minutes ago. You didn't see her pick it up off the floor?"

"No, I was too busy paying attention to the psycho with the axe." He speaks a little too loudly, because a lady three rows ahead angrily shushes us.

It doesn't matter, because the credits start to scroll a minute later. Lights brighten the dark crowded theater and the many occupied velvet seats. This wasn't some obscure horror flick. It was a sold-out showing of a summer blockbuster.

The abrupt ending has Rocky glowering at the movie screen. "That's it?"

"She survived," I tell him and brush off crumbs from my lap. *Ugh, why does popcorn have to be so messy?* I peer back at the credits. "What more is there?"

"How about, what is she going to do now that all her friends are dead, her house was set on fire, and she's wanted for three different murders that she didn't even commit?" He pushes at his black hair, some strands hanging disobediently in his face.

"Valid points, but normally horror movies end when the main characters survive. They don't unpack the trauma of surviving." That endnote hangs heavy in the air, and I watch Rocky work his jaw into a tighter scowl.

Okay, so this movie might've been a bad idea, but I didn't know Rocky would draw comparisons to himself. But maybe I should have known. I *am* the horror movie buff. And technically, Rocky is the "final boy" of his own childhood.

The true sole survivor of his entire familial line.

It doesn't help that the president of the Historical Society organized a Float on the River event for this weekend. Where the lovely citizens of Victoria, us included, can tie off colorful inner tubes and sunbathe over the bodies of Rocky's deceased family. Unknowingly since the Wolfe family deaths are largely buried and forgotten, but still.

It also doesn't help that Varrick got the event canceled earlier today. Rocky's skepticism is at an all-time high with that act of kindness, considering Varrick is the fucking *reason* his family is dead in the first place. So if this was his attempt at currying favor with Rocky, it didn't work.

He's never been more on edge.

Which puts me more on edge.

Eerie music floods the movie theater, and Rocky and I aren't rushing to exit. We stay seated in the very back row while people rise with their candy wrappers and emptied popcorn buckets to leave.

I don't invoke Varrick's name in this hallowed space. It's like calling upon a hell demon. All it does is draw more and more rage out of Rocky's eye sockets, and right now his irritation hasn't even simmered down.

He squeezes the fountain soda, his gaze cemented on the scrolling credits like every single name has personally affronted him.

"This movie is bullshit," he tells me. "How is this a happy ending at all?"

"She's alive. That was the goal."

He cocks his head in thought, then nods once. "Alive but fucked-up."

"She was already a little fucked-up before the murder. And the fire."

He stuffs the soda in the cupholder. "But at least give me a fucking *ending*. That was the middle." He swings his head toward me. "And I know you love this genre, Phebs, but it's depressing as shit."

"It's hopeful," I counter. "Someone always survives . . ." I pause. Wait, that's wrong. "Unless you're *Cabin in the Woods*, *Cloverfield*, *Final Destination 5* . . ." I scrunch my face. "Okay, maybe it's not a hard-and-fast rule."

He raises his brows at me. "And here I was about to say I'd watch all the depressing-as-shit movies with you as long as you don't spoil them."

I suck in a breath. I did spoil those, didn't I? "Oops?"

"Don't act so sad about it."

I am grinning. "You still watched *The Ring* with me after I spoiled that one when I was fifteen, and in my defense, who hasn't seen *The Ring*?"

"Someone who wants peaceful dreams."

I throw a kernel at his face. He catches it in his mouth, and his accompanying satisfied smile is to both my delight and my misery.

I make an annoyed *humph* sound because I was *not* trying to feed him.

Rocky relaxes back in his seat, and we overhear some older ladies gabbing mindlessly as they exit. "They're already saying it's going to a Thornhall. Either the boy or the girl."

They must not notice the boy Thornhall is in the movie theater beside me. "There's still so much summer left," her friend says. "Varrick couldn't have already chosen."

"The de la Vegas wouldn't print it in the *Weekly* if it weren't true. It didn't even say *allegedly*. The Wolfe inheritance is going to a Thornhall."

"*Most likely* going to a Thornhall," her friend clarifies. "I still think it'll end up with a Koning."

That's promising. Another win for us after planting rumors in the local paper. We turn back to each other, but in our peripheral, we both spot the teenage girls who work at Seaside Griddle side-eyeing us. They cover their mouths to whisper-giggle too loudly, "Oh my God, it's Grey and Phoebe."

A girl squeals. "Do you see the way he's looking at her?"

Rocky has another smug smile on me, and I launch a second kernel at him. Right in his mouth. *Ugh, enough.* Now I really am feeding him.

I should probably thank Sidney for her heroic recap of Grey Thornhall defending my honor at Trent's party. I never thought people here would *swoon* over the idea of me and Rocky getting back together.

The toxic ex-husband is no more. How easy perceptions change.

Slowly but surely, I've been seen out more with Rocky all summer. But we haven't set a date for when we'll be official in public. We haven't planned out some big reveal.

Should we have?

Ignoring the spectators, Rocky leans into me and roots a hand on the back of my chair. "You know what I think?" His intense gray eyes are heavy on me. I smell his intoxicating musk and the expensive leathery cedar cologne he spritzed tonight. He's rolled the sleeves of his black button-down to his strong forearms. Veins spindle toward his wrists. My lungs inflate as he's inches from me, my skin tingling.

"What?" I whisper.

"That you're attracted to the morbid, fucked-up shit."

I grind away an abrupt smile. "Or it's attracted to me," I counter. "I'm a magnet for the macabre. Perfect example." I wave a hand at his face. "Gruesome. *Terrifying.*"

His hot breath hits my ear. "You should be terrified of what I'm going to do to you tonight."

I almost snort, but the danger pulsing in his dark gaze is a tether drawing me in. I'm letting him as his eyes travel over me in the least platonic way conceivable. My imagination runs rampant with flashes of Rocky pounding inside of me.

My breath becomes shallow.

Especially as his fingers graze the fallen spaghetti strap of my red sundress. His knuckles brush my skin. A shiver ripples along my entire body at the sensitivity.

Caging more breath, I go very still.

He lifts the cotton fabric back to my shoulder and pushes

strands of my dark blue hair off my neck, exposing more sensitive flesh. What is he doing?

His closeness is a heady, inviting rush. I want to crawl toward the feeling with everything in me, but a weird panic screams, *Run away!*

Self-preservation. This is what I've been taught.

Protect our identities.

Do not give in to my desires. To the longing for Rocky.

We've never had a real kiss with a real audience.

I tilt my head slightly to meet him head-on. It causes our lips to nearly skim. *People are watching.* I hear the two teenagers whispering at an audible octave as they take their sweet time to reach the exit.

"I told you they're really together, Grace. *Look.*"

Yes, yes, we are together! I want to shriek it like a banshee. But my lips are padlocked on instinct.

Is it too early?

Is there a right time? Should we actually map this out? Strategies, logistics, things . . . my mind melts into molten lava.

Because Rocky hasn't ripped his gaze off me. He suddenly tears the popcorn bucket from my hands, setting it on the ground.

"*Rocky*," I warn. "I'm not a movie theater litterer."

"I had no idea." He skates another coarse hand through his hair. "It's not like I haven't been to the movies with you a hundred fucking times." His dry tone is just drowning me in confusion. I can't tell if he's ready to leave or not.

"I always went with your sister," I correct him. "You just tagged along."

He lifts his brows. "Could that be because you both were

trying to sneak in flasks of vodka, and I didn't want you to get caught underage-drinking in a fucking Cineplex?"

Out of all the lawless things we've ever done, that has to be bottom tier. "That was one time," I whisper, my gaze dropping to his lips. Heat roasts my cheeks as he notices. "And don't act like a moral authority. You literally stole our flask and drank half of it."

"It was good liquor. And I've never been a *moral* anything." He cocks his head at me, like I've forgotten who he is.

I direct my scorching face away from him, and I freeze. Is it my paranoia or is the theater still half full? I know my relationship has been B-level entertainment for this town, but that *B* doesn't stand for *Blockbuster*.

Rocky rises to his feet, but before I can follow, he suddenly seizes my hips and lifts me. He places my ass on the top of the theater chair, and I clutch his biceps like he's thrown me halfway across the room. What the hell? *What the hell?*

I can't catch my breath. This is . . . this is *hot*. One of his hands settles on the bareness of my thigh where my sundress rides up. And his hard gaze dives into me, searching me at rapid, unrelenting speed.

My legs dangle on either side of his waist, and I almost, *almost* wrap them around him. I almost bring him closer. I'm clutching his arms in a death grip. My heart is pounding out of my rib cage.

Then my eyes dart to Grace and her friend, who've settled back in theater seats. They're texting hurriedly on their phones.

Rocky pinches my chin and turns my head, forcing my attention on him.

I slap his hand away. He clutches my cheek more fiercely,

showing me it's okay. His eyes practically ram each word inside me. *It. Is. Okay.* We can be physically affectionate out in public. I touch his hand against my face, not shoving him aside this time.

This can't be happening.

I did wake up this morning, right? And why is it so hard for me to believe that he'd choose tonight to rip away the façade? "You aren't . . ."

"Yeah, I am."

And then he bends down on one knee, his good knee, thankfully. And I nearly black out. "Rocky . . ." My heart accelerates to thrilling, volatile speeds—the speeds we love living at, him and me.

He reveals a velvet black box from his pocket. I half expect to see a Ring Pop inside. We're still just pretending.

"Our lives aren't going to fade to black. This part is making the movie." He opens the box, and my heart skips a beat while my eyes well and lips go wider and wider. Overwhelmed. I am so overwhelmed, because I know this elegant gold pear-cut diamond ring. He's already slipped it on my finger before.

In Miami.

The only time we went through the steps to have a fake wedding. It came right after the Melon Drop in Nashville, and I'd never been more head over heels for Rocky than when we pretended to get married. Our relationship, whatever we could really call it, had never been so all-consuming, adrenaline fueled, and messy. Just how I loved it.

I remember how a sexy silk wedding dress dripped down my body, but his eyes had been on mine the entire night. I wished for that job to never end, for the fantasy to play out for eternity.

We did all the stupidly romantic newlywed things. Cut the

five-tiered cake. Smeared a line of buttercream on his cheek. He retaliated with one down my lips. We were supposed to be a young, playful, crazy-in-love couple who couldn't keep their hands off each other.

We teased and taunted. He grazed his fingers up my thigh, just to slip off the lacy white garter, and it felt like I was being touched for the first time. Shivers ran up my body. I lit up in my own skin—I only ever lit up with his hands, with him. I wanted to chase after those electric touches all night long.

I could. We were married.

The after-party led us to an exclusive Miami club. Our fake friends were there, but so were our real ones: Hailey and my brothers. I remember being in the dance pit with Rocky. Grinding, breathing heavy, kissing. His hands all over me. My hands all over him. The strobe lights stroking our sweaty bodies, and I never wanted to let go of that feeling with him.

But I did.

We did.

My feelings lived inside every job with Rocky, and every job had an ending. The fantasy popped, only to be built into a new one. He was my stepbrother. We were college dormmates. Strangers. Coworkers.

But here, in this town, he's just my Rocky. I'm just his Phoebe. And our relationship has never been so real.

"Phoebe," he says, his soul-burning eyes never leaving mine. "Marry me again."

The squeals and applause around us have my ears ringing. I can barely even hear myself say, "Yes," but Rocky knows. He's standing, slipping the gorgeous ring on my finger for the second time.

His lips rise.

A smile spreads across my face. The secrets we share nestle

affectionately in my body. I ease backward from him, just a little. "If you want it, come and get it," I taunt.

His large hand cocoons the side of my face. He slides those same fingers into my hair, raking them against my scalp. Then he yanks my head backward and whispers hotly against my ear, "I've already gotten it."

My heady, drunk-in-love smile bursts inside me, and he pulls me tighter against his strong build—his lips on mine in an erupting kiss. It explodes my senses.

Marry me again.

I'm stifling a moan, melting into Rocky's possessive, demolishing kisses. His tongue slips sensually against mine, and I kiss as fervently back, curving my arm around his neck. Then Rocky cups the backs of my thighs and hoists me off the chair. I meld against his firm chest while we make out like we're fighting for oxygen.

If my fake relationship with Jake was chaste and PDA-free, my real public one with Rocky is going to be next-level raunchy.

I smile into the sultry kiss.

I'm already obsessed with this.

"Get a room!" a teenager shouts, and Rocky flips him off while we're lip-locked. As the passionate seconds burn into minutes, I sense we've cleared the theater. It doesn't stop us. But me scrounging for breath does.

As he lowers me, I slide down his body. The bottoms of my strappy white heels thump to the popcorn-littered ground. Rocky tugs down my cherry-red dress, which bunched on my descent.

My lips sting like he's still on them, and I intake a big breath to stop panting. "Just to let you know," I say, "you might be remarrying the town's newest Victoria's Sweetheart. I heard I'm in the running for the annual competition."

"Yeah?" He soaks in my haughty smile. "Tricked the whole town into thinking you're a sweetheart? How's that crown of lies sitting?"

"Like victory." I clutch the seat behind me, my face so flush seeing his smile. "But to warn you, you also might be with the callous bitch of Victoria. I'm sure some Jake defenders will wish I ended up with him."

"I'm the real callous bitch."

"Trying to steal my reputation?"

He lets out a tight laugh, glances behind me in short thought, then drops his eyes to mine. "I've loved the heart-breaker of Malibu, the virgin of Manhattan, the angel of Boston, the slut of Las Vegas—you think I wouldn't love the bitch of Victoria?"

"Rocky," I whisper out, the sudden declaration of love pummeling me, even after he just proposed.

He holds my face again, his thumb caressing my cheek. "I've loved you in every way, in every fucking place. But this place is getting the best of my love."

I can barely breathe again. "Why's that?"

"Because it's not confined anymore, Phebs. Everyone can see it now. You get that?"

It overwhelms me. "Yeah," I murmur, feeling it. "I really do." It's all slamming into me. Strength surges inside my full lungs. "We were taught deceit is the most powerful tool, but the truth hasn't made me feel weak."

He looks me over. "What do you feel?"

"Indestructible. Loving you loudly might become my new favorite obsession."

His slow-rising smile crawls across his mouth. "Try not to come so hard in the street when you scream my name."

I glare. "Not *that* loudly."

He laughs and brings me closer to his chest, nestling a kiss into my hair. I stare down at my hand, the diamond ring, and my eyes glass all over again.

He never sold this ring. He held on to it for four years. And he says he's not sentimental over things.

Liar.

THIRTY-SEVEN

Phoebe

I'm on a high tonight from the real proposal, and *nothing* can bring me down. Not even a run-in with human garbage.

Trent Waterford exits Baubles & Bookends with a stream of book clubbers. We've regrettably walked right toward him after leaving the movie theater. So when we see him and he sees us—Rocky's arm securely over my shoulders—it feels a little like a John Wayne film. Glaring. Silence. *Fuck you* staredowns of lethal proportions.

Only instead of Trent reaching for a pistol at his hip, he procures a cellphone. He puts it to his ear. "Hey, Trevor, my boy." He watches Rocky's eyes darken. "Whatever you're up to, cancel it. Let's grab a drink at the Gulp. Whiskey on me." He drops the phone down, just to say to Rocky, "Your baby brother says, 'Fuck you.'"

Rocky takes one hot step forward.

Trent recoils a little. Ooh, he's scared.

I smooth my lips as a smile forms.

"You hurt my brother," Rocky sneers under his breath,

"and I promise it will be the last thing you ever fucking do. I will end you, and you best *fucking* believe I have the means to get away with it." He works for the CIA, after all.

"Great, Trevy," Trent says into the phone, not responding to Rocky. "I'll see you there." He keeps the phone to his ear as he steps off the curb and jaywalks across the road.

I scowl out at his quick stride away. "Do we follow him?"

"No. Trev will be fine. It's better I'm not in sight. It might provoke Trent into doing something worse. He'll probably have a couple drinks with him and go home."

Home. "You mean the home we're all sharing?"

"Yeah." He clasps my hand. "But at least that fuckbag won't be there for a few more hours."

I grin. Night definitely not ruined.

Once we're inside the mansion, we can't make it up to my bedroom fast enough. My lips sting from the forceful hallway kisses. My body hums like a bell being tolled over and over.

We're all fire and engulfing passion when we push into my room. I tear myself off Rocky to capitalize the pursuit. "It's not that easy," I pant, backing up farther and farther. "Haven't you heard? I'm impossible to catch."

"Not that easy?" His hot gaze sears me. "Funny, considering I've caught you a thousand times already." He flicks the lock closed.

I raise a brow. "One less time tonight." My shoulders thump into the muraled wall. Breathless.

I've been staying in his late aunt's bedroom. Daphne Wolfe. She must've loved nature. Sweeping wildflowers, bees, butterflies, rabbits, foxes are painted all over her walls. Field guides on birds and falconry stock her bookcases. And the gilded leaves and twisting vines of a stunning chandelier hang above us. It's one of the lighter bedrooms at Stonehaven when most weigh heavy with moody greens and darker velvets.

Rocky sheds his black button-down, then he's unbuckling his leather belt. "Fiancée. Wife." He slides the leather out of his loops, and I feel myself clench, aching for him inside me. "Lover."

"Enemy," I taunt. "You. Can't. Have. *Me*."

He never breaks from my gaze while he unbuttons his black slacks, then unzips. He has them down his toned thighs. Soon, his pants are off completely. And so are his boxer briefs. He's sculpted muscle and primed arousal. Ready to take me.

I can barely capture my breath. His unyielding dark confidence chokes out the room.

"Keep squeezing your thighs together, it's not going to help you," Rocky says in a deep threat. "I'm going to spread you wide fucking apart."

I'd like to see you try. Words knot in my throat. I'm doing everything not to melt against this fucking wall. Just feeling the wedding ring on my finger quickens my heartbeat.

Several feet still separate us, and the tension is killer, especially as he says, "You keep staring at my cock."

"I'm not," I combat, a weak lie.

"No?" He hasn't moved an inch since he undressed. He's buck naked while my high heels and red sundress are still on, and I love this. I love how I can drink in all of Rocky and so clearly see how strongly he desires me.

I chew my bottom lip when I glance at his erection again. God, it's actually infuriating how *beautiful* his cock is, especially hard.

Rocky takes another threatening step forward. "You're not

thinking about how I'm going to ram every inch in you?" He draws a finger across his long length to demonstrate just how many inches. My pulse skips.

"Nope." I cage breath and slip my hands up my dress, only to draw down my lacy pink panties. I pull them past my high heels and throw them aside.

His cock twitches. He's standing at mouthwatering attention. I tell myself to move, to let him chase me, but I'm pulsing so much between my legs, I can't pick up my feet.

"Yeah, keep staring, you little fucking *liar*," Rocky growls out. "The only reason I'm this fucking hard"—he closes in on me, his voice deeper, rougher—"is so I can penetrate your tight, wet *cunt* and hear you scream."

"Rocky," I warn. It sounds like a moan.

"Like that, but louder."

Fuck me.

I almost buckle at the knees. Somehow, I find the strength to push off the wall, and I circle Rocky like he's my prey. His eyes track me like I'm his.

I suppose the truth is somewhere in between.

Biting my lip, feeling my smile, I walk backward toward the four-poster bed. He stalks forward.

"Wife," he repeats with force.

"Husband." My tone isn't sweet either. Then I turn around to run, but he's fast and seizes my hips. I put up a feeble fight as he pushes my chest into the mattress, my heels scraping at the floorboards. There is literally no time to sit up, no time to think. Rocky pins me with his muscled build. He hikes my dress to my waist, and as he captures my wrists, stretching them above my head, he makes good on his threat. He thrusts so deep into me.

My lips break open with a gasp and slight moan. *Fuck.* "Fuck," I cry out.

"What was that?" he taunts back with a heavy grunt. "Phoebe wants more?"

"Fuck. You." My growly moan is smothered into the mattress.

He fills my pussy without a condom, and the heat of his cock is sending my mind on a dizzying voyage. I. Can't. Think. Can barely move as he fucks me from behind and bears his warm chest against my back with greater force. Deeper—he drives so deep, deep in me.

I shut my eyes for a moment. That's when shit gets bad. I open them, and I don't see Rocky, just the headboard. I feel my body jostle as he rams into me, and I tighten as a flash of Carlsbad strikes my brain. I freeze more and scramble for the ability to speak. *Tell him.* "Miami," I choke out.

He stops moving inside me.

I have a regret when I say the safe word. Regret because I don't like acknowledging how screwed up I might still be from a situation that occurred a *year* ago, and this is basically signaling, *I am not okay.* When all I want to be is okay.

The regret instantly decays once Rocky tilts my head so my eyes crash against his. Only care in his gaze. He hasn't pulled out. His body shelters mine, and he strokes my hair out of my face. "Breathe with me," he whispers.

I inhale deep the same time he does. Exhale. Inhale. "Sor—"

"No," he glares. "Don't fucking apologize."

His pissy tone actually makes me smile. "Fine, I won't," I snap back.

"Good." He studies me.

Flush coats my cheeks again. He turns my head more to him and presses a kiss to my lips. It's a sultry, deep kiss that summons more heat from me and loosens my body. I grow wetter around him.

"Fuck," he curses against my mouth, then catches a breath to ask, "You need another minute?"

"Mm-hmm." I want him so badly. "Face me?"

"Already plan on it." That's when he draws out, then flips me. Our eyes stake each other with hostility and longing. He picks me up. Tosses me higher on the bed. While he retrieves a condom, I unstrap my heels. He's quick to rip the packet, sheathe himself, and return just as I toss the heels aside.

He captures my thighs, splitting me open.

"Rocky," I cry, shoving his chest. *"No."*

"Phoebe." He confines my hands to the mattress. "*Yes*. You can keep being a brat all you fucking want." He bows over me, his knees spreading me wider. "You're still going to take all of me." I love being trapped beneath him.

Don't let go.

Never let me go.

He flexes into me. *Oh God*. My hips buck up on instinct. He grinds harder. Once again, I'm so full of Rocky. This time, our eyes stay fastened. He devours me inside out with his gaze. Even as his hand ravages me, wrenching my dress down. Teasing my nipples. Cupping, journeying.

Then he grips my face. Holding me so close to him with each thrust.

It's deep, rough sex where I'm digging into his back for closer. *More*. He can't go deep enough. He can't be close enough. My body is alive beneath Rocky.

Every sensation blows me apart. We come together, and I moan into the pit of his hand. My body rattles. My eyes fucking *roll*. I can't even hear his curses and groans. My ears are ringing.

Coming down from a climax is just as enjoyable. Where he brushes my sweaty hair out of my face. Then places a loving kiss on my lips. I can barely move. I'm still throbbing, but I manage to whisper the truth: "Thanks for being patient with me."

"Thanks for recognizing I can't read your mind all the time."

"So you're admitting you can *sometimes*."

"I can read your *body*." He stands off the bed. Condom trashed, he collects a pack of cigarettes, then lights one between his lips.

I like watching him mosey naked around the room after we fuck. Sometimes, I think he knows it, too.

"What's my body saying now?" I ask while I lie on my stomach. I'm hugging a fluffy white pillow under my head.

The bed undulates with his return. "You want me to fuck you again."

I snort. "*Fail*. Try again, buddy."

He stares at my bare ass. My dress is bunched above my hips. Not really doing its job to cover my bottom or tits. He leans over to me, and I tense in anticipation. He pauses, staring right at my face.

I glare. "Shouldn't you be looking at my body, not my eyes?"

"I am doing both," he mumbles, cigarette between his lips. Then he squeezes my ass before slipping two fingers into my pussy.

Do not twitch.

I try to act like this is nothing, but feeling him inside me again is driving another need into me. I want *more*.

Rocky smokes with his right hand, fucks me with his left, and all the while, his eyes stay fixed on my glare.

He blows smoke away from me. "You know what your soaked cunt is saying now?"

"I hate Rocky."

"You need my cock."

"Oh, now I need you?" I swallow an aroused knot, because I am crumbling at a vicious rate. "Okay, yeah, Rocky." I nearly whimper in impatience, and I catch his wrist, tearing his fingers out of me. I go to crawl on top of him, but he pushes me back down.

"Let me get a condom first, Phebs."

I groan like he's torturing me. "You did this to me."

He nearly smiles. "Thank *God* you're also as patient as me."

"Don't kid yourself, we *are* the same."

"Not in every way. Clearly." He lets the cigarette burn between his lips while he sifts through the condom box. He picks one out, and right before he rips the foil, he pauses. His brows crinkle. His abs contract into more defined ridges.

I frown. "Rocky?"

He runs his fingers over the foil packet, then he snuffs out the cigarette and returns to the box. He dumps out all the condoms on the dresser. He's examining each one.

I slip the straps to my dress on my shoulders. "What's wrong?" My pulse is skidding. He's *very* particular about his condoms. A fun fact I learned when we had sex for the first time. He only uses a specific brand, an ultrathin kind.

I slide off the bed and walk toward him. "Are they not the ones you like?"

He bought that box himself. He always buys the condoms.

Rocky raises a hand at me to stop for a second.

I stand in the middle of the room. "Rocky . . ." Fear steals my breath. Because his silent rage is so lethal and he's doing his best not to aim it at me. I can only think, *This isn't just bad*.

Whatever he sees is devastating.

THIRTY-EIGHT

Rocky

That motherfucker.

Everything in my vision is bloodred. I've shot past pissed. I'm volcanic, about to fucking explode. It takes a hard, furious blink just to push past anger to recheck several of the condom packets.

Yeah.

There are puncture holes in each one. I just came inside Phoebe wearing a defective condom. I might've been coming inside her this entire *fucking* summer using pinpricked condoms.

"How bad is it?" Phoebe asks, her constricted voice saying she already knows whatever is wrong is god-awful.

"He gave me a key to your bedroom." I throw a foil packet back on the dresser with the others. "Night one, he gave me access to your bedroom, so it'd be easy for me to sleep with you all summer."

"Wait. You're talking about Varrick? As in my dad?"

I still can't look at Phoebe. I grip the dresser in a lunge. My knuckles whiten, and I just inhale through my nose so I don't scream. "He gave me a key—"

"I heard you, but he gave you that key to keep Trent out of my room."

"That's what he told me, and he got me, Phebs, because that one thing, I didn't question. I believed him. Why *the fuck* did I believe him?" I straighten up and clutch the sides of my neck with two hands.

"Can we . . . can we just think about this for a second?" Phoebe sounds out of breath. I'm sure she is putting two and two together. The condoms. My rage.

"Sure." I slide my hands off my neck. "I'm thinking about how he invited us here this summer so he could have easy access to our bedrooms. Our belongings. I'm thinking about how many times he could've easily come in here while we were gone, while you were working at the club. We kept our burners on us. We kept all our IDs, all our extra papers, in a storage unit out of town. We didn't consider . . ." Acid drips down my throat, and I take a searing breath. "We didn't consider needing to protect our fucking *protection*."

She's dead silent behind me.

"You're going to say I'm overreacting." I smear a hand over my mouth. "That there's no way he'd try to get his own daughter pregnant. What's the motive? But this is *exactly* why I thought our parents even wanted us together in the first place. So we would have a fucking *baby*. So they could get their little shill." It's why I resisted being with Phoebe for so long.

I never wanted them to use us.

I always knew they could.

My blood won't cool. I rake a hot hand through my hair. "It's not far-fetched to think Varrick would want the same, and it's not a stretch to think he'd do worse to make it happen.

He has no *real* emotional ties to us. Everything he's done is smoke and mirrors so we wouldn't see what he really wants at the end of the summer."

"I need . . ." Phoebe trails off in a haunted daze.

I turn to her for the first time. She's not blinking. Not moving. "Phoebe." I head toward her, but she reanimates and bolts over to her purse on a tufted chair.

"I need to call Hailey." She raises the phone in the air, trying to find a signal. Once she's able to locate enough, she puts the phone on speaker, and my sister picks up after the second ring. "Hails, you back at Stonehaven yet?"

The line crackles. "Been here."

"Can you check your condoms? See if any have been tampered with."

"Ohh-kay, yeah."

We hear rustling and then Jake comes on the line. "Is something wrong with your condoms?"

"Yeah." I state one harsh word.

"Fuck," Jake curses.

"Uh, no, no—mine are okay. They look fine. Don't they, Olly?"

"Foil intact," Oliver declares.

I rub my eyes.

"Thanks," Phoebe says stiffly.

"Phoebe—" Hailey starts.

"We'll talk more later. It's a . . . situation." Phoebe's staring tensely at me. "But it's becoming evident someone has been trying to get me pregnant. For who knows how long?"

I drop my arm, my brows knitting together in confusion. Why is that a question? It's clear this started this summer. "What do you mean?"

"I mean," Phoebe says slowly, "that I gave Hailey my box

of condoms *months* ago. A box that I no longer needed because you're picky about the brand and type, but they'd been mine, in my room—"

"Your room at the loft?" I question.

"Yeah, but look who ended up pregnant, Rocky." Phoebe lifts her phone to her mouth. "Hails, were you using those condoms around the time you could've gotten pregnant?"

She takes a beat. "Yes."

Fuck.

Hailey chimes back in. "B-but this implies that someone broke into the loft."

"Can we confirm that, Jake?" I ask him. "Did you have hidden cameras anywhere?" I sincerely wish he spent months being an overly anal landlord to the point of intrusion.

"No, but Baubles & Bookends has security cameras. I'm sure facing their entrance, and the apartment door is in view. It'd probably capture him trying to get in."

"The Wolfes own the bookstore," I remind him. "We not only have a problem accessing the footage, but he also could've deleted it."

"I know the store clerk. I can buy the footage," Jake assures. "We'll see if he thought that far ahead to delete it."

I pray he did not.

"Phoebe," Oliver pipes in. "Polar bear?"

She's staring off at the wildflowers on the wall. "I think . . . platypus."

"Hang in there. It'll be okay," he reassures. "Rocky, you're staying with her?"

"I'm not going anywhere." I grind my jaw, unable to look away from my girlfri—my *wife*. She's my wife. I told her I wanted to marry her again tonight.

Phoebe hangs up after we all confirm we'll keep in touch.

She takes a ragged breath. "How long do you think my dad has known we've been together?"

"Your mom insinuated it was a while."

Her face contorts in fury but also hurt. "It's my fault Hailey is pregnant—"

"We don't know that yet, and it would *never* be your fault. You didn't know they were defective condoms. If you did, you never would've given them to her." We're both burning at such a hot temperature, I wait to near her.

Her features twist in more pain. "What if he did this to my mom, too? What if this is all happening all over again? Everything is repeating itself, and we can't escape it."

"I don't believe that."

She looks up at me like she wants to wield the same belief.

"If we are stuck in a cycle, Phebs, that means *nothing* is in our control, and I refuse to believe that. I refuse to believe we can't get out. We're getting out. You are not your mom. You've already proven that by giving up the role she won't let go."

Her eyes redden with emotion.

"Hailey isn't Addison," I say just as strongly. "She's proven that by choosing to protect you and Oliver over the job. We're going to dictate how this ends. We already have been. It's not over."

Phoebe nods, but her face breaks apart at a thought. "We can't control if I'm pregnant or not."

I rub a hand across my mouth, glancing at her body. These are conversations we've been avoiding. The future. *Our* future. Kids.

I feel like I'm being run over by a semi.

"Should I take Plan B?" she asks me.

"Is that what you want?" I ask her.

"Is that what *you* want?" she volleys back.

Jesus Christ. I scrub my face two times, then let my hands fall. "How about we start with a pregnancy test? I don't know how long I've been fucking you with damaged condoms."

She nods quickly. "Yeah . . . yeah." She's frozen in fear.

I go grab my wallet off the dresser. I flip open the leather and pull out a gold ring from the pocket.

I slip it on my wedding finger.

Coming back to Phoebe, I hold out that same hand. She gets emotional seeing the ring, and I tell her, "I don't need to be engaged to you. I don't even need to have another wedding to know you're my wife, Phoebe Graves. I'm devoted to you under any name, in any place, and whatever happens next, that will never change."

She takes a deeper breath, then clasps my hand tight. "Where are we going?"

"The 24-hour drugstore is open. We're getting a pregnancy test."

THIRTY-NINE

Phoebe

"This goes in my top ten," I tell Rocky quietly in a bathroom that has to be violating at least four health codes. The tub is cracked. The showerhead is leaking, the sink dripping. And I'm fairly certain black mold is creeping out of the air vents.

"Top ten what?" Rocky reaches into the plastic drugstore bag.

My arms are tightly crossed. "Top Ten Most Unexpected Nights." I did not think Rocky would get down on one knee or that I'd need to buy a pregnancy test or that we'd end the night in a run-down, crappy motel two hours from Victoria. "Did it make yours?"

"Top five, for sure." He holds out a blue box to me.

I cringe at the pregnancy test, then peer back at the door. "Who do you think will make it here first?" Our siblings, plus Jake, are meeting us at the motel. Room 102. A staggered arrival. It lessens the chance that the Michael Myers wannabe will suspect that *we* know he's a literal disgusting *creep*.

Rocky isn't answering me.

I stare at the scuffed doorknob. "My money's on Nova."

"Betting your pocket change on your most overprotective brother."

I glance back at him. "Who would you bet on?"

Rocky rips the box open while staring at me. "Nova." He flashes a dry smile.

I force one back, then my eyes fall to the test and my grimace re-forms.

"It doesn't have cooties," he states.

I scowl. "Did I say it did?"

"You're staring at it like it's going to leap out and lick your face."

Rotating to face him fully, I avoid elbowing the stained sink. "Great, maybe you should take it then."

"I would if I could, but that's not how this works." He plucks out the stick and the mini pamphlet of directions. "You want me to hold your hand?"

I drill a *Fuck you* glare into him.

He's not intimidated. "You want to wait for my sister and do this with her?"

"I want to wait for the person who'll jump out of the closet and say, *Aha! Gotcha! This is all one big joke!*"

"Okay, a stranger hiding in the motel closet is some horror shit that's not going to happen. So let's stay in fucking reality."

"As if this isn't horrifying?" My voice cracks. *Fuck*.

Rocky stares deeply into me until I look away again.

I didn't realize just how relieved I'd been learning I *wasn't* pregnant until this moment—when I'm faced with another scare. Only this one feels a hundred times worse. Because my own *dad* could've baby-trapped me.

I blink out of my heavy thoughts and reach for the stick in Rocky's hand.

He retracts it from me. "Let's talk about this first."

I swallow a pit in my throat and manage to ask, "Do you want to be a father?"

I'm surprised when he doesn't volley the same question back at me right away and instead answers, "Not really. Do you want to be a mother?"

"I've literally *never* pictured it." I stare at the tile floor. "Even now, the image is just so . . . blank." I look up at him.

Rocky's gaze skims me head to toe. "Do you know if you want kids or not, Phebs?"

"Like now or ever?"

"I know you don't want them now. It's very fucking clear. I meant *ever*."

I touch my wedding ring absentmindedly. "You know what would be *really* unexpected, we just married each other and we're on different sides of a deal-breaker."

"We'll figure it out," he says quietly.

"Will we?" I try not to cry. My burning eyes feel swollen from restraining waterworks on the drive here. I'm used to bolting the emotion behind closed doors. Being numb. What I'm trained to do. Just carry on. "I don't know, Rocky . . ."

He tenses more. "Don't know what?"

Fuck being closed off. I'm done pushing it down. Even if this part hurts. I rip the feelings out with the words. "I don't know if I ever want to be a mom. I don't know if I ever want to carry a child in a body that barely feels like mine sometimes. I don't know if I want to be a parent when the only road map we were ever given was so fucked-up, it's impossible to follow. And then I think I do know . . . I think I know that I don't want any of it."

He seems stunned, either that I just purged my feelings in one breath or by my answer.

I try to inhale. "You better say something."

"You don't want kids," he realizes.

"I honestly . . ." I swallow. "I just can't see that changing. It would take decades for me to feel differently, and by then, I'd be too old to have—"

"I don't want kids either, Phebs."

"Never?" I ask.

"Never." He nods. "After all we've been through . . . I've never wanted to bring something so innocent into a world so corrupt."

I wince. That hurts for some reason, and I figure out why very quickly. "Hailey."

"I know," Rocky says in a deep breath. "I know. Hailey is going to have a baby. And it's a blessing that Oliver or Jake will be the father. Your brother is so unfettered. He won't let life drag that child down, and Jake—Jake is fucking *noble*. He was practically born to spawn a litter of golden retrievers."

I frown. "You don't think the world could use more German shepherds?" It's what Hails says Rocky would be if he were a dog breed.

He glances at the pregnancy stick, then back at me. "I'm not going to say I'd be a bad father, because that'd be a lie. In the end, I think I'd cut out to be a great one."

"Cocky," I tease.

His lips tic up, rising with mine. "All I'm saying is that you don't have to think you'll be a bad parent to not want a baby. You can just not want one. Because I do know that we would be great parents."

"Yeah?"

"Yeah, we both would try to give a kid *everything* we never had and *everything* we ever loved, and I know this because we're going to give my sister's kid absolutely *everything*."

It swells inside me, and I nod strongly, knowing he's right.

I would do anything for Hailey's baby. Absolutely anything and everything. Just like I've always done for her.

I inhale the deepest breath yet. It's audible when I exhale, and I say, "You're really good at this."

"Talking?"

"Making me feel better. Just when I was about to feel guilty for never wanting to have kids of my own while my best friend is pregnant."

He raises his brows at me. "Fuck your guilt. We have way more shit to worry about." He's still holding the pregnancy test.

"Right." I tense. "I might be pregnant." I reach for it.

He lets me take it this time. "If you are, we'll figure it out together. But at least we know we're on the same page."

Letting out another breath, I nod. "I just pee on it?"

He reads the directions to me. I shimmy my panties down my ankles, reluctant to put my butt on the toilet seat. I just squat over it. Rocky stays in the bathroom while I piss on the stick, but he keeps his eyes on the door.

I can tell he's listening for noises.

"Is someone here?" I ask.

"I think I heard a knock."

"I'll get it." I hurry. Wipe. Wash hands. Set the test on top of the box. Do not want to be around that thing.

Rocky gives me a hard look like I'm being a scaredy-cat.

I flip him off on my way out. I swear I catch his smile before I leave him behind.

Even though I fully expect to see Nova, I peer through the peephole. Okay . . . unexpected thing number whatever of the night. I yank open the door. "Trevor? Did you speed here?" I notice the parked Honda. He took my car.

"I ditched Trent early at the Gulp." He enters the motel, fisting a bottle wrapped in a paper bag.

I lock the door, including the chain. "Were you drinking and driving?"

"No, I barely had any whiskey. I faked it." He plops on one of the squeaky twin beds and unscrews the alcohol.

Rocky is still in the bathroom. His voice sounds muffled, like he's on the phone.

Just me and his little brother, who withstands me like a cold sore. I sink down on the other bed, facing him. "You okay?"

"Fine." He takes a large swig.

Concern tosses my stomach. "Everything went okay with Trent?"

"Yeah."

He's not the best liar among us, so I can tell that's not the total truth, but I don't press. In our shared silence, Trevor offers me the bottle.

I stiffen. "No thanks. Baby might be on board, so . . . I need to figure that out first."

"Shit, yeah." His frown deepens. "Sorry."

The apology surprises me. I don't like that he's not teasing me hard-core or calling me PG. This feels wrong. My eyes flame. "If Trent fucked with you tonight, I will mutilate him."

Trevor lets out a short laugh. "No, you wouldn't."

"I would shear off his nuts."

"Please, PG, you're embarrassing yourself." He's smiling a little bit. "We all know I'm the only one with a kill list."

"That you're no longer using," I tell him in a tone that says, *You better not be.*

"Oh, so you can chop Trent's dick off, but I can't?"

"I'm older."

"So, when I'm twenty-five, I get full castration privileges. Got it."

"I will *always* be older than you." I shrug my rigid shoulders. "We all will, Trev. That's the beauty of being the youngest, you get full *protection* privileges when we all take turns worrying about you. I don't know why you hate it so much."

"I don't," he says under his breath right when the bathroom door opens. Rocky comes out, and Trevor raises his bottle at him. "Heard you're going to be a dad."

"We don't know yet, shithead. You get wasted, you're spending the night here."

"Already planned on it." He gets comfy on the single bed, not taking his shoes off, and grabs a remote.

Also did not expect to room with Trevor tonight. Maybe the motel has a king available.

This must've been a "failed" stagger since Nova, Oliver, Hailey, and Jake arrive practically two minutes after Trevor. Soon, we're all crammed into the musty motel room, and I sit beside Hailey on a bed, while on the other, Trevor flips through TV channels on mute.

I hold Hailey's hand. She looks around at the motel room, and I wonder if she's remembering how this all started. With me and her and boxes of hair dye in a crummy little motel. En route to Connecticut. Now we splurge and have our hair professionally dyed at the salon from time to time. I don't even hate the upkeep just to have it blue.

Her eyes meet mine. "This could be the end to something awful and the start to something great. That's what I told myself a year ago, you know," she whispers. "Things could be better than they were."

"They have been." I had such low hopes for how things would pan out living honestly in a cutesy small town. I would've never thought how much could change. How much I could change.

She smiles down at my hand in hers. The diamond ring. "I loved Miami." She peeks over at Jake and Oliver, who talk quietly with Nova and Rocky in the corner of the room.

"You love Victoria more," I say with a growing smile.

"Yeah," she breathes. "That's why it's scary to lose him."

Him. She sees the town as Jake. My heart pangs. Hailey and I look over at the guys as they break apart their team huddle to face us. The timer for the pregnancy test hasn't gone off yet.

Trevor sits up on the other bed, seeing the severity in their expressions. Even Oliver is way more uptight than usual. I send my brother a look like, *What's going on?*

He lifts his shoulders and brows, then takes a sharp inhale like, *Shit's fucked-up. What can I say?* I watch him slip on designer sunglasses, which means he's sick of me reading his reactions.

I try not to worry about him. He wouldn't want me to.

"What were you talking about?" I grimace at Rocky. "I hate to even want this, but please tell me Trent is still alive."

"No one killed Trent," Rocky says, running his fingers through his hair. "We're discussing the possibility of Varrick not wanting a team in the end. If his motive is solely to have a baby."

"What?" My face falls.

Hailey squeezes my hand, like she's already thought about this. She's comforting *me*. When I should be comforting *her*. She's the pregnant one. I might be . . . I might not be.

Nova snatches the paper-bagged bottle from Trevor. "He means Varrick isn't a team player. Never has been. Why would he believe Rocky would ever work with him?"

"He doesn't believe that I would." Rocky sounds so assured. "Because he's not going to work with us. That's not what this has been about."

"If it's just about having a baby to raise as a grifter, then . . ." I can't process this. "He could've had one any other way. Adoption. Gotten another woman pregnant."

Rocky arches his brows. "Honestly, I think it's a *fuck you* to Elizabeth, Addison, and Everett for not telling them he had children two decades ago. He really wants revenge, and we're caught in the fucking middle."

My blood runs cold. "So, what is he going to do?"

Nova chugs from the bottle, then wipes his mouth with his bicep. His anger is palpable. Jake is rolling his sleeves to his forearms. Oliver sends me and Hailey tiny, fleeting smiles of reassurance.

Rocky works his jaw before saying, "He could steal the baby and run."

Oh.

Okay, yeah. It hits me like a brick wall. I feel like I just got knocked out. "My dad might kidnap Hailey's baby. That's what you're saying?" I refuse to acknowledge that I might be pregnant.

Oliver leans on the dresser, blocking Trevor's view of the TV. "Nicolas Cage did it in *Raising Arizona*. Maybe our dad has a thing for the actor." He holds up his right hand. "*Raising Arizona*." Then lifts his left. "*Matchstick Men*."

"That's the film about con artists?" Jake asks.

"Yep," Rocky says.

"I hate that movie," Trevor mutters, trying to switch channels with Oliver in the way. "Too predictable."

"Okay. Okay." I let go of Hailey's hand, needing to stand up. "So, easy fix. Varrick can't know Hailey is pregnant. He has to be dealt with ASAP."

"He will be. That's the plan," Rocky reminds me.

There've been two jobs happening at once.

I know.

There will be two ropes pulled.

Rocky looks around at everyone, at Hailey, at me, as he says, "This stays here. Do not act like you hate him more than you already do. Don't act like he's the scum of the fucking earth. Do exactly what you've been doing."

I'm more nervous than I have been. All I'm going to want to do is stab him between the eyes. "Everything about this is dangerous."

"Yeah," Rocky agrees with me. "And the next generation of Tinrocks and Graveses will be dangerously ours. He's not getting shit."

FORTY

Oliver

Tonight is too heavy. Love a motel though. I try to hang on to the new location change. The ten p.m. swerve.

Fun. Cool.

I'm not that surprised we needed to get out of Victoria for a night. Needing safe places to reconvene is pretty typical.

Problem: The twenty-pound weight plates on my chest have quickly amassed into a hundred pounds.

I can't throw them off.

Cannot breathe.

Beside the TV behind me, my sister's phone is counting down to her pregnancy test results. I don't want to be here when it beeps. She doesn't need me for comfort. Rocky has that handled.

I twirl a finger in the air as I walk backward to the door. "Making a vending machine run. Text me junk food orders if you want anything." I make a peace sign on my way out.

I shut the door. Leaning against it, I inhale.

Exhale.

Breathing should help. Why is that not helping? I tug at the collar of my shirt, grimacing, and I make my way toward the outdoor vending area.

Crickets chirp, and moths flap beneath the dulled lights illuminating the concrete pathway. The heat is sticky. Cumbersome. I dig my phone out of my khaki slacks.

I know what has me so fucked-up.

I know my brother and sister would not approve of this. So I cast a quick glance backward, then I dial a number. Phone to my ear, I stroll toward the flickering lights above two vending machines.

"Spider," she answers fast.

Mom. I run my tongue over my molars. My eyes scald faster than they should. I can control this. I can control this. I can . . . not.

I press the heel of my palm into my eye socket. *Fuck.* "Can I ask you something?" I train my voice to stay steady. To carry no weight.

"Anything."

Her voice is pure sunshine. It's not even manufactured. I saw myself in her. I thought, *I don't pretend. I just am this way.* I'm not made to feel like I'm sinking.

I'm made to break up conflicts between Nova and Rocky.

I'm made to take the risks no one else can take.

I'm made to cut the tension when the room is strained.

So, why do I just want to fall down and scream? Hailey is safe. She's safe. She's not hallucinating. She's okay. That should be enough.

I adjust my grip on my burner phone. "Did Dad ever have an interest in kids when you were working with him?"

"In what way?"

"Did he want them?" I reach the vending machines and lift

my dark sunglasses to my head. One is snacks, the other drinks—just Fizzle products. I fish out my wallet.

"Well . . ." She trails off, thinking. "We always talked about what kids would look like—the four of us. The way you would when you're young and not thinking it'd happen right away, but for us, it was about, *How does this work with our work?* We all had those conversations. Made pros and cons lists, wondered if it'd be worth the risk, and little did we know, it'd just fall into our laps. Brayden was all alone, and Addy and Everett weren't going to leave him with Varrick. And then you three were a big surprise not long after we left Victoria."

"So those conversations you had about little baby grifters," I say lightly, propping my phone with my shoulder and taking out a couple dollar bills, "it was hypothetical for all of you?"

"We were in our early twenties. None of us wanted kids that young, spider. It was a big, big risk." I hear her voice go unsteady. "I mean . . . it wasn't unusual for Varrick to want to take the risk. Why are you asking this anyway?"

"My brain. Cycling through the ways I came into this world." I feed the bills into the machine and say, "By immaculate conception."

She laughs.

"By force," I add.

Her laugh cuts into a sharp breath. "No."

"By accident on your part."

"Yes."

"By accident on his part."

She's quiet.

"By manipulation."

"I . . . I don't know. I can't know if he messed with my birth control. That was a long time ago."

"Did you ever suspect it?"

The phone is dead quiet for a solid fifteen seconds. I check to ensure I didn't lose connection. I wait for her to respond in case she's not alone.

"I did . . . once or twice. Addy thought maybe he switched my pills with placebos, but to be honest, spider . . ." I've rarely heard my mom cry. Even now, she sucks in a noise that'd follow tears. "I didn't want to believe it. Because that'd mean he wanted you three, and I wanted you all to myself."

I press a hand on the glass. More weight slams down on me. I thank her. Tell her I need to go. We say our goodbyes, and I tap a couple numbers on the vending machine's keypad.

Do not freak out, Oliver.

I watch a Payday dispense. My eyes can't stop burning. *Breathe.* I put a hand on my taut chest, then quickly collect the candy bar.

It's too heavy.

I squat beside the machine. I balance my forearms on my knees. *Breathe.* I gasp for air. *Breathe.* I stare up at the lights blinking in and out. *Breathe.* Oxygen won't reach my lungs, no matter how much I try to inhale.

I tear the wrapper. I break the candy bar in half. Caramel and nuts. Then again into fourths. I can't breathe. I can't even remember the last time I ate candy. Going to need to run this off . . . No, because how can I even eat it when I'm suffocating?

I hate this feeling.

I want nothing to do with this feeling.

How do I get rid of this feeling?

"Oliver?"

I can't even see him. A hot, disorienting film coats my eyes. I just hear Jake and his hurried footfalls. Relief is so far away.

I might pass out. I might actually pass out squatting beside a vending machine holding a Payday.

A *Payday*, it's hitting me like another fifty-pound weight plate. Right as Jake crouches down in front of me. Right as he clasps the side of my jaw. Right as he tells me, "Oliver, *Oliver*, I'm here. It's okay, hey—"

"Jake," I choke out and fall on my ass, trying to kick him back. My hands are covered in peanuts. Jake is deathly allergic to *nuts*.

He rests a knee beside me. Not giving up on me, and that about rips something inside me—because I'm going to kill him. I am actively killing him while he's helping me.

It takes all my energy to chuck the candy bar down the pathway. Several feet away from us. I scrape my hands against the pavement.

He sees the nuts. Instead of bolting away from me like he should, he props his arm on his bent thigh and intakes a weird breath.

"Go," I choke. *Breathe*. "Koning."

"You're having a panic attack. I'm not leaving you."

I can't argue with him. I don't have the breath. Quite literally. Which makes me want to laugh, but I can't even laugh.

"Just concentrate on me," he suggests. "Just focus on the things you can see."

I stare at his picturesque jawline. His eyes—a shade Hailey calls cerulean blue. Like the summer sky, she said. "Think . . . I can get . . . high in your eyes," I say.

"Are you flirting with me while you're struggling to breathe?"

Yeah. He's ridiculously attractive. I've never been attracted to a man before Jake, so it's been doing quite the fucking number on my body and brain. "Might as well . . . One of us could be . . . dead soon anyway." *Breathe.* I gasp.

"I feel fine. *Oliver?*" He cups my face as black dots dance in my vision. I manage to refocus on his features. On his sheer concern for me. You'd think he loved me. Jake exhales when he sees me catching my breath, then says, "There are better ways to get me to straddle you."

He is kneeling on either side of my lap. I am enjoying it, but . . . "I wish I were faking this," I say with a slow breath, then eye him. "You're within two minutes of peanut exposure. You're positive you're fine?"

"My throat is just scratchy." He reaches down in his pockets. Right one, then left. He goes rigid. Must be empty.

I pat mine, then pull out an EpiPen from my back pocket.

Jake frowns.

"Didn't want you to die on me, Koning. I memorized your fatal flaws."

He takes the EpiPen. "How many are you hiding?"

I put a finger to my lips. "Secrets. I'd have to do very bad things to you if I showed you any more."

Jake sits beside me against the stucco wall. Not near the peanuts I smeared on the ground. He glances over at me. "How many times have you had panic attacks?"

"This has only happened once. When I was sixteen." I tip my head toward him. "To be a kid again." I laugh weakly and it catches in my chest.

He smiles only a little.

"Tough crowd," I tease, pressing my head back to the stucco. "The first time, Hailey found me."

"Where were you?"

"Four Seasons in Austin. Beautiful suite. I got back late, late from a job where I found myself in a pickle. To get out, I pretended I'd been mugged, attacked." I mime knuckles to my jaw.

Jake's mouth drops. "No, you didn't."

"I did punch myself in the face." I stretch my legs out. "I did it well, too. Gave myself a busted lip and a black eye." I swallow a knot. Check on him. *He's breathing fine.* "It's not doing it that overwhelmed me. I like pushing myself. It was the anticipation of being lectured for it. I cared too much about being benched. I didn't want to be treated like a child needing a time-out."

"Who disapproved?"

"Everett. Hailey's dad hated when I improvised to that level. I think he thought I'd be the reason they'd get caught, eventually. I had way more faith in myself, but looking back, I was just sixteen." I roll my stiff neck. "I'm made of mistakes that I learn to let go of. The only way to move on."

"And Hailey found you?"

"Yeah." I nod. My eyes feel swollen picturing the memory. "I was waiting for her parents to get home. I'd been in the suite, sitting on the couch holding a bag of ice to my face. And it hit me." I turn my head to him. "The weight."

Jake frowns. "What'd she do?"

"Hailey things." I smile a little. "She walked in while I was gasping for air, sat on the coffee table, and bent her head to mine. Forehead to forehead. She was forcing me to just stare into the pits of her eyes."

I instantly breathed deeper. Her inhales were mine. Her exhales were mine.

She whispered, "You're okay, Olly. You're bleeding, but you're okay."

"Don't move," I murmured.

"I won't."

I look over at Jake beside me. Bullfrogs croak around us. "You aren't going to ask what has me so bent out of shape this time?"

"I was getting there. I just like hearing you talk about Hailey."

"Her name does sound great coming out of my mouth."

He side-eyes me with a headshake and a slow-rising smile. "Stop."

"What?" I up-nod him.

"Making me think about you fucking her."

"You don't want to envision heaven on earth?"

"Says the monster under my bed."

My brows spike and a smile spreads. "How long have I been in your bedroom wreaking havoc?"

"Oliver—"

"Do I crawl out and slip under your covers?"

"Oliver," he groans, his eyes dipping to my lips. *"Stop."* Now I just want to kiss him, but he said stop, so I won't.

Our gazes keep flitting over each other, and our heads turn.

"There she blows," I say as Hailey strolls over to us.

She's digging in her studded purse. "You need more cash?"

"I had a panic attack," I admit, then tilt my head to Jake. "He found me."

"Oh." Her concern floods her gray eyes. "You're okay?"

"No, Jake still hasn't kissed me," I say. "I'm dying inside."

Jake sends me a hard look like I'm being dramatic.

"You better kiss him," Hailey says to Jake, fishing a dollar bill in the machine. "It sounds like his life depends upon it."

I swing my head back to Jake with a smile.

He's trying not to grin. "You're good." He means I'm good at getting what I want.

"I think that's the first time you haven't called me bad."

He glances at Hailey, then to me before he cups my jaw and presses his lips against mine. The forcefulness of his kiss, the way he urges my mouth open right before I can, makes my brain do a jig. His tongue slides hot against my tongue, and a groan rolls out of my throat.

Fuck.

I pry away first. His breath is more ragged, and I tell Hailey, "We're monitoring his heart rate, signs of a rash, weird breathing patterns—you and me. I almost killed him with a Payday."

She grabs Doritos out of the machine, eyes widening. "The motel is supposed to be safe, and you both are finding creative ways to die."

"I am an artist," I quip.

Jake laughs.

So does Hailey, and without prompting, she comes and sits on Jake's lap. His arms curve around her hips. She leans her head into his chest to listen to his heart while eating Doritos.

I hold her legs sprawled across my thighs. "Who's craving Doritos? You or Baby?" I ask.

"Since it's not pickle-flavored, probably me." She crunches, then puts a finger to her lips to be quiet, listening.

Jake stares down at her with the affection she deserves. During this summer, I've stopped feeling like I could lose Hailey to him. I've started feeling like the loss will be Jake. He's what we're both going to lose in the end.

Anything can happen.

Including us throwing our luggage in our cars and riding away from Victoria with new IDs, new names. I've thought about trying to convince him to come with us, but that'd entail giving up a crown and a name.

I wouldn't blame him for holding on to all he knows. In a

way, I have been, too. Life as the chameleon, transforming into hundreds of people, is all I've ever known. Staying as Oliver Graves this long is the unfamiliarity, the change.

"He has a nice-sounding heartbeat," Hailey tells me. "Strong."

I smirk. "Must be all the butterflies flapping."

His chest rumbles against her as he laughs.

"He's laughing," Hailey says, slipping me a smile. "I think he likes us."

"Who wouldn't like you, Hailstorm?"

Her lips hike before they turn down, and I wonder if she's thinking, *Trent, hopefully, dislikes me*. I try not to think about the job. It's the first time I've ever worked this closely with Hailey. We're work buddies now, and if I thought it'd be like working with my sister, I was dead wrong.

I worry about Hailey at every juncture. Because I know she hasn't been taught everything that we have, and she's hiding a pregnancy on top of it all.

Her pregnancy . . . Fuck. Heaviness descends again. I lower my sunglasses to my eyes.

"What was the panic attack about?" Hailey asks in the quiet.

I trace a bruise on her leg. "Oh, you know, the usual. Dad baby-traps Mom. Only she manages to get away without him realizing for over two decades. Then Dad retaliates by trying to baby-trap his daughter." I stare out. "The same things that happened to my mom are happening to my sister and to my . . ." I turn to Hails.

Her eyes are downcast while she fiddles with her fingers.

It makes me smile. Her flushing cheeks. As if we haven't had sex a thousand times in a thousand different places.

Old love does not rust. I feel it in my bones when I'm with Hailey Tinrock.

"My love," I whisper.

She reaches forward and holds her kneecaps. She's closing in on me, and I edge closer to her face and brush my nose against hers.

Her smile fights through. "Olly." Her voice is a furtive whisper. "I have a secret."

"Tell me."

"Not all the same things are happening again." Her lips begin to rise. "The timer went off. Phoebe's not pregnant."

Relief slams into me. Hailey lifts the sunglasses up to my hair to see my eyes pooling. I don't stop the emotion. Yet, the pain isn't ceasing. I came into this world because of a selfish man. My child is likely coming into it because of him, too.

Unless this is Jake's baby. For the first time I'm wishing for a Koning to be born. It'd be safer for the child to not be a Graves. Who knows if that's my dad's intention? To have a baby with his DNA.

FORTY-ONE

Rocky

Phoebe twirls as we enter Stonehaven's stainless-steel kitchen, one that'd be the envy of any chef. It's wiped clean this late at night. I flip on the lights as Phoebe takes a dramatic curtsy, a crystal tiara nestled in her blue hair and MISS VICTORIA'S SWEETHEART sash draped across her body.

She's genuinely happy, and amid all the unknown about this high-risk job, it's hard not to be with Phoebe. We've never been more on the same page in the same book. I know whatever happens, I will have her and she'll have me.

I bring my hands together. Clapping. "Way to milk the victory lap."

She flips me off with two fingers. "Not everyone is as humble as Jake."

"Obviously."

"*Obviously*," she snipes back, and I smile right as the thirdborn Koning walks into the kitchen wearing a sash and crown. Hailey, Oliver, and Trevor in tow.

Oliver applauds less mockingly. "Mr. Victoria's Sweetheart. Long may he reign."

"Six years in a row," Hailey says while Phoebe takes off her tiara and places it on her best friend's head. *Cute.* Hailey grins.

Jake tugs open the fridge. "I voted for you, you know," he tells me.

"Thanks, Jake," I say dryly, resting my elbows on the island, keeping an eye on my brother as he screws off the cap to a beer. "Like I was attempting to win a dinky little trophy."

"A beautiful, elegant *crown*," Phoebe rephrases.

"A cheap piece of plastic."

"Crystal," Hailey corrects, reaching up and touching the tiara.

Phoebe crosses her arms haughtily. Her smug smile on me. "Sounds like a sore loser."

"I'm chronically annoyed at everything and everyone," I remind her. "Losing the title of Victoria's Sweetheart isn't changing that." I force a smile.

She's about to respond when we hear a loud *thump* and shattering. I'm a bullet. Sprinting, racing toward the noise.

Fuck, *fuck*. At the bottom of the wooden staircase, Varrick has thrusted Nova up against the green wallpaper, pinning the side of his face to what remains of a broken mirror. Pieces of glass and gold frame are broken at their feet.

"HEY!" I yell, tearing Varrick off Phoebe's brother. I wedge myself between them. Neither one moves a muscle. Their eyes are screaming at each other.

"Nov?" Oliver asks in the background, a soft *Are you okay?*

Nova isn't tearing his glower off Varrick. He isn't touching his face, not even as blood trickles down his cheek from a massive cut.

I push Varrick in the chest, backing him up even more. "What the fuck was that?" Did he finally break?

He exhales through his nose. "This isn't how you establish *trust.*" The Bennet brothers are thankfully not here tonight. They've been staying less and less at Stonehaven due to the rumors of Varrick narrowing down his choice to a Thornhall, and Trent likes to creep in past three a.m. to avoid me.

"Nova?" I ask him.

"He caught me," Nova says, which tenses the entire room. "He found out I bribed the clerk at the bookstore to hand over security footage of the past year. He knows I've been combing through videos. To see if he ever broke into Phoebe's loft."

What we all asked Nova to do.

I cock my head at Varrick. He's viscerally angry. "Are you upset because you were caught?"

"Ask me, Brayden," Varrick retorts, his glower veering to me. "All you have to do is *ask*. I told you I'd be honest."

"Great." I drop my hand off his chest. "Did you break into the loft above Baubles & Bookends?"

"Yes. I was profiling you. Of course I did."

Is that all you were doing? I want to ask. *Were you not rifling through boxes of condoms?* I know not to lead him there. And the others know not to open their mouths and question him. That is *my* role. What *I* am trained to handle.

"You would do the same," Varrick says as if it's just smart business. "You're doing the same right now." He stares around at everyone. "You're here to be closer to me, to learn more about me."

No. It's not why we're here.

It's not why we accepted the invite to summer at Stonehaven on day one.

But I nod a few times, letting him believe what he wants to

believe. He watches Phoebe put the inside of her elbow to her mouth. She's sheet white, and she bolts for the nearest bathroom. Hailey runs after her.

I'm actually concerned, only because she just made herself sick on purpose.

Varrick thinks she's pregnant. We've kept Hailey's prenatal vitamins in Phoebe's bedroom for him to find if he ever decides to snoop again. It's safer if we direct his attention off the real baby.

The twisted things we do to keep one another safe.

As our eyes meet, I tell him, "We've just *recently* been betrayed by our parents. We're *shaken.* Give us some leeway here."

Varrick eases, his warm hand on my shoulder. "Just remember, I'm not them."

"I know." *You're worse.*

Nova storms away, and quickly, I assure Varrick, "I'll talk to him," and I chase after Nova as he barrels out the heavy front doors.

"Nova!" I yell, the wolf knockers clattering behind me as the doors bang shut. He's skipping steps as he heads down the winding staircase cut into the rock. The stone is wet, but solar lights illuminate the pathway in the dark. "Nova! Winchester!! Slow down, man!"

Nova lands on the wooden dock. I'm hot on his heels as he walks around to where Oliver's speedboat is tied off. The *Salty Miss* sways against rough waves.

"You really want to sleep on that tonight?" I question. "You're going to hurl, and your face—"

He just now touches his cheek. Just registering he's been cut. His face broke the mirror. He sees the blood on his fingertips.

"It looks deep," I tell him, hovering while he reaches for the rope tied around a metal cleat. *"Nova."*

"What?!" He straightens up, his pain so forceful, I feel asphyxiated the second he looks at me. Like he's shoving all the torture down my throat. "Better *me* than my brother."

Meaning Oliver's cut from his shaving mishap did not scar. The one on Nova's face—yeah, that is going to leave a lasting mark.

This isn't a typical bad night from a shitty job, the way he's making it out to seem.

We're both breathing hard, and Nova points back up at the mansion. "He's not the first father figure who's hit me."

"But he's the first one who's actually your father."

He shifts, turning his back to me, crouching to unspool the rope.

"It's almost over. Just come back inside, man. You're going to worry your sister and your fucking brother." He ignores me. "You're worrying *me*." Not that he cares.

"I can't stay there right now, Rock. I'm getting a room at the Harbor Hotel." His voice is final, resolute. There is no swaying Nova Graves tonight.

Understood.

I tell him I'll untie the last cleat. He reaches out for the *Salty Miss*, about to climb on board. Then he twists back to me. "Do me a favor. When all this is over, the next time you see that motherfucker"—he takes a hot breath—"give him a *fuck you* from the last Wolfe."

It barrels into me.

Who I am.

The real last Wolfe alive.

FORTY-TWO

Jake

Niall Greensboro has been my family's butler for as long as I can remember. He drove me to boarding school when I'd been too scared to ride alone in the helicopter. And when I got older, was no longer scared, he offered to take me anyway. On those long drives, we talked about books, movies, normal topics kids want to chat about with their parents.

But I've never deluded myself into thinking he's a father figure. He has a loving wife who lives in a midsized cottage down the street. His daughter is a microbiologist in Providence. He's here because my family trusts him, and he's remained here because we pay him well.

So when he calls me this morning to tell me he's quitting, I make it a point to meet him at the estate. Warm sun streams through the kitchen, and Niall pours bourbon into two glasses. "It's just not the same since your mother passed."

"I thought the parties had died down." Looking around the room, I don't see any broken bottles on the floor or holes in the wall. The shattered windows have been replaced from the last rager three weeks ago—the party where Phoebe was drugged.

Niall pushes the glass toward me. "They have. Your brother must have gotten some sense in him, or the repair bills were adding up."

"Or his reputation was taking a hit." I raise the glass to my lips.

Niall sighs heavily, disappointment etching his brows. "That too."

"It's not Maxwell Abbot, the staff manager, is it?" I ask him, thinking about Everett Tinrock's alias. I'd hired him for the con, but if he's not treating my staff well—

"*No.*" Niall waves a hand. "No, Maxwell has been a fantastic manager." He laughs. "If you ask me, he's a little too lenient with the time off, but . . . everyone here loves him."

That's good and terrible at the same time, since I'll have to find a replacement once Everett leaves town. "Then what is it?" I ask.

Niall stares out the window at the yard. Groundskeepers mill about the bushes, trimming the hedges, planting new annuals for the summer and fall. Cosmos and sunflowers. "Things are different now. I don't know how to explain it. There's just a shift here, and I think it's time for me to move on."

His gaze descends upon me with a great deal of concern. "Have you ever thought about that?"

I don't follow. "About what?"

"Moving on." His brows rise. "It's not too late for you, you know. To get out. Take whatever your mother left you and go. Start fresh somewhere else. Build another life. You don't need to be tied to all this." He waves a hand around the room.

It sounds like a question he'd been ruminating on for a while. I can imagine most of the staff have whispered about it.

Why doesn't Jake just take the money and run? Leave the headache to his belligerent older brother. He'd also never ask me a question so personal unless he knew he wasn't going to work for me again.

"I wish it were that easy, Niall."

"Why can't it be?" he wonders. "This was never your legacy." I see what he wants to say. I hear it in my head: *You're just the thirdborn heir.*

"It was never my legacy," I agree. "But I made it my purpose."

He meets my eyes in understanding, and he raises his glass to me. I finish the drink with him, and we discuss severance. My body feels weighed down, especially when he asks me what I'm doing tonight for the Fourth of July.

"The Bennets are having a party," I tell him. "If you want to swing by for the fireworks—"

"No, that's all right. Me and the missus are visiting Sabrina in Providence. We have plans for a family cookout."

I smile. "That sounds great, Niall."

Before he leaves, he gives me one last look, and I'm struck by the sheer pity in his eyes. "Take care of yourself, Jake."

I can't muster a smile this time. I just nod and watch the door swing behind him.

Air. I need air.

I head out into the gardens. The fresh flowers and warm breeze don't hit me. So I keep walking and walking. Until the tennis courts come into view—and my heart drops straight out of my chest as I see two figures alone on the court together. Her platinum-blonde hair is unmistakable, and his self-assured arrogance could never be replicated.

Hailey *and* Trent.

Trent *and* Hailey.

They stand near the net only inches apart.

She didn't tell me she'd be here. My pulse thumps in my ears. Adrenaline starts to surge. I run. Too worried to think clearly other than *get to her.*

My feet slow to a tortured lull as soon as I see my brother drop on one knee. Color drains from my face. My despair doesn't register that *this is the plan.*

It feels too fucking real.

I keep walking. Each footfall beats a heavy pulse in my eardrums. Trent stands up just as I make it to the gate. He slips a ring on Hailey's finger, and when he sees me approach, he quickly turns back to his bride-to-be and swoops her around the waist, twirling her.

I can't stomach it. I rush the court. "Put her down."

Trent sets Hailey on her feet, her windblown hair hiding her face. My brother wears the biggest self-satisfied smirk. "Jacob. Don't tell me what to do with my fiancée."

My throat dries. "What the fuck is going on?" I'm not looking at my brother. "Hailey?" She wears a black tennis dress like he'd invited her onto the courts. *She didn't tell me she'd be here.* Was it to save me from this? The agony of watching the woman I love being proposed to by the brother I hate.

"We're getting married," Hailey says wistfully, her gaze pinned to the giant diamond on her finger. She either doesn't want to look at me or can't bring herself to.

"Today," Trent tells me.

"What?" I'm dumbfounded. *That* is not part of the plan. Today? Already?

Trent's smile only widens. "Why wait, right?" He takes Hailey's hand. "I need the town to understand I've never been interested in Phoebe Smith. I've been secretly in love with her best friend this whole time. This nonsense about me wanting Grey's wife was *truly* a misunderstanding."

My stomach knots. "And what do you get out of this?" I ask Hailey.

Her cheeks flush.

Trent doesn't let her answer. "She gets to be Mrs. Trent Waterford. A title that *every* woman in this town would have died for. And I get to be the husband *you* can't be, Jake. The one that will let her privately have as much fun as she wants." He tilts his head toward her. "Isn't that right, Hay-Hay?"

Hailey's cheeks flush. "It's a good deal."

"It's a *great* deal." He keeps his eyes on me, his smile a fixed feature as he relishes my misery. "I'd invite you to the wedding, but we're eloping to the courthouse." His fingers thread through her hand.

I'm going to be sick.

She doesn't look at me.

I want to go with her.

I want to make sure she'll be okay.

I want to stop my brother if he tries to consummate this sham of a fucking wedding.

My wants turn into *cant's* as I watch them both walk away. How is it that this is the plan, and yet everything feels so out of my control?

FORTY-THREE

Hailey

BITE OR GET BITTEN

Victoria, Connecticut

The orange sun hangs low. Partygoers begin lighting sparklers. Little embers glow in the hands of kids as they race around the lawn waving the burning sticks.

I try not to look at any children.

I try not to think about the little flutters in my belly. *Nerves*, I tell myself. Just nerves. It's not the baby moving. If I think too hard about my pregnancy, I start thinking about Oliver, then Jake, and I need to be here.

I cannot lose time. Not today.

It's imperative I stay cognizant. Aware of my surroundings. And it's not like my mission is a particularly elaborate one. I have one purpose tonight.

Avoid Trent Waterford . . . my husband.

It's just a piece of paper, Hailey. It's real in the sense that everyone believes it. It's real in the sense that Hailey Thornhall is me. It's real in the sense that Jake was truthfully hurt. I didn't mean for him to see the proposal. It wasn't part of my plan.

I'm sorry, Jake.

It's fake in my heart. This marriage is *fake*.

I let the wind whip my flowy white Vera Wang dress and soothe my burning face. My hair is in tamed waves.

The Bennet estate resides on the highest hill in Victoria, overlooking the rest of town. It's my first time here, and I love how the coastal breeze rushes stronger on this hill and brings cooler weather tonight.

People mingle at teak picnic tables, carrying plates of seafood and summer salads from the catered spread. On a normal occasion, I'd be giddy with excitement, soaking up the Fourth of July party atmosphere with a lemonade and mini crab cake. Phoebe and I would be chatting on the porch swing while fireworks shoot overhead.

But normal is not on the schedule for tonight.

For one: I have never been this popular at a party.

Ladies from town have stopped me too many times to count. Asked to see my ring. Prompted me for *all* the details on how Trent proposed and how our whirlwind romance began. I smile and give the talking points Trent and I agreed upon. Each time I recall the fake events, I have to stifle a gag.

Just when I think I can slip away, the younger crowd descends upon me near the arched pergolas on the lawn. Among the twentysomethings, I recognize Sidney Burke's group of college friends and Chelsea Noknoi from VCC.

I hold out my hand when they ask to see the ring. "*Hailey*." Chelsea gawks. "Is this *the* Grace Kelly engagement ring?"

"A replica," I reply into a forced smile that I hope looks genuine enough. The Cartier ring has an emerald-cut diamond set in between two baguette-cut ones. "But exactly 10.47 karats like hers."

"Trent is so romantic," Rachel Rawlings says wistfully.

"We would have had a longer engagement, but he doesn't want me to have to work at VCC anymore, and I need health insurance, so . . ." I flush and avert my eyes to the ground.

"I wouldn't be ashamed of a quick marriage," Rachel assures me. "Elopements are in."

"I almost wish I did it," Chelsea adds. "Wedding planning is so stressful. Giddeon and I still can't decide on our caterer. Then you have to think about table settings, flowers—it goes on and on. You're lucky to bypass the headache."

The other girls voice their approval.

"But I will miss you at VCC," Chelsea says and gives me a hug. My stomach sours uncomfortably. I don't like lying to her. I don't really love lying to anyone in this town. It had been nice being so honest somewhere.

"Are you moving to the Koning estate?" Valentina de la Vega asks.

I nod. "When the summer ends . . . or when Varrick Wolfe chooses an heir. Whichever comes first."

"I heard Damian and Sandon might leave Stonehaven early. You know, after the rumors Varrick has narrowed it down to a Thornhall," Valentina says. "Is that true?"

Val is an MBA grad student, and her family owns the paper. I always thought she'd make a terrific journalist. Sadness rushes through me. I might not see what becomes of her. "I know they haven't been staying as often," I mutter.

Rachel waves her hands in excitement. "Wait, wait. Who cares about that? What were Trent's vows? Start from the beginning—"

"Hailey! There you are!" The booming voice belongs to

my very best friend. Phoebe pushes through the throngs of girls. “Oh my gosh, *finally*, we need to talk. Sorry, everyone! I have a thing that I have to sort out and you know . . .” She’s already grabbing my hand and pulling me away from the group.

I can’t fight off my smile. “Thank you.”

“No need to thank me, I’m officially on errand duty.” She crinkles her nose. “How you like this role is beyond me.”

“Less pressure.”

“Less fun,” she refutes, swinging my arm like we’re skipping through a meadow. We share a smile.

The Bennets are known for their lilac plants. Hundreds of purple flowers cascade from bushes and trees. So unlike the meticulously trimmed hedges and rose garden of the Koning estate. The overgrown lilac shrubs and the canopy of trees remind me of a fairy tale. But I wonder if this is more *Wizard of Oz* than *Cinderella*.

Nothing feels real. Not even the glass slipper.

Phoebe draws me up toward the stone mansion. While I’m a principal on this job, Phoebe’s role is to make sure we’re all in the proper places at the right time. “I must say, Hails, you’re really killing it.” She speaks under her breath. “I don’t think I could’ve moved the timeline up this fast.”

I know what she’s implying.

Trent wasn’t supposed to propose and marry me on the same day. I’d planned for a short engagement that would at least last the rest of the summer.

“That was unexpected,” I whisper back. “I think Jake walking in on the proposal pushed Trent there.” I still can’t shake the look in Jake’s eyes. The *real* hurt. Real despair. Trent inhaled it like a noxious drug, and he couldn’t help himself from twisting the knife just a little more.

She bumps my shoulder with hers. “The proposal was all you.”

Once Trent believed I was as moldable as clay, he realized I’d be amenable to any arrangement he offered. He never really doubted that I wouldn’t want him. He thinks most girls in town would suck his dick for the pleasure of saying they did.

Rocky was right. He wasn’t hard to manipulate. Only difficult to make sure he doesn’t want me sexually.

Which . . . brings me back to how he believed I was clay.

The day before the proposal, Trent flipped through books in my bedroom at Stonehaven. He barged in, and I told Jake it was okay. To wait in the hall. “You’re an interesting creature, Hay-Hay.” He shut the novel hard. “How would you feel if I asked you to . . . I don’t know, fuck Oliver?”

I shrugged, trying not to gulp. “I wouldn’t mind.” *I would very much mind.*

“And if I watched? Because I do think he’s into you. My brother might be, too, but he’s blah.” He thought he was being flirty and cute. He was not. “You could do so much better.”

“Like . . . you?”

“Of course like me. We could be a team, you and I.” He curved his arm over my shoulders. “Rule the world.” He spun his hand across the air. That’s when he laid out our arrangement. How we could benefit from a marriage together.

I agreed.

After that conversation, I thought there might be a slim possibility he’d want to consummate the marriage . . . with Oliver in attendance.

I did not expect him to say, “I booked a room at the Harbor Hotel for tonight. I think you must be doing it all wrong.”

I got nervous. “Doing what wrong?”

He laughed, looked over at me in the car. He was behind the wheel. I was in the white designer dress he bought me, the one I'm wearing now. "I'm going to teach you how to fuck, Hay-Hay. You can thank me later."

"I . . ." I was speechless. "Why do you think I'd need help having sex?"

"The way you kiss. Very bad. That needs help first. I might have Oliver assist there."

Oh, okay, I thought.

"You'd like that?" he asked, as if he was doing me a favor.

I shrugged, my blood frozen over. I wouldn't even call what Trent and I did at the courthouse a *kiss*. My lips hovered over his. He retracted like I was a moldy wall . . . one he needed to clean first, apparently. Then he planted a kiss on my cheek.

For show.

My head whirls with the memory. My bones ache with the longing for Oliver and for Jake. It rose minute by minute while I was there. And it rises minute by minute when I'm not with either of them here.

I wonder when it'll engulf me.

The yearning.

Phoebe draws me close to a lilac tree. More secluded. She squeezes my hand like she can see I'm not all present. My mind . . . am I wandering?

I focus as Phoebe says, "Trent is high on his own supply tonight. Everyone wants to talk to him. I don't think he'll be looking for you until after the fireworks."

That's good.

That's good.

"The wedding . . ." Her voice sputters out when I avert my gaze to the flowers.

No one knows what really happened. Trent drove me here to the Bennets' party as soon as the marriage license was filed. I haven't told her about the conversation in the car.

My throat dries. My lips feel wind chapped.

I shouldn't be at this party.

I need to leave early, I think.

"Phoebe." I turn.

She's not . . . she's not here anymore. My pulse spikes. Was she ever really with me? Did I hallucinate her? *No*. She held my hand. Phoebe was holding my hand. Now my hand is empty. Children giggle and race in front of me, sparklers crackling, the heat nipping me as embers drift into my skin.

The fireworks boom.

It's too loud.

I blink, and Oliver is suddenly beside me. His hair darker. He's letting the natural color grow out. Wind whips at his linen shirt while he pulls off a strand of lilacs. He starts twisting the thorny stems together. "You forgot your earplugs?" he asks conversationally, his gaze everywhere but on me.

I breathe easy with him next to me. "Yes."

His playful smile inches upward. I wait for him to come behind me and cover my ears.

He doesn't.

The job. Right. He can't touch me. I'm married to Trent.

Or . . . what if . . . what if Oliver isn't real? "Olly?" I jolt at a firework *boom*. When I look back, he's closer beside me. "Are you real?"

His eyes snap down to me. Then he subtly surveys our surroundings before he slips a lilac behind my ear. His knuckles brush against my cheek.

Real.

He's really here.

I'm overwhelmed. I almost burst into tears. And I ache for his arms to wrap around me. I want Oliver to pick me up. I want him to swing me around. I want to go to bed with him and Jake, and I don't want to be married to a man who won't listen to what I have to say. I want to be with men who never tire of listening and learning. I want to be with men so curious, they could fill their hours picking my brain and they let me scour theirs.

I want to be with Oliver Graves.

I want to be with Jake Koning Waterford.

This is it, I remind myself. This will be the end of something awful and the start to something great.

"Hailstorm." Oliver is bent to my height. He has a hand on my cheek. "Where'd she go?"

"I-I can't be here, Olly." I lick my lips and speak lowly. "He bought a hotel room for the night."

He straightens up, looking around. "You eat something bad, Hails?" He reaches casually for his phone. "You might be coming down with food poisoning."

Yes. "Food poisoning." I nod. "Probably the crab cake."

"The crab strikes again."

"Will you tell Trent I feel sick?"

"And that you needed to leave early. Sure thing." He winks, then smiles brightly at someone else. "Phoebe."

"Hey?" Her brows scrunch, trying to make sense of me and him. He shouldn't be hovering around me. That's not part of the plan. He came to check on me, I realize. He saw I wasn't okay. She's carrying two cups of lemonade.

"Where have you been?" I ask her.

"You . . . you said you were thirsty." She's confused. "I told you I'd get us lemonade. Do you not remember?"

I shake my head rapidly.

"Okay, we're leaving," she says fast.

"It was the crab. I might puke."

"Me too." She gives Oliver one cup, then grabs my hand. My heart pounds in my eardrums.

Everything is happening so fast now. The sun has set. Sparkling reds pop into the sky and bathe the lawn in crimson.

My nerves ratchet up.

Time stops when I glance back at Oliver. As his glimmering eyes train on mine, as he mouths, *The webs we weave.*

Oh, the webs we weave . . . when we come together to deceive. An old Tinrock-Graves motto. Our history. One we're keeping and remaking.

For a moment, I pretend this night has no beginning, middle, or end. It's just *now.* And then I remember my older brother—and the pretending vanishes.

There's no pause for Rocky. No real break or a moment to breathe.

Not when he has the hardest job of us all.

FORTY-FOUR

Rocky

BITE OR GET BITTEN (CONTINUED)

Fireworks explode in the night sky, lighting up the Bennets' lawn in various colors. I need to stop fiddling with my watch. *Fifteen times* in the past twenty minutes—yeah, I am on literal edge. This isn't a run-of-the-mill job anymore. Not with Varrick involved. Not with how much is at stake.

One saving grace: I don't have to corral horses or babysit a mansion from being obliterated by a bunch of drunk fucks. Thank God.

The Bennets' Fourth of July party is respectably *tame*. A true blessing to the rest of my senses. The only blistering sound comes from the incessant fireworks popping overhead. But that, I can definitely live with.

At a picnic table, I stab my fork into a piece of Chantilly cake and scan the party for Phoebe and Hailey. I've seen them here and there. They've been mingling with guests all night. Doing their part.

Next to me, Jake takes a gulp from a bottle of gin (yes, a bottle), his death glare has been pinned across the lawn on

Trent. But Trent left his picnic table five minutes ago, so now Jake is just glaring at a fucking tree. "I hate him."

"We know, sweetheart." I swallow the cake and check my phone. "You've been plotting murder with your eyes for the last hour." *No texts.*

I crack my neck.

Jake doesn't reply to me. He's been burying his emotions in booze all night. It's his role as the aggrieved brother, and I'm only worried because I've never actually seen Jake Waterford plastered. He's assured me alcohol doesn't loosen his lips, but I'm not in the mood for rolling the dice tonight. My phone buzzes.

We're ready.

The text comes from Varrick's burner phone. My stomach instantly knots, and I set my fork on the plate. "Varrick just invited me onto the boat to watch the fireworks," I tell Jake. "You going to be okay?"

"You care," Jake points out. I think he'd even smile if he weren't knee-deep in hatred and grief.

"Yeah, I do," I state just as plainly.

The admission surprises him. He opens his mouth to reply, but his eyes trail past me into a deep, confused frown.

I follow his gaze. Oliver is coming toward us. Where's Phoebe? I scan and just barely catch sight of her and my sister hand in hand as they trek higher up the hill. Hailey peers backward one time, and I see a lilac in her hair.

I see the twisted vine of lilacs in Oliver's hand.

Jesus fuck. He did not put a flower in her hair tonight when she's newly *married.*

Oliver swings a leg over the picnic bench. "Boys." He up-nods Jake. "Dropped your crown, Koning." He places the lilac wreath on his head, then winks at him.

I glare. "You're doing too much."

"Leave him alone," Jake defends.

Oh my God. I can't deal with whatever they are right now. The *booms* are shrill in my ears, and all the bright blues, greens, and purples try to heave me to somewhere outside of Boston. The Fuckup.

My little brother. A lake house shed. Gardening shears in another guy's neck. I blink out of the memory, and I realize, "Have you seen Trent anywhere?"

"Not since he left the table," Jake says.

The firstborn Koning has been the most popular person here outside of Hailey, and he's suddenly MIA? His friends are gazing up at the fireworks. He should be with them.

Oliver does a casual scan. "No sign of your brother either."

My gut drops out from underneath me. *Fuck*. "I'll find him. Don't wait for me. I won't be coming back." I hike my leg over the bench. "See you around, Jake."

"Wait." Jake catches my wrist, stopping me. His blue eyes hit mine in deeper concern. Worry. I see what he's asking me. *Is this going to be the last time we see each other?*

Maybe. If this job doesn't end well, this will be our goodbye.

My ribs knot, but I don't dole out any false hope. I just nod to him, then say, "Try not to change too much, Jake. Places like this need more people like you."

I feel his eyes on my back as I walk away.

I don't have a crystal ball. I don't know if things will go right. With Trevor missing at the same time as Trent, they're already going wrong.

My brother has been under Trent's wing for weeks, I

remind myself. They could be conversing somewhere on the other side of the house. The Bennets aren't letting anyone but staff and family inside, so I don't bother checking the mansion.

I slip between servers handing out Prosecco. I ignore the several men who call my name. I act as if it's too loud over the fireworks to hear.

I search without appearing like I'm on a life-or-death hunt for Trevor.

Trent likes to flaunt his relationship with my brother *in my face*. Clearly, he's not dangling shit in front of me if I can't find him.

As elbows brush me, as the scent of grilled corn and seafood floods my nostrils, as faces are bathed in color, I feel like I'm fifteen again. Rolling a dead body in a tarp. Carrying it through the woods with Oliver. Twisting my knee.

Then I find Trevor in the shadows on the Bennets' property. All the breath I'd been caging rushes out of my lungs at once. I inhale deeply and pick up my pace into a jog just to reach him, then slow when I'm feet away.

He stands slumped, his back against a lilac tree.

As soon as the fireworks light up his gray eyes, and I see the absolute torture in them, I know something is very fucking wrong.

"Trev," I whisper when I reach him. "Did he hurt you? Hey—" I hold his face as his gaze drags against the earth. I lift his head, and when I look into his eyes, I see *pure* fucking agony. My muscles sear inside out. "What'd he do?" I am two seconds from dragging Trent into the grill and making a burger out of his fucking face.

Trevor shakes his head just once. "He didn't . . . he didn't hurt me, Rock."

I can't untense. "You hurt him?"

He shakes his head again. I track his gaze down the hill. He's staring at . . . Trent, who sips bourbon and rolls his eyes at his so-called friend, then snickers like a fucking prick.

Trent is accounted for then.

Trevor's jaw tightens. He looks away, then scuffs the ground with his leather shoe. "I can't do it anymore." Pain lances his voice. His nose flares as he tries to control his emotions.

"Yeah?" The word sticks to the back of my throat. "Which part?"

"All of it." Trevor looks up into the firework-lit sky. "The things he says about people . . . about our sister . . . I can't . . . I can't fake it. All I want to do is tell that bastard *exactly* what I think. I hate that I can't. I hate that he just gets to . . . I hate it." His eyes redden; he's trying to stop himself from breaking down.

I put my arms around him and bring him into my chest.

This ends his position as Trent's friend. Our reunion again. So, if he wanted, he could push me off, but all he does is hold on.

Trevor has always wanted my role. He's always wanted to be in a position where he'd manipulate a mark face-to-face. I never thought that, finally given the chance, he'd hate it.

I doubt he thought he'd hate it, too.

He adds in a tortured breath, "I'm not as good as you."

My heart. *My* kid. "You're right," I breathe out. "You're better, Trev." I never wanted this for him. I *never* wanted him to be me. The fact that he can't stomach it—maybe I did one good thing here.

He winces up at the sky. "I'm screwing this up. Tonight."

"We can make this work. Just go back to Stonehaven. You're out."

His nose flares. "I can help with the boa—"

"*No.*" I glower. "Go . . . be with Sidney. Be a fucking teenager for once in your life." *Forget about this*, I want to add. But he's already pulling out his phone, I hope to text her. Sidney officially moved into the Reynoldses' boathouse last weekend. Completely cut off from Weston Burke, her new independent life is being funded by Hailey and Phoebe's meager savings. How long that'll last—no clue. I have bigger issues to deal with.

Trevor's eyes flit up from his phone. "What are you still doing here?"

I push away. Time to go. "Thanks for the reminder, shithead."

When I'm five feet down the hill, he calls out, "Rocky." I turn, and his eyes soften on me before he gives me the middle finger.

I smile, and I give him two back.

His lips rise.

I hang on to that.

I have to. Because I can't look for Phoebe. The very last thing I need to do is see her face before I go to the boat. My resolve won't last.

And I need to do this—for all of us. Pull the rope. Bite or get bitten.

Let's sit in the bow," Varrick suggests, fisting the neck of a champagne bottle. We're not on his boat. But I *love* how he's calling the shots here. So fucking gracious of him.

We're technically on Oliver's speedboat. The *Salty Miss* is moored at sea among dozens of other vessels for the Fourth of July. From catamarans to large yachts to other midsized speedboats.

Varrick agreed to take the *Salty Miss* to the Bennets' party—the mansion and private docks in view from the water—mainly for privacy. His yacht needs staff to operate it. This boat, we can drive ourselves.

The air is a mess of noise.

Of sizzling and hissing fireworks. Of boisterous laughter and chatter and pumping music from other boats and onshore. My temples pound as we congregate in the curved bow seating. I lean closer to just hear him speak.

"I want to make this right," Varrick tells his son. He pours champagne into Nova's flute, then mine, then his own. Only the three of us on the boat. "You should feel like you can ask me anything, and maybe I didn't make that clear enough from the beginning."

Varrick isn't desperate to regain Nova's trust—not when he barely had it in the first place. But he does want to maintain this relationship, especially since keeping Nova close ensures he's close to Phoebe.

I told Varrick I had news to share about his daughter. That I needed to do it somewhere private and that the Fourth of July was probably the best time. He believed me because I wasn't lying, so he said, "Let's bring Nova. I need to make some inroads with him, too."

I let out a laugh. "Yeah, you do. Good luck with that," I told him.

His lips quirked. "I'm not shocked I produced a stubborn son. Their mother is the same."

I never considered Elizabeth as *stubborn*. Maybe she has always been stubbornly determined to protect her children from him.

Nova is clutching the champagne flute so tight, I'm surprised it doesn't shatter in his fist. His cheek is stitched and bandaged. *Boating accident*, he's told people in his gruff *don't ask me more* Nova way.

Honestly . . . he shouldn't be here.

I didn't want Nova to come, but the mental fuckery I'd need to perform just to talk Varrick out of it was too much. So that is precisely why this boat meeting is a three-person affair and not two.

Nova runs a hand over his head. "I have questions that I know you won't answer."

"Try me first." Varrick sips the bubbling liquor. "Have some faith, Nova."

I tilt my ear to them, listening while I scan the water.

"Fine." Nova glares. "Where are you from?"

"America. Now, where exactly was I born? Toledo."

"Ohio?" I raise my brows.

"You know your geography," he quips with a smile into another sip. I hate this conversation already.

"And Elizabeth?" Nova nods over at him.

"Huh." Varrick leans back with a breathy laugh of surprise. "I would've thought she'd trust her own children with that information."

The godmothers never wanted us to incriminate them. To find their origins.

Let me make this clear—I don't give a fuck about what Varrick has to say. I don't care if he's being honest. If he's blowing smoke. We will never *really* know if he's spouting facts or feeding us lies. I believe mostly what I can see.

We saw him on camera breaking into the loft.

We saw pinpricked condoms in Phoebe's room.

We saw him shove Nova into a fucking mirror.

So now, we're entertaining him the way you would a guest at a dinner party. He thinks he's placating us—fine.

Placate me, bitch.

"She never told me," Varrick says, "but I suspected Beth was from Jersey. Addison, New York, originally—her accent would fight through in the early days. Your mother is likely Italian, maybe Scillian. Or even Greek. Probably had parents or grandparents who immigrated over here through Ellis Island."

I want to dump my liquor in the ocean. I don't drink it as I ask, "These are your unproven theories of how many years? When did you first meet?"

"They were nineteen. Though they said they were older at the time. I was around twenty-one, twenty-two. Young. Ran into them at a bar on the Upper East Side. We had mutual acquaintances. The rest, as you know, is history."

"Romantic," I say dryly.

He grins. "You remind me of me. Phoebe of her mother."

"Yeah?" I tilt my head, appraising him before I lean forward. "Funny you say that, considering we're in a bit of a . . . situation. Kind of the same one Elizabeth found herself in."

"Phoebe's pregnant," he says with a satisfied smile. "I know." He raises his champagne, congratulating me.

I raise mine back, not hiding my surprise. Only I'm more surprised he filled the blank in for me. Rookie mistake. "How'd you figure it out?"

"A dad always knows."

Sick fuck.

Nova is crawling out of his skin. He has to ditch the champagne and stand up. Varrick is confused at his volatile reaction. He's trying to make sense of why Nova wouldn't want Phoebe to be pregnant. He's wondering if Nova knows he's the cause.

"It was an accident," I say, capturing Varrick's attention.

"Me and Phoebe. Unplanned. Surprise pregnancy, whatever you want to call it."

"I assumed."

I'm sure you did.

Fireworks whizz overhead. Just intermittent pops in the sky, slowly building to the climax. I've been to enough of these extravagant parties to know no expense is wasted on the two-hour firework show.

Whistling, whooshing, and crackling in the night sky draws eyes upward and off us. Varrick's face lights in greens as I tell him, "Nova knows me and Phoebe don't want kids."

This takes him aback. "No?"

"No." I shake my head tensely. His mind is working overtime right now. I try to guide him in a direction. "You want a kid?"

"Pardon?"

"You want a baby?" I enunciate very clearly. "A child to raise?"

He searches my face so rapidly. All he can likely see is pure fucking rage. "What are you getting at, Brayden?"

"Let's cut to the fucking chase." I set the glass in a cupholder. Varrick does the same. We stand at the same time.

He threads his arms over his chest, his brows pleated as if he's patiently awaiting me. "You go first."

"Fine. I'm not going to work with you after we pull the rope on Trent. *None* of us want to work with you, and I think you know that. I think you've always known that we'd never be one big happy team."

"I did." He smiles a little, impressed. "Keep going." Sizzling gold embers rain down behind him.

"We've figured out you want a baby. For whatever reason. You want to tell me why?"

"You six turned out to be great assets to Beth and Addy. Better than they even give you credit for, and I know you'll never trust me to the extent that you trusted them. Even if they've burned you now."

"But a child will trust you?"

"My child will." Varrick arches his brows. "You don't understand the pain Beth caused me. By lying. Taking my kids away from me." He points at Nova. "She did what we said we'd do *together*, educate our children in the family business in *our* way. How she betrayed you—multiply it times a *hundred*. So I would love nothing more than to raise my daughter's child. It will . . . *destroy* Beth. Do you know how much she loves Phoebe?"

Yes. "I'm aware."

Varrick drops his arm. "So let's make a deal, all of us."

"Let's make a deal," I repeat in a biting tone.

"I'll leave Victoria if you give me the baby."

Yeah.

I knew this was coming.

"I'll raise them as my own," he continues, purple hues bathing his pitiless face. "You'll never hear or see from me again. You get what you want. A town without me in it. I get what I want."

Revenge and a little pawn of his own making.

I start laughing. Barrel-chested hard laughter while we lock eyes. His features become a brick wall, but he can hide in every musty fucking corner all he wants, trying to scurry away from me. It doesn't matter what he makes me believe anymore. "You think you're going to ride away from Victoria as the Lone Wolfe?" I ask, using the name the town has adopted for him. "With a billion-dollar fortune still at your disposal?"

"We can work out those finances." He's scouring my eyes

for what I'm thinking, feeling—what I might do. "We can share."

"We can't." I step forward—so close our forearms touch. "Because here's the thing, Varrick, you aren't the Lone Wolfe. You aren't the Big Bad Wolfe. You're just a fucking termite who's eaten away at my family tree." Fireworks pop, sizzle—paint our livid faces purple again. "And you've been gnawing on his." I motion my head toward Nova. "His sister. His mother." Another step forward.

"Brayden—"

"Phoebe isn't pregnant."

His face falls. I devour his sheer shock, then his torment at realizing . . . he was conned. "No . . . ?"

"Surprise," I say dryly. "There is no baby."

"No, there . . ." He squints at me as fireworks explode in aggressive, quick succession. "You're lying." He begins to smile. "If it's Hailey, we can work something out. This isn't the end—"

"This is the end," Nova cuts in. Before I can send him a warning look to stay out of this, he shoves me so hard, I careen into the seat.

And then he tells his father, "Never again."

Nova barrels into Varrick with an unrelenting, merciless impact, forcing him overboard. And they plunge into the dark water . . . together.

Fuck, fuck, fuck! I bend over the boat. I see no one. No heads pop out of the rough ocean. The current is strong tonight. The water lights up in gold as fireworks crack one after the other. There is no pause in the sky.

Nova is killing his father.

Nova is going to drown with him. Because he's not trained to hold his breath beneath the water like I am.

"NOVA!" I scream, and on impulse, I wave over at neighboring boats. "They fell in! Get help!!" Ladies on a yacht understand my frantic energy. Phones go to ears. This needs to appear like a drunken accident, but also, we actually need EMS.

I'm going to kill Nova if he's not already dead.

They're not coming up for air. No one is coming up.

I don't think anymore. "I'm sorry, Phoebe." She might lose more than a brother tonight. Quickly, I step onto the seat, the edge of the boat, and I dive into the water. Salt burns my eyes. It's so fucking dark.

I swim around, diving and coming up for air. People yell at me from a neighboring speedboat. Saying they're looking, too. I dive again around where they fell in. I swim deeper and deeper, and that's when I feel a sinking body.

Familiar.

Brother.

Hers.

I know him. I know him too well, and I should've known he would do this before I could. It was supposed to be me.

Me pushing Varrick into the water. Me dragging Varrick down. Me hoping Varrick wouldn't drown me with him. Me hopefully coming up for air and acting like I accidentally fell in.

Now, I'm wrapping my arms around Nova's body. I kick to the surface. Nova is all heavy soaked muscle. He's gone. *He's gone*. Not breathing. Not moving. I breach the water, and I keep him against my chest while I kick my legs toward the swim platform of the *Salty Miss*.

I grit my teeth and scream between them.

It takes so much fucking energy to lift him onto the platform. When I'm on the hard surface with him, I check his pulse. *None*. I start compressions on his chest.

"Oh my God! Oh my God!" I hear a lady on the nearest boat.

"Call 911!" another screams.

"Is someone still in the water?!" they're shouting at me.

I act like I can't hear. Like I'm too busy trying to save my wife's brother, and I fucking am. I give Nova mouth-to-mouth, then restart compressions. I feel his ribs crack beneath my pumping hands. "Come on, Nov. *Come on.*" My eyes sear, burn, scald. He can't die. He can't die tonight. *Please don't fucking die.*

Please, Nov.

Please.

This is my job.

My responsibility.

To protect them. To protect him.

I can't lose another family member to the water. "Come on, Nov!" I shout with another hard compression. His face is pallid. His head jostles with my movements.

I scream.

A tortured, furious, agonized scream tears through me like an animal I've never let out—that I've never been allowed to release—not in my entire life. *Don't fucking die.*

Don't die.

Please.

It should've been me.

One minute is an eternity. The next time I blow air into his lungs . . . Nova begins to choke. Quickly, I turn him on his side while he coughs up the sea. Relief is a sledgehammer against my body. After he gets it all out, I collapse backward.

We're both spent. Exhausted. Breathing too hard as we chase after oxygen and stare at each other for a long, long moment.

Fireworks blast around us. He can read my pained gaze that says, *You weren't supposed to go in with him.*

That wasn't part of the plan.

It was *always* supposed to be me.

His eyes are bloodshot. "I had to . . ." He pants. "I had to make sure he wasn't coming back, Rock." He wanted it to be over.

We summered at Stonehaven to get closer to Varrick. So he'd believe we were desperate for his help with pulling the rope with Trent. So he would never suspect that we'd want to kill him.

The explosions in the sky, the commotion, the booze, the accidents—it's all around us like it was ten years ago at a lake house somewhere outside of Boston.

The first time we buried a body.

We knew tonight we'd try to drown one instead.

FORTY-FIVE

Phoebe

He's going to be okay," Oliver says.

"Are we sure about that?" I frown deeply. We both stand on the paint-chipped back porch of the seven-bedroom 1900s mansion in the Berkshires, the property Nova bought months ago. The same property the guys have used as a meetup spot for small jobs outside of Victoria. Morning light breaks across the rolling hills. Tranquil. Almost peaceful.

I'd say it's picture-perfect pastoral imagery, if not for the six-foot-one brooding Nova Graves standing in the backyard with a canister of gasoline. He runs a hand over his buzzed head and cranes his neck back toward us.

"You know I can hear you both," he says into a deep scowl.

Oliver steps off the porch onto the soft grass, and I follow him to our brother's side. A large painting with an ornate gold frame sits on a pile of wood.

"We weren't trying to whisper behind your back," I tell Nova.

"Yeah, we're not assholes." Oliver stuffs his hands in his pants pockets, a smile in his eyes.

Nova blinks between us. "I'm *fine*."

"It's okay if you aren't," I tell him. "It's only been three days since our dad died."

Varrick Wolfe's death was ruled an accident. No foul play. A final notch in the morbid fate of the Wolfe family. He was quietly buried in the plot next to his late wife.

Nova's grip tightens on the gasoline canister. "You mean since I killed him."

My heart skips. "We promised never to say those words out loud."

"First and last time." Nova turns to the painting. It's not just *any* art. The oil painting is an original by William-Adolphe Bouguereau. It depicts the fight between a demon and a man who'd been a fraud. An imposter. *Dante et Virgile* was Nova's favorite painting after he sold a fake to the Musée d'Orsay.

For him to wake up this morning and want to burn it panicked both Oliver and me. We forced ourselves into his car, and he complained the entire drive here.

The reality is that Nova protects all of us. *Has* protected us from the dawn of time. Every escape. Every last-second recovery. He'd been behind the wheel to drive us away from danger.

And three days ago, he was willing to die for us.

Rocky told Oliver and me what happened on the boat. How Nova was finishing the job in the only way he knew how. But if Rocky hadn't pulled him out of the water . . .

My eyes burn and my throat becomes swollen. I just—I need Nova to know that we're here for him. Whatever he goes through next, we're going to protect him.

It's our turn.

"Are you sure you want to do this?" I ask as he untwists the cap to the canister.

Oliver pops a piece of gum in his mouth. "We could wrap it in cellophane. Bury it."

Nova exhales and shakes his head before he dumps the gasoline onto the painting.

Oliver whistles. "Just so we're clear, I don't approve of lighting several million dollars up in flames."

Nova doesn't stop. "It's too risky to try to sell it, and Rocky thinks it's cursed."

A gust of wind blows through. I hold down my minidress with one hand to keep myself from flashing my brothers. "Is that why you're burning it?" I ask in confusion. "Because of Rocky's superstition?"

"Maybe he has a point," Nova says. "It's a bad omen."

"Rocky has a point?" My mouth gapes.

Nova sends me an instant glower. "You're not telling your husband I said that."

Emotion pools through me so viscerally. So suddenly. My heart swells.

Nova tilts his head at me, our eyes latched. "Phoebe . . ."

"You called him my husband," I say softly, tenderly, holding on to this moment.

Nova sighs. "Let's not make it a thing."

"Oh, it's already a thing," I say.

"A big thing." Oliver smiles.

Nova forcefully tosses the empty canister to the ground. "Isn't that what he is to you?"

I inhale the crisp morning air. "Yeah, he is. I just didn't think you'd acknowledge it."

"I have two eyes."

"And apparently a heart." Oliver grins.

Nova scowls at the ground. “Maybe somewhere in there. But I don’t know . . . I don’t think someone with a heart would feel what I’m feeling.”

“Which is?” I ask in a soft whisper.

Nova lifts his head to meet my eyes, then Oliver’s. Sudden emotion hits him and his face breaks. “Relief.”

Oliver grabs the back of his neck, pulling him into his chest. I wrap my arm around Nova’s waist, and he spreads his arm across my shoulder. Our little sibling huddle is indestructible. Powerful. I feel ten years old again in the backseat of a car, smashed between them as we flee a city in the middle of the night.

The only comfort of starting over was starting over with them.

The sound of gravel catches all our attention and jolts us apart. My heart lurches until I recognize the convertible pulling into the driveway.

“What is she doing here?” Oliver frowns.

The woman who raised us, birthed us, made us who we are, exits the driver’s side door.

“I invited her.” Nova removes a pack of matches from his pocket.

My stomach twists painfully, especially when I see Addison in the passenger seat and Everett sitting in the back. There’s only one reason I can think of for Nova to call her. He’s going to leave with them—he’s going to choose to keep grifting. But it wouldn’t make any sense. He can barely call Elizabeth *Mom*.

Oliver’s face collapses. “Nov, you didn’t want us here, but you invited her?” He shakes his head in confusion.

Nova nods. “To say goodbye. They’re leaving town. She texted me this morning.”

“*They’re* leaving?” My stomach doesn’t unsettle. Why? Shouldn’t I be happy that they’re going away?

Our mom comes closer, golden-blonde hair tucked back into a claw clip, strands hanging delicately over her face, and she pulls off her Louboutin red-bottom heels when she approaches the grass and walks barefoot until she's across from us.

Her eyes flit to each of us, emotion pooling in this silent moment. "Sweet spiders," she says into a staggered exhale.

This is goodbye? My heart throbs. My head fogs. "The job isn't done," I blurt out. "You can't leave." *Why does this hurt? This shouldn't hurt.* I've barely seen her this summer anyway.

Is it because her departure feels more permanent? How many times has she ever returned to the same alias after leaving a job for good?

Never.

"My part is done, bug." Her eyes glass. "It's time for us to go."

"But if we have the money . . ." I think about the Wolfe fortune. "You three don't need to keep going. You can settle down. You can retire . . ." My voice trails off at the look in her eyes. Disappointment like I'd forgotten who and what they are.

"Phoebe, we don't only do this for the money. You know that."

My heart caves.

Oliver smiles weakly. "Sticking it to the man?"

"That's Addy's mantra," she says. "And I will go where she goes. But you can't beat the lifestyle."

"The money doesn't hurt," Nova says.

She smiles. "It never does." Her gaze returns to me, her expression softening. "Hold tight to Rocky, bug. I've always loved that you had him." *I know.* "You have what I never found in a man. Love that you can always trust. I never wanted your life to completely mirror mine. I'm so glad it hasn't." It crashes into me—that all the times she wanted me with Rocky, it'd been in hopes I'd turn out different from her.

Hot film burns my eyes.

She tells us, "I respect what you built here, and we're not going to mess it up for you kids. This life . . . it's yours."

"You're releasing us," Nova says in realization.

Tears well up in her eyes. "As much as a mother can, spider." She pulls a pair of sunglasses from her coat pocket and puts them on, hiding her emotion quickly. "Well, we had a good run. Nova. Oliver . . ." Her gaze lands on me. My name can't get past her lips because her chin starts quivering.

We immediately close the distance between each other until we're in a tight hug. My body shudders. *She's leaving for good.*

All the pain.

All the betrayal.

It fades away in this moment to make way for new beginnings. She kisses the side of my head, her voice full of honey-sweet velvet, like those summer days when I was six, seven, eight. I'm just a little girl wanting her mom to think she's the bravest, most beautiful thing in the world.

"Phoebe," she says. "I love you *so* much."

I believe her.

I hear the flick of a match and feel the heat of a fire behind me as flames eat away at the painting.

"Mom . . ." My voice cracks. "I love you, too."

Nova, Oliver, and I drive back to Victoria, our luggage from Stonehaven crammed into the trunk. We're all moving into the Koning house (Jake's side) while lawyers go over the Wolfe trust and settle the inheritance of the estate.

Nova makes a detour down Main Street before we head to Jake's. It takes him twenty minutes to find a parking spot, all the lots full today. He's been grumbling curse words about shitty parking jobs and looks like he wants to key an Aston Martin that took up *two* spaces.

When we're finally parked, I shut the car door with a *thump* and put my hand over my eyes to block the bright midday sun. "Did we miss the ceremony?"

Oliver's on his phone. "Nah. Hailey says it won't start for another five minutes. She's at the fountain if you want to see her."

Yes, very much. But a wave of guilt assaults me when I see Oliver's shoulders slump. He puts his phone back in his pocket and tries to fake a smile. But I can see the truth . . .

He's in pain.

He's hurting.

Hailey is still married to Trent. *The job isn't done*. As long as she's Mrs. Trent Waterford, Oliver can't be around her. Not really. Not how they both want.

How long will this last? It's a question no one has the answer to, because the most important thing in a long con is . . . patience.

I leave my brothers to hurriedly push through the crowds. They gather around a tall sturdy oak tree tied with a white ribbon. In lieu of a funeral for Varrick, the beneficiary of the Wolfe trust has chosen a memorial service to celebrate the entire Wolfe family. Seeing the amount of people coming out for *Rocky's* family—it pushes emotion into me.

I try to keep it together, especially when I find Hailey sitting on the fountain, a book in hand. Her husband stands beside her, scrolling absentmindedly on his phone. I'd like to say Trent is doing his best impersonation of being a complete douchebag, but it's just who he is in his soul.

"Hails, there you are." I capture Hailey's attention. She glances up from her book as I dig out a pill bottle from my crossbody bag. "I have your prescription."

Trent gawks at me. "Could you be any less discreet, Phoebe?"

Hailey quickly takes the pills from me and shoves them in her purse. She mouths a *Thanks*.

I glare at Trent. "Just helping a girl out, Trent."

The morning after the Fourth, Hailey confessed to Trent that she had an outbreak of herpes, and she'd need at least a few weeks before it cleared up so they could have sex.

By the disgusted look on his face, I'd say he'll let her take as long as she needs. We've got to thank Carter for the prescription. It only sucks that this is another dent in Hailey's reputation. But she's made it clear she's willing to run it over with a Mack Truck to get this done.

"Can you give us a minute?" I ask Trent.

He sighs in annoyance. "Sure. I need to find Collin anyway." He's promoted his childhood best friend back to the number one position.

I plop down on the fountain ledge beside Hailey. She has on a chain-link necklace and her usual snakebite lip piercings. "The godmothers left," I whisper.

She looks up from her book, and I see the puffiness around her eyes. "I know."

I suck in a tight breath. "Your mom called you?"

She nods, her eyes misting over. "I wish they could have stayed for us . . . but I think they were okay leaving, knowing we have each other."

I sniff back emotion and nudge her shoulder. "Dynamic duo. Like Thelma and Louise."

Her nose crinkles. "They die at the end."

I think harder. "Harley Quinn and Poison Ivy?" Nova would be proud of that comic book pull.

Hailey's lips lift. "That actually kinda fits."

Katherine Rhodes walks over, clipboard and scissors in her arms, and interrupts us. "Hailey," she says. "As the beneficiary of the Wolfe trust, would you like to cut the ribbon?"

Hailey closes her book. I give her a smile of encouragement, even as my throat dries.

Before his death, Varrick had filed paperwork naming Hailey Thornhall as the sole beneficiary of the Wolfe trust. She's set to receive the entire estate in a couple weeks.

She'll own Stonehaven, Baubles & Bookends, dozens of other properties in town, and have amassed a multibillion-dollar fortune.

But she'll still be married to Trent fucking Waterford, and no one is safe until he's gone for good.

THREE MONTHS LATER

FORTY-SIX

Jake

THE HEIR OF NOTHING
Victoria, Connecticut

"I want to get this done today. Your lawyers said before the end of the summer, and now we're in October. Do any of them own a calendar?" Trent complains over the phone. "If I have to sit through another earnings call, I might blow my brains out."

Oh, that couldn't happen soon enough.

Three months. I haven't been talking to Hailey in *three* months. We see each other sparsely, only when she's on Trent's arm. And I try not to make this any harder on her by stirring up a conversation that lasts more than a hello and goodbye.

Most of the time, she's holed up on her side of the Koning estate like Belle from *Beauty and the Beast*, only the Beast is my soulless brother.

"If you would let me talk," I say, exasperated. "I only have one more paper for you to sign. Then it's finalized." Trent had a breakthrough four weeks ago when he realized he'd rather be flying to Malta on a private jet than stuck in a boardroom dealing with investors and managing his stake in Koning. The Wolfe fortune he inherited by marriage is worth double what he has tied up in the beer company, all without the corporate politics and headaches.

He has convinced himself—or someone has slowly, surreptitiously planted the seeds—that transferring his stake to me, making *me* the majority owner, is the equivalent of settling me with the world's worst case of gangrene.

He gets off on watching my limbs necrotize.

He gets off on flaunting his wife in front of me—the woman he knows I love.

But who knew transferring forty percent ownership of a multibillion-dollar company takes longer than a few weeks. The back-and-forth and legal paperwork have been torture. Especially knowing that every day wasted is another day Hailey has to live with him.

"You're sure?" Trent asks. "Because I'm not coming all the way over there for this to be a joke."

I roll my eyes. "You live in the guesthouse. Just cross the lawn."

Even owning Stonehaven, he's refused to move there. He thinks the inconvenience of living on a rock in the middle of the sea is enough to sell it. He's been considering offers for months.

Yesterday, Phoebe told me, "Hailey says he wants one big house with less property to manage. They're thinking of building on the coast."

Another reason to get this done today.

I already own all of the Koning properties. We closed on them last week. I didn't need to buy them from Trent. He gave them to me to saddle me with mortgage debt, property taxes, and costs to maintain.

Until he finds a more permanent residence, I'm letting him live rent-free in the guesthouse. Trent knows it's not out of the kindness of my heart.

I do it to be as close to Hailey as I can be.

Before ending the call, Trent agrees to come over.

"That him?" Rocky leans a shoulder on the doorframe to my home office, his chin dipping to my phone. His black hair is damp, like he just took a shower. He holds his favorite Seaside Griddle mug.

I'm not the only one who's been trying to be near Hailey.

Her brothers and Phoebe moved into my house months ago so that they could keep an eye on her. Their presence here has been a saving grace, because I don't know what would've happened to me had I been alone all this time. Some days I stay up through the night, watching the grounds outside from my balcony. Making sure I don't find a platinum-blonde girl running across the yard, chasing a hallucination.

Phoebe has assured Oliver and me that Hailey is sleeping. "She says she's focused on her health. She wants to carry the baby to term, so that's where all her energy is going." Thinking about Hailey sends sharp stabs through my chest, so I bring my attention back to Rocky. He's watching me quietly.

He knows I'm thinking about his sister. I always am.

"Trent is coming over," I confirm. "He's going to sign the last document."

Rocky pulls out his cell. "It will finalize the transfer?"

"Yeah." I inhale deeply, trying to let it sink in, but it practically floats over me. It doesn't feel real. I'm not sure when it will.

Rocky stares at me in deeper concern. "This is where you smile, Jake."

I lift my shoulders. "Not sure I can."

"Great. Well . . ." Rocky texts on his phone. "At least you finally get to see the fun part."

My brows arch. "There's a fun part?"

"You think we would've been doing this our entire lives if it was *all* doom and gloom, sweetheart?" He slips his phone in his pocket when a blue-haired girl fills the doorway.

"What's doom and gloom?" Phoebe asks, and turns to Rocky. "Besides your face?"

He shoves a hand at her mouth, and she grins wildly, snapping her teeth at his palm like a turtle. Seeing their love so in my face every day hasn't been as hard as I'd thought it'd be. I'm really happy they can be together for real. The months I pretended to be Phoebe's boyfriend almost feel like a fever dream.

"Trent is coming over," I warn her.

Rocky drops his hand off her face and rounds his arm over her shoulders.

Her face twists. "Ugh. Thank you for the heads-up."

"To sign the final paper," I add.

Her mouth parts in surprise before her eyes light up in a smile. "Oh—wait, this will be fun."

Rocky eyes me as if to say, *Told you so*.

It doesn't feel fun when I spot Trent through the window crossing the lawn with Hailey trailing him like a shadow. It was no surprise he'd bring her. She's the equivalent of a bulletproof vest and an armed firing squad anytime he sees me.

Her hair has grown to the middle of her back. She wears a baggy black Lamb of God shirt over her cargo pants. She keeps her head down, reading a paperback as she walks. My chest tightens, and the three of us quickly leave my office.

We meet Trent and Hailey on the back patio before he has time to set foot in the house. Trent steps onto the cobblestone with an annoyed huff at the sight of Phoebe and Rocky. "You both are like a fungal infection that won't go away."

"What a coincidence. The feeling is mutual," Phoebe snaps, and then smiles sharply.

Trent returns the smirk before looking at me. "You need to ask yourself, Jacob, why these two keep loitering around you."

"They're fine." I set the paper on the glass table, pen on top.

"They're leeching off your money." Trent steeples his hand on the document, his eyes on me. "I don't want to see my baby brother being taken advantage of."

I smile tiredly. "Sure."

Phoebe nods toward the door. "Hey, Hails, want to come inside? I have some cronuts from the new bakery—"

"No," Trent pipes in. "Hay-Hay is on a diet."

"I am?" Hailey frowns like this is news to her, but clearly Trent has noticed she's gained weight and assumed it's from food.

Trent nods and waves a hand. "And *this* is what it looks like to protect someone you care about."

I suck down a more vicious retort. *Don't engage*. I need this done. I do the foolish thing and look at Hailey. She's closed her book over her thumb and watches a caterpillar crawl along the banister. The urge to pick her up is a straitjacket to my soul.

It takes all my energy to look back at Trent. "Can we get this done?" I ask my brother.

"Give me a second." He takes his sweet time reading over the *single* piece of paper. He sees how brutal this is for me, being in eyeshot of her, and he's not wasting the opportunity to twist the knife harder.

I hold my breath when he picks up the pen.

I can't blink when he signs his name on the bottom line.

"Done?" he asks me.

The question feels so weighted. So heavy. I'm in a fogged haze when I say, "Yeah . . . done."

Trent steps back and lets out a deep exhale like the stress of the world just left his body. "Good luck, Jake. You're going to need it with running all of"—he twirls his fingers—"this." He turns to Hailey. "Come on, Hay—" He stops when his phone buzzes in his pocket.

He pulls out his cell, his brows furrowing. "Hold on . . ." He pushes off the patio and steps onto the manicured lawn, walking a few yards to take his call out of earshot.

Phoebe swipes the paper from the table. "I'll go fax this." She leaves for my office.

Hailey doesn't meet my eyes. She doesn't even look at her brother. She's focused on the caterpillar.

None of us talk. It almost feels like breaking the silence will stop the momentum.

I just watch Trent. As the minutes pass, he gets more and more flustered. A hand goes to his head. He grips his hair. Flush ascends the back of his neck, rising slowly to his jaw. He starts gesticulating wildly. His expression morphing from confusion to irritation to a darker rage.

"Hailey, get behind me," Rocky urges.

She brings her book with her and slips behind him without a single glance at me.

Seconds later, Trent grips his cell in his fist and storms over with fury-filled eyes. His anger. His wrath. It's only directed at one man.

FORTY-SEVEN

Rocky

THE HEIR OF NOTHING (CONTINUED)

"What the fuck did you do?" Trent sneers, barreling toward me. He's a slingshot, but I'm a wrecking ball swinging toward him. When I step forward, unafraid, he loses balance and staggers back on the lawn. He rights himself before he eats grass.

Hedges flank this area of the backyard, and beyond the neatly pruned wall of green lies the morning sun glistening against the sea. Beautiful scenery, as summer has slipped into early fall, made exceedingly *gorgeous* when Trent Waterford begins to lose his ever-loving mind in front of me.

I force down a smile.

It's easy when I'm still uncertain if he's going to redirect his anger onto Hailey. I stop at the edge of the patio, putting enough distance between Trent, his brother, and my sister to ease my nerves.

"Me?" I point a finger at my chest. "I didn't do anything," I say simply. "What are you even talking about?"

He pushes at the sleeves of his burgundy button-down, like

he's about to fight me. I would absolutely love for him to try. The cherry on top of the shit sundae he's about to force-feed himself will be my knuckles in his eye socket.

He huffs, "This was *you*. Don't give me that bullshit."

I glare. "Again, don't know what you're talking about, Trent." I put a hand on the stone pillar on instinct. To block him from reaching my sister. "Maybe you want to clue us all in."

He cranes his neck to look up at his younger brother, then to the table where Hailey is currently sitting, but he's noticeably eyeing the glass surface.

The paper he just signed to give Jake the other half of the beer company, the paper that just made Jake the sole heir of everything Koning—that paper is no longer there. It's inside with Phoebe.

Trent pales. "Where's the document?" He rushes toward the patio.

I drop onto the lawn and instantly block him, my forearm to his chest. "I don't think you're allowed in this house."

Trent snarls. "I don't give a *shit* what you think." He thrusts my chest, but I barely sway. I'm not letting him get an inch farther. He shies from the ruinous look in my eye. "JAKE!" he shouts. "Where's the fucking document?!"

"Already faxed to the lawyers," Jake says calmly. "It's done, man. You can't reverse this."

Trent blows back like he's been sucker punched. "No . . . no . . ." His hands fly to his head while his mind reels over the crumbling state of his reality. His life has been slowly disintegrating brick by brick for months, but he's only just realizing he's underneath the wreckage.

"This has to be a prank." He nods to himself and laughs shrilly, his phone squeezing in his fist. "Okay, which one of you fucking *losers* decided this would be funny? You?" He points his phone at Jake. "Nice try, baby brother."

Jake crosses his arms. "I didn't prank you, Trent."

"Sure, right, *yeah*. Just cut it out." Trent shifts his weight uneasily. "I see right through this. You got some weirdo to prank-call me and tell me my wife's no longer the beneficiary of the Wolfe fortune."

"What?" Hailey perks up in fake confusion.

"It's a lame prank, Hay-Hay," Trent assures her. "That money is still yours." He mouths to Jake, *Mine*, with a conceited prickish smile.

I've dealt with too many marks who can't accept they've been fooled. He's far from the fucking first.

Jake raises his hands. "I have no idea who called you. I don't know anything about this."

Accurate.

Jake has stayed as far away from the legal holdings of the Wolfe estate as possible. It makes him more innocent in what's just occurred.

"I have an idea who it was," I chime in, staring at Trent as he slowly spirals toward his fucked reality again. "The trustee of the Wolfe estate, I'm guessing."

Trent is barely breathing.

I continue. "They called me earlier this morning and said a second trust document was found in a locked safe at Stonehaven. A newer one. Apparently, Varrick changed his mind on who he'd like to inherit his wealth upon his death. Signed, notarized, and legally valid—he's given everything to the other Thornhall." I consume his slow-building rage. "To me."

This is all true.

I was there with Varrick and a lawyer when he *legally* made me the beneficiary of his trust. A second document that would supersede the one he had *legally* filed to name Hailey heir. This was all a part of the Koning job.

The Heir of Nothing.

Only, Varrick was supposed to be here to see this part. He was supposed to be alive to still reap all the benefits of the Wolfe fortune and be able to *legally* change his mind once again and take it away from me. But he's not here.

And I'm the last Wolfe standing.

"You?" Trent puffs out a stilted laugh. "How *convenient*. A second document. In a mysterious locked safe."

"Not a mysterious safe. It was in Varrick's office."

"No, I would've—"

"You would've known about it?" I cut him off. "Because you've visited Stonehaven *so many* fucking times since Varrick died."

Trent seethes quietly.

I raise my brows. "You refused to rifle through the mansion because of the *arduous* five-minute boat ride to and from the island." Ego. Hubris. Laziness. Never thinking any harm can come to him. Never thinking the rug will be ripped from under his feet because he's been protected by Mommy his entire fucking life.

He slides two hands through his hair, disheveling the strands as he pulls them back. "No, *you* did this." His angry finger returns to me. "You planted it. Whoever found it—"

"The trustee of the estate found it."

"Hay-Hay!" Trent yells. "Come here!"

"Hailey, don't," Jake says.

"*Wife*," Trent threatens between gritted teeth.

I get in his face. "Speak to my sister like that again and you will be choking on this lawn and eating my *fucking* shoe."

Trent doesn't pry his attention off my piercing glare, but he yells to Hailey, "Did you let the trustee of the estate into Stonehaven?!"

"No, you did," she says. "Don't you remember? He asked if he could go through Varrick's office. You said yes."

Trent is confused. He's unsure if he did approve this or not. He did. Flippantly. After two glasses of whiskey and a line of coke. Oliver had been there.

"It's real," I tell Trent. "The new trust document. You can call the lawyer who notarized it. The trustee has his number."

He does call him. This isn't a scenario where we need Everett Tinrock to pose as a lawyer and fake a notary. Though, we have done that plenty of times before.

Trent speaks to a real lawyer, who assures him this is all legal and that Varrick simply had a change of heart. When Trent gets off the call, he smears a hand down his mouth.

"You want to legally dispute it? Fine, but you won't win," I say. "It's not forged. Varrick was of sound mind when he signed it. And the entire town knows he was wavering between me and Hailey, and in the end, he chose *me*."

Trent begins shaking his head.

"The Wolfe fortune isn't yours," I tell him. "Not by marriage, not by *anything*. And after—what?—five minutes ago"—I tilt my head—"neither is the Koning fortune. Your baby brother, the one you love so fucking much, is the sole heir of everything."

The thirdborn finally has the crown.

It only took two deaths, a three-month-long fake marriage, and a summer spent in my deceased family's mansion with the con man who murdered them.

Top three hardest jobs of all time. No question.

Trent can't stop shaking his head. "He's not . . ." He stakes a glare at Jake now. "Dad will clear this up. He knows I would *never* just hand you everything."

"Dad?" Jake frowns. "Dad has been in Sweden since Mom died. He has no shares or interest in the company. He never has. What's he going to do?"

Trent lets out a low chuckle. "Jordan won't like this—"

"Jordan is going to rehab." Jake names their other brother. The secondborn. "I already told him I'd help him out under the stipulation he checks himself into a facility and stays sober. He's not going to vouch for you."

Trent stops shifting his weight. He fumes in place, his eyes pinging from me to Jake. "You two fucked me."

I raise and lower my brows, not admitting to shit verbally.

Then Trent zeroes in on Hailey. "*You.*" His lip curls. "Did you know about this? Were you a part of this fucking . . . thing, too?"

Hailey has her knuckles to her cheek, acting sheepish. He sees right through it. She's basically smiling.

"You fucking bitch—" He makes one furious step toward Hailey, and I cut off his path in an instant. I throw my fist into his mouth, *hard*, and he stumbles backward again, his ass meeting the ground this time.

"Fuck," he grunts. He doesn't get up. He spits out blood. Glaring at me like I'm picking on a guy when he's down. *How unfair.*

"What'd I say?" I glare. "Don't mess with my fucking sister. You want to fight someone, I'm right here. Stand the fuck up." I motion to him.

He stays seated. His forearms on his bent knees.

Yeah. That's what I fucking thought. All these petulant little pricks are the same. They always go after the girls because they know they're physically stronger than them and want a guaranteed win without injury or harm.

I watch his eyes veer again, and I rotate slightly to see Phoebe emerge from inside the house. She leans a shoulder in the doorway to the patio. Her lips stretching higher and higher at Trent's disgrace.

I tower over Trent, and he's rethinking what he wants to say to my wife because his eyes drop to my foot.

"Wow, *TK*." Phoebe feigns surprise. "Is it true? Are you really, like, losing billions of dollars in one day? Does this make you . . . broke? Like, do you have money to pay your mortgage—oh wait, do you even have a mortgage? Are you . . . are you homeless?" She gasps, a hand to her mouth, which she turns into a middle finger.

I grind down a smile. Phoebe grins at me, which makes it harder not to share in this sweet, *sweet* victory.

Trent's face flames bright red in humiliation, in hatred. "You think you're better than me . . . *Phoebe*?" He says her name with a mocking high pitch. I know where this is going.

I crouch down to his height on the ground. "You call her a cunt, a whore, or anything in the realm and I *will* put your face in the fucking ground. I think I saw a pile of dog shit over there. You want to eat it?"

"Fuck you," he mutters under his breath, unable to even meet my eyes now.

"What was that?" I turn my ear to him.

"I could have you arrested for assault," he says more clearly.

"Self-defense," I say assuredly.

He laughs.

"You came at Rocky first," Phoebe chimes in. "I saw it."

"Me too," Hailey adds.

Trent is more surprised at Hailey turning on him. It's been

sinking in. Rapidly, then slowly, then quickly again. "You . . . ?" He's cringing.

Right then, "Spirit in the Sky" begins playing in Jake's hand—a ringtone he's set for someone. He doesn't answer right away, so the song continues as Hailey rises from her chair and comes to the edge of the patio.

"I'm filing for divorce," she tells Trent. "Today. You weren't a very good husband."

He lets out a stunned noise. "You were a shitty wife who never put out."

"That's because you said cruel things to me—"

"Oh *please.*" He winces like she's full of shit. "I was nothing but *nice* to you."

Hailey raises her phone and plays some voice recordings. I hear him say, "You little freak," and "I wouldn't fuck you if my life depended on it," and "You're lucky I like your money," and "You better do what I say like a good little wifey." *Yeah, fuck him.*

My blood runs hotter, and she plays enough that he gets the idea. He's breathing like he's scaling a vertical wall.

"It's been really hard on me," Hailey admits. "This afternoon, the town will know how badly you've treated me. How you just got with me because you thought I'd be heir."

He's losing color in his face. "The town?"

"*Victoria Weekly* has these audio recordings, and they're going to publish my story. How I've been confiding in your younger brother. How Jake helped me escape you. How I'm pregnant."

"You're pregnant?" His eyes widen on her.

Hailey lifts her shirt to show her round baby bump, and his lips part in fragments of shock before she says, "With Jake's baby."

Jake's neck almost breaks, he looks to Hailey so fast. I also have a record scratch inside my brain, but I don't wear my surprise.

As far as I knew, Hailey was still unaware of the father.

She nods to Jake in confirmation.

He puts a hand to his mouth. The song cuts out but quickly restarts again as the person calls twice. "I need to take this," Jake says, and he steps onto the lawn, shooting me an urgent, pleading look to take care of Hailey while he leaves. As if I haven't done that my entire fucking life.

Trent is in a daze. Emotionally, mentally, and physically kicked down.

"I wouldn't stay here if I were you," I tell him. "And by *here*, I mean Victoria. There's nothing left for you in this town. Take whatever offering Jake gives you because it's going to be a hell of a lot better than living here. A place where everyone sees you as Trent Waterford, the gold-digging husband who was such a piece of shit to his wife, she ran to his younger brother for solace. You can't spin it. You can't fight it. Just take the fresh start and go."

He takes labored breaths.

"Oh, and don't worry about the bet, man. You know, the one you made me at the beginning of summer? Where you said you'd be the richest man in Victoria? As it turns out, that man is actually me."

Trent blinks like he's trying to throttle himself awake from this nightmare.

"I know you likely don't have twenty grand to spare," I say. "And I don't really need it. That's pennies to me anyway."

He's caving forward. Head in hands like he might puke. A full minute passes before he's able to pick himself up. After wiping the grass off his ass, he leaves without looking at any of us. His eyes are on the ground. The tail-between-the-legs walk of shame.

And the job is finally done.

I turn around to Phoebe and Hailey, who hold hands and dance on the patio. Shimmying left and right to an Avril Lavigne song playing from a phone. They're both sporting humongous grins, and it's a little infectious.

Their happiness. Setting my sister free of Trent is a massive boulder lifted off everyone, but mostly off her and Jake and Oliver. When the song finishes and they're out of breath, Hailey's attention travels to where Jake vanished.

I see the way she intakes a staggered breath. The way her head almost imperceptibly tilts and her eyes glaze.

I see her longing for him.

To be with him, and once the story hits the *Weekly* this afternoon, she can be.

"Jake's baby?" I ask her.

She turns to me, fiddling with her fingers. "I just found out yesterday." Phoebe doesn't seem surprised, so I'm assuming she went with Hailey to the doctor.

"Does Oliver know?"

Hailey nods. "I told him first. He was . . ." She chews her lip as a smile forms.

I lift my brows. "Oliver," I finish for her. *He was Oliver.* He was happy for Hailey and likely did not care that the baby is Jake's, because Oliver Graves will love my sister just as fiercely and deeply as he already did, just like he'll love that baby like it's his child anyway.

I know because I know him.

I know all of them.

FORTY-EIGHT

Jake

Jeez Louise." The lighthearted voice comes through the phone. "Your oldest brother is a snake. A little bitty toothless garden one that thinks it has venom and a bite. I hope you flung him into the woods."

"Where are you?" I ask him, phone to my ear while I trek across the estate grounds with a lengthy, assertive stride.

"Look to your right, Koning. I'm coming at you hot." Oliver isn't lying. I roll to a stop in the middle of the lawn as I see him bounding in from the stables. He's horseback on a black Dutch Warmblood that I've loved since I was seventeen, and he rides him like a Texan cowboy with strength and reckless freedom. His grin could light the sky on fire.

I laugh into a bright, weightless smile and lower the phone to my side. All the pressure of this morning flits away in one moment, one second, of just *seeing* Oliver Graves. His devil-may-care spirit never wanes, not even when he slows from a gallop to a trot to a walk as he nears me.

"Howdy there, good-looking." Toothpick between his

teeth, his smile stretches with mine. Our conversation on the phone drifts out of my brain.

I study his natural composure and ease on the horse. "I thought all of you hate horses?"

"Rocky and Phoebe don't like animals," Oliver clarifies, leaning forward and patting the Warmblood's neck with affection, "because they think they can smell their lies."

"You don't feel the same?"

"I believe animals can sense what humans can't. But all animals love me, and I love them." Oliver smiles at the horse, which is very relaxed in his presence. "No scent of deceit on me." His glittering eyes return to mine. "Some feelings you don't need to fake."

My lungs reinflate.

"You can smile, Koning. I won't think you're into me. I already know you are."

He's something else, something that I never want to go away, and the frustrated noise in my throat produces an actual smile. "You called." I nod to him.

"You came, or technically *I* came." He winks, then stops the horse a couple feet from me. "You don't need to concern yourself with the wily affairs of your brother." He dismounts, boots thudding to the ground. "It's already taken care of. The monster under your bed does more than just tickle your—"

"Oliver."

"Uh, he wants me to be serious," Oliver groans while staring at my lips, then shifts the toothpick with his tongue. My blood stirs, a carnal urge to do more than kiss him, and at the same time, my smile returns. Oliver seems more than satisfied by both reactions. "What's this one's name anyway?" he asks, smoothing a hand across the Warmblood's side.

"Formally, Knight Rider—I just call him Kit." I come up,

and the horse softly nickers, a vibrating hum of contentment in his throat. I stroke his muzzle.

"Kit." Oliver smiles more at me than the horse. "Well, good thing I'm here. He would've been on a trailer headed for Kentucky by now."

Trent's last rebellion against me—he was apparently trying to sell my favorite horses as if they were his own. "How'd you know about it?" I ask.

"Oh, he told me the whole thing. Pays to be friends with garden snakes. Keep Your Love's Lover's Enemy Close is the name of a very fun game."

"Yeah?" I run my fingers through my hair. "Is that what you think I am—Hailey's lover?"

We haven't defined anything between the three of us. Not once during the summer. Those fever-dream nights of unencumbered affection and quiet solace and hot curiosities filled with challenge ended the minute we left Stonehaven. As expected, they faded with the summer haze and made way for the tortured yearning of the fall.

I've tossed and turned ever since. I've had the worst sleep of my life being home. Being alone. I've realized that having sex with Hailey to help her sleep was more selfish on my part, and maybe Oliver's, too. I think we were all taking care of one another and using one another to feel something more. We were too afraid to fully commit to a relationship with parameters and definitions and hard, rigid lines outside the bedroom.

It was easy to slip into helping the girl we loved and just leaving it at that. It was even easier to fall for the man who loved her.

It's the first week of October, and I don't know where we all go from here now. But I'm not afraid. As I'm standing here in front of Oliver, even knowing Hailey is carrying my child, even knowing this makes no sense—the three of us—fear can't grab hold and choke.

I think, maybe, that's the beauty of being with people who cast aside doubt and nourish belief like it's a wall that can't be knocked down. *Together* feels like a fortress.

"Terms, labels, semantics," Oliver muses. "Hailey's lover. Hailey's midnight fuck. Hailey's past. Hailey's present. Hailey's baby daddy." He spots my surprise, bowing toward me. "Yes, I know." He rocks back. "She told me earlier. I figured she likely already told you, and if she didn't"—he sucks in a breath though his teeth—"I'll ask for forgiveness later." He reads me well. "She did tell you though."

"Like ten minutes ago."

He laughs. "You're still in shock."

"Yeah." I look him over, then shift more uncertainly. "A little worried about you."

Oliver smiles through his eyes. "I'm happy the baby is a Koning and not a Graves. I promise I'll love your child and teach her how to be bad in a very good way." He wags his brows.

I freeze. "Her?"

He winces in realization. "She didn't tell you you're having a daughter?"

My pulse skips, and I let out a laugh, my eyes trying to well and burn. *Hailey and I are having a daughter.* "No, she didn't."

"Fuck." He skims me head to toe. "Want to pretend you heard nothing?"

"I don't think I can." I slide my hands against my neck. *My daughter. Hailey.* "Oliver." I stare longer at him. The air shifts between us like a crack of electricity, quickening my pulse, raising the hairs on my arms. Because our gazes tunnel too deep. His breath hitches just slightly. I feel like we're colliding, even when neither of us moves a muscle. "I'm not just Hailey's," I tell him. "I think I've become yours, too."

"I think you might be right," he whispers, our eyes scouring at a dangerous speed. "What are you going to do about it, Koning?"

"I'm making sure this isn't just a summer fling. It can't be the finish line, and if you don't move the goalpost, I will."

"I'll move it with you," he says. "I'm used to doing the heavy lifting."

I start to smile. "Yeah?"

"Oh yeah. I suspect you'll need me."

"I suspect you'll need me, too," I say as our gazes roam so freely. I feel like we're inside of each other in this field, and we haven't even physically touched. "Move in for good," I spell out clearly. "Live with us at this estate."

He breathes deeply through his nose, his lips curving higher. His eyes shining brighter. "I'll have to check my other offers."

"Your other offers?" I glance at his lips, then watch him back away from me with a smile like dynamite and kerosene, and I am so gone, so fucking taken by him, looking away would feel like the real death of me. "Are you playing hard to get right now?"

"Keeps things interesting." He grabs Kit's leather reins, then gives me a salute. He laughs lightly. "Don't look at me like that."

"Like what?"

"Like I'm torturing you." He's amused and chews on the end of the toothpick. "I've already let you fuck me once." I have been inside Oliver, but that's not nearly as deep as I want to be.

"I don't think once was enough."

Oliver stays fixed on my gaze like he's the one falling down the rabbit hole. "Agreed."

After trekking back to the house alone, I only find Rocky. He's balancing backward on two legs of a patio chair, his actual legs kicked up on the table while he plays *Candy Crush* on his phone.

"Where's Hailey?" I ask on instinct, anxious to see her.

Rocky drops his feet off the table. "She went to the bookstore with Phoebe. I didn't want the girls hanging around here in case your brother throws a temper tantrum. I suggest you go make him an offer before he decides he has nothing to lose."

They're very good at preempting worse-case scenarios. It makes me wonder how many times they've encountered marks who like to retaliate after being humiliated. How many times they've needed a quick escape. How different this must be since they're not fleeing the place of the con.

"Will do." Before I go deal with my brother, I walk over to Rocky. "About your sister."

"About my sister," he says darkly. I can't see a situation where Grey/Rocky/Brayden wouldn't be protective of the people he loves, no matter who's on the other end of his aim. "If this is another conversation, Jake, where you tell me you aren't *serious* about her, your face will be the one I put in that pile of dog shit."

I let out a laugh. "It's the opposite, actually. All I want is to be serious with Hailey. I can't imagine not being with her after all of this, Bray."

He smiles hearing his birth name. "And Oliver?" It's like he already knows. There is no real question in his eyes.

"And Oliver," I say deeply.

He nods. "You love them."

"I love them," I state more firmly. "I will take care of them the rest of my life, and I know you guard all of them with yours. So I needed you to know where I stood."

"I already knew, and I could lie, but I won't." He forces a dry smile. "It is nice hearing it out loud." He checks his watch. "You need help with Trent?"

"I'll call you if I do."

"Great. You better go."

The conversation with Trent is thirty minutes of a pulsing migraine. I offer him our family's flat in London—one bedroom, one bath, in serious need of new plumbing. He takes it like I'm doing *him* a favor and starts packing his bags right then, right there.

"This small town is overrated trash. I always knew I'd be in a city. Spend your days bored out of your fucking mind, Jacob. There is *nothing* here."

Everything I've ever loved has been in Victoria.

I'm stuck taking calls regarding the beer company for hours longer than I want. By the time I rip myself away, my head is pounding, and my pulse spikes with anticipation.

Noon.

It's past noon.

Hailey. I can't think anymore. I'm going out of my mind. Grabbing the keys to my Porsche, I exit quickly. The blue car is parked in the large horseshoe driveway.

I only slow when I open the door and look back at the looming mansion. Ivy spindles up stone. Red rosebushes in bloom. Wind catches and rustles the trees, and afternoon light strikes the windowpanes.

It's beautiful.

I smile fondly. Kate would've loved to see the haunted mansion evicted of its ghouls. "I'll call you later, Kate," I whisper. My little sister can't come back. Kate Koning Waterford was pronounced dead, but she'll be thrilled to hear the news.

We keep in touch as often as we can. Even if it's only through phone calls, it's good to hear the light and happiness in her voice. It's what I hoped for her.

Climbing into the car, I start the engine and peel out.

My grip tightens on the wheel the whole drive into town. Waves of realization crash into me like I'm waist-deep in the ocean, being swallowed by the sea. I'm going to have a life where I can love a girl and she won't be a tool used by my mother or a toy by my brother.

I'm going to be able to keep Hailey and our daughter safe.

In the town she loves.

It overwhelms me. Throttles me, and I'm just barely holding it together when I shift gears and parallel park one street over from Main, which is blocked off from cars. Locals are preparing for the annual Harvest Festival next weekend. Fall decor is being erected—scarecrows, pumpkins, hay bales, apple baskets, the humongous HARVEST FESTIVAL banner stretching across the street.

I lock the car and jog over to Main. I can't see the bookstore from this far down the road. Not with all the ladders, wooden crates, and people milling around.

Please still be there.

I didn't think to call. I just assumed they still would be, but it's been hours since Rocky told me where Phoebe and Hailey went.

My stride is long, urgent, and I search left and right for her. I duck under a strand of acorns and feel locals staring, whispering, *knowing.* People I've known my whole life as I raced through this street as a child with no responsibilities and then as an adult with heavy pockets of errands and to-do lists.

"Hi, Jake." Some reach out. "Sorry to hear about your brother. I had no idea . . ."

"Thanks, Nathan," I say when he pats my shoulder. Hailey's story in the paper has definitely made its rounds. I pass him and hear more. "You doing okay, Jake?" and "I always knew Trent was a bad apple, Jake" and "Good for you, Jake. Helping that girl."

I will give her full credit when I'm less preoccupied. I respond, "Have you seen Hailey Thornhall?"

Ladies point giddily down the street, and that's when it dawns on me that the town is rooting for me and Hailey to be together.

My pace picks up.

"Weather's going to be great for the fest, Jake!"

"That's great, Amber," I call back, distracted. I am very distracted . . . by a critical hunt for a beautiful platinum-blonde girl.

I slow as the bookstore comes into view. Phoebe fiddles with the extension of a paint roller while Rocky holds an aluminum ladder in a lunge, chatting with his wife. The chalkboard sign out front reads, BOOKSTORE CLOSED FOR RENOVATIONS.

The Baubles & Bookends logo is already partially painted over.

Hailey isn't there.

Disappointment tries to drop my shoulders, but I hurry

forward in the middle of the street. Then my feet drift into a frozen state beneath me.

Hailey is at the fountain with Oliver.

Red paint streaks her soft cheek, and Oliver dabs the bottom of his shirt at her face. He must've wet the fabric in the fountain. As he cleans off the red splotch on her cheek, he grins down at her and likely flirts.

She acts disinterested, but he's able to pull a teeny-tiny smile out of her, which just illuminates his features. It's like a lighthouse calling me home. I am tugged forward. Slowly moving again.

I won't tire seeing them together. It's time-capsuled love. Old love. And Oliver is right, it doesn't rust. It's made to endure through harsh climates. So the fairy tales and icicle dreams can't melt in the winter.

My love is new. Born into the magic of summer. Made to reach December.

The two, I believe, coexist naturally.

Oliver spots me first, his smile stretching. He rotates Hailey, and the second she sees me, her expression obliterates my senses.

She looks like she's free-falling.

I feel like I'm being shoved. I keep heading to her. Walking, walking, closer, closer. Until my pace quickens; I'm needing her in my embrace, wanting her wrapped around me.

I jog.

Her hands fly to her mouth as her eyes pool. She's nodding. She extends her arms.

I collide with her and pick her up against my chest to applause and my racing heartbeat. I slide my hand into her hair while she touches her forehead to mine.

We're smiling while I whisper, "'All the night-tide, I lie

down by the side of my darling—my darling—my life and my bride.'"

She laughs through her tears. "'In her sepulchre there by the sea.'"

"Not her sepulchre," I say.

"No?" She closes in on my lips.

"No." I'm about to kiss her. "Just in our kingdom by the sea."

FORTY-NINE

Rocky

Midnight. Don't be late. 

I read the incoming text from my sister and pocket my phone. Only to see Jake beside me, checking the same message on his.

We aren't in a hurry to leave. It's not close to midnight yet.

Resting my forearms on the metal railing of his catamaran, I loosely grip a beer bottle as the sun starts to set over the water. No, at the beginning of everything, I did not think I'd be here—willingly having a beer on *Jake's* boat, without any plot or scheme, like he's become my best friend (whatever that means).

Then again, I would've never believed I was born in this town.

My home. Ripped away as a baby.

Standing beside Jake, a beloved figure of Victoria, a guy I could've grown up with in another lifetime, I feel more like

Brayden Wolfe—the son and the brother who came back for his family. Who got justice for the ruthlessness they met.

I stare out, not just at the water or the sinking sun. From Jake's slip in the marina, he has a perfect view of Stonehaven. The mansion on a lone island.

Jake places his arms on the railing beside me, pinching the neck of a Koning Lite. "What are you going to do with it?"

"I have some ideas." I lift my beer to my lips. "I'm definitely not living there."

"The boat ride," he guesses. "Too far out."

I swallow beer. "It's haunted."

Jake gauges my seriousness, then laughs hard. "Oh, man, of all the things you've encountered in your life, you choose to be afraid of the make-believe."

"Bad luck is so far out of my control," I say honestly. "And so are ghosts."

His laugh sounds light. Free. He's dropped 180 pounds of burden with Trent gone. It's been two weeks of peace without that fuckbag, and I can't wait to keep counting. The calm, though, is strange for me.

I swallow more beer.

Jake rotates his bottle in his hand. The label facing him. "I'm thinking of selling it."

My brows jump. "The family business?" I let out a long whistle. "The end of the Koning dynasty."

It's why Trent would've never sold the company outright and freed himself from the headache. Not only has this been in Jake's family for generations, but it's one of the oldest, most recognizable beer companies in America.

It's prestigious and known *as* a family company. To sell to a corporation will be seen as a betrayal to the Koning name and its values. But something tells me Jake has never upheld the same values as his family anyway.

"I never saw myself handling any aspect of the company," Jake says. "And I want to make sure I'm there for Hailey and our daughter, not pulled to board meetings and on the phone 24/7."

I read him. "You were always going to sell it," I say, realizing that now. "You were never going to run the company."

He raises the beer to his mouth. "I've already made calls. I think I can get at least fifty billion for it."

Holy shit. A deep laugh rumbles out of me. "You trying to rival me as the richest man in Victoria, Jake?"

"I think I'd have to sell another company for that."

"True."

There was no long discussion about who the Wolfe fortune would go to when Hailey would be overridden. They all agreed, before I even said a word, that it deserved to be with the real last remaining heir.

"It was always meant to be Rocky's," my sister said.

I wanted it to be theirs, too. Everyone is set. I have properties to give and so much money to divide between us, it's mind-blowing.

Since they know I'm loaded, I was flabbergasted the godmothers and godfather never asked for a penny. They only requested the money for the Koning job that was promised at the start. One million each from Jake, and they were gone.

All this time, I'd believed the worst in them, and I don't know—some days, I start to believe the worst was the man they were running from. Maybe they really weren't manipulative at all. Then I remember the mindfuck Everett put me through when it came to Phoebe, and I return to hating them.

After a long swig, I say, "The loft above the bookstore."

"What about it?"

"I want to buy it from you."

He begins to smile. "You're going to live there with Phoebe?"

"We'll probably renovate first." Need to rip up some bloodied floorboards from when Trevor was stabbed. I think about my little brother. "I have a feeling Trev will stay with us until he can find an apartment on the street." That'll be interesting as fuck since Phoebe and he get along like a feral cat and a stray dog. I slide my fingers through my hair. "Sidney moved into your pool house?"

"Officially, yesterday." She didn't have the funds to cover rent at the Reynoldses' boathouse on her own, so Jake is letting her stay for free. Always the hero.

I tip my beer to him. "Heard you lost two servers at the club, and you didn't even need to fire them. They just walked out on you."

"They gave me their two weeks' notice."

"I told Phoebe to give you a two-hour notice." I swig beer.

"Thanks, jackass." He rotates the beer, staring back at the water. "I'm glad they quit on their own terms."

I make a face. "So you wouldn't have to fire them?"

"I would've figured out how to keep them, but I like that they get to work together and own something."

Like *Mystic Pizza*, I realize, and I roll my eyes and laugh. Fuck. How did I not make the comparison before? Instead of owning a pizza shop, the girls now own the bookstore. It's in their name. It's not mine anymore.

"They're so fucking cliché," I say, but I can't help but smile.

Jake smiles off mine. "Did you get everything you wanted?"

I nod slowly in thought. "Yeah. I did."

Revenge.

Love.

Power.

"And I keep thinking, *Was it worth the cost?* But I barely had to pay a cost." I glance over at Jake. "I keep waiting for the reaper to come collect."

"You and Phoebe have been paying the cost your whole lives," Jake says. "He already collected."

That almost breaks me. I bend into a lunge and dip my head toward the railing, my eyes scalding. His hand stays on my shoulder, and I recognize that he deeply understands what Phoebe and I have been through. He endured the emotional turmoil of loving a girl inside a job where you can't be together, where you have to see her with another man and protect her from the same horrific man. He did it for three months.

I've done it for over ten years.

FIFTY

Hailey

Three minutes till midnight, Phoebe and I trek through the old cemetery in Victoria wearing woolen coats and laced boots. Leaves crunch beneath our feet, and fog hangs low over lichen-covered headstones. It's eerily quiet, except for the hoot of an owl. I'm unsurprised to see my best friend grinning like we're at Disney World.

I've always loved how much Phoebe loves the strange and scary.

She makes me less afraid.

Her hand reaches out to mine, almost unconsciously, and I clasp her fingers as we hike farther off the path and the hill steepens. I place a protective hand on my round belly. She's a kicker, in a hurry to meet the world, but it's definitely not time yet.

December, she'll be here.

I can make it two more months.

Olly says her restlessness is because of all the books we keep reading out loud. She senses the world is so much bigger than the cramped darkness she's inside now. I already love her, as she fights to escape her confines. Like a princess in a tower.

I step over a root.

Phoebe touches the gold heart-shaped locket at her neck. "You think we're the first here?" she whispers.

"I told them not to be late," I whisper back. "I think we're the ones cutting it close."

She scoffs. "We're *early*. Like by ten minutes."

I raise my brown leather Tiffany Gondolo watch that Jake gifted me. He'd seen me admiring it online. "Late by like one minute." I put the watch in her face.

She scoffs even louder. "Nonsense. All you have to do is spin that little knob on the side and we're ten minutes early. Turn back time, Hails."

"I'd rather not," I say too deeply, my eyes flooding as they meet the depth of hers.

She squeezes my hand, and I squeeze back as she says, "Me either."

In the very beginning, it might've just been two girls, Elizabeth and Addison, who likely went by other names. Just as likely their childhood friendship didn't start over something so innocent—a shared snow cone on a hot summer day. Likely, that was just a story.

I'm satisfied letting theirs go, no longer plagued with needing every fragmented detail. Fiction or fact—their story has no bearing on ours anymore. We've been writing our own. Pens in our hands. Indelible ink that won't be easily scrubbed away.

I know Phoebe has been tormented at the idea of our story mirroring our moms', of history repeating itself, but she forgets one important thing.

In *our* beginning, there weren't just two girls.

As we come into a clearing at the deepest part of the cemetery, the boys of our childhood turn around to greet us.

We are the last ones to arrive. "Just like old times," Phoebe says to me, and we share a grin, remembering a long-ago job at a coed boarding school. Where we all snuck out into a graveyard and passed around a bottle of booze.

Only now, Oliver has an aluminum flask, and they're no longer boys. They're hardened, timeworn confidence men.

Rocky looks like he's hating every moment of this, but that couldn't be further from the truth. Especially as Phoebe approaches him and he slides an arm around his wife.

I join the huddle, closing the circle as I slip beside Jake.

Our newest member. My pinched smile puckers my cheeks the longer his affectionate gaze touches mine, as though he loves me.

He does love you, Hailey. Oh, to be loved in a small town. Not just by one man but by *two*—Oliver perches an arm on Jake's shoulder, and his grin drops down to me. It's a little dreamy, but I'm certain I'm awake.

Even my dreams have never felt this peaceful and happy.

"Nice of you both to show up five minutes late," Rocky says dryly.

"*Thirty seconds* late," Phoebe corrects, jutting a finger at him.

He seizes her wrist. Just to hold her hand. "I see we're playing the lying game."

"We're here now," I chime in. "Fully intact. All truths."

"Yeah, just in time." Rocky arches his brows. "Nova was thirty seconds from calling Search and Rescue."

"That was you," Nova retorts, blowing on his cold palms.

Jake and Oliver laugh.

Rocky flips them off with his free hand, and Trevor swipes the flask from Olly to raise it in the air.

"Toast first," Trevor says.

No one knows where this is headed. He might just want to drink. Rocky has been trying to get our brother to lay off the alcohol.

Then he decrees, "To the dead."

Oliver is amused. "Is this a circle of remorse? Are we paying respects to the people we've offed?"

"Not so fucking loud," Rocky chastises.

Phoebe scowls. "I'm not toasting to that *creep*." Her dad.

Nova looks like he'd love to light this conversation on fire. Rocky, not far behind.

"No one is asking you to, PG," Trevor snaps, then he slowly catches all our eyes around the circle. His arm goes back in the air. "To Rocky's family." He motions his flask over to the row of chipped headstones beside us.

All of Brayden Wolfe's siblings, his mother and father, who'd been moved into the rear of the cemetery to be hidden and forgotten.

"To my family," Rocky says to our brother. "The one that's alive."

My eyes mist as Rocky looks at me. He mouths, *Sister.*

I mouth back, *Brother.*

Trevor smiles, then drinks to that, and Oliver steals the flask back before my brother downs the whole thing in one gulp.

"Let's get this over with," Nova mutters, crouching to pick up a large shoebox on the mossy earth. Everyone but Jake begins to dig in pockets or grab things they'd set aside on the ground.

Rocky, a manila envelope. Trevor, a plastic grocery bag.

Oliver, a waterproof container. Phoebe has her things in her purse, and I dig for a makeup pouch in my messenger bag.

The midnight hour has my mind buzzing.

A waxing moon as our light, we stare around at one another and exchange softer, fond expressions of our strange adolescence and lifetime spent together. Every city, every town, every short and long job.

Our story, as it's been written. "And so," I begin, narrating the legend we created as kids in a graveyard, "there once was a silver-tongue."

Rocky's dark smile crests. He places the manila envelope in the shoebox Nova outstretches to him.

"A seductress," I say to my very best friend.

Phoebe grins, then dumps her old burners into Nova's box.

I add, "A getaway." Nova lifts the shoebox, showing he's already placed his fakes in them.

"A chameleon." I smile over at Oliver, who wags his brows at me, then pops open the stuffed waterproof container. He slides out checkbooks, burner phones, credit cards with fake names, and photo IDs into Nova's shoebox, then raises a finger and says, "Attendez," in a smooth French lilt. *Wait*.

We do wait for him as he reaches back into his peacoat pockets, digging out another stack of plastic IDs and passports. Jake gives him a look, like *What the hell?* Which only causes Oliver to grin. "I've been many people, Koning." He places the rest in the box. "Sorry for the intermission, Hailstorm."

I try not to blush when he winks at me, and I clear my throat to say, "A mastermind."

Nova extends the shoebox to me, his shadowy smile present.

Before Phoebe and I moved to Victoria, we got rid of most

of our fake IDs. But I kept one just in case we needed a quick exit. A backup plan. I plop my old burner phones, a credit card, a checkbook, and one fake ID inside.

Done.

I release a breath and turn to Trevor. "A psychopath."

Trevor overturns his plastic bag into Nova's shoebox. Putting his fakes with the others.

I finish, "And a king."

Jake bends his head, pressing a kiss to my hair. He doesn't have any forgeries to dispose of. He's never had a fake alias. A fake name.

The irony is that all our names are fake. None have ever been real. Except, these are the realest versions of ourselves, here in Victoria, and maybe that's why it's easy to give Nova our old, fake identities one by one.

Those we've kept around for side jobs and emergencies. Those we don't really need anymore.

Phoebe asks Nova, "How are you destroying them?"

"Incinerator," he replies, putting the lid on the box. Our old identities are going up in flames.

We all decided it's safer to remain in Victoria without ties to the past. We've never been in one place for this long, and preserving who we are now is more important than trying to become someone else.

"Is this the end?" Trevor asks us. "Are we seriously never going to pull another job again?"

Oliver smiles first, then Rocky, and it feels infectious. I catch Phoebe's big grin. Nova smiles down at the earth, and before I know it, my cheeks hurt, too.

"Once a spider, always a spider," Rocky tells him.

"Translation?" Trevor asks.

"We're going to protect this town and our identities here

for the rest of our lives. In the way we all know how. Anyone who's a threat to us becomes a mark."

Rocky never lied when he said he'd never quit grifting. He's conditioned to protect us, and even when the dust has settled, he'll still set his sights on the people who kick it up.

I look at Olly. "Our final web is Victoria."

He smirks. "I do love trapping prey."

"And predators," Phoebe adds.

"Always," Rocky says deeply.

Trevor begins to really smile, happy we aren't disbanding. We're just doing things our way now.

"I gotta head out," Nova says, tucking the shoebox beneath his arm.

"Midnight booty call?" Phoebe teases.

"No, I'm exhausted," Nova says. "You all are fucking exhausting."

"Let the old man sleep," Oliver quips.

Nova must really be tired. He doesn't remind Olly that he's only minutes older than him. In the moonlight, the long scar on his cheek is more noticeable. I know Rocky wanted to protect Nova from killing Varrick by being the one to do it, but I think it had to be Nova in the end.

Phoebe said he's more at peace.

He gives us a tired, stiff wave, but we all know he'll wait in his Pontiac near the exit. Just to ensure we all make it out of the cemetery okay.

Trevor trudges in the same direction. "I do have a booty call."

"Ew." Phoebe grimaces.

"*He's* your actual brother, PG." Trevor points toward Nova's shadow.

"One was a joke."

Trevor opens his mouth, but Rocky cuts in, "Go fuck your girlfriend. Don't waste time antagonizing Phoebe."

Jake sighs. "We really need to go over what shouldn't be said when the baby is born."

"Yep." I nod in agreement.

Trevor strolls down the slope, hands in his pockets. He fades into the darkness. Then Oliver walks backward in the same direction out of the cemetery.

I find myself drifting.

Not a mental drift.

A good drift as my feet—one in front of the other—follow Oliver, and Jake isn't so immune to the pull. His strong arm curves around my frame, warming me, and he smiles as Oliver lifts his flask and toasts, "To Baby." We still haven't decided on a name for her yet.

Baby, she's been for now.

Oliver drinks, then makes another toast to endings and beginnings.

"And middles," I add.

"Why a middle?" Jake asks me.

I look from him to Oliver. "That's where most love is made."

Their emerging smiles cause my face to heat, and I hope I never stop blushing. I hope love always kisses my cheeks with fire.

When we're farther down the hill, I cast one glance backward. Phoebe and Rocky linger behind together, as they've done most of our lives, stealing a clandestine moment at the headstones.

And I smile softly.

FIFTY-ONE

Rocky

Past midnight now, we're the last to leave the quiet cemetery. As Phoebe and I head out, she takes one more peek at the four crumbling grave markers. "Will you move them?" she asks, collecting her blue hair into a ponytail. "To be with the other Wolfes? Daphne and Brent?" My late aunt and uncle.

"I don't want to disturb them." I steal the hair tie off her wrist. "I might just get new headstones made." I bite the hair tie, and Phoebe moves in front of me. She tries not to melt like a fucking Popsicle while I pull her hair into a pony for her, using two hands.

"Admit it," she says, her back bumping into my chest.

"You're obsessed with me doing your hair," I mumble. Taking the hair tie out of my mouth, I say clearly, "Can admit."

"Not that."

"Then what?" I finish tying off her pony.

She spins around to face me. "You're sentimental. You cherish *things*."

"People."

"*Things*. Example number one." She waves back toward the illegible headstones that I'm ninety-nine percent sure I will replace.

"That's people adjacent," I argue, watching her continue to walk backward over limestone, roots, and fallen leaves. I stay so close, knowing she's going to trip at some point.

"Example number two." She flips me off with her ring finger, showing off the glinting diamond.

It almost makes me smile seeing it on her. Remembering Miami, marrying Phoebe in this diabolical, overly handsy way that fueled something in my soul—it was real in a lot of ways, even if it was part of the job.

I nod to the ring. "Also people adjacent."

She wags her pointer finger. "That's the thing, bucko—" She stumbles.

I seize her hips. She's panting hard while I keep her close to my chest. "Bucko? Wow." I widen my eyes. "Did you suck a gallon of helium behind the headstone?"

She starts grinning. "Must be the moon."

"Must be." I pull her up, resisting the urge to fuck her against a tree. She's more careful this time, but not much more. Because Phoebe likes being caught by me, and I love catching her.

"Sentimental items are people adjacent," she argues. "It's the same thing. They're all *things*."

"No," I state plainly, shaking my head.

"*Yes*."

"Phebs, you can't tell me my fucking toothbrush has any sort of special meaning. Other than ensuring I don't need a root canal."

She clasps my hand. "We're headed toward example three."

"Are we?" I say dryly, not needing her to tug me in the direction. I walk beside her, keeping her hand in mine, knowing where we're going. We trek down the hill toward the winding road that leads out of the cemetery. Lit by the orange glow of cobwebbed lampposts.

It's eerie as fuck. Do not love. Definitely want to leave.

Phoebe so clearly wants to stay, which makes me not in a hurry to go at all. I'm hooked on her, on her smiles emerging out of her usual scowls as she tries to make this dumb point. And then the point feels like the least dumb thing in the world.

It feels like the only thing that matters.

The only thing that exists.

The only thing I love.

The only thing.

Her.

So when she waves her hands like Vanna fucking White at the black Corvette parked on the pavement, I'm already falling in love with Phoebe Graves all over again.

"Ta-da!" Phoebe reaches the curb next to the sixties Stingray. "You cried when you first got the keys."

It is a *beautiful* fucking car. One I coveted when Varrick had possession of the vintage collection belonging to my late grandfather William Wolfe. Now, over a hundred classic cars are mine.

"I cried." I arch my brows. "Was that before or after you passed out from professing your love for fourteen fucking hours to me?"

"That definitely did not happen." Her collarbone juts out as I stalk her backward until her spine hits the Corvette's passenger door.

I pin her against the car, my legs splitting hers apart. "I thought we were spinning tall tales." She's breathless. I look her over. "No?"

"No." She smothers a smile and tries to catch her breath. "Admit it. You're sentimental. This Corvette means something to you."

"You still don't get it." I thumb the gold heart-shaped locket that hangs between her breasts. She's breathing like I'm chasing her, and it drives oxygen out of my lungs, too.

"Get what?" she whispers.

"That I'm mostly just sentimental over you." I thread my fingers through her hair, pulling out the pony I'd already tied. She's buckling against the car, and I want all over her. But I edge out the moment of collision by lifting the gold heart off her breastbone with my other hand.

The chain is still around her neck. I know what her mom used this locket for.

"What's in your heart of lies?" I whisper.

Her smile isn't just taunting. It's tender and . . . *sentimental.* I feel the emotion swelling inside me. "Open it and see," she says very quietly.

So I click the spring on the heart, and it unfolds. We keep such few photos of ourselves, so the second I see her and me from this summer—where I'm kissing her and sliding my hand into her hair like I am right now—my love for her blisters my gaze.

"No lies," she whispers, her voice shaking with the powerful rapture I feel. "My heart only holds the truth."

THREE SUMMMERS LATER

FIFTY-TWO

Phoebe

I do a lazy scour of the family room at Stonehaven, in search of someone. Floors have been polished, chandeliers dim for a moody ambience, dark damask wallpaper restored, and all nooks and crannies have been checked for black mold. Biohazard-free.

Livable for longer than a summer. But this is not my place of residence. Even though I love things that go *boo*, I wouldn't live somewhere that could potentially cause Rocky grief every time he's ready for bed.

I rotate in a circle and tap my lips. "I wonder where she could be? Is she . . . under the pillow?" I swipe the quilted pillow off the tufted love seat. "Nope, not there."

Giggles emanate from the arched window. Two teeny-tiny combat boots stick out from the bottom of a thick purple curtain.

"Is she"—I creep closer—"behind the tea cart?" I glance around the tea cart, only to hear bright snickering.

"Is she—"

"Boo!" A little girl in a black jean skirt bounces out with the cutest giggles ever.

As I said, I *really* love things that go *boo*. Particularly this gap-toothed toddler with light brown pigtails and big enchanting gray eyes that immediately steal hearts. I should know; she stole mine the minute Hailey gave birth to her and I held her in my arms.

Really, I think she stole seven hearts that night.

I gasp. "Were you hiding there this whole time?"

"Uh-huh." She nods robustly and rocks on her feet.

"What a terrific hider you are, little miss. Your mommy will be so happy to know."

She presses her tongue against her tiny baby teeth in a cheek-dimpling smile, her shoulders rising a little bashfully. It reminds me of Hails.

"Auntie Phoebe." She enunciates very well for not even being three yet. "You hide now," she says, but goes and scurries back behind the curtain with a giggle.

"You ready?" Rocky saunters in, slipping his phone in his back pocket. "The nine-a.m. tour group is one room over."

Shit. "Did you get the thing resolved?"

"The thing," he whispers, like I'm understating this. "You mean the tourist who pissed in my great-grandmother's vase?"

"Yeah, that thing." The caretaker called us and said there was a "situation" from a tour group last night. I thought we were going to show up to something far worse. Like a busted pipe leaking through the walls. Or stolen trinkets, like the Sèvres porcelain or bronze wolf figurines.

Instead, it was the mysterious case of the pissing tourist. Which is extra funny, because out-of-towners are called "skunks."

"Really putting *skunk* in *skunk*," I tell Rocky now.

That makes him smile. "It's resolved."

"Yippee—"

"Where is she?" he cuts me off, instant *I will go to war* levels of defense in his voice. And Rocky says Jake is the Arthurian knight.

"I think she went up the chimney. Pulled a reverse Santa."

"Funny." Rocky nods to me a couple times, relaxing as he sees her little combat boots beneath the curtain. "How long have you been working on that one?"

"You get my on-the-fly material."

"It fucking shows," he whispers lowly.

I flip him off subtly at my side.

"And if you'll all just pool right in here." Susie, a college student and one of our excellent tour guides, directs a group of ten inside. "This is where the Wolfe family would gather, especially during stormy days when boating to town would guarantee seasickness to even the most experienced sailors."

I take one step to collect my niece when she decides to spring out and proudly yell, "Boo!"

Tourists laugh, some clap, and she giggles, swaying side to side. Her lack of stranger danger drives Rocky out of his mind.

He scoops her up fast.

"Oh dear, *her eyes*," a lady says. "They're stunning." This is the fourth eye compliment and it's not even ten a.m. yet.

"Thank you," the toddler says very clearly, her shoulders lifting again. She shies away with a little giggle-smile into Rocky's chest. Too precious. Will easily murder for. Thankfully none of us have ever had to.

"These are the owners of Stonehaven," Susie says, introducing us. "Grey Thornhall and Phoebe Thornhall. They're the reason the public can venture inside this historic home and truly appreciate its significant part of Victoria's rich history."

Rocky didn't do it for the kudos. He'll say he did it for the money. But he's not pocketing a dime. All proceeds from Stonehaven tours go back to the town.

I think he did it for them.

I glance over at the humongous oil painting hanging over the fireplace mantel of his brothers squished on a couch and his parents on either side and his mother holding him in her arms. No longer hidden in a musty secret room under a canvas tarp, but alive for all to know, for all to see.

"We appreciate you all coming out," I tell them. *But we have to go.* I must not evoke enough hurriedness.

An older woman acknowledges the toddler perched in Rocky's arm. "And who's this little adorable girl?"

"Hi," she greets cheerfully with a wave, no hesitation. "I'm Winter."

I try not to panic because her name *is* Winter. She's allowed to introduce herself. There is nothing wrong, but we were told as kids to never tell anyone our names. Even when asked. Because our parents were afraid we'd give someone the wrong one.

When we leave the mansion and board the speedboat, I'm a little shaken by the interaction. My pulse hasn't calmed down.

"Phebs?" Rocky bends toward me with a toddler life jacket.

I'm seated in the copilot's chair. Winter on my lap, humming to herself.

"I'm fine," I whisper, trying not to appear freaked out. Last thing I need is for Winter to sense she did anything wrong.

She did everything right.

I hold her securely.

"She's safe," Rocky whispers to me, fitting her little arms through the life jacket. She has on a black-striped tee with embroidered red strawberries.

Hails said she's been on a strawberry kick all summer because "Auntie Phoebe wears 'em and I wanna, too!"

I crinkle my nose to stop from getting emotional.

She's safe.

"Uncle Rocky, no," Winter whines as he buckles the vest tight. She tries to pinch at the clasps, but it's too tough for her tiny fingers. "Unbuckle. Unbuckle." Her brows crease, a panicked look in her eyes.

I almost crumble.

Rocky stays firm. "It's for your safety, Winter. You wear life vests around water."

"Unbuckle. Unbuckle." She kicks her legs and looks up at me for help.

"Oh no," I tell Rocky. "We're about to meet a toddler meltdown."

"Unbuckle, please. Unbuckle." She's near tears. Okay, now she's full-on blubbering.

Rocky curses under his breath, and I make an executive decision and unbuckle her. He gives me a headshake. Though not a hard one. His lips twitch up a little.

Maybe at the notion that I'm not calling Hailey to ask for step-by-step instructions on what to do. It even surprises me how quickly I can make some choices without consulting others whether it's okay or right.

"It's a five-minute boat ride," I defend. "I'll hold her tight."

"Fine. Don't tell Jake." He mans the wheel, staying on his feet.

"Wasn't planning on it."

Winter immediately calms. As happy as a clam. She sprawls back against my chest like she's sunbathing. Her arms spread wide as she feels the wind in her pigtails, the same light brown shade as Jake's hair.

Rocky and I share a smile. Even loving her to the deepest core, we haven't changed our minds about having children of our own. He had a vasectomy years ago, and there hasn't been a day when I've wanted a baby.

If anything, I'm more resolute in our decision to not have kids. I'm happy as Winter's auntie.

The town is bustling with tourists and locals when we make it to shore.

Docks are pristinely clean. Beaches raked. Storefronts all have fresh coats of paint. Everything about Victoria seems brighter, livelier.

In large part, because of Jake. He contributes sizable amounts of money to Victoria the same way that Rocky does through the Stonehaven tours.

Together, Jake and Rocky have given more to this community in the past three years than the Konings and the Wolfes did in the past decade.

"Hold hands, Winter," I tell her once we're in town on foot.

She grabs my hand and Rocky's as we cross the street.

"Jump," Winter says, and Rocky and I lift and swing her together over the cobblestone sidewalk. She giggles. "Jump!" We do it again and again.

The bookstore comes into view, and we let go of her hands. Winter *races* to the entrance, yanking at the locked doors with all her might. Then she presses her back to the glass with a smile like someone will come help her if she's sweet.

"Does she remind you of Oliver?" I ask him.

"Every fucking day."

I don't have to unlock the bookstore. Hailey opens the doors from the inside. We're closed on Mondays, and we all meet here for coffee and breakfast from Seaside Griddle. Not to plot a job.

Just to catch up.

The store isn't Baubles & Bookends. For almost three years, it's been The Bleeding Shelf: Books & Merch. A decal of the logo—a knife stabbing a heart on top of a book, blood dripping off the blade—covers the front glass door.

Just the right levels of romance and horror.

The bells *ding* as we go inside and the door shuts behind us. It's a typical bookstore except for the iron shelves, the black walls with waves of pink, and stocked merch from various slasher flicks. Rocky jokes about my portion of the store being a Hot Topic, but we make a pretty penny off the campy *Scream* T-shirts.

And he has purchased way too many kitschy mugs for me to believe he doesn't love it.

"Mommy. *Mommy.*" Winter immediately embraces Hailey's legs with a big squeeze.

Hailey hugs her daughter with so much tender affection. My best friend has grown out her brown roots. These days, she only leaves the ends platinum-blonde. My hair is still a dark shade of blue. I watch Hails straighten Winter's crooked skirt. "Did you have fun with Auntie Phoebe and Uncle Rocky?" she asks her.

Winter nods robustly.

"What'd you do?" She fixes her droopy pigtail.

"Hid in the castle."

"Hid," Hailey repeats, her eyes widening on me, then her brother.

"For fun," I say fast. "Hide-and-seek."

Hailey eases.

Rocky leans on the checkout counter, looking between us too intrusively before the door *dings*.

"Daddy!" Winter bounds over to Jake. He's carrying white paper bags with the Seaside Griddle logo and a lilac box of donuts. I quickly snatch them.

"Thanks, Phoebe," Jake says before lifting Winter up, her arms already outstretched to him. Almost instantly she sinks her head against the crook of his neck. He sways her side to side so soothingly. Like he's done since she was a baby.

She's not bouncing around or squirming. I swear she's this little quiet angel when she's with Jake, especially when she's reading with Hailey.

He leans down just to kiss Hailey in a tender hello. He whispers something to her, and Hails nods back with a little red flush. I love that my best friend got her romance. Times two.

As Jake straightens up, a protective hand on Winter's back, the little girl looks like she's being lulled to sleep on his chest.

I put the bags and donut box near the register. "You have to be giving her to us coked out on sugar."

Hailey plucks a fairy-tale children's book from the shelf. "She's feeding off your energy."

"We're calm," Rocky and I say in unison, to which Jake and Hailey look at us like we're deranged.

We're not high-strung. We are *very* mellow. Chill.

No time for them to put up a strong rebuttal, the doors chime as Trevor pushes into the store with a blonde girl in four-inch heels and the cutest baby-pink minidress.

Sidney Burke.

Yes, they are *still* together. Not only does she work full-time at *Victoria Weekly*, she lives with Trevor in the apartment across from the movie theater.

While I go behind the checkout counter, she immediately

approaches me and throws a white Chanel purse on the surface. "Skank."

"Bitch." I unearth a pair of red Jimmy Choos from under the counter. We return our previously borrowed items. Strangely, we wear the same shoe size. More strangely, we are *very* good friends.

I would have never, ever, ever imagined I'd be close with Trevor's girlfriend, but the more she hung around while Trevor had been living in the loft with me and Rocky, the more we just kind of . . . clicked. There was also one tearful night when she opened up and even apologized to Rocky for coming on to him so hard.

The two of us had a major heart-to-heart that ended with tissues, a bottle of Pinot Grigio, and a burnt sheet of chocolate chip cookies that set off the fire alarm.

"You on for cocktails tomorrow night?" Sidney asks. "Val said she can come." Valentina de la Vega also works at the paper.

"Yeah, I can make it."

"Hailey?" Sidney asks. "Girls' night. Cocktails at the Gulp?"

"I'll be there." Hailey flips through a kids' book, but she's smiling at the pages. I feel that same smile in me. We've never stayed anywhere long enough to form bonds outside of each other, let alone being allowed to be honest to cultivate them. For the first time, we've made a couple lasting friendships.

"Me too, Mommy?" Winter asks expectantly.

"Next time, Win." Hailey smiles, pressing the book against her Black Sabbath tee and giving her daughter all her attention. "You'll be right alongside Mommy."

Winter smiles up at her dad and whispers too loudly, "I love Mommy."

"Me too, baby," he says, his blue eyes lovingly on Hails.

"Shoot." Sidney checks the time on her phone. "I have to go, Trev. Late for work." She swipes the heels, then kisses Trevor. He catches her hand, making her slow down, and he gives her a much longer kiss, which causes her to smile.

Cute, cute, *cute*. I can cop to it. Trevor might have *some* moves, but even thinking about them makes me want to hurl a little.

It's not even that he's young, because he's not. He's twenty-two now. It's just . . . that's *Trevor.* After Sidney leaves, Rocky asks his brother about his job.

A normal, ordinary kind of job.

Trevor has been refurbishing some boats at the marina for fun. He's always been a tinkerer. Fabricating money boxes and such. Rocky loves that his little brother has chosen to fix things rather than destroy them.

Nova barrels into the bookstore like he's escaping a zombie apocalypse. "There are way too many fucking people out there."

"It's summer," we all say.

I go to the merch wall. "You just need a Jason Voorhees machete." I pluck off the plastic weapon. "Tell the sweaty zombies to fuck off."

"Fuck!" Winter shouts.

I point at Nova.

He points right at me.

"You said it first," I contend.

He groans out, "Fuuu . . . dge."

"Nice save, Winchester," Rocky says with one clap.

Now Hailey points at her brother. "You are just as bad."

"What?" Rocky grimaces, then turns to Trevor, who's nodding while stabbing his pancakes. "Oh come on, I'm not that fucking—"

"Ah." I point my fake machete at him.

"Fine. Whatever." The three of us might have been born inside a swear jar.

Winter waves heartily at Nova until he acknowledges her with a nod and a "How you doing, Winter?"

"Happy, happy," she says certainly.

Nova gets soft and reddened in the eye. It's probably why she often tells him, "Happy, happy." I think she knows it makes her big strong uncle ooey-fucking-gooey.

"Was the boat ride almost teary, teary?" Hailey asks me, knowing it can go in either direction.

"Meh, she was fine." I hang up the machete and grab a plastic wooden stake out of a bin near the Buffy merch. Then the bell *ding*s.

Oliver pushes inside with two trays of coffees and a contagious smile. Realizing we're all here, he grins. "Saved the best entrance for last."

Hailey collects the trays from him, and she rises on the tips of her toes to kiss Oliver. He nuzzles extra-playful kisses in her hair. So sweet and endearing that she has trouble hiding a smile.

Winter wiggles down her dad's body. "Uncle Olly!" She circles Oliver's legs with bright giggles.

"She's moving so fast, I can barely see her," Oliver says. "Whoa. *Whoa*. She's no match for me though. I'm gonna get her." She shrieks into belly laughter before he's even snatched her around the waist. He holds her upside down. Her pigtails flopping.

She's grinning from ear to ear.

"Anyone seen Winnie?" He looks around, swinging her side to side. "Where'd she go?"

"I'm right here!"

"Oh my gosh. There she is. An upside-down creature."

"Girl," she corrects.

"A girl." He gasps. "I've never heard of a girl before."

"Mommy's a girl."

"That's right." He tickles her toes. "How clever you are."

She giggles so happily.

I like looking over at Jake whenever Oliver is with his daughter. He wears this soft reverence in his eyes that even the best con artists would have trouble manufacturing.

Once Oliver sets her down, she tugs on his pant legs. He squats to her height. "Yes, baby?" She hugs him extra tight, then whispers in his ear. He holds her little hand and asks, "You know where it is?" She nods. "Okay, go find it. Hurry."

Winter races down the aisle. We all keep one eye on her, even if we're acting like we're not.

Oliver goes to the checkout. "Another one bites the dust, apparently," he says, plucking a coffee out of the tray. He hands it to Jake. "The van Hoffs just moved out of the Burkes' house."

I didn't love oh-so-very-snooty Mrs. van Hoff, who had far too many "suggestions" to "improve" Victoria Country Club, so I'm not incredibly heartbroken. Still . . . "That's the fifth family that's moved in and out."

"Cursed." Rocky raises and lowers his brows.

"Bad energy, probably," Oliver says, hanging an arm around Jake and sipping his own coffee. No one mentions the third family we ran out of Victoria. They made the van Hoffs look saintly.

Trevor washes down his pancakes with coffee before saying, "Tear it down."

"It's one of the historic homes," Jake says. "It can't be demolished."

Rocky tips his head. "We could if it has a rotten foundation."

"But it doesn't."

"Obviously." Rocky blinks hard with widened eyes of annoyance. "We could say it did."

"*No*," Jake decrees.

Oliver grins over at him. "So honest. So pure."

"Not a bad thing," Jake replies. None of us disagree.

Jake and Oliver have this intense stare-down that ends with Jake clasping my brother's jaw and stealing a strong kiss.

I smile, especially seeing Oliver grin against Jake's lips. If anyone asks them what they are—which they inevitably do—the three will simply say they're life partners.

She's still Hailey Thornhall, and Jake was adamant that he didn't want Winter to be a Koning or Waterford on paper. Despite the prestige of being a Koning, he'd rather not saddle her with a name related to a family that he never cared for.

They landed on Winter Thornhall. A name so fake sounding to me that I instantly fell in love the second Hailey said it.

Especially because it's real.

Winter comes racing back with the little book, but instead of veering straight for Oliver, she skids to a stop in front of Trevor first. She hugs his legs, then he crouches down and feeds her a tiny piece of pancake.

"Mmmmm," she says to him with a gleeful scrunched nose, then opens her mouth wide for another bite. I'm not sure who loves Seaside Griddle's sweet potato pancakes more. Her or Trevor.

Rocky catches my attention as he leans too confidently, too

coolly, too darkly against the checkout counter. Arms loosely crossed. He's hot.

And perfectly unsuspecting prey.

I twirl my plastic stake like I'm Buffy as I stalk toward him. "You won't see me coming," I warn.

"Because my eyes aren't right on you," he says.

"You better watch out."

"I'm terrified," he deadpans.

I whirl around in a cool maneuver, about to stake him in the heart, but Rocky disarms me so quickly by seizing my wrist and spinning me around. Just as swiftly, he pulls my back against his chest and cages my arms against my breasts with his flexed biceps.

My pulse spikes in the best way, and I'm glad my back is to him because my grin is too fucking wide. I naturally rest my weight against my Rocky, and his arms stay wrapped so tightly around me.

His Phoebe.

Not letting go.

We end up staying in this protective, loving embrace while Winter licks her syrupy lips and returns to Hailey. She waits patiently for her mom to take her hand, then they sit on the floor together. Winter scoots between her mom's legs as Hailey opens the little picture book the toddler found.

As soon as Hailey sees the book, she looks up at Oliver with raised brows, both of them pierced. Yes, she wears most of her piercings. "This one again?"

"Can't knock a girl for loving spiders, Hailstorm."

That makes us all smile in a way.

Winter already starts to sing, "The itsy bitsy . . ." She trails off, waiting for more of us to join in so she's not all alone, and we collectively carry the tune of "The Itsy Bitsy Spider"—

some more theatrically than others. Rocky is practically monotone.

". . . spider climbed up the waterspout," I sing, doing the hand movements with Winter and Hails. "Down came the rain and washed the spider out."

Winter's favorite part comes next. She stretches her arms in the air. "Out came the sun and dried up all the rain!"

"And the itsy bitsy spider climbed up the spout again," we sing and then clap and holler like it's the best damn song of this generation.

Don't let him fool you; Rocky is very happy. We all really, really are, and it becomes even clearer, more vivid, more burrowing when Hailey asks Winter, "How old are you?"

"Two and a . . . a half!"

My smile hurts.

"Can you tell everyone your name?"

"Winter." She looks up at her mom, then around at all of us. She proudly picks herself up off the bookstore floor. Hands twiddling, her bright innocent smile bursting. "I'm Winter Thornhall."

We applaud, and I try to keep the emotion at bay.

But it's a futile battle when she spins to Hailey and says, "You're Mommy." Then she points at Jake. "Daddy!" She rocks on her heels toward my oldest brother. "Uncle No-va." Her big gray eyes sparkle on Oliver. "Uncle Olly!" She spins around. "Uncle Trev." She giggles. "Uncle *Rocky*." Then her big beautiful eyes are on me. "Auntie Phoebe. I love you."

"I love you, too." My voice breaks.

"Don't be sad, Auntie. Why are you crying?"

I intake a sharp breath. "Your Auntie Phoebe isn't sad," I say while Rocky rubs my wet cheeks before I can. Hailey shares my tears, and we smile at each other into a soul-filling, beautiful laugh together before I tell Winter, "I'm so happy you know who we all are."

The truth still finds a way to overwhelm me, even in the smallest of moments in the quirkiest of towns. I can't think of a better life than this one we all made together.

Honestly.

Acknowledgments

Some books and characters will never leave us, and there is something incredibly special about the Webs We Weave series that we know will last a lifetime. It's been one of the most rewarding, thrilling, emotional experiences for us to reach *Dangerously Ours* and finish a story that first began when we were fourteen.

Exactly two decades ago.

Saved to a floppy disk and left in a tin box for years, our childhood story, *The Reign of Spiders*, was unearthed—and we finally returned to it as adults. It became so much more, but at its core, it was always about kids raised as con artists who learned to heal from the trauma of their strange upbringing. We'd like to believe that the pieces of our youthful past are as much a part of this series as the pieces of our present.

And in the present, this series has been full of so much tremendous love because of the readers who've picked up these books. Thank you for meeting the Tinrocks and Graveses, and we hope that at this point you've come to love them, too.

When we look back, we're going to cherish all the beautiful readers we've met through this series. All the tour stops. All the readers wearing strawberry merch. (Phoebe would be proud!) All the spiders. All the smiles and hugs.

Thank you for showing up for the Webs We Weave series, and for us.

Thank you to our mastermind agent, Kimberly Brower, for always championing us and the stories we love to tell. Thank you to the Berkley team and to our brilliant editor, Kristine Swartz, for helping make this series the absolute best it can be.

Thank you to our friends Jenn, Lanie, and Shea for all the support and love for over a decade. Thank you to more extraordinary, beautiful friends who've rooted for the Tinrocks, the Graveses, and these books. You've simply filled our hearts the past few years: Haley, Alyssa, Juana, Andrea, Maria, Marissa, Rowena, Zoë, Abby, Angelina, Andressa, Margot, Em, Laura, Marie, Sarah Green, Olivia, Kenny, Allyn, Priyanka, Julia, Cass, and so many more.

We wish we could name everyone. There are so, so many of you we can picture who've made such an impact on us through this series. We feel lucky to have made these heartwarming memories, and we're so grateful for you.

Thank you to our mom for fueling our childhood passions. Without you, this story would've never existed when we were fourteen. Let alone twenty years later, when we turned thirty-four.

And lastly, once again, thank you—the reader. For sticking with this merry little gang of heathens and for embarking on this twisty, turny tale of belief, truths, lies, and love. Trust us, we couldn't imagine a better way to say goodbye.

—xoxo, Krista & Becca

KEEP READING FOR A PREVIEW OF
KRISTA AND BECCA RITCHIE'S

ADDICTED TO YOU

AVAILABLE NOW!

I wake up. My shirt crumpled on a fuzzy carpet. My shorts astray on a dresser. And I think my underwear is lost for good. Somewhere between the folds of the sheets or maybe hidden by the doorway. I can't remember when I took them off or if that was even my doing. Maybe *he* undressed me.

My neck heats as I take a quick peek at the sleeping beauty, some guy with golden hair and a scar along his hip bone. He turns a fraction, facing me, and I freeze. His eyes stay shut, and he groggily clings to his pillow, practically kissing the white fabric. As he lets out breathy snores, his mouth open, the strong scent of alcohol and pepperoni pizza wafts right towards me.

I sure know how to choose 'em.

I masterfully slip from the bed and tiptoe around his apartment, yanking on my black shorts—sans panties, another pair gone to a nameless guy. As I pick up my ripped gray tee, tattered and practically in shreds, the foggy image of last night clears. I stepped through the threshold of his room and literally tore my clothes off like the raging Hulk. Was that even sexy? I cringe. Must have been sexy enough to sleep with me.

Desperate, I find a discolored muscle tee on his floor and manage to tug it over my shoulder-length brown hair, the straight strands tangled and greasy. That's when I find my woolen hat. Bingo. I smack that baby on and hightail it out of his bedroom.

Empty beer cans scatter the narrow hallway, and I stumble over a bottle of Jack Daniel's, filled with black spittle and what looks like a Jolly Rancher. A photo collage of inebriated college girls decorates the door to my left—thankfully not the room I exited. Somehow I was able to dodge that Kappa Phi Delta horn dog and find a guy that *doesn't* advertise his conquests.

I should know better. I swore off frat houses after my last encounter at Alpha Omega Zeta. The night I arrived at fraternity row, AOZ was hosting a theme party. Unaware, I stepped through the four-story building's archway to be met with buckets of water and guys chanting for me to rip off my bra. It was like Spring Break gone awry. Not that I have much in the upstairs department to show off. Before I convulsed in embarrassment, I ducked underneath arms, wedged between torsos and found pleasure at other places and with other people.

Ones that didn't make me feel like a cow being appraised.

Last night I broke a rule. Why? I have a problem. Well, I have many problems. But saying *no* happens to be one of them. When Kappa Phi Delta announced that Skrillex would be playing in their basement, I thought the crowd would be a mixture of sorority girls and regular college folk. Maybe I'd be able to land a normal guy who likes house music. Turns out, the demographic centered on frat guys. Lots of them. Preying on anyone with two boobs and a vagina.

And Skrillex never showed. It was just a lame DJ and a few amps. Go figure.

Deep, *male* voices echo off the marble balusters on the balcony and staircase, and my feet cement by the wall. People are awake? Downstairs? Oh no.

The walk of shame is a venture I plan to avoid all four years of collegiate society. For one, I blush. Like intense tomato-red. No cute flushed cheeks. Just rash-like patches that dot my neck and arms as if I'm allergic to embarrassment.

The male laughter intensifies, and my stomach knots at the nightmarish image spinning in my mind. The one where I stumble down the stairs and all heads whip in my direction. The look of surprise coats their faces, wondering what "brother" of theirs decided to hook up with a flat-chested, gaunt girl. Maybe they'll throw a chicken bone at me, teasing me to eat.

Sadly that happened in fourth grade.

Likely, I'll sputter unintelligible words until one of them takes pity on my flaming red leopard spots and shuffles me out of their door like unwanted garbage.

This was such a mistake (the frat house, not the sex). Never again will I be forced to hoover tequila shots like a vacuum. Peer pressure. It's a real thing.

My options are limited. One staircase. One fate. Unless I happen to grow a pair of wings and fly out of the second-floor window, I'm about to face the walk of shame. I creep to the balcony and suddenly envy Veil from one of my newer comics. The young Avenger can vaporize into nothingness. A power I could surely use right now.

As soon as I reach the top step, the doorbell rings and I peek over the railing. About ten fraternity brothers are gathered on leather sofas, dressed in various versions of khaki shorts and collared shirts. The most lucid guy nominates himself for door-duty. He manages to stand on two feet, his brown hair swept back and his jaw intimidatingly squared. As he answers the door, my spirits lift.

Yes! This is my one opportunity to dash out unseen.

I use the distraction to glide down the steps undetected, channeling my inner-Veil. Halfway to the bottom, Squared-jaw leans on the door frame, blocking the entrance. "Party's over, man." The words sound cottony in his mouth. He lets the door swing shut in the person's face.

I hop over two more stairs.

The bell rings again. For some reason, it sounds angrier.

Squared-jaw groans and yanks the knob hard. "What?"

Another frat guy laughs. "Just give him a beer and tell him to piss off."

A few more steps. Maybe I can really do this. I've never been a particularly lucky person, but I suppose I'm due for a dose.

Squared-jaw keeps his hand planted on the frame, still blocking the passage. "Speak."

"First of all, does it look like I can't read a clock or furthermore don't know what *daytime* looks like? No shit, there's no party." Holy . . . I know that voice.

I stay planted three-quarters down. Sunshine trickles through a tiny space between the doorframe and Squared-jaw's tangerine-orange Polo. He clenches his teeth, about ready to slam the door back in the other guy's face, but the intruder puts his hand on it and says, "I left something here last night."

"I don't remember you being here."

"I was." He pauses. "Briefly."

"We have a lost and found," Squared-jaw says curtly. "What is it?" He edges away from the doorframe and nods to someone on the couch. They watch the scene like a reality rerun on MTV. "Jason, go grab the box."

When I glance back, I notice the guy outside. Eyes right on me.

"No need," he says.

I sweep his features. Light brown hair, short on either side, full on top. Decently toned body hidden beneath a pair of faded Dockers and a black crew-neck tee. Cheekbones that cut like ice and eyes like liquid scotch. Loren Hale is an alcoholic beverage and he doesn't even know it.

All six-foot-two of him fills the doorway.

As he stares at me, he wears a mixture of amusement and irritation, the muscles in his jaw twitching with both. The frat guys follow his gaze and zero in on the target.

Me.

I may as well have reanimated from thin air.

"Found her," Lo says with a tight, bitter smile.

Heat rises to my face, and I use my hands as human blinders, trying to cover my humiliation as I practically sprint to the door.

Squared-jaw laughs like he won their masculine showdown. "Your girlfriend is a skank, man."

I hear no more. The brisk September air fills my lungs, and Lo bangs the door closed with more force than he probably intended. I cower in my hands, pressing them to my hot cheeks as the event replays in my head. Oh. My. God.

Lo swoops in behind me, his arms flying around my waist. He sets his chin on my shoulder, hunching over a little to counter my short height with his tall. "He better have been worth it," Lo whispers, his hot breath tickling my neck.

"Worth what?" My heart lodges in my throat; his closeness

confuses and tempts me. I never know where Lo's true intentions lie.

He guides me forward as we walk, my back still pressed against his chest. I can barely lift up a foot, let alone think straight. "Your first walk of shame in a frat house. How'd that feel?"

"Shameful."

He plants a light kiss on my head and disentangles from me, walking forward. "Pick it up, Calloway. I left my drink in the car."

My eyes begin to widen as I process what this means, gradually forgetting the horrors that just occurred. "You didn't drive, did you?"

He flashes me a look like *really, Lily?* "Seeing as how my usual DD was unavailable"—he raises his eyebrows accusingly—"I called Nola."

He called my personal driver, and I don't begin to ask why he decided to forgo his own chauffeur that would gladly cart him around Philadelphia. Anderson has loose lips. In ninth grade when Chloe Holbrook threw a rager, Lo and I may have been discussing illegal narcotics that were passed from hand to hand at her mother's mansion. Backseat conversations should be considered private among all car-participants. Anderson must not have realized this unspoken rule because the next day, our rooms were raided for illegal paraphernalia. Luckily, the maid forgot to search in the fake fireplace where I used to keep my X-rated box of toys.

We came away clean from the incident and learned a very important lesson. Never trust Anderson.

I prefer to not use my family's car service and thus embed myself further in their grips, but sometimes Nola is a necessity. Like now. When I'm slightly hungover and unable to drive the perpetually drunk Loren Hale.

He has knighted me as his personal sober driver and refuses to shell out money to any cab services after we were almost mugged in one. We never told our parents what happened. Never explained to them how close we were to something horrible. Mostly because we spent that afternoon at a bar with two fake IDs. Lo guzzled more whiskey than a grown man. And I had sex in a public bathroom for the very first time. Our indecencies became our rituals, and our families didn't need to know about them.

My black Escalade is parked on the curb of frat row. Multimillion dollar houses line up, each outdoing the last in column sizes. Red Solo cups litter the nearest yard, an overturned keg splaying sadly in the grass. Lo walks ahead of me.

"I didn't think you were going to show," I say and skirt past a puddle of barf in the road.

"I said I would."

I snort. "That's not always accurate."

He halts by the car door, the windows too tinted to see Nola waiting in the driver's seat. "Yeah, but this is Kappa Phi Delta. You screw one and they may all want a piece of your ass. I seriously had nightmares about it."

I grimace. "About me getting raped?"

"That's why they're called *nightmares*, Lily. They're not supposed to be pleasant."

"Well this is probably my last expedition into a frat house for another decade or at least until I forget about this morning."

The driver's window rolls down. Nola's deep black curls caress her heart-shaped face. "I have to pick up Miss Calloway from the airport in an hour."

"We'll be ready in a minute," I tell her. The window slides up, blocking her from view.

"Which Miss Calloway?" Lo asks.

"Daisy. Fashion Week just ended in Paris." My little sister shot up overnight to a staggering five-foot-eleven inches, and with her rail-like frame she fit the mold for high fashion. My mother capitalized on Daisy's beauty in an instant. Within the week of her fourteenth birthday, she was signed to IMG modeling agency.

Lo's fingers twitch by his side. "She's fifteen and probably surrounded by older models blowing lines in a bathroom."

"I'm sure they sent someone with her." I hate that I don't know the details. Since I arrived at the University of Pennsylvania, I acquired the rude hobby of dodging phone calls and visits. Separating from the Calloway household became all too easy once I entered college. I suppose that has always been written for me. I used to push the boundaries of my curfew and spent little time in the company of my mother and father.

Lo says, "I'm glad I don't have siblings. Frankly, you have enough *for* me."

I never considered having three sisters to be a big brood, but a family of six does garner some unique attention.

He rubs his eyes wearily. "Okay, I need a drink and we need to go."

I inhale a deep breath, about to ask a question we've both avoided thus far. "Are we pretending today?" With Nola so close, it's always a toss-up. On one hand, she's never betrayed our trust. Not even in the tenth grade when I used the backseat of a limo to screw a senior soccer player. The privacy screen was up, blocking Nola's view, but he grunted a little too loud and I knocked into the door a little too hard. Of course she heard, but she never ratted me out.

There's always the risk that one day she'll betray us. Cash loosens lips, and unfortunately, our fathers are swimming in it.

I shouldn't care. I'm twenty. Free to have sex. Free to party. You know, all the things expected of college-aged adults. But my laundry list of dirty (like *really* dirty) secrets could create a scandal within my family's circle of friends. My father's company would not appreciate that publicity one bit. If my mother knew my serious problem, she'd send me away for rehab and counseling until I was fixed up nicely. I don't want to be fixed. I just want to live and feed my appetite. It just so happens that my appetite is a sexual one.

Plus, my trust fund would magically vanish at the sight of my impropriety. I'm not ready to walk away from the money that pays my way through college. Lo's family is equally unforgiving.

"We'll pretend," he tells me. "Come on, love." He taps my ass. "Into the car." I barely stumble on his frequent use of *love*. In middle school, I told him how I thought it was the sexiest term of endearment. And even though British guys have staked a claim to it, Lo took it as his own.

I scrutinize him, and he breaks into a wide smile.

"Has the walk of shame crippled you?" he asks. "Do I need to carry you into the threshold of the Escalade too?"

"That's unnecessary."

His crooked grin makes it hard not to smile back. Lo purposefully leans in close to tease me, and he slips a hand in the back pocket of my jeans. "If you don't unfreeze yourself from this state, I'm going to spin you around. Hard."

My chest collapses. Oh my . . . I bite my lip, imagining what sex would be like with Loren Hale. The first time was too long ago to remember well. I shake my head. *Don't go there.* I turn around to open the door and climb in the Escalade, but a huge realization hits me.

"Nola drove to fraternity row . . . I'm dead. OhmyGod. I'm dead." I run two hands through my hair and begin to breathe like a beached whale. I have no good excuse to be here other than I was searching for a guy to sleep with. And that's the answer I'm trying to avoid. Especially since our parents think Lo and I are in a serious relationship—one that changed his dangerous partying ways and reformed him into a young man that his father can be proud of.

This, picking me up from a frat party with the faint smell of whiskey on his breath, is not what his father has in mind for his son. It is *not* something he'd condone or even accept. In fact, he'd probably scream at Lo and threaten him with his trust fund. Unless we want to say goodbye to our luxuries from our inherited wealth, we have to pretend to be together. And pretend that we're two perfectly functioning, perfectly well-kept human beings.

And we're just not. We're not. My arms shake.

"Whoa!" Lo places his hands on my shoulders. "Relax, Lil. I told Nola that your friend had a birthday brunch. You're covered."

My head still feels like it'll float away, but at least that's better than the truth. *Hey Nola, we need to pick up Lily from frat row where she had a one-night stand with some loser.* And then she'd look at Lo, waiting for him to explode in jealousy. And he'd add: *Oh yeah, I'm only her boyfriend when I need to be. Fooled you!*

Lo senses my anxiety. "She's not going to find out." He squeezes my shoulders.

"Are you sure?"

"Yes," he says impatiently. He slides in the car, and I follow behind. Nola puts the Escalade in gear.

"Back to the Drake, Miss Calloway?" After years of asking her to call me anything, even *little girl* (for some reason, I thought that would entice her to drop the whole act, but I think I only offended her instead), I gave up the attempt. I swear my dad pays her extra for the formality.

"Yes," I say, and she heads towards the Drake apartment complex.

Lo nurses a coffee thermos, and even though he takes big gulps, I'm certain that the caffeinated beverage does not fill it. I find a can of Diet Fizz in the center cooler-console and snap it open. The dark carbonated liquid soothes my restless stomach.

Lo drapes an arm across my shoulder, and I lean into his hard chest a tiny bit.

Nola glances in the rearview mirror. "Was Mr. Hale not invited to the birthday brunch?" she asks, being friendly. Still, anytime Nola goes into question-mode, it jostles my nerves and triggers paranoia.

"I'm not as popular as Lily," Lo answers for me. He has always been a much better liar. I blame it on the fact that he's constantly inebriated. I'd be a far more confident, self-assured Lily if I was downing bourbon all day.

Nola laughs, her plump belly hitting the steering wheel with each chortle. "I'm sure you're just as popular as Miss Calloway."

Anyone (apparently Nola too) would assume that Lo has friends. On an attractiveness scale, he ranges right between a lead singer from a rock band you'd like to fuck and a runway model for Burberry and Calvin Klein. Although, he's never been in a band, but a modeling agency did scout him once, wanting him for a Burberry campaign. They retracted the offer after seeing him drink straight from a nearly empty bottle of whiskey. The fashion industry has standards too.

Lo should have lots of friends. Mostly of the female kind. And usually they do come flocking. But not for long.

The car travels along another street, and I count the minutes in my head. Lo angles his body towards me while his fingers brush my bare shoulder, almost lovingly. I make brief eye contact, my neck burning as his deep gaze enters mine. I swallow hard and try not to break it. Since we're supposed to be dating, I shouldn't be afraid of his amber eyes like an awkward, insecure girl.

Lo says, "Charlie is playing sax tonight at Eight Ball. He invited us to go watch him."

"I don't have plans." *Lie.* A new club opened up downtown called The Blue Room. Literally, everything is said to be blue. Even the drinks. I'm not missing the opportunity to hook up in a blue bathroom. Hopefully with blue toilet seats.

"It's a date."

Silence (of the awkward variety) thickens after his words die in the air. Normally, I'd be talking to him about The Blue Room and my nefarious intentions tonight, making plans since I am his DD. But in the censored car, it's more difficult to start R-rated conversations.

"Is the fridge stocked? I'm starving."

"I just went to the grocery store," he tells me. I narrow my eyes, questioning whether he's lying to play the part of a good boyfriend or if he really did make a Whole Foods run. My stomach growls. At least we all know I didn't lie.

His jaw tightens, pissed that I don't know a fib from a truth. Normally I do, but sometimes when he's so nonchalant, the lines blur. "I bought lemon meringue pie. Your favorite."

I internally gag. "You shouldn't have." *No, you really shouldn't have.* I hate lemon meringue. Obviously he wants Nola to think he's an upstanding boyfriend, but the only girlfriend Loren Hale will ever treat well is his bottle of bourbon.

We stop at a traffic light, now only a few blocks from the apartment complex. I can taste freedom, and Lo's arm begins to feel more like a weight than a comforting appendage across my shoulders.

"Was this a casual event, Miss Calloway?" Nola asks. *What? Oh . . . shit.* Her eyes plant on the muscle tee I snatched from the frat guy's floor. Stained and off-white with God knows what.

"Umm, I-I," I stammer. Lo stiffens next to me. He grips his thermos and chugs the rest of his drink. "I-I spilled some orange juice on my top. It was really embarrassing." Was that even a lie?

My face flames uncontrollably, and for the first time, I welcome the rash-like patches. Nola gazes sympathetically. She's known me since I was too shy to say the Pledge of Allegiance in kindergarten. Age five and timid. Pretty much sums up my first years of existence.

"I'm sure it wasn't that bad," she consoles.

The light flickers to green and she redirects her attention to the road.

Unscathed, we make it to the Drake. A towering chestnut-brick structure juts up in the heart of the city. The historic 33-story complex boards thousands and teeters into a triangle at the apex. With Spanish Baroque influences, it looks a cross between a Spanish cathedral and a regular old Philly hotel.

I love it enough to call it home.

Nola offers a goodbye and I tell her thanks before hopping from the Escalade. My feet no sooner hit the curb than Lo clasps my hand in his. His other fingers run over the smoothness of my neck, and his eyes trail my collar. He sets his hands on the openings of my muscle shirt, touching the bareness of my ribs but also concealing my breasts from Philly pedestrians.

He observes me. Every little movement. And my heart speeds. "Is she watching us?" I whisper, wondering why he suddenly looks like he wants to devour me. *It's part of our lie*, I remind myself. *This isn't real.*

But it feels real. His hands on me. His warmth on my soft skin.

He licks his bottom lip and leans closer to whisper, "In this moment, I'm yours." His hands run through the armholes of my shirt and he settles them on my bare shoulder blades.

I hold my breath and immobilize. I am a statue.

"And as your boyfriend," he murmurs, "I really hate to share." Then he playfully nibbles my neck, and I smack him on the arm but fall victim to his teasing.

"Lo!" I shriek, my body squirming underneath his teeth that lightly pinch my skin. Suddenly, his lips close together, kissing, sucking the base of my neck, and trailing upward. My limbs tremble, and I hold tightly to his belt loops. He smiles, in between each kiss, knowing the effect he has on me. His lips press to my jaw . . . the corner of my mouth . . . he pauses. And I restrain from taking him in my arms and finishing the job.

Then he slips his tongue inside my mouth, and I forget about the fakeness of his actions and believe, for this moment, that he's truly mine. I kiss back, a moan caught in my throat. The sound invigorates him, and he pushes closer, harder, rougher than before. *Yes.*

And then I open my eyes and see the absence of the Escalade on the curb. Nola's gone. I don't want this to end, but I know it must. So I break the kiss first, touching my lips that swell.

His chest rises and falls heavily, and he stares at me for a long moment, not detaching.

"She's gone," I tell him. I hate what my body eagerly aches for. I could so easily hike a leg around his waist and slam him against the building. My heart flutters in excitement for it. I am not immune to those warm amber eyes, the ones that a functioning alcoholic like Lo carries. Endearing, glazed and powerful. The ones that constantly scream *fuck me!* That torture me from here until eternity.

With my spoken words, his jaw hardens. Slowly, he peels his hands from me and then rubs his mouth. Tension stretches between us, and my very core says to *jump*, to pounce on him like a little Bengal tiger. But I can't. Because he's Loren Hale. Because we have a system that cannot be disrupted.

After a long moment, something clicks in his head, horrified. "Tell me you didn't blow some guy."

Oh my God. "I . . . uh . . ."

"Dammit, Lily." He starts wiping his tongue with his fingers and dramatically takes what's left of his flask and swishes it in his mouth, spitting it out on the ground.

"I forgot." I cringe. "I would have warned you . . ."

"I'm sure."

"I didn't know you were going to kiss me!" I try to defend. *Or else I would have found toothpaste in that frat's bathroom. Or some mouthwash.*

"We're together," he says back. "Of course I'm going to fucking kiss you." With this, he pockets his flask and aims his sights on the entrance to the Drake. "I'll see you inside." He spins around, walking backwards. "You know, in *our* apartment. That we share, as a *couple*." He smiles that bitter smile.

"Don't be too long, love." He winks. And part of me utterly and completely crumbles to mush. The other part is just plain confused.

Reading Lo's intentions hurts my head. I trail behind, trying to unmask his true feelings. Was that pretend? Or was that real?

I shake off my doubts. We're in a three-year-long *fake* relationship. We live together. He's heard me orgasm from one room over. I've seen him sleep in his own puke. And even though our parents believe we're one small step from engagement, we'll never have sex again. It happened once, and that has to be enough.

Photo © Kelley Raye

Krista and Becca Ritchie are *New York Times* and *USA Today* bestselling authors and identical twins—one a science nerd, the other a comic book geek—but with their shared passion for writing, they combined their mental powers as kids and have never stopped telling stories. They love superheroes, flawed characters, and soul mate love.

VISIT KRISTA AND BECCA RITCHIE ONLINE

KBRitchie.com
KBMRitchie